T[illegible]
THE FIGHTIN' FOR ONE LOW PRICE!
A $9.00 VALUE FOR ONLY $5.99!

NEBRASKA NYMPH

The long-haired cowpoke faced Spur squarely. "You wouldn't be one of those homesteaders, would you?"

"No. I'm no farmer, but I'm not a rancher either. Fact is, I'm a lawyer," said Spur.

"You don't look like no lawyer to me," said a Spanish-accented voice.

"Why the hell don't you go back where you came from?" said a white-haired old hand.

Spur felt the tension increase. The men were outraged, scared. If he said the wrong thing, he could set them off like firecrackers....

MOUNTAIN MADAM

Landower eased away from a wall ahead of McCoy and stopped, his feet wide, his hands at his side in the classic gunfighting pose.

"Whenever you're ready, McCoy," Landower shouted. "Now's the time for action instead of using that big mouth of yours."

McCoy walked to within 20 feet of the other man. A woman screamed. People on the boardwalk between and behind both men scampered out of the possible line of fire.

"Anytime you want to die, Landower, I'm ready...."

The *Spur Double* Series from *Leisure Books:*

NEVADA HUSSY/WYOMING WILDCAT
SALT LAKE LADY/DEADRIDGE DOLL
SANTA FE FLOOZY/LOUISIANA LASS
TEXAS TART/MINER'S MOLL
WYOMING WENCH/PORTLAND PUSSYCAT
SAN FRANCISCO STRUMPET/BOISE BELLE
KANSAS CITY CHORINE/PLAINS PARAMOUR
BODIE BEAUTIES/FRISCO FOXES
DODGE CITY DOLL/LARAMIE LOVERS
DAKOTA DOXY/SAN DIEGO SIRENS
COLORADO CUTIE/TEXAS TEASE
MISSOURI MADAM/HELENA HELLION
RAWHIDER'S WOMAN/SALOON GIRL
INDIAN MAID/MONTANA MINX
ROCKY MOUNTAIN VAMP/CATHOUSE KITTEN
SAVAGE SISTERS/HANG SPUR McCOY!

SPUR

NEBRASKA NYMPH

MOUNTAIN MADAM

Dirk Fletcher

LEISURE BOOKS NEW YORK CITY

A LEISURE BOOK®

April 1996

Published by

Dorchester Publishing Co., Inc.
276 Fifth Avenue
New York, NY 10001

Printed in the United States of America.

SPUR

NEBRASKA NYMPH

CHAPTER ONE

Kearney County, Nebraska
April 1874

AL PARKER wiped early morning sweat from his sunburned brow as he filled the last bucket at the outside water pump. The air hung crisply over his farm with the first hints of summer as the sun's rays slowly stretched over the flat land. Parker hefted the bucket, cursing softly as the water slopped over the side and spilled onto his trouser leg.

Then he heard it.

Riders approaching—two, perhaps three. From the west. Not many men riding this time of day, Parker thought, resting the bucket on his spattered leg and squinting into the darkness. A gray trail of dust rose along the track that led to the Parker farm.

The hair on the back of his neck rose. Parker felt the old queasiness boil up in his gut. The threats—the angry looks from the ranchers in town. Could they be riding against—

"Al! Al! Hurry up with the water!"

"Get on inside!" Al screamed, letting the bucket crash into the dirt as he turned and ran toward the farmhouse. His wife, Gilly, darkly pretty, stood in shock in the doorway.

"What's the matter, Al?"

Parker raced past her, gripped her arm and pulled her into the farmhouse with controlled strength. He grabbed the Winchester off the rack by the fireplace, filled his pockets with extra rounds, slammed the door shut and bolted it, then knelt before the parlor window facing the trail.

"Git down, Gilly," he said. "We have company. Could be them ranchers who were threatening me in town the other day."

Gilly's face, not yet worn by the strains of farm life, clouded with confusion.

"What? Whatever are you talking about? What threats?"

Parker grimaced. He had avoided telling Gilly, didn't want to upset her. They'd just moved into their new farm six months ago and things had been tough.

"Never mind. Just get Kris and go on into the kitchen. Stay clear of windows. Find a spot on the floor and don't budge. I pray to God that I'm wrong, but—"

"Al!" Gilly's hand touched his shoulder. "You're shaking!"

Parker gathered his strength and willed his body to remain still. He wasn't scared—even though that's what everybody said back in Atlanta—he was just angry. "Get Kris and do what I say!"

"All right, if you think so—"

"Do it!" he roared, so loudly that Gilly backed away from him and ran into the kitchen were their two year old daughter tearfully awaited breakfast.

Parker's glance flew from one side of the view the window afforded him to the other, scanning the entire terrain. The dust trail had dispersed, melding into the deepening gold of the morning. The riders must have dismounted, turned off the trail, or—

A window shattered, sending deadly shards of glass through the air. Gilly's scream echoed through the house.

"Gilly!"

"I'm fine, and so's Kris." Her voice was taut with fear.

"Stay put!" Parker ran to the opposite window to get a better view. Still no sign of the men—they must have dismounted and walked in. Parker saw a hint of movement out of the corner of his eye—he smashed the window with his rifle butt and planted two rounds into a newly-built shed, the rifle's recoil nearly knocking him backward. Parker had used it once or twice before. He'd always told himself he had to learn how to shoot. He hated firearms.

Sharp, stinging reports of rifles slashed through the air from three directions simultaneously. Fear mounting within him, Parker ran from window to window, from the parlor to the bedroom, as rounds slammed into the house. He peeled off random shots and was reloading as another window shattered somewhere in the house. Gilly's screams punctuated each new blast.

I should have told her, Parker thought. His hands shook and he spilled a cartridge to the floor. He cursed and finished reloading, then blasted as much lead as possible at the unseen gunmen, hoping to God he'd get lucky and hit at least one of them. He didn't care about himself —it was Gilly and his sweet Kris he was protecting. He'd been an idiot to leave the comfort and safety of Atlanta to drag his family into this.

Lead shot past him and slammed into the split pine wall behind. Blinded with anger and fear, Parker's untrained hands fired round after round, the fury at the unjust attack building up within him. After a moment, all was silent. He poked his head up and peered out the window. Still no one in sight, but the air was filled with smoke.

"Hey, you in the house!" a gruff voice called. "Parker. Come on out. We don't want to hurt you. We're just having a little fun. Ain't we, boys?"

A few laughs rang out. Parker, taken completely by surprise by this new approach, didn't budge. He tried to determine the men's positions by their voices, but it was no good. He didn't know where they were holed up.

"Hey Parker, we just want to talk to you. What's the matter, afraid, little man?"

"I ain't that stupid," Parker called, then ducked and moved to a new position at another window. He didn't want his voice to give away his exact whereabouts. Being inside the house was an advantage, he thought with grim satisfaction.

"Hell, you were stupid enough to try your luck at farming. This is the worst goddamn'dest excuse for farm I ever did see."

"Leave us alone!" Gilly's voice shouted from the kitchen. "We never hurt you!"

"We will. As soon as we've got your word that you'll pack up and move out of Kearney County forever—go back to Atlanta or Augusta or wherever the hell you're from. We don't want your kind. There's no room for homesteaders in the Platte River Valley."

"We've got every right—who the hell put you in charge?" Parker screamed. "Get the hell off my property or I'll—"

"You'll what?" the gruff voice said. "We hold all the aces, Parker. Get you, your ugly brat and fat-assed woman onto the next train heading East or we'll blow you all to bits."

Parker crawled to the kitchen, where he found Gilly huddled in a corner, protecting a fidgeting Kris with her body. She started at the sound of his hands and knees shuffling across the floor, then relaxed when she saw his face.

"Al, I—" she began.

He shook his head. Gilly nodded, then stroked Kris' hair.

"We have to leave," Gilly whispered.

"No."

"You don't care what happens to us?"

Parker's face was set.

"Is that it?" Gilly asked, her voice rising. "Or is it what your friends'll say back in Atlanta?"

He looked up at her sharply.

"Please, Al. Think of me and Kris."

Parker shut his eyes tightly.

"You still in there? Come on out where we can see you, or we'll blast you all to kingdom come. That way, even though we won't be rid of you, at least you won't be fencing up prime grazing land. Course, they'll need to dig three more graves on boot hill."

"We're staying!" Parker yelled out the kitchen window, rage mounting slowly inside him. He looked back to Gilly. Her face fell; she turned from her husband and cradled Kris in her arms, as tears silently splashed down her cheeks.

Parker's news was greeted with several rounds that shook the house with their fury.

"You didn't hear me, Parker," the gruff man said, when the firing quieted. "You ain't got no choice. Go homestead somewhere else, if you're bound and determined to be a piss-poor farmer, but not here. Come on out of there or we'll come in shooting."

Parker glanced again at Gilly, but she wouldn't look at him. He snaked along the floor to the parlor and poked his head above the windowsill. If he left the farmhouse they'd probably kill him, but they might leave Gilly and Kris alone. Parker rose to his feet, beating down the vomit that churned in his stomach.

"Don't shoot!" he called as he gripped the door handle. "I'm coming out!"

"Al! Don't!" Gilly screamed from the kitchen.

"Stay put, woman!" he said, then opened the door. Slowly, his rifle in hand, Al Parker stepped into the full sunshine.

"Throw down your weapon," a man to his right said.

Parker laid it on the porch, then kicked it away.

"Why me?" he asked, his voice trembling. "I'm not the only homesteader in the county. There are plenty more, the Craigs, the—"

"You're the newest one," the unseen man said in his gruff voice.

"But—but why can't you—"

"Shut up, you blubbering asshole! If you wanna live in Kearney, be prepared to die for the honor. You got that straight?"

Parker's fears ate away at his determination. His farm, the work he'd done so far, meant nothing. All that mattered was getting Gilly and Kris safely out of Kearney. "All right. I got it straight. Look, can't we talk about this man to man? Why don't you show yourselves? I thought only cowards hid in shadows?"

A grumble emitted from his right. Parker was sure one of the men—the one doing the talking—was crouched behind a stack of old lumber near the barn.

Three men rose from their hiding places—

evenly spaced around the farmhouse. He had to crane his neck to see the third. All wore nondescript clothing and had kerchiefs hiding their lower faces.

"Here we are. Nobody calls me a coward," the gruff-voiced man said. "Especially not an asshole farmer. Why don't you get your wife to come on out too? I could use a good fuck right now." The man lewdly grabbed his crotch and laughed.

Parker's face flared with color. The man had gone too far. To his amazement he found courage. Without thinking out his actions he ducked, rolled across the porch, and had the Winchester in his hands before any of the men could stop him. As he took aim on the leader he felt a sharp, searing pain tear through his left shoulder. He screamed and dropped the rifle to the floor, where it discharged crazily into the farmhouse wall.

"Asshole!" the leader shouted. All three men had ducked back under cover.

Parker pulled himself in through the door and slammed it shut with his foot as the air filled with the sharp, acrid stench of gunpowder and piercing blasts from discharging rifles. Gilly cried out from the kitchen as Parker scrambled to his feet, the pain pounding in his shoulder. He ignored it and returned fire, moving from one window to the next, aiming for the spots the men had last hidden themselves in.

He heard a crash and twisted his head back in time to see a flaming torch fly through the air and land on their bed. The quilts and blankets instantly caught fire.

"Get the water buckets!" Parker called to Gilly as he ran for the bedroom. He grabbed a quilt from the rack by the door and slapped it at the base of the flames but backed away as they increased in heat and roared up toward the ceiling. The curtains had caught on fire too as the flaming torch had passed through them. Within moments Gilly appeared, bent over with the weight of two filled water buckets, but Al pushed her back from the inferno-like heat. He took the buckets and dumped their contents on the flames on the bed.

Water sizzled and evaporated. Angry red and orange flames licked up the walls as thick black smoke rose from the bed. Sputtering and coughing, Parker stepped back again. The water was no good; the fire had had too much of a start.

Wallpaper peeled and crackled as it burned; caches of pitch deep inside the wallboards exploded and sent out spurts of acrid white smoke.

"Jesus Christ!" Parker yelled.

Gilly turned away and ran into the kitchen. He met her as she turned back to him, holding a sobbing Kris. Gilly's eyes shone like those of a madwoman.

Over the increasing roar of the fire they heard occasional rounds from outside. Smoke filtered into the parlor from the bedroom, and Gilly screamed as flames broke out noisily in the kitchen. Parker ran there—another torch had been tossed into the house.

"What can we do?" Gilly asked, looking at the front door. Parker knew the men would never let him leave the house alive. He put his arms around Gilly and Kris and held them for a moment, then kissed his wife tenderly, though his body shook.

"I'm going out. If they kill me, stay in here as long as you can."

"But Al—"

He shook his head. The flames crept closer on both sides, approaching them with frightening speed. "I made a mistake. We could've left and never come back. I'm sorry, Gilly." He turned and ran for the door as the roar of the fire increased tenfold. Waves of heat radiated throughout the farmhouse. Gilly took three steps toward him, one arm cradling Kris, the other outstretched to him.

Parker opened the door. An instant later a round slammed into his chest, the hot lead piercing his heart and driving through his body to exit out his back. Parker saw blinding white light for a second, then fell lifelessly to the porch floorboards.

Inside the house, Gilly glanced out the broken windows. Were the men gone yet? Kris coughed and screamed in her arms. Gilly's eyes, blinded by tears and the smoke, couldn't properly focus. She finally saw the prostrate form of her husband lying on the porch, a dark red stain over his left breast.

"No!" she screamed harshly, startling the

child in her arms. Tears streaming down her cheeks, Gilly started for the door. Timbers crackled and twisted above her. She looked up in time to see the roof fall toward her as it burst into flames, crushing and burning them before Gilly could open her mouth to scream again.

CHAPTER TWO

THE HOMESTEAD Act passed by the United States Congress on May 20, 1862 spelled the end of the open prairies west of the Mississippi. This act provided the head of a family or an individual over the age of 21 with up to 160 acres of land, free of charge. The family simply had to take up residence on the property, cultivate and improve it for three years, and then the land was legally theirs.

Before this act huge tracts of land belonging to the U.S. government were bought and sold, sometimes at enormous profits. In 1852 the *Free Soil Democracy* stated, "That the public lands of the United States belong to the people, and should not be sold to individuals nor granted to corporations, but should be held as a sacred trust for the benefit of the people, and should be granted in limited quantities, free of cost, to landless settlers."

The debate raged politically for ten years,

with two homesteading bills drafted: one failed to pass, the other was vetoed by President Buchanan. Finally the Homestead Act of 1862 was passed. This opened up the West for countless settlers. Many of those who came were poor, homeless or adventure-seeking. Many more returned home, driven back by the hostility of the land, their own ineptitude at farming, droughts, and insect plagues. Those who stayed tamed the land and parcelled up the once free prairies, often infuriating ranchers who ran their cattle over the formerly open range. The widespread use of the newly invented barbed wire sparked outcries from ranchers, but the farmers had to protect their crops. Hostilities often grew violent. In Kearney, Nebraska, in 1874, things got downright deadly.

General Halleck was a cold, unfeeling man, Spur McCoy thought as the train screeched to a stop before a freshly-painted sign bearing the words KEARNEY, NEBRASKA. Spur hadn't more than a day off work in the last six months, and he'd already received his new assignment. Still, Spur realized that Halleck used him so much because he was the only United States Secret Service agent west of the Mississippi. Hell, he hadn't seen his office in St. Louis for months.

Spur retrieved his carpet bag, rested his favorite Spencer over his shoulder and walked off the train to the small Kearney station platform. At 6'2" and 200 pounds, well tanned, with green eyes, reddish-brown hair and a full moustache set off by sandy mutton chop sideburns, Spur was a man everyone noticed. Especially the ladies. They never seemed to mind when he spent an afternoon or evening with them.

At thirty-two he was one of a handful of Secret Service agents in the country. An excellent horseman, crack shot with most any gun, and skilled in hand-to-hand combat, knife and stick fighting, Spur McCoy was a man able to take care of himself.

Spur watched a smartly dressed woman with an ample bosom wait patiently for the passengers to leave the train, then pertly step into the passenger car where she was lost from Spur's view. Not bad for a first glimpse of a new town.

Spur turned and walked through the station and down the main street, a broad expanse of dust and mud with six blocks of unimpressive false-front buildings on both sides. The railroad had come to Kearney to ship beef to St. Louis, and Kearney had grown. Since 1862 homesteaders had been moving into the area, in turn producing more business all around. Kearney in 1874 was a bustling small prairie town, growing bigger each year.

On the surface, it wasn't an exceptional place. Spur had seen many similar towns—so many he couldn't possibly name them all. But General Halleck had warned him that the town wasn't as peaceful as it appeared to be. Two weeks ago a farmer, his wife and two year old daughter were burned to death at their farm outside

Kearney. There were also conflicting reports that the farmer, one Al Parker, had taken a slug through the heart, but the bodies were so badly burned it was impossible to be certain.

Word around town had it that the deaths were not accidental, and were a warning to the other homesteaders in Kearney County: *Move or we'll burn you out.* The ranchers were furious over the homesteaders' lavish use of the newly introduced barbed wire. The farmers were trying to save their crops from the stampeding feet of cattle, but the ranchers were used to running their cattle wherever they damned well pleased and the barbed wire was ending that.

This situation was becoming more common throughout the West, but in Kearney some ranchers evidently decided to relieve their frustrations with violence, Spur had been told. If it had been an innocent homestead family murdered by ranchers, it was Spur's job to discover the murderers and hand them over to the proper authorities. He also needed to diffuse the tension between rancher and farmer in the Platte River Valley.

Spur checked in at the Calico Hotel, dropped his bag and rifle in his room, then headed for the nearest saloon. It was Peterson's, the only one in town, a two story building with a fancy sign.

McCoy pushed through the bat-wing doors into the fairly clean, smoke-filled saloon.

"Hold it right there, asshole!" a man's high-pitched voice said.

Spur's hand automatically flew to the holster he had tied down on his right leg, but quickly realized the words weren't directed at him.

"Fuck you," another man said, snarling as he leaned against the bar. He was twenty-five, with an angry expression fired with whiskey. His clothes indicated his occupation: farming. Blond hair spilled around his weathered face. Spur noticed that although the man appeared to be relaxed, his hands hung loose but ready for instant action.

The other man stood across the saloon, in shadows. Spur could faintly make out his outline, and the glint of steel where a kerosene's light penetrated that far.

"Damned sodbuster! Take back what you said!" The voice was turgid with emotion.

"I don't know what you're talking about." The farmer's words were smooth and easy. He drained his whiskey glass, set it back on the bar, and motioned for another.

Spur gauged the reactions of the few men scattered around the bar, and was surprised to see a pretty woman in a red, frilly dress that matched her red hair sitting at a table near the center of the bar, apparently unafraid.

"I heard what you said about ranchers—goddamn it!" the man in the shadows said. "Look at me! Turn around and face me like a man!"

Having received his drink, the farmer downed it, threw the glass to the floor, and spun around. In a smooth, easy style Spur greatly admired, his hand slipped to his right, gripped the pearl handle of the Colt Peacemaker, and swung it up, perfectly aimed at the man. He could have blasted the rancher into the next world in a split second. Instead, he grinned insolently.

"I don't give a fuck what you think," the farmer said slowly, enunciating each word carefully.

As he watched the scene play itself out, he realized the man wasn't drunk. This confrontation confirmed Halleck's message—there was tension between the farmers and ranchers. He'd walked in on a fine example.

The shadowed figure took three steps forward. The man was dressed in ranching work clothes, his jaw freshly shaven, black hair perfectly parted in the middle framing his anger-marred fleshy face. A fattened rancher, Spur decided immediately. His hand hovered over the handle of his Colt .44.

To Spur's surprise, the red-dressed woman rose to her feet, standing almost between the men.

"Put your guns away, boys. The boss doesn't like blood messing up his floor." The woman turned her tightly-packed body to each in turn, smiling.

"Git out of the way, Roxanna," the rancher said. "I'm gonna blow that damned farmer to hell."

"The hell you are, Fred! The only blowing that'll be done around here I'll do, thank you!"

The saloon rocked with laughter.

"Relax, Roxanna," the farmer said smoothly. "You know better than anyone in town that ranchers got no dicks."

"Goddamn you!" the rancher said, and started to draw his iron.

The woman rushed him, then kicked the gun from the rancher's hand. It rattled to the floor.

"Leave me alone, Roxanna!" the rancher said as he grabbed her wrists. She fought back, laughing, and finally wrestled her way free of him.

Roxanna pushed back a wisp of hair that had fallen from her head and planted her hands on her hips. "Go on back home, Fred. No sense in getting thrown in jail for nothing. Go on!"

"No woman tells me what to do," Fred said menacingly.

This set up another round of guffaws from the men in the saloon. Spur glanced back at the blond farmer. He just caught the man holstering his weapon and walking out of the saloon.

"Showed up by a woman!" one man said, slapping another's back.

The rancher walked past Roxanna and stomped out the door after the farmer. With the excitement finished, the men went back to shuffling cards, drinking, and smoking. Roxanna laughed again as if the incident had been a joke and sat at a table.

Spur bought a whiskey and stood next to the bar. He downed the shotglass of booze in one gulp and the bartender wordlessly replaced it. McCoy sipped his second drink as the man next to him turned and stared at Spur.

"I don't recognize you," the man said after a few moments. Light brown stubble covered his cheeks and spilled down on either side of his thin face. A pinkish-red scar snaked along his right cheek. He stood about two inches shorter than Spur's six feet two, slightly leaner as well. What held Spur most about the man's face were the blue eyes. They seemed infused with deep, violent emotion.

"I'm new in town," Spur said, after summing up the man as he'd been analyzed.

"That wasn't a smart thing to do," he said. "Roxanna breaking up that fight. She should have let them have it out. I'd have liked to seen that farmer blast that rancher into hell."

"Why?" Spur asked.

"Because he's a rancher. That's good enough reason for me. If only Roxanna had—" He trailed off.

Spur sipping the biting, warm liquid. "You a farmer?" He damned well knew the answer.

"Yeah. Carl Lanford."

"Spur McCoy. I take it this isn't the first confrontation between farmers and ranchers here?"

"Shit no! It's been going on for years—but now with barbed wire we can fence those bastards off our land. Now the ranchers are really getting mad, cause we can fight back. At first they just stampeded across our fields, knocked over our buildings, that kind of thing. But two weeks ago the Parkers were murdered. Ranchers have gone just about as far as they can."

"You think some ranchers killed these Parkers?"

"Damn straight. Hell, I don't like to come into

town. I hate it here. I come in twice a week, maybe once a week, to buy supplies for my farm. Too many ranchers flaunting their money and power here to suit my tastes. But of course, there's other reasons for coming to Kearney—like that red-headed bitch that broke up the fight."

Spur glanced over at Roxanna, who sat entertaining a young man at his table.

"I see what you mean," Spur said conversationally. At least it wasn't difficult to get people to talk. Lanford might know plenty. "Someone got killed?"

"Yeah. The Parkers. Al and Gilly and their kid. Christ, they were good people. Hard working, from Atlanta. Just trying to make a go at farming, though they never really fit in well around here. They moved to Kearney County about half a year ago, homesteading. Now they're dead—and those damned ranchers killed them!"

"You know that for sure?"

"You're goddamned right I know for sure! Christ, word got around town real quick. Some think the men went there to scare the Parkers away, but that something went wrong and they killed them. I don't think so. Those ranchers went out there to kill the Parkers as a warning. Can't be any other way."

"I see. Any idea who did it?"

Lanford snorted. "If I did they wouldn't still be breathing. I got my suspicions, but nothing for certain." Lanford glanced up at Spur. "You seem mighty interested in all this, McCoy."

Spur shrugged. "Just making conversation."

The men were silent for a few moments, and Spur collected his thoughts. Things were heating up in Kearney. He'd come at the right time, before the whole country erupted into a farmer-rancher war with heavy losses on both sides.

Spur understood the problem from both viewpoints. Unfortunately, the ranchers and farmers couldn't do that. The hardest thing to accept, Spur thought, is change. The West was changing and the men who lived there had to as well.

"Who were those two men just now?" Spur asked.

Lanford started somewhat—then recovered and downed the rest of the drink. "The ranchers are getting more ornery, more sure of themselves," he said, ignoring Spur's question. "I hate all ranchers—I'd kill them all if I could. Especially that one," he said, motioning to the door through which the rancher had recently departed. "Things like this happen all the time—in the saloon, on the street, even in the general store. Hell, I heard about Roxanna going at it hot and heavy with some cowboy, only to have a rancher pull him off her to go at it. The rancher got his pants down before the farmer got back on his feet and the two men set to fisting it out. It ended with the rancher chasing the farmer butt-naked out into the street." Lanford's face grew dark. "But now it's gone beyond that. They're ruling this area, squeezing the life out of us."

"Think the farmers will retaliate for the Parker killings?"

"Hell, I don't know. Maybe. I wouldn't put it past some of the men I know. They're not only scared, they're damn mad. If the ranchers killed the Parkers, who's next? That's on my mind every night when I go to sleep. I go to bed with a loaded rifle." The man's face suddenly looked haggard, and Spur wondered how much sleep the man actually enjoyed. "Shit, I should be moving on." Lanford set the glass down and walked toward the door.

"Good talking with you," Spur said to the retreating man, then swung back to the bar.

The situation in Kearney was as volatile as the message from General Halleck had indicated. Spur had met many ranchers and they weren't ordinarily the type who would kill three innocent people in cold blood. The local sheriff, a man named Gardner, Spur remembered from the telegram, hadn't had any luck in finding the Parkers' murderers, and had called to the U.S. government for help.

Spur figured it should be fairly easy—if the killings were done by ranchers, that automatically narrowed the number of possible murderers. Certainly no farmer killed the Parkers, unless there was some sort of rivalry or fight that Lanford didn't know about. Not likely.

Spur turned his back on the bar and leaned against it. Roxanna, the fancy woman, approached him slowly, her hips swinging gently and her breasts bouncing with each step.

She kept her eyes down as she approached him. When she stood three feet away she halted, riveted her stare on Spur's crotch, then after a few moments looked up and smiled deliciously at him, her pink tongue visible between her lips.

"What's your name?" she asked in a high, light voice.

"Spur McCoy, ma'am." Spur tipped his Stetson to her.

"McCoy. Want to come to my room for some fun?" She moved closer until she fitted her feet between his. A warm hand traveled down between their bodies and rested on the lump between his legs, pressing and fingering. "I'm good. I'm real good."

Spur felt his body responding, but with an effort moved away from the woman.

"I just got into town. Business. I don't have the time."

She looked down at the growing bulge between his legs and laughed shortly. "*He* thinks differently," she said, extending a slender finger toward his crotch.

Spur smiled. "He doesn't think. I do."

Roxanna put her hands on her hips and sighed. "Okay. Maybe next time. How long will you be in town, Spur?"

"A week, probably; maybe longer. Depends."

"On what?"

Spur looked directly into her eyes. "On how much rest you give me."

She laughed again, a hearty, musical laugh unfettered by common standards of femininity.

"I can say this for you, Spur McCoy. I like your style. Is the rest of you as inviting?"

"I don't have many complaints," Spur said, deadpan.

Roxanna laughed again. "Next time, Spur. It's you and me." She sauntered off to another prospective customer.

Spur smiled and swung back to the bar. He lifted his glass to down its contents.

"Ranchers!" a man near him said, and followed it up by spitting on the floor.

CHAPTER THREE

WE SHOULD have waited, he thought as they continued to ride through the endless, dusty prairies that made up the vast majority of the state of Nebraska. It was too light yet. They should have waited until night, so they could cover their tracks better. The blond-haired man glanced over at his riding companion, staring straight ahead, eyes riveted on the position of the still unseen ranch that was their destination.

He was a strange one, Hiram thought, and smirked as he looked away. But he'd worked for worse, and when the man had approached him in a saloon in a town he happened to be passing through, the man's offer of pay sounded interesting. Hiram remembered how he'd been wondering how he'd pay for his next drink of whiskey.

After the stranger had set a full whiskey bottle before him at the bar and said, "Drink up," he propositioned Hiram—$30 for an afternoon's work. Hiram had taken the offer—and he didn't mind if he had to kill.

But this guy was a strange man. All show and no guts, he thought. He wanted another man dead. That was common enough, but this guy seemed crazy about it. Couldn't talk or think of anything else.

His partner—Hiram didn't know his name—drew rein and motioned for him to do so as well. His eyes flickered nervously back and forth, constantly on the alert, his full attention now turned toward detecting the presence of other human beings.

No one was around. They hadn't been followed from Kearney. Hiram relaxed as they rested their horses. It was at least an hour until sunset, maybe two. They should have waited.

"I know what you're thinking," the stranger said suddenly. "I can see it on your face. We shouldn't have come out here until sundown. I know. But I need the light to look around the place. I've been out there once before, earlier today, but I've got to get the lay of the land."

"I see," Hiram said, surprised by the man's forethought. Perhaps he was more than he appeared to be.

"Let's go."

They nudged their horses into action, bolting them forward due north. Hiram looked over at his partner; the man clenched and unclenched one fist.

* * *

Spur walked into the whitewashed wooden structure that bore a carefully painted sign: SHERIFF'S OFFICE. It was dark—the building had few windows and those were small. He stepped into the office area, with desk, an impressive shelf of books. potbelly stove, and a framed oil painting of President Grant. Behind this were two cells: the local jail. Both were empty.

A man swept the corner of the jail, carefully moving piles of dust closer to each other until they merged into one large mass. He looked up as the door banged shut behind Spur. He was 50, stood 5'8", balding. The remaining hair was short-cropped and black, streaked with gray. The prominent nose poked out between two friendly, honest eyes. The man's face was fleshy, guarded.

"Sheriff?" Spur asked.

"That's right," he said, placing the broom in the corner. "Jerry Gardner."

"I'm Spur McCoy. Just got into town a few hours ago."

At the mention of the name Gardner's face suddenly grew serious. "Mr. McCoy, am I glad to see you. Have a seat." He motioned to the chair that sat before his plain wooden desk.

The two men settled down facing each other.

"I really need your help," the sheriff began. "I've—I've done my best, but there's been so much trouble I haven't been able to keep track of it. And all my ideas—they just don't add up." Gardner stared out the window, the afternoon sun hitting his face harshly, turning it into a mass of wrinkles and worry lines. "I'm not the best lawman. I'm old and tired."

Spur shook his head. "I don't think so. Tell me why you brought me here."

"Didn't your man—"

"Yes, I got General Halleck's version, but I want it from you. Don't leave out anything."

Spur listened to the sheriff's story. It matched Halleck's information.

"That's as much as I know," Gardner said. "And I couldn't do anything."

"Bullshit, Gardner," Spur said. The man felt sorry for himself, had lost his self-confidence. That could kill a man faster than a drawn revolver. "You wouldn't be behind that desk if you weren't either capable or crooked, and I don't think you're crooked."

"Thanks," Gardner said.

"Only a sheriff who cared about his town would send for help. I don't think less of you for it, and neither should you."

"Hell, McCoy, sometimes I think it's time I stepped down. I don't have what I used to."

"Why?" Spur asked. "Because you can't draw as fast as you could thirty years ago? Or because your shoulders hurt sometimes, or your brain doesn't work quite as well as it used to?" Spur smirked. "I don't want to hear any more of *your* problems, sheriff. Fill me in on *Kearney's* problems. What's happened in the last few days?"

Gardner sighed, then leaned back. "No more murders, thank God. Ahh—little things. Fences being cut. Cows moving from one herd to another overnight, or disappearing completely. Crops torn up by careless hooves. Still, it's not over yet."

"Why?"

"Folks are upset here. You can see it in their faces, read it in the way they walk down the street. They aren't friendly anymore—not until they've decided which *side* you're on." He shook his head. "We used to be neighborly. I don't like this."

"Have there been any more threats?"

"Sure," Gardner said. "All the time. They don't amount to much. But they're fuel for the fire, that's for certain."

Spur was silent for a moment. "Where should I start looking?"

Gardner sat up and fumbled through the papers on his desk. "I've got it here somewhere—damn!" The man took a pen, dipped it into the well, and scribbled on a piece of paper for a few minutes while Spur sat and watched. "I forgot to do this earlier," he said. "I knew I didn't do something."

Occasionally the sheriff would pause, place the pen's point to his tongue, blackening it slightly, then resume writing. In a few minutes Gardner handed Spur the paper.

"Here's a list of the ranchers in Kearney County that I know are more than a mite angry at the homesteaders. I'm not saying either side's right, but these men have suffered the most of the farmer's wrath."

"Why's that?"

"They have property near farms, or run their cattle over what used to be open range, although technically it was owned by the government. I've listed them in no real order, just as they came to mind. As you can see, I've also included little descriptions of each and directions on finding their ranches."

"Fine," Spur said. "Any suggestions on who to contact first? Who'd be the most productive for me?"

Gardner shrugged. "Don't know. Maybe the Tates, although it's only one of them that dislikes farmers—that's Roscoe Tate, as you can see."

Spur read the list over carefully. There were six names. He waited for the ink to dry before folding it and tucking it into his pocket.

"Are the ranchers organized? Do you think the attack on the Parkers was a group effort? Think they may be getting some sort of secret band together to drive the homesteaders out of Kearney?"

"Damned if I know," Gardner said defensively. "It's a possibility, and one that I've thought of before, but there's no proof."

"No one witnessed the Parker killings?"

The sheriff shook his head. "No one I can find."

"And no one saw anyone ride toward the farm that morning, or away from it?"

"Damnit, Spur, I've already gone over those questions a thousand times in my mind. No one saw anything—or if they did, they aren't talking."

"Sorry, Gardner. I have to ask."

He lifted a hand and waved it in the air as if to dispel the tension. "I know. I'm sorry I yelled. This thing's been pressing on me for two weeks now. The whole town's in an uproar about it, and even some of the ranchers are angry, probably because they think they'll be blamed for the murders. In a way, they're all responsible.'"

Spur rose. "Thanks for the information, Gardner. I'm sure I'll find those killers."

Gardner rose and extended his hand. "It's great to have you here, Spur. God knows I can use your help."

They shook hands and Spur headed out into the dusty street.

Sunset. The two men stood and stretched their aching limbs amidst the shelter of a willow thicket. They were on the grounds of the Lucas ranch, a mile from the farmhouse. As the sun set a cool breeze blew up for a few brief seconds, stirring the trees around them into noisy action, then quieting as the wind died. A full moon hung in the eastern sky.

"Now?" Hiram asked, looking at his boss. He was eager to get this over with. Hiram wanted his pay and a good meal in his stomach within three hours.

"Soon."

Hiram turned away from the man then, to hide his look of disgust. The man was losing his courage. He'd waited too long; the anger or fear or bitterness had passed and it was too late.

"I've thought it over. We'll wait, get him while he sleeps."

"Sleeps?" Hiram asked incredulously.

"Right. We wait six hours."

Hiram had turned half-dumb by the time the luminescent moon had climbed directly overhead. Finally his employer gave the signal and they mounted their uneasy horses. By moonlight they picked their way toward the ranch-house, glowing white in the darkness.

"No noise," the stranger said. "We take him alone—quietly. No shooting until or unless there's no other way." He lowered his voice substantially as they neared the house. "We'll knock him out, take him outside."

"Right," Hiram said, wondering what tortures the man had in mind for his enemy.

They drew rein a quarter mile away in another clump of willows, tied up their horses, then walked silently toward the still ranch-house.

No lights shone from the windows; the bunk-house as they passed it was quiet. The ranch lay sleeping as they approached the house. It was a one story, unpretentious structure.

Which room was the bedroom? Hiram hoped the man knew. He sweated. This wasn't the kind of work he was used to. He liked things noisy—guns blasting, men falling to the dirt—not sneaking into houses at night.

The man walked up to the front door and turned the knob. It moved and the door swung open. Apparently the rancher wasn't expecting trouble. They walked in and turned immediately to the right, then down a hallway. At its end they came to a half-shut door. His boss pushed it open—a man lay snoring.

Motioning the other man to be quiet, they walked to the bed. Hiram's employer hefted his rifle and struck the man sharply on the head. He grunted and lay still, his breathing at a much reduced rate. He was unconscious.

They carried the man's limp body from his bed and down the hall, finally outside. As they hefted it back to their clump of willows the man flinched, rolled his head from side to side. Hiram, holding his legs, dropped them and punched the man's jaw. His head fell sideways.

Moments later Hiram stood still, holding up the man's body by the armpits while his employer pushed a noose around his neck. The other end of the rope stretched over the highest branch in a walnut tree that grew near the willow grove. Once the noose had been tightened, Hiram dropped the man to the ground.

"Roll him over."

Hiram did so and watched as the other man tied the wrists tightly together behind his back.

"Now we wake him," he said, smiling.

"Why don't we just hang him and get it over with?" Hiram asked. "What's this about waking him up?"

The other man ignored him and produced a bucket of water which he'd apparently hidden earlier. Hiram's employer threw the bucket's contents over the man's face.

He spluttered and shook his head, fighting off the sensation of drowning.

"Fred Lucas," his boss said. "You're going to die."

The man's eyes weren't open yet, and Hiram wondered if the man heard.

"You're finally getting what you've been deserving for a long time."

Lucas woke fully, blinking against the icy cold water that continued to slide down his forehead.

"Let's get him up."

Hiram rushed to the end of the rope and the two men hoisted Lucas off the ground. After securing the rope around a tree trunk Hiram's boss yanked it twice. Lucas gagged, retched, kicking the air while struggling to free his hands.

"Hold him still," the man said after standing in front of Lucas. Hiram rushed around behind him and gripped the man's legs. His employer produced a six-inch blade from a sheath that hung from his belt. It gleamed in the moonlight as he plunged it deep into Lucas' gut, grunting with the effort.

It cleaved the skin neatly. He thrashed the blade, bursting the internal organs, ripping the man's belly apart.

Lucas groaned in agony and tried to kick free of Hiram's hands. Blood spurted out, staining the ground where it dropped. He finally pulled the blade out, slimy with blood and dark tissues.

"Enough," he said, then stuffed a piece of

cloth into Lucas' mouth. "Don't want anybody to find you before you're dead."

Hiram watched the man stoically; a messy death, sure, but where's the excitement? The adventure? He sighed. At least he'd be paid.

"Let's go."

The two men made their way through the willows to the horses. No one had been alerted. Hiram pulled himself up into the saddle and frowned. It had been a good night's work. One man was happy, another dead. That's the way of life, Hiram thought as they rode quietly from the area. He drew up alongside the man. He'd been wrong about him. The guy knew what he wanted and had gotten it.

"When do I get paid?" Hiram asked.

The other man halted his horse. They were well away from the ranch.

"Now." He reached into his vest pocket.

Hiram tensed. Was this a trick? Would he pull out a revolver and blow him to hell?

No. The man produced a small bag and handed it to him. Inside he found three ten dollar gold pieces. He pocketed the money.

"Thanks."

Hiram turned away from the trail that led back to Kearney. On to the next town, the next job, and a warm woman who'd share her bed with him for a few hours.

CHAPTER FOUR

THE TATE Ranch, situated five miles outside of Kearney, was one of the largest in the area. With its four sections and 5000 head of cattle the Circle T sprawled over the flat land of the Platte River Valley and swept up into the plains.

David Tate, twenty-eight, his curly red-brown hair spilling around his handsome face, moved closer to the man lying wheezing and coughing on the bed. David's face was concerned. His father was dying, and nothing could be done about it.

Three doctors had already examined him—one brought in especially from St. Louis—but Dick Tate's disease had mystified them all. Now, six months after his father had first contracted the mysterious illness, David Tate ran the ranch, with the advice and guidance of his mother, Amanda.

As he approached his father, David choked back a grimace of pain. Dick Tate looked ancient, far older than his fifty-five years would indicate. It wasn't the harshness of ranch life, nor the power of the relentless sun that had carved the age onto the man's face—it was the strange wasting disease that sapped his strength.

"David," his father said slowly, coughing out the word.

"How you feelin', Father?" David sat on the edge of the bed and gazed down at his father. After six months it was still hard for him to see his father in this condition.

The man waved off the question. "You know how I am," he grumbled, and set into a coughing fit. When he'd quieted, Dick Tate looked up gravely at his son. "How's the ranch? Everything fine?"

David smoothed on a smile. "Yes. No problems I can think of."

"Bullshit," his father said softly. "There's always problems on the Circle T or any ranch. Don't hold back on me now, son. There's nothing I can't take."

"You always knew when I was lying, didn't you?" David asked, then brushed back salt and pepper hair from his father's head. "No real trouble. We lost twenty head—probably to rustlers. There's no sign of them anywhere."

His father frowned. "Twenty head? Shit."

"That's what I said," David said, laughing softly. "Along with that, one of the cowboys—Cole was his name, I think—came to the back door and asked to talk with mother. She refused, of course—he had no right—but he pushed past her anyway and went in. He asked her for something, and as soon as she'd left the room he rifled it of everything he could carry and then left the ranch and the county in a damn big hurry."

"What'd he take?" Dick asked huskily.

"A bag of silver dollars—"

Dick winced.

"A pair of candlesticks—oh yes, and a book. I don't remember which one."

"Not too bad."

"That's why I didn't want to disturb you. You've got to save your strength. Don't worry about the ranch—everything's fine, or will be when you're back to normal."

Dick shook his head. "I'll die in this bed, son. You know that."

David couldn't speak.

"How's Roscoe been lately? He hasn't been in to see me for two days."

The young man suddenly found words.

"Roscoe's an idiot, as you well know. He's trying to stir up trouble in town against the homesteaders."

Dick snorted. "What?"

"Yeah. I heard all about it when I rode into town this morning. Seems he wants to drive the homesteaders out of the county. I think he'll use any means."

"He didn't have nothing to do with the Parker killings, did he?"

David sighed. "Don't know. In fact, I don't

know what Roscoe's capable of doing anymore. The hot-headed ranchers are still badgering the homesteaders and I don't think it's gonna stop soon. Roscoe's in the middle of it, trying to keep the situation alive, rustling up support in the other ranchers to drive the farmers out of the county." He shook his head. "I don't like what he's doing, Father. It's not right."

"And you don't like Roscoe, do you?"

David lowered his eyes. "He's not the same since he came back. He's tougher, wilder. And I think he's jealous of my position, running the ranch."

"Can you blame him?' Dick Tate smiled. "If he hadn't run off ten years ago he'd be in your place now. Not many men can accept the consequences of their actions." Dick Tate dissolved into a coughing fit.

A moment later David turned to the second story window to see Roscoe riding toward the house.

"Here he comes," David said.

"I remember the day he left. He said he was tired of ranching and wanted to see the world. So he took that $500 from the safe—his *inheritance* he called it—and left."

"I remember too. It was my eighteenth birthday—what a shitty day to pick for doing a thing like that."

"Don't be too hard on your brother," Dick said. "He's blood. Roscoe's had a rough life, same as us. I think he's touched in the brain now, just a bit. Watch him, David. Don't be too obvious, but let me know what he's up to. God knows we certainly don't want any trouble, here on the ranch or anywhere in the county. If he is doing this—stirring up hard feelings against the farmers—I don't know what will happen. Someone's got to stop him."

"Me?"

Dick shook his head. "No. Roscoe'd never take to you giving him orders. It'll have to be Amanda or me. I don't know if we have any control over him anymore. Oh, we could kick his butt off the ranch, if it comes to that. But Roscoe seems—untameable, like that one bay I never could break."

"I know what you mean," David said, then heard the scraping of feet behind him. He turned and saw his brother standing in the doorway.

"Untameable, am I?" Roscoe asked in his guttural voice. "I take that as a compliment." The man crossed his arms over his chest and laughed heartily. "That's what Roxanna calls me."

At thirty, Roscoe Tate was in fine shape. He was 6'2", barrel chested, with powerful arms and legs honed by years of tough work. A brown moustache curled down around his mouth, and green eyes stared intently at all that came into his field of vision. His hard chin, planed jaw and hair-swept forehead all combined to make him popular with the ladies—those who charged and those who did not.

"Hello, Roscoe," Dick said. "Nice of you to stop by."

Roscoe's face didn't alter. "I've been busy, so

I haven't had time to come up here." He moved into the room and turned his attention to David. "Well, little brother, since you're running the Circle T shouldn't you be out there doing something?" He pointed toward the window.

Rage welled up inside him but David wouldn't show it in front of his father. "I'm filling Father in on the ranch. That's work, but I'm not surprised you didn't recognize it."

"Oh yeah? Sounded like you were talking about me—untameable, wasn't it? Now that doesn't sound like ranch business to me." His smile faded and his neck tightened. "That sounds like my business."

"Can it, Roscoe!" Dick Tate said, a little too forcefully, and he collapsed into a coughing fit.

"See what you've done?" David gestured toward their father. "Can't you think of anything but yourself?"

"Seems like you're doing a lot of thinking about me," Roscoe said.

"That's right. You're part of the ranch—at least, you're living here, though you're not doing an inch of work. That concerns me, as does everything connected with the Circle T."

"Look, little brother, if you were cold and dead do you know where I'd be right now?"

David stiffened visibly. He wouldn't give his brother the satisfaction of an answer.

Roscoe's green eyes shone excitedly. "If you were dead, I'd be running the Circle T." He walked two paces closer and clapped a hand down on David's shoulder. "Think about that, little brother."

David wrenched from his brother's grip and turned back to his father, who had finally ended his coughing spell and lay wheezing.

"I'll do what I can about that little matter," David said to his father, then turned to leave the room. His brother caught his arm but David pulled free. "Keep your fucking hands off me, Roscoe! I don't know who the hell you are, but you're not my brother. Not anymore."

"What a relief!" Roscoe said grimly. "To think after all these years—"

"That's enough!" Dick Tate said from his bed.

Both men turned to look at him.

"Roscoe, I'll not have you treat your brother that way. Not on the Circle T!"

"Come on, Father. You know I'm just—"

"I don't give a good goddamn what you're doing! You won't do it in my presence, or in my house."

Roscoe's eyes narrowed. "Are you telling me what to do, old man?"

David spun and wildly threw a punch at his brother, which Roscoe easily deflected.

"You can't even fight like a man, baby brother. Maybe that's your trouble—you're not a man."

"Don't listen to him," Dick said to his younger son. "You remember what I said." His voice grew husky and harsh. "Now leave. I need some sleep." He pulled the quilts higher and settled back onto the goosedown pillow.

"Glad to get out of here," Roscoe said. "I'm going to get a drink. God knows I need one."

David shot past Roscoe out the door. Roscoe's

laugh echoed in the bedroom as David walked down the hall and stairs, then out the front door into the blinding Nebraska sunshine.

"Jesus Christ!" David said. Roscoe had lost all control, all feelings. Or had he? Perhaps he was just drunk. Roscoe got drunk every day, David knew. But he hadn't smelled liquor on the man's breath. Why the hell didn't his father kick Roscoe off the Circle T? Could he still feel anything for his son who treated him so cruelly? David shook his head and stared out over the vast expanse of the Tate ranch. Someday, he knew, it would be his. He didn't want it right now—God no. He didn't want his father to die. But he would get it eventually. When that day came, he'd be certain his brother never set foot on the Circle T again.

Roscoe Tate ambled down the stairs and went into the first floor study where he poured a drink of whiskey. He swallowed it straight and repeated the process. A warm glow radiated from his stomach, soothing his nerves and making him feel fine and happy.

His asshole brother David was up to something. He knew it. Roscoe could feel it in his bones. Maybe he shouldn't have said all those things in front of his father—but hell, the old man was almost dead. In a week or two—three at most—it wouldn't matter anymore. It was not that he wanted the Circle T. He'd hate to be saddled with the work, problems and headaches. Let his brother run the spread. He could loaf and drink and play with the fancy ladies in town.

Roscoe wanted the Circle T to grow richer and more prosperous year by year. Then when there was sufficient money in the bank he'd withdraw, say, ten thousand dollars and leave, never to return.

The plan had almost worked before—he'd stayed away for ten years. But his money had run out long before that; he had taken too little and spent it too fast.

Roscoe had a plan now—a better plan. With the money he'd find a good town and open a saloon. Bring in a few fancy women from St. Louis and let the cowboys and homesteaders drink and fuck their money out of their pockets and into Roscoe's.

His stupid, snivelling little brother wanted the Circle T. What an asshole! Roscoe poured another drink, then wet his mouth with the burning amber liquid, feeling it wash around with its fiery power.

He knew he'd better get rich quick or it'll be too late. Opening a saloon in a boom town farther west would do the trick, and he'd have the strongest whiskey and prettiest women anywhere around.

Roscoe shook his head. He was daydreaming again. He had to concentrate on the present, on his immediate plans. He'd heard that they'd lost twenty head, rustled from the ranch. That would cost whoever did it. He'd heard rumors around town that some farmers were killing cattle and hiding the carcasses. There was also someone else rustling in the area. These problems didn't make for good cattle business. If any upstart homesteaders were picking off cattle branded with a capital T and a circle—he wouldn't rest easy until he found who was doing it.

The thought of the homesteaders jolted a nervous twitch over his left eye into action. He hated them. Those stupid sodbusters, their weak women and scrawny babies. He wished every one of them would keel over dead or move out of the Platte River Valley. The trouble was, he also knew the homesteaders wouldn't move out by themselves. They needed help. Roscoe grinned, thinking of the kind of help he could give them.

His attention was drawn to the family Bible, with its glorious gold-stamped leather spine four inches thick. Roscoe stared at it for a moment, then smirked as he worked out his plan and poured another drink.

CHAPTER FIVE

SPUR McCOY went back to his hotel, the Calico. He asked the clerk how the food was in the dining room.

"Tolerable. Just got a new cook hired on. The last one made everything taste like stewed dog. They're just putting supper down now."

Spur thanked the man and headed into the dining room. After a filling meal of a thick steak, mashed potatoes and gravy, corn and peas, topped off with coffee and apple pie with cheese, Spur went up to room 201. He had made sure he got a room situated at the end of the building, facing the street, near the outside stairs.

Spur reached out to push the skeleton key into the door's lock beneath the handle—and the door slowly swung into the room. Spur tensed and kicked the door fully open.

He heard a surprised yelp and saw a beautiful young woman sitting on his bed, her knees drawn up, the booted feet resting on the edge of the mattress. She had been playing solitaire—the cards were spread out on the quilt. When she saw Spur she lowered her feet and stood.

"Hello," she said in a high, musical voice. She looked about twenty, just under five feet even, with milky-white, smooth skin. Cascades of blonde ringlets spilled over her shoulders and back onto the skin-tight, white, high-necked bodice of her satin dress. Spur looked at her thrusting breasts. A dimpled chin and high cheekbones gave the woman a stunning face.

"Good evening, ma'am," Spur said, tipping his hat. "Mind if I ask what you're doing here?"

"Not at all, Mr. McCoy—but it's Miss."

He looked at her use of his name in surprise.

"I checked the registry," she explained. "I'm Ginny Burriss. I saw you walking into the hotel earlier, and I wanted to meet you."

Spur liked this woman, and not only physically.

"Why?"

The woman's gaze dropped to the floor. "Well, when I saw how tall and strong you are, and how handsome . . ." Her cheeks slowly flushed red. Ginny lifted her head and looked at Spur. "I just had to meet you, Mr. McCoy. You're such a man, like one I'd see in my dreams."

Spur smiled. He had heard this kind of overture from women before, and it never failed to surprise him.

"Thank you, Miss Burriss. I take that as a

compliment. You're certainly beautiful yourself."

"Really?" She looked at him in wonder. "Maybe I am. Oh, and call me Ginny, Spur. Do you mind if I call you that?"

"You can call me anything you want." Spur closed the door half way for propriety, then hung his hat on the knob and turned back to an expectant Ginny Burriss.

"I hope this doesn't shock you, my being here this way," she said. "But I—I just had to meet you." She suddenly raced across the room and flung her compact, rounded body against Spur. Ginny clasped her arms around him and buried her head against his powerful chest, grinding her thighs against his.

"Not shocked at all, Ginny. As a matter of fact, I like it."

She broke free of him. "You do?" she said, delighted. "I'm so glad. I never have any fun—cooped up at home all day. That's why I had to meet you." Her eyes grew intense. "Let's hurry." She turned her back to Spur. "Unbutton my dress, Spur, quickly. I can't wait much longer!"

Spur deftly freed the pearl buttons from their satiny prisons until the back of the dress lay open. Meanwhile, Ginny removed her boots, pressing her firm bottom against Spur's crotch. He pulled the bodice down and reached in to cup her warm, firm breasts and squeeze the nipples.

"Oh Spur, yes! Play with them! Your hand

feels so good!" Ginny sighed at his ministrations for a moment, then whirled around again. She pulled down, then stepped from the dress, which she threw into a corner.

Spur walked to the door, closed and locked it, and pushed a straight chair top under the door knob. He didn't want to be disturbed.

"You look better and better," he said, feeling warmth flow to his groin while he stared at her silk-clad body. The chemise did nothing to hide her perfectly formed breasts, the nipples already pushing out firm and erect against the smooth cloth.

"Don't just stand there, Spur," she said. "Undress me!"

McCoy slipped the chemise off her body, then bent his head to take one perfect breast in his mouth. He sucked and licked the nipple, taking it between his teeth and gently chewing.

"Oh God, Spur, yes!" Ginny's face flushed as her hand found his crotch and pressed firmly against it, manipulating his hardness mercilessly, hungrily. "Eat my tits!"

Spur switched to the other breast, taking as much as it as he could into his mouth. Tasting, then sliding back until only the hard, reddish brown nipple rested between his lips. As he ate Spur slipped down Ginny's drawers. His hand went to her fury patch and rubbed the outer lips.

Now naked, Ginny ripped at Spur's clothing, apparently unembarrassed. She unbuttoned his shirt with one hand while fumbling at his fly with the other. Spur laughed.

"Relax, Ginny. I'm not going anywhere."

"I know, but it's been so long." Then she smiled. "You are going somewhere." She took his hand, kissed it, then pressed his fingers inside her. "You're going right in there!"

Spur returned the smile and allowed the woman to remove his boots and shirt, then he unbuttoned his pants and slid them down along with his drawers. Ginny's eyes lit up as Spur's penis swung up in its full hardness.

"God, Spur, he's so big!" she said in awe. "It's the biggest one I've ever seen!" Ginny grasped it and squeezed gently.

"Come on," Spur said. "On the bed." He flipped the cards onto the floor.

"No. Not yet."

To Spur's surprise Ginny knelt before him and sucked his entire shaft into her throat.

Spur's knees nearly buckled at the incredible warmth surrounding his penis. Ginny's eyes closed as she worked on him, and Spur couldn't help but take her head in his hands and gently, slowly pump in and out of her mouth, each trust surging his passion higher.

After a few moments of this Spur pulled away from her.

"You've done this before, Ginny Burriss!" he said.

She rose and dropped back onto the bed on her back, then lifted her knees and spread them wide. Spur looked hard at her lush crotch.

"I've done a lot of things, Spur McCoy."

He moved to her then, putting a hand between her legs, parting the lips and thrusting his fingers inside her as she squirmed in delight. Spur stretched out on her body, fingering her, pressing his mouth to hers. They parted and he thrust his tongue into the woman's warm mouth, searching, probing as was his finger deep inside her. The lashing kiss ended as Ginny turned her head and Spur's tongue slipped out.

"Enough of this teasing," she said pouting. "Put it in me!"

Spur removed his finger and raised his body slightly, feeling her hands grip and guide him.

"Now, Spur; now!" She cried out in need.

Spur rammed into Ginny in one swift thrust that pushed her body higher on the bed. The woman cried out as his hugeness filled her, then gasped for breath.

"Oh Spur, yes! Yes!"

Spur pulled back, then began thrusting his entire length into her slot. His head dropped and attacked her left breast, chewing the nipple, then switched to the right one. Ginny gasped as he pumped into her, meeting his thrusts with her hips, forcing him to the fullest possible penetration.

"That's good, Ginny!" Spur cried as he rammed and bucked. The ancient bed squeaked noisily as they wrestled. Ginny threw her legs up around Spur's thighs, resting her feet in the hollow of his back. The new position seemed to transform her; a series of cries erupted from her mouth and her eyes closed in ecstasy.

"Oh, fuck me, Spur! Harder!" Ginny's breasts flushed bright pink and her body shook with an internal explosion. "Oh, it's never been so good!"

Spur found it increasingly difficult to control himself as he watched the woman's pleasure continue to grow. He finally felt the old surgings in his groin.

He increased the intensity of his thrusts tenfold, his hips blurring as the sexual friction between them sent a surge of power into his loins. Spur's body jerked violently as he shot deep within her, his eyes screwed shut as she sighed and wrapped her arms around his sweaty back.

After a few shuddering seconds, locked together in an erotic embrace, Spur's body collapsed on top of her. She sighed and lay motionless under his slick, warm body, their chests fighting each other for breath.

Suddenly conscious of his weight pressing down on the tiny woman, Spur gently withdrew and lay on his side. They both rested—panting, worn out, unable to speak.

"Spur McCoy," Ginny finally said, breaking the silence of the moment. "That was worth waiting for!" Her eyes shone as she looked across the bed to him.

He planted a kiss on her bare belly and she giggled. "I have to agree, Ginny. You exhausted me."

She pouted again. "Really? I'm just getting started. Can't you go one more time?" She took his flaccid penis in her hands, rolled it, squeezed it. Slowly it awakened and grew hard and proud.

"There," she said. "I knew you could do it!"

Spur never ceased to be amazed at the sexual capacity of women. Not that he complained.

"Lie on your back," Ginny said, trying to roll him into position. As he did so she straddled his thighs with her legs, then holding his penis, slowly impaled herself on it. "Oh God! That's the heaven my fahter's always talking about—you hard and all the way up inside me!" She brought a hand down and massaged herself rapidly as she bounced up and down on him. Spur laid back, his hands behind his head, and watched the woman work herself out on him. He was tired, but not too tired to enjoy the sight of Ginny Burriss arousing herself on his body. Her full breasts bounced majestically above her, and he suddenly felt hungry.

Spur sat upright, catching Ginny around the waist to balance her, and sucked a breast into his mouth.

"Eat it, Spur! Suck on my titty!" She bounced harder on him, her buttocks slapping against his thighs with a steady rhythm—the music of sex.

Ginny's other hand dropped behind her and Spur felt her fingers on his balls—cupping, squeezing, setting his whole body on fire. Then she slid one finger up beside his penis up into herself. She sighed and arched her back twice in rapid succession, her mouth forming an *O* as she climaxed again and again, sitting down harder onto Spur's penis.

Spur cupped her buttocks in his hands, holding her a few inches off his body as she stopped bobbing, then thrust up into her until their crotch hairs intermingled. He drove it up inside her in quick, contrapuntal thrusts, his breath choking out in ragged gasps as he squeezed her soft bottom and blindly bucked upward, finally spilling his seed out in heart-stopping spurts while Ginny shivered above him.

Spur lay as if dead, his chest pounding, his penis spasming still buried to the hilt in the beautiful young woman. She slowly rose off him and dropped to the bed.

Neither spoke for several minutes while they struggled to recover from the exertion. Spur finally lifted himself up on one elbow to look at Ginny, who slept softly beside him.

Who was this woman-child? Spur wondered.

She opened her eyes then, smiled and nestled her body against his. Spur wrapped his arms around her, pressing his face down into her hair. It smelled lightly of lilac.

"I can't tell you how much this has meant to me," Ginny said. "I don't mean—well, it's not like I think we're going to get married. But these few times I can be with a man—that's what makes the rest of life worthwhile. My father—" she sighed. "He doesn't let me have any fun. If he knew I was here with you I can't imagine what he'd do." She shivered. "But let's not talk about him."

"Whatever you want."

She suddenly turned on him. "I want you to kiss me, Spur. Hard on the mouth. Please?"

She sinuously turned her body around, threw

one leg over his and moved up against him. Spur kissed her deeply and was rewarded by hearing her moans issuing from deep within her throat.

As he broke it Spur shook his head. "You're something else, Ginny Burriss."

A few moments later they dressed, then sat on the bed. Ginny bent down to retrieve her cards.

"I want to see you again, Spur. Before you leave Kearney. Okay?"

"Try to stop me," he said.

She laughed happily, her face radiant.

Then the door burst open. The wooden frame splintered and the chair bounced across the room as they stood in shock.

CHAPTER SIX

SPUR AND Ginny glanced up at the hotel room's door. A hefty, red-faced man squeezed into a black preacher's suit stood raging in the doorway. Wind-blown, coarse black hair, cropped close around his skull and hanging down longer against his neck, seemed to add to the man's wrathful appearance.

"Painted whore!" he spat. "Heathen slut! You'll burn in hell for this, girl!"

Spur rose. "Who the hell are you, and what are you talking about?"

"Servant of the devil!" the man hissed at Spur, then stalked across the room and grabbed Ginny's arm. When she resisted he drove his palm down hard against her cheek.

Spur's fist slammed into the man's jaw, jolting him away from Ginny.

"Are you all right?" Spur asked the woman.

"I'm fine."

"Idolatrous hussy! You'll burn in hellfire for

your lustful sins!" The man glared at them. "I didn't raise my daughter to go around—"

"Your daughter?" Spur asked. Ginny nodded meekly.

"—visiting strange men's rooms at night unescorted! It's tantamount to fornication! For the Lord saith, 'Verily, he who lies—' "

"Save the Bible quotes, Rev. Burriss. Your daughter's unharmed. Ask her." Spur cursed under his breath. He'd bedded the preacher's daughter. Great.

"You servant of Satan! Fornicator!" The big man's neck shook as he prated, the rippling flesh intensifying its reddish colors. He rubbed his chin where Spur's fist had smashed it.

Good, Spur thought. He's afraid to get hit again.

"I'll not have you polluting my daughter with your un-Christian ways!"

"Father, I—"

"Shut your mouth, whore! I'll deal with you later. Now get on out into the hall."

"But—"

"Get!" the man thundered.

"Maybe she wants to decide," Spur said. "She's not a little girl any more."

"Stay out of this, sinner! This is my daughter and she'll do what I say. Right, girl?"

Ginny nodded meekly and moved slowly from the room, frowning. She gave Spur a half-hearted smile and disappeared. She's got to break free from her father, Spur thought.

"Don't think you can come into town and bed every young unmarried woman you see. Just because you've fornicated your way across this God-fearing country doesn't mean that you'll do so with my daughter!" He stabbed the air with his finger. "Watch yourself, stranger. You're lucky I caught you before anything could happen!"

"You scare me, preacher. I'm shaking in my boots."

"Goddamn you!" Burriss roared.

"Ginny's not a helpless child. She must be eighteen, nineteen. Plenty old enough to do what she wants with or without your approval."

Fire shone in the reverend's eyes. "That kind of heathenish talk has put lots of girls into trouble, and then what became of them?"

"She's a grown woman, Burriss. You can't live her life for her. Let her do what she wants."

Burriss threw back his shoulders, closed his mouth and marched past Spur out the door.

McCoy shook his head. Ginny Burriss had one hell of a father to cope with. As much as Ginny enjoyed sex, Spur couldn't imagine why she stayed with her father. He certainly wouldn't have thought that she lived with such a man while they had been in bed together—Spur had seldom had a more enthusiastic woman.

Ginny Burriss cowered in the corner of the parlor, shielding her face from the blows the reverend rained down on her. Tears spilled freely from her eyes.

"I'll teach you to go to men's hotel rooms!" Rev. Burriss thundered. "How dare you disobey my orders! You were to stay here while I was out!" He slapped her face again. Slashes of red rose on her delicate skin, marring her beauty. "Have you been tarnished by Satan? Have you been possessed by a spirit? One that forced you against your will to do such wicked acts?"

"No!"

Burriss' face grew in hatred and blood lust. "I think so, girl. I think I know the cure. God is telling what I must do to cleanse you of your wicked nature." His powerful forearms wrapped around her waist and he easily lifted her, then lay her face down on his lap. Avoiding his daughter's blows the reverend hiked up the back of her dress, then savagely ripped the drawers from her body. "An exorcism of pain, my dear! Avaunt thee, Satan! I will drive you out by the powers of the almighty hand!"

Reverend Burriss stared down hungrily at her perfect white buttocks. He delicately caressed her bottom, then lifted his hand.

"Prince of darkness, leave this poor girl!" The hand contacted Ginny's exposed flesh with such force it squeezed out fresh tears. Ginny kicked and screamed as the second blow cracked across her cheeks, then another and another.

Burriss felt a warm glow within his broadcloth trousers as he spanked the woman, and the tightness against his fly grew with every repetition.

"Leave this woman!"

"Father, stop!" Ginny cried helplessly, then twisted on his lap, driving her elbow into his crotch.

Blinding pain shot through the man's body;

his mouth hung open in soundless horror. Ginny broke free and scrambled across the floor, then stood.

Stunned at her luck in eluding her father, Ginny straightened her dress and faced him.

"All right, Father. You want to know about me? About the real Ginny Burriss? I'm not the woman you think I am—or the little girl. I've slept with lots of men. Dozens of them. I've seen every size, shape and color of pricks and I don't intend to stop doing so."

Burriss groaned in pain as he rubbed the damaged area. "Goddamn you! You nearly unmanned me!"

Ginny smiled. "That's not much of a job. Father, haven't you been listening to me? I'm the whore of Babylon you always warned me about. I'm one of those women who spread their legs for any man. You know why? Because it feels good—better than anything else. It tells me I'm alive, makes me feel like a woman."

Burriss face flushed. "Ginny!" He winced.

"That's right. I even made love with that man you found me with! We'd just finished." Her eyes sparkled as she relived the moments. "I tore off my clothes and then he sank it deep into me! Does it shock you, Father, your good little Christian daughter talking this way?"

"I'll have no more of that kind of talk in my house! If you've fallen from the ways of the Lord I won't keep you under my roof!"

"You should know, Father. Fallen from the ways of the Lord! You're the most hypocritical man I know." She moved her head sharply, sending lustrous black hair cascading around her shoulders. "Don't think I don't know where you go when you sneak out nearly every night!"

Burriss sputtered, then regained control. The pain had ebbed. "Where?"

Ginny was astonished, not only at the look of fear that flickered across her father's eyes, but also at her own daring. Is this really me talking, she asked herself, or was she possessed by some errant spirit? No. She was tired of her father's tyrannical ways and she wouldn't bear them any longer. Imagine the pleasure she'd been denying herself! Now that she'd made love again she knew there was nothing else in life so sweet.

"Tell me!" Burriss thundered.

Ginny paused a moment; she wasn't sure where her father went, but she had suspicions. She decided to play them out. "Peterson's. I've seen you looking at that fancy woman, Roxanna Stafford. You probably sleep with her twice a week. How much do you pay her, Father, or does she let you do it for free because you're holy?"

Burriss' face washed with relief. He halted rubbing his crotch. "Young lady, you're in a shitload of trouble now." He rose from the floor where he had sat.

"Father, swearing again!" She clucked. "Not a very Christian way to act." She frowned. "Don't you understand, Father? You don't own me anymore. I won't listen to a word you say."

"Fine. So go off and take up with strange men," Burriss said. "What happens if you get knocked up? If you're been fucking so many men it's bound to happen. What then? How will you raise a baby without a husband? And what will that make you—and your baby?"

"I don't care. I don't have to, since I have this Indian herb that takes care of that." She smiled sweetly. "One day when you were gone I met an Indian woman in town, and she told me about it. She was a Christian, of course, but she remembers the old ways. I've thought of everything."

"Not quite. No man will marry you. Oh sure, they'll talk about you, probably relieve themselves at night thinking about you, but they'll never give you their name. No man will. Because you'll be a whore, anybody's woman."

Ginny burned in embarrassment for a moment, then shook her head. "I don't care. I could get a job in a saloon."

Burriss laughed heartily. "That's choice. You, a fancy lady. The preacher's daughter. It'll make me the laughing stock of the country."

"You already are."

Burriss' eyes shone with flashes of intensity. "Don't speak to me like that, hussy! You may be a loose woman, but you're still my daughter. Be out of here as quick as you can! I'm sure it won't be too hard to find a warm bed to sleep in."

"Fine with me!"

Burriss' face suddenly softened. "Ginny, I'm sorry you've fallen into these evil ways. Won't you pray with me to rid you of the wicked spirit that has set its evil grip on your very soul?" His eyes filled with paternal tenderness.

Ginny, confused, looked away from him. That was time enough for Edward Burriss to grab his daughter, shove her into her windowless bedroom, and lock the door with the skeleton key.

"Father!" Ginny screamed, pounding on the door.

Burriss pressed against it, feeling it vibrate against his body. He imagined his daughter's white buttocks streaked with pink, shaking in fright as his hand raced down toward them with ultimate authority.

McCoy woke with a grunt to greet the hot morning sun that shot directly parallel with the floor, across the bed where he lay. Spur rubbed his eyes, stretched and walked to the pitcher and basin where he splashed cold water on his face, stinging him to full consciousness, then dried with a stiff towel.

After he'd bathed and eaten three eggs, two cups of coffee and a pile of bacon in the dining room he walked to the livery stable and hired a fine looking bay horse and saddle. Just before he mounted, Spur pulled Sheriff Gardner's list from his pocket and studied it. The Circle T seemed as good a place to start as any. He pushed the paper back into his pocket, slid into the saddle and headed east out of Kearney.

Dust-laden heat suffused the bleak area. Plains stretched around him with monotonous regularity, the sky a deep blue bowl arching above. He rode easily, not tiring the horse, collecting his thoughts.

Spur finally saw the well-painted sign supported by two high posts over a gate: CIRCLE T RANCH. He went in through the gate and rode alongside pens and hay barns approaching the two story wooden structure—the largest ranch house Spur had seen. The Circle T must be doing well for the Tate family. Perhaps they'd have a lot to lose if homesteaders moved into adjacent property. Perhaps they—or Roscoe Tate, as Gardner had pointed out—were responsible for the Parker killings.

He rode past a huge corral and finally halted the bay at the hitching post outside the great house, slid to the ground and tied up his mount. Spur turned and approached the front door just as a gunshot blast rocked the house with a deafening sharpness.

CHAPTER SEVEN

SPUR RAN to the house as the sound of the shot died. He gripped a window frame and peered inside. A table, bookcase, chairs. No firearms, bodies, people. Spur bent at the waist and ran toward the window opposite the one he'd checked on the other side of the porch. Again, nothing suspicious. The Secret Service man knocked loudly on the front door.

Moments later it was opened by a plump, fifty-ish woman with blue eyes, a pinched face and a decidedly cold manner.

"Can I help you?"

"Sure hope so, ma'am. I'm Spur McCoy. I just heard a rifle blast inside the house and hoped you were safe. Has there been any trouble? Do you need any assistance?"

She shrugged, sending a few curls loose from the bun on her head. "No more trouble than usual. My sons were fighting and got too rough.

You've come at a bad time, I'm afraid. I'm Amanda Tate."

Spur tipped his hat. "Pleased to meet you, Mrs. Tate."

"So what brings you to the Circle T?" She stepped aside and motioned him into the house. "Please, come in." Amanda Tate closed the door behind him. "This way." They walked to a comfortably furnished parlor—overstuffed chairs, velvet curtains shielding out the hot sun.

"I'm here to ask about the Parker deaths last week."

The mention of the name brought color to the woman's white face. Her hands went to her throat.

"I see. Are you friends of the Parkers, perhaps family?"

"No," Spur said. "I never met Al or his family. But I've heard talk that they were killed—someone set that fire, it was no accident—and I'm trying to find out who did it. That's why I came out here to see what I could learn."

"Have you been to the sheriff? I'm sure he must have conducted an investigation." Her voice was steady, controlled, but disturbed.

Spur decided it was time to lay out his cards. "Mrs. Tate, I—"

"Amanda. Please call me Amanda."

"Amanda. I know there's been trouble between the ranching and homesteading factions of this area. I think the deaths of the Parkers have something to do with this. What do you think? After all, you live here—you might know what goes on."

She shook her head. "I'm sorry, Mr. McCoy."

"Call me Spur." He shot a smile to her.

"Fine, Spur. I don't get to town too often, and I don't follow local gossip. I'm afraid I can't be of much help to you."

"But surely you've heard something—"

"Rumors. Only rumors." She shook her head. "When I think of those poor people trapped in their house while it burned down around them . . ." She closed her eyes and shivered.

"Do you think ranchers may have been responsible for their deaths?"

Amanda Tate glanced at Spur abruptly. "You don't mince words, do you, Spur? But I hardly think you should ask me these questions; I'm just a rancher's wife."

"Then perhaps I could speak with your husband?"

"Sorry. Daddy's not feeling too well," a low voice growled behind them.

Amanda and Spur turned. "Spur McCoy, meet my son, Roscoe Tate."

The men exchanged nods.

"This your new suitor, Mother?" Roscoe asked wickedly.

"Ignore him," Amanda said. "I usually do."

"Perhaps he could tell me about the Parkers' murders?" Spur suggested.

"I'm sure he could tell you some things about homesteaders in general," Amanda clasped her hands at the waist. "Couldn't you, Roscoe?"

The man stared at McCoy. "I haven't seen you around here before."

"Just got into town yesterday."

Amanda turned to Roscoe. "Well, go on, son. Start spouting your story about the homesteaders. You know, how they're carving up the plains and ruining ranching. About how barbed wire fences cut across prime grazing land and the best drive routes. Go on, Roscoe! You've been talking about nothing else for months!"

Roscoe shrugged. "It's like she said, McCoy. I figure outside of two years they'll cut our profits way down. So much so that it's only sense to be worried about the homesteaders."

Amanda laughed. "Worried? You worry? The only think you worry about is eating and sleeping and drinking and loving! You don't care for the ranch and you know it!"

Spur shuffled his feet, feeling out of place in a domestic squabble. Amanda looked at her son for a few moments, then threw her hands up in disgust and turned to Spur.

"Trying to talk sense into this boy is like trying to convert a priest. He already shot a hole in my brand new wallpaper this morning. Roscoe, why don't you go into town and blow off some steam! You could use it, and I could use the peace and quiet!"

"I love you too, Mother," Roscoe said, then left.

Amanda sighed. "That's Roscoe."

Spur nodded. The man seemed to fit the general pattern—he definitely hated farmers. Did he hate them enough to kill them? Spur didn't know. Yet.

"Can I get you some coffee?"

"Sure. I'd love some."

Amanda sighed. "I don't know about Roscoe sometimes. It seems he's a child who hasn't grown up yet." She disappeared toward the kitchen.

Roscoe Tate walked into the bunkhouse, surprising two hands sleeping it off there. They scrambled out of their bunks, dressed only in their drawers, and faced the owner's son.

"Sir, we wasn't trying to ditch work, it—"

"Cut the shit," Roscoe said, "and put on your pants. I don't care if you work around here or not. But I've got a job for you." He took a flask out of his pocket and offered it to the men when they had finished dressing. One was Anglo, the other Mexican. The Anglo eagerly opened the flask and drank the burning whiskey as Roscoe talked.

"There's one man—at least—snooping around the ranch. His name's Spur McCoy. I don't want him or anyone else doing that. You understand me?"

The Mexican received the flask, raised it and the liquid spilled down his throat. He nodded in mid-drink.

"Why not, Mr. Tate?" the other asked.

The Mexican handed the flask to Roscoe, who wiped off the bottle and drank deeply. He then screwed the top back into place, and slipped it into his pocket.

"I don't want this ranch going up in flames! He may be a homesteader, or a gun they hired. I don't want anything harming the Circle T." He looked toward the door and saw Spur walking out of the ranch house. He motioned the two men to look at Spur.

"That's him. See him?"

"*Si.*"

"If you catch him sneaking around, checking up on things here, looking into our windows or just plain acting suspicious, let me know."

"And if we think he's dangerous, about to do something?"

Roscoe belched and ran the back of his hand over his lips and moustache, wiping them dry.

"Kill him."

Spur led his bay mare to the edge of the broad, shallow Platte River for a drink. He left the horse there, tied to a bush, then stretched out leaning against a cottonwood, thinking.

The low drone of insects permeated the afternoon stillness until he heard a splash and a feminine voice. Spur jumped to his feet and walked to the river. Five hundred feet downstream a natural depression had caused a pool of deep water to form, and in this pool Spur saw a naked woman bathing.

She lifted the crystalline water above her head to cascade down over her body, splashing off the nipples and sliding past her smooth thighs. Her body shimmered in the sunlight.

Spur wondered if she knew he was watching. If so, she didn't mind an audience. He approached the pool, hands stuck casually into his pockets, his head down low so that the Stetson's brim cut off the water's glare. She noticed him then, and smiled as she saw him drawing closer.

"Hello!" she called. "Come in. It feels wonderful."

It certainly looked wonderful, Spur thought. He debated for a moment. Not wise to turn down an invitation from a naked woman, Spur thought. As he undressed he looked at her more closely.

She was a real beauty, perfectly formed, the lines and curves of her body flowing into each other in pleasing patterns. Her skin was honey-golden in the sun, almost matching the long brown hair piled and knotted on her head. The face below it was sensuous: full, luscious lips, deep eyes, high cheekbones and just a touch of mischief.

"Get those pants off and come in here!" she said. "I usually bathe alone but I sure don't mind company."

"Do you do this often?" Spur asked as he stepped out of his pants and walked naked to the river. Despite his best intentions a partial erection swung before him. The woman's eyes widened as she watched it, mesmerized.

"God, you're packing a big piece there, stranger!"

"And you've got two fine, huge tits on you, lady!"

He entered the water and splashed ten feet to her. At this point the water level centered around their waists. Spur looked and saw her dark patch inviting him. He slipped down a hand and touched it.

"Nice! Real nice!" the woman said, and took Spur's penis into her hands, fondling it to full hardness as it floated in the water.

Spur bent at the waist and sucked in the woman's left breast, forcing as much of the warm mass into his mouth as he could, then moved back and concentrated on the nipple, sucking, licking, and biting it. The woman's hand grew more insistent at Spur's crotch and he finally had to throw it off him before he prematurely exploded.

"Watch that!" Spur said, pulling his mouth from her breast. "I almost shot my load!"

"Um. I love a man who talks dignified to a lady." She giggled and took his penis again, and pulled him toward the bank with it. "Let's go over there and do this right."

"No. I've got a better idea," Spur said. He turned the woman around, pressed her back gently so that she'd bent over, then pried her buttocks apart.

"I like the way you think," she said, shivering.

Spur guided his erection to the right spot, then bucked forward and slipped up into the woman.

"Oh yes! Ride me! Shove that thing deep in me and make me feel like a woman!"

Spur grabbed the woman's waist as he pumped into her, their bodies sending water splashing crazily in all directions. The unexpected sex, brazenly performed in the open, excited Spur more than he had expected. He looked down to watch where their bodies met and grunted.

"Oh, drive that huge thing up me!"

Spur's thighs slapped against the woman's buttocks as he pounded into her. She gave a cry and her breathing grew more erratic as he furiously thrust and withdrew. One moment her head slipped below the water but she surfaced a scant second later, coughing and pushing back to meet Spur's thrusts, forcing him deeper into her body.

Spur felt the woman tremble with orgasm and finally let go, ramming savagely into her as colors danced before his eyes, his body shaking with an internal explosion.

He thrust one last time and then pulled out from the woman. She stood and turned to look at him.

"God, that was wonderful! Just what I needed."

"We haven't been properly introduced yet," Spur said, fondling her breasts. "I'm—"

"No!" the woman said, putting her hand before his mouth. "Don't tell me your name. I never want to know that." She gripped his penis and pumped it vigorously below the water's surface. "We don't need to know each other's names, now that we've known everything else." She slipped closer to him, kissed his lips briefly, then let him go and walked toward the other side of the river.

"Hey!" Spur called, following her. "Aren't we going to see each other again?"

"No," she said. "I'm just passing through. But it was fun, and thank you for a wonderful time."

She splashed off and Spur stopped, watching her move, her buttocks gracefully swinging in the sunshine, glistening and throwing off pellets of silvery water as she ran.

Who the hell was she? Spur asked himself as he went back to the river bank and found his clothes threwn over it. He laughed and leaned back, staring straight up into the dazzling sky, at peace with the universe.

Except for those who killed the Parkers. The glow of satisfaction the exciting woman had provided to him vanished.

Who had killed the Parkers?

CHAPTER EIGHT

SPUR SWAYED gently in the saddle as he rode back to Kearny. Afternoon sun slanted across the plains before him, charging the earth with gold and orange hues. The bay whinnied a complaint and stamped a hoof into the dust-laden trail.

"Easy girl. We'll be home soon."

The horse relented and continued its pace. Spur scanned the horizon—unbroken save for a few rises or farm buildings pushed up against it. When Spur swung his gaze back to the trail directly before him, he noticed a rider approaching fast.

He didn't change his horse's gait, though all his senses were keyed to the rapidly approaching figure of a rider, horse and dust track. Someone was heading somewhere fast.

A few minutes later Spur identified the man—he was Sheriff Gardner. Where in hell was he going? Spur wondered. Soon Gardner reined in his horse five feet from Spur. The animal stamped and shook, lathered, nostrils popping with breath.

"Spur!" Gardner said. "Shit, am I glad to see you!"

"What's up, sheriff?"

"Trouble. Fred Lucas was murdered last night. Stabbed in the gut and hung until he strangled or bled to death."

Spur grimaced. "He's a farmer?"

Gardner shook his head. "A rancher." He patted his horse's neck and rubbed his shoulder. "Nope; it looks like the farmers are reacting to the Parker killing. They're returning fire with fire."

"Know of anyone who'd do such a thing?" Spur asked as the two men dismounted and stood in the center of the trail.

Gardner shrugged. "Half the farmers within twenty miles could probably be talked into killing a rancher. You know how things are."

"Yeah. Where's the Lucas ranch?"

Gardner turned and looked around him. "A half mile west of here you'll see an old burned-out farm. Turn right there and ride due north for four miles. You can't miss it."

"You've already been there?"

Gardner nodded. "I came out here looking for you, thinking you had gone to see the Tates. What'd you think of them?"

Spur frowned. "Don't know. Amanda Tate seems normal enough, but that Roscoe—"

"He's quite a character, isn't he?"

"Does he get on well with other people around Kearney?"

"No. He's pretty much a loner. Hasn't made many friends since he came back." Gardner sighed. "He's just plain ornery, if you ask me. Well, I should head back to town. You going to the Lucas place?"

"Yeah," Spur said. "You find anything there?"

Gardner shook his head. "Nope. Doubt if you'll do much better, but it's worth a try. No one saw or heard anything; a cowboy found him early in the morning, hanging from an old tree, his stomach a mass of slashed flesh and dried blood." Gardner scowled. "Who the hell would want to kill Lucas? He was one of the finest men around."

"Maybe some angry farmer who doesn't take kindly to seeing his friends get killed."

"Guess you're right; one senseless murder for three."

"See you around, Gardner. Thanks." Spur stepped into the saddle and rode toward the landmark, leaving the sheriff standing by his mount.

It wasn't a long ride but Spur had time to think before he arrived at the Lucas ranch. The next killing magnified the Kearney problem. If the farmers were indeed striking back and Lucas's murder wasn't unconnected, twice as much danger now existed for the citizens of Kearney County. He not only had to find the Parkers' murderers, he also had to discover

Fred Lucas's killer and try to halt the tensions rapidly worsening in the area.

"Great," Spur said. "My problem just got twice as complicated."

A half hour later Spur rode into the Lucas spread. It was typical of ranches in Nebraska, with several corrals, barn, bunkhouse, and a one-story ranch house, all woodframed and shiplap sided.

Seven cowboys idled the day away in the shade of a huge spreading oak that must have been transplanted from back east. One strummed a guitar, the others sat or laid back, hands clasped behind their heads, drifting on memories of earlier times, softer companions.

As Spur's approach became audible over the music the men looked up in various stages of alarm. As Spur halted his horse at the edge of the gratifying pool of shade the men relaxed. This was no farmer.

The men must be idle because their employer was dead.

"How're doing, men?" Spur asked.

"Fuckin' fine," one said.

"You work for Fred Lucas?" Spur stepped to the ground beside his mount, then tied it to a hitching post nearby.

"We used to," the same man answered. "Now we work for Mrs. Lucas, we think. What's it to you?"

A ring of nervous eyes scanned his every movement, gesture, and expression. He shrugged to ease off the tension he sensed in the men.

"I heard in town that Fred Lucas had been shot last night, and that another family—can't remember the name—got burned up in their house a few weeks ago."

"So?" a man with a thin beard shot back.

Spur shrugged again. "So I was thinking of moving into Kearney, but these killings and farms being burned up and all are making me think twice about it."

Another man—gruff, unshaven, black hair flowing onto his shoulders, moustache drooping around his mouth—stood up.

"Ain't no danger unless you're a rancher," the man said. "Shit, the farmers are behind Fred Lucas's murder. They have to be!"

"Why?" Spur asked. "Because he's a rancher?"

The area suddenly grew still. The long-haired cowpoke faced him squarely, his left eyelid twitching.

"What's wrong with that, stranger? You wouldn't be one of those homesteaders, would you?"

Four more men stood, hands placed jug-handle style on waists or tensely held into fists.

"No. I'm no farmer, but I'm not a rancher either. Fact is, I'm a lawyer. That's why I'm interested in Fred Lucas's death—the legal aspects of it."

"You don't look like no laywer to me," said a Spanish-accented voice with a high, nervous sound.

"Why the hell don't you go back where you came from?" said a white-haired, grizzled old hand who'd probably worked twenty spring drives.

Spur felt the tension increase. The men were outraged, scared. If he said the wrong thing he could set them off like firecrackers.

"Yeah! Get the hell off this ranch!"

"Enough!" a high voice said behind Spur. "I've had all I'm going to take of this!"

Spur turned and saw a stunning woman approaching, her head held high, half-shrouded by a length of black lace that hung down from a simple hat. Her firm, enticing body was tightly wrapped in a black dress accented with black lace and jet buttons which travelled its entire length.

Her clear, calm face with prominent cheekbones, languorous blue eyes and fine, full lips peered out from behind the veil that partially obscured it.

"That'll be the last outburst of poor hospitality I'll ever hear on the Lucas ranch. Do I make myself clear?"

The men grunted their assent.

"Mrs. Lucas?" Spur said.

"Yes. I'm Lorna Lucas." She extended a hand.

Spur grasped it for a few seconds. "Spur McCoy."

"You're here to inquire about my husband's death?" she asked with a steady voice. Her eyes betrayed no emotion.

"That's right, ma'am. If it wouldn't be too much trouble."

"Not at all." She turned and dismissed the men with a flip of her chin, then held out her arm for Spur to hold as they walked to the simple frame house.

Lorna Lucas couldn't be much past thirty, Spur thought. Her fine bearing and features betrayed a heritage of careful breeding and vast quantities of old money. Her skin was so fair. Scandinavian? Spur wondered.

"I don't know how much I can tell you," Lorna said, as they strolled. "My husband was asleep—at least, I guess he was." She smiled briefly. "I hope you won't take offense at this, but I didn't sleep with my husband. We had separate bedrooms. So, I'm assuming he was attacked in his sleep, dragged out there, and then killed."

"Did you hear anything unusual last night or early this morning?"

"No. I slept right through to five-thirty, my usual rising time. So you see there isn't much to tell."

"I'm sorry to put you through this again, Mrs. Lucas."

"It's nothing. I'm used to blood and pain and death. I'm just not used to it happening to my husband. It was so—" She paused a moment. "Unexpected? Death always is, I suppose."

"And you saw no one or nothing around his body to betray the murderers?"

"Absolutely nothing. They'd ridden off long before his body was found—hours earlier. I'm sorry if you've wasted your time coming out here," she said. "But let's have a glass of sherry and talk." She suddenly clasped his hand. "I need to talk to someone now."

Spur nodded, meeting her earnest gaze with calm, self-possessed eyes. Delighted, she led him into the house and to a glass of dry sherry. The wine wasn't the best quality, but he didn't turn down offers from beautiful woman. Ingratitude had never been Spur's style.

They talked for a half hour, general chatter, Spur thought, then he politely excused himself and left. After poking around the farm for a few minutes, and investigating the place where they'd found the body, Spur rode back to town.

He tied up the bay before Peterson's and walked in. His throat was dry from the ride. He also knew from Gardner's list that this was a good place to catch Jack Parsons.

Parsons was a rancher who'd been vocal in his opinions concerning homesteaders and their use of barbed wire, Gardner's list had told him. Parson's ranch lay three miles east of Kearney, but he might as well talk to the man while he was in town, at least get a chance to sum up the man. Parsons usually hit Peterson's around noon when he came to visit friends in Kearney, and apparently did so nearly every day.

Walking into the saloon Spur knew he could pick out the face if he wanted to waste an hour or so, but when he saw Roxanne decided to save time. He walked over to her and she smiled up at him from the table over which she was slumped.

"Hello, Spur. Nice to see you again. Are you ready?"

He smiled. "Maybe later. Do you think you could tell me something first?"

Roxanna pursed her lips, then spread them expansively. "Anything you want."

Spur turned around one of the straight-backed chairs, straddled it, and moved closer to the table opposite Roxanna. "Tell me if Jack Parsons is in this room. Don't make it obvious, but if you'd point him out I'd appreciate it. Could you, Roxanna?"

"Sure. But what do I get out of it?" She pouted gorgeously. "I mean, when I do a man a favor I expect him to do me one back." She batted her incredibly long lashes a few times, then straightened her back and thrust out her huge breasts. "See anything you'd care to do a favor with?"

Spur laughed. "Lots, Roxanna, but I don't have the time right now. I'll owe you one. How's that?"

She sighed. "What are you, a preacher? One of those Bible thumbers like old man Burriss? Let me tell you, Spur; that's not the only thing he thumps!"

"Roxanna, please," Spur said, touching her wrists acorss the tabletop. "I need your help."

"Okay. Now, where is he?" She raised a painted fingernail to her lips as she searched the room. Moments later she turned back to Spur. "I've found him. He's at the first table, the one closest to the door, wearing a brown hat and beige shirt. A tall man with a moustache."

Spur spotted him. Parsons didn't seem to notice the attention he was receiving. The man drank and smoked continuously, pouring shots from a whiskey bottle and pulling cigarettes from a pile of the neatly rolled sticks.

Spur turned back to Roxanna. "Thanks. I owe you one."

"Hey! That's two you owe me!"

"Fine. I appreciate your help." Spur pushed off the chair and walked in Parsons's general direction. He'd decided not to talk to the man at that time—he was too drunk to be of much good. But he could test the man nonetheless.

Beside Parsons's table Spur feigned tripping and landed directly on Parsons.

"What the hell?" Parsons yelled, then shoved Spur off him as he stood and glowered.

"Excuse me," Spur said in a slightly intoxicated voice. "I tripped."

"I guess you did! Why don't you watch your feet, clodhopper!"

Parsons's somewhat handsome face was streaked with sweat that burned down his flushed cheeks. Brown hair and browner, red-veined eyes; a tall, lanky build just under six feet; hairy arms and chest where it showed through the beige shirt and black vest, made up the file on Jack Parsons.

"Sorry," Spur said, brushing off his shoulder.

"Keep your goddamned paws off me!" the man bellowed. "You'd best get the hell out of here, stranger! I'm in no mood for clumsy fools!"

"I apologized. You'd better be happy with that, 'cause that's all you're going to get from me."

"Then leave me alone!" Parsons stuffed the

cigarettes into his vest pocket and grabbed the bottle. He moved to another table and sat, his back toward Spur.

McCoy grunted and exited the bar before anything more could occur. One thing was clear—Parsons was hostile. If Parsons was one of those guilty of the Parkers murders he may by now know Spur was poking around town checking up on things—others must know by now.

That could make things tougher.

CHAPTER NINE

THAT NIGHT, bats flapped across the inky sky, their bodies and furry wings silvered by the moon. Owls spoke from tangled bushes and rose in a flurry of activity, while below a snake slithered across the cold sand.

One hundred feet from the snake a circle of twenty masked men rose suddenly, their already hushed conversation cut short by the unexpected sound. Two scouts broke from the group and wandered slowly into the surrounding terrain.

"Nothing," one of the two said as they returned.

The men settled before the fire again. Around them cottonwoods stretched their branches sixty feet up. The natural copse marked an underground water source—probably a runoff from the Platte River. It also formed an ideal setting for clandestine meetings. Lovers had coupled there, rustling the leaves with their passionate gyrations. Tonight the men who gathered there showed desperation on their faces. In dim flicker of firelight—screened by the trees, the men themselves and the undergrowth—they talked.

One of those who sat back, thinking, not participating in the talk was Thomas Standler. He didn't belong here. He didn't want any part of this meeting, or the men running it.

He looked at the leader. He thinks he's so tough, does he? Thinks he can clear all the homesteaders out of the Platte River Valley. He'd do that even if it meant killing every one who wouldn't move.

Standler himself had been suffering because of the fencing and the formerly free-to-use grazing land. Some of his best had been taken from him less than a month ago. Still, he'd seen bad times before and had weathered them. Standler figured he'd do so again.

"We've got to wipe them clean off the plains!" the leader said, a big man with a gruff voice, his face hidden with a kerchief as were the other men's. The man's eyes reflected the fire's meager light as he continued to talk. His guttural voice was forceful, but quiet. This gathering didn't want uninvited guests stopping by. "They're going to kill the cattle business if we don't do something about them! We'll all be on our butts, broke, if we don't get rid of them now!"

Standler sighed. This guy's tune never changed. He'd been droning on and on like this for at least an hour. He didn't recognize the man. He almost had the voice pegged but not quite. Standler was there because he had to be, not from worry about the homesteaders.

A friend of his had stopped by his ranch that afternoon, telling him to be *in the copse* one hour after dark. Thomas tried to put off the invitation, but he man seemed angry about his hesitance. The meeting was for the protection of the ranchers, the man had explained. Didn't Standler care about his ranch? Gary had the distinct impression that if he didn't attend the meeting he'd be sorry later.

Now he didn't know where all this would lead.

"Fred Lucas was deliberately killed in cold blood last night, by some damned asshole farmer tryin' to break our spirit. Well, we won't stop bothering them until they're gone from our land!" The man's voice grew in volume. "They won't scare us off!"

"I thought Lucas got killed in retaliation for the Parkers," someone in the gathering said.

The leader's head turned toward the speaker, his eyebrows low. "Who said that?"

No information was volunteered.

"Goddamn you!" he said. "Forget the fucking Parkers! They're dead and gone. Let's concentrate on getting the rest of the homesteaders out before they destroy our ranches. Hell, any of you who're soft on the farmers should get the hell out of here. Right now. We don't need your kind, and I'll deal with you later."

A few grumbles and grunts ran through the assembled men but they soon died. Thomas

Standler knew he should speak out, make a stand or leave. But here among his fellow ranchers he sensed the safety of a common cause. However he felt about the homesteaders, he couldn't disagree with the leader that ridding themselves of the sodbusters would work to all their benefit. He was afraid if he stood and walked away he'd be shot as a traitor to the cause. So he sat, lost in the circle of the men, and thought.

"What's the next move?" one rancher asked.

The leader jumped on the question. "Another burning. This time we'll be sure no one gets hurt. We'll hit a farm—one I'll choose at that time. I wouldn't want the farmers forewarned. We'll herd them outside, burn down their house and maybe a few other buildings, then tell them to move or we'll kill them. Simple as that. That should be enough to send them scurrying back east as soon as they can find transport." He laughed, a low, dirty laugh. "And good riddance to them."

"What if they don't leave?"

"Then we hit another farm."

"Do we kill the farmers of the other place, like you said we would?"

The leader shrugged and grasped one hand in the other before him. "That depends. Leave it to me."

"Who killed the Parkers? Was it an accident? I'm still not clear on it." The question was anonymous.

"Shut your goddamned mouth!" the leader spat. "Don't ask stupid questions! I'll need three good men to do the job. It'll be tomorrow morning. Any volunteers?"

"Why the hell ain't you going?" one man asked.

"Come on, men. I need three volunteers to ride out tomorrow morning, put a scare into a family, and torch their place. Sounds like a lot of fun, right? Who wants to do it?"

No hands raised. After a few seconds, he nodded. "Then I'll have to find some men. As for you men—act normally. We won't have another meeting unless tomorrow's strike goes bad. Everybody understand?"

The men nodded assent.

Thomas Standler, though, did not. A doubt throbbed in his mind, one that chilled him. He didn't think the Parkers had accidentally been killed, and the leader had done nothing to quench his fears. Thomas thought they'd been killed, and that that had been the plan all along. Why the smokescreen, though? The leader was obviously the type who enjoyed killing—at least as far as homesteaders went.

"When the farmers move we'll make them pack up that barbed wire and take it with them. We don't want it here! And we'll stamp their crops into the dust and everything will be back to normal. I can feel it, men; I can feel the day when the ranchers once again rule the valley, and the tall grass stretches out unbroken on all sides."

Thomas smirked. Not likely, he thought. Not if the homesteaders were bold enough to kill Fred Lucas. At this rate, they'll kill each other off and no one would be left in Kearney County but the merchants and the sheriff.

Will the next homesteading family be killed? And if so, who will be the next ranchers to follow him into hell?

Thomas shivered. He didn't like this business at all.

Carl Lanford dropped his pants and drawers, then climbed onto Roxanna and thrust into her.

"Hey, watch it, big boy!" Roxanna said, wincing in pain. "You've got a thing bigger than most of the men in this town put together!"

"Shut up, Roxanna. I'm thinking." Lanford's mind was preoccupied while he enjoyed the woman's warmth and moist tightness. Though his hips moved mechanically his mind raced in other directions.

It was their move now, he thought. Now that Fred Lucas was dead the ranchers and farmers were even. He was certain no farmer would raise a hand against a rancher until it was clear the ranchers weren't going to leave them in peace.

The thought of the Parkers brought renewed vigor to his strokes. Roxanna groaned as he filled her to capacity, then nearly slipped out on the backstroke. His sharp, bony knees pressed against her soft skin, raising bruises where they continually banged against her. Lanford's sweat mingled with hers as he strained to work out his problems.

Lanford suddenly lowered his gaze to Roxanna's face, now transfixed with pain and ecstasy. Furious at the interruption, he pulled out and slapped her thigh.

"Turn over," he growled.

Roxanna moaned and lifted herself heavily up, then over. Lanford took her waist in his hands and pulled her into a kneeling position, then rammed into her from behind. Roxanna sighed as he sank in.

Now less distracted, Lanford was barely conscious of his intimate connection with the woman. Nothing like sex to clear your head, he always said.

Lanford banged into Roxanna and mulled over his problem. Being a farmer, the ranchers threatened his existence. If he was faced with death at the hands of the ranchers, he'd welcome the opportunity to take down as many of the bastards as he could before he dropped to the ground.

Not that all ranchers were bad, Lanford thought. Sure, some were the meanest sons of bitches you'd ever care to meet, but others were downright friendly. A few were worse than others, he thought grimly. At least his troubles in that area were now over.

Lanford had done his part in harassing the ranchers—all the farmers had been talked into it at one time or another. He had to admire people who could stand up to the treatment they'd received.

He remembered the men who'd shot him dirty looks in the street, or the time he'd found a threatening note tied to the carcass of his favorite dog, or the morning he'd found his chicken coop blazing away—chickens prematurely roasting loudly within it.

He could kill them. Easily, one by one. Lanford's attention switched to the present, to the woman he thrust into. She squirmed beneath him as their bodies slapped together.

Lanford finally groaned and slammed into Roxanna with such force she fell to the bed. The man's buttocks thrust crazily as pleasure spread through every nerve in his body, his mind's eye filled with images of his enemies' bloodied corpses.

CHAPTER TEN

SPUR ATE in the Calico Hotel's dining room, then walked outside into the cool evening air. The street was quiet—Kearney wasn't a thriving city—so he climbed the outside hotel stairs and sat at its top, leaning back against the railing, letting his thoughts drift as he digested his meal.

McCoy found a cheroot in one pocket and stuck it between his teeth, then lit a stinker match and soon had its tip glowing in the darkness. He inhaled and slowly blew the biting blue smoke into the air.

"Spur!"

The voice cut through the night. He jumped to his feet and searched the area. No one was visible.

"Spur McCoy!"

The voice was high—a woman, or a young boy.

"Who wants to know?" he boomed into the

darkness. Still no signs of life. If the voice wasn't echoing and bouncing off several buildings, it could be originating from his right.

"I have a message for you," the voice continued, now directly behind him. Spur sprung around, only to realize the voice had echoed off the hotel's wall.

"Show yourself!" he called.

"No."

The word was followed moments later with a small heavy object dropping to the dirt before the stairs. He raced down them and crouched over it. A piece of paper had been tied around the rock.

Crude, Spur thought, but effective. He picked up the rock and strained to hear the sound of departing feet, but detected only silence. A search would be fruitless.

He returned to his position at the top of the stairs and broke the twine, then unrolled the paper. Spur had to move over two feet to use light from a nearby hotel room's window to read. The lettering was in an unschooled hand:

Meet me in back of Petersons in one hour.

No name or indication of its sender. Spur frowned, crushed the paper, threw it and rose, then stood looking at the door. Roscoe? Spur thought. Or Jack Parsons? What about some other rancher who didn't like Spur nosing around the place? It could also be a farmer with news, or perhaps someone totally unrelated to the murders.

Spur drew heavily on the cheroot and finally turned and walked down the stairs and into

Peterson's. If he had to meet the unknown party behind the saloon, he might as well slip in a little early and check local sentiments concerning Fred Lucas's untimely death.

Peterson's was noisy and dusty, stank of tobacco and stale whiskey and sweat. McCoy got a drink and stood at the bar, listening as conversations drifted past him.

Most of the men discussed matters of daily living; Spur head the words *horse,* and *herd* frequently. The fifteen men situated around the saloon drank, smoked and talked, but Spur heard no mention of Fred Lucas's death.

McCoy casually ambled around the saloon, as if he couldn't find a comfortable place to sit or stand. Once he'd heard the subject of the conversations around him he moved on.

After the fifth or sixth such move the name Lucas stood out above all the rest of the words.

" . . . got shot last night."

"You're joking," another voice said.

"No. You didn't hear? Lord sakes, it was all over town."

"Tough. Lucas didn't deserve it."

"Hell no!" the first man said. "I think it was some damned homesteaders, if you ask me!"

Spur moved to look at the men. One, lean, tall, smooth-shaven over a hard jaw, had a gun tied to his leg. He spoke again.

"Maybe. We'll never know for sure."

"Sheriff Gardner just didn't try hard enough!" a bright-eyed younger man said. "I'll bet ya we could find out who killed Lucas better'n any lawman."

The older shook his head. "How you gonna do that? You don't have the time or the brains."

"I got everything I need. It was a farmer, right?"

"Could be." The man swallowed the last of the whiskey in his glass. "I don't know."

"And you don't care, right?" The younger man gripped the other's vest at his midsection. "Look. Lucas died at the end of a rope. You wanna be next?"

"Get your hands off me," the older man said sharply. The other complied. "Of course I care, Kenyon! I'm no fool. But I don't see what getting upset about it's going to do. Now leave me alone; I've got some thinking to do." He turned way from the other man.

"Wise up, Waters!"

Spur idly turned from the men as Kenyon walked away. Kenyon and Waters—the two names were on Gardner's list, possibly trouble-makers. Could be something. At least he'd have to keep the men in mind when he had more evidence or information regarding the death of Fred Lucas.

Spur estimated a half hour had elapsed since he was summoned. He put his drink down and wandered out the back door and into the night air. An alley stretched behind the saloon, with a row of mostly one-story buildings abutting it on both sides. The alley was dark save where moonlight slanted in between shadows. A perfect place for a meeting.

He quickly chose the best spot to wait; one with his back to a solid wall where his vision was unblocked by buildings. Spur moved up against the brick wall that must've been the rear of a store or office building and settled against it, preparing for the wait.

Fifteen minutes later he heard a scuffling in the dirt down the alley ten or twenty yards to his right. Someone walking—clumsily. He waited.

Moment later the scuffler came into view—a woman. In a flash of moonlight Spur recognized her—Roxanna Stafford, the saloon fancy lady.

He relaxed then—she couldn't be the contact. Roxanna stepped into the middle of the alley and looked around her. Spur froze. Was she the one who'd summoned him there?

"Roxanna?" Spur said from his hiding place.

"Yes?" She clutched her bosom, looking around her. "Who's there? Is that you, Spur?"

"Yes." He stepped from the shadows into the light.

"Good. Got my note, I take it?"

"Yes."

"I wondered if I'd paid that boy a nickel for nothing, but I guess he was honest."

"Roxanna, what's this all about? Why the note and all this secrecy?"

"Because it excites me," she said. "I like to be in dangerous situations with handsome men."

"I see. What did you want to talk to me about?"

"Not here. Let's sneak up the back stairs and go into my room. No one will see us, so no one will suspect us."

"Of what?"

Roxanna shook her head. "Never mind. Come on, lover boy!" She held out her hand. Spur took it and they walked to the stairs, climbed them side by side, and went into Roxanna's room.

"Whew!" Roxanna said, laying a hand on her ample bosom. "That just makes me tingle!" She shivered and moved her body back and forth, gently falling into a swaying motion while her gaze locked onto Spur's eyes.

"Fine. Let's talk. That is why you wanted to see me, isn't it?"

She halted and frowned. "All right, Spur McCoy. I can see I'll never get you in my bed. And it's not just the money I'm thinking about, Spur. Honestly. You're—you're kind of nice."

Spur smiled. The woman seemed sincere. At least she loved her work.

"Okay. I asked you here because I heard you were looking for information."

Spur feigned innocence. "Information? About what? What gave you that idea?"

"You know what I'm talking about," Roxanna said. "Information regarding the deaths of the Parkers."

Spur shrugged. "Maybe."

"Don't worry," she said, flapping her hands before her. "I won't give away your secret. I don't know why you want to know about the Parkers, but you do, don't you?"

Spur nodded. "How'd you know?"

"I hear a lot in my line of work," she said, then smiled. "Men like to talk after doing it, you know? Anyway, this afternoon a customer mentioned that you were snooping around, trying to find out as much about the Parker killings as you could."

"So?"

"So, a week ago another of my customers was a cowboy. He'd been out riding range and saw three men riding toward the Parker ranch. It was early—just before dawn—on the day the Parkers were killed."

"Three riders?" Spur asked.

She nodded. "He was too far away to see faces. I asked him if he did, because he seemed interested in it. He was convinced that they'd been the men who'd killed the Parkers."

"What about the men's clothing, hat types, perhaps their horses?"

She shook her head. "I asked him that too, just out of conversation-making, but he didn't see anything more than three riders heading toward the Parker ranch."

"Did he see them come back by there later that day?"

"No."

"When did he tell you this?"

"Wednesday, last week. One week after the Parkers were killed."

"What was this cowboy's name?"

"I don't know." Roxanna blushed and turned away from Spur. "I don't remember their names too often, unless they're regulars—you know. But I'd remember that guy if I ever saw him naked again—he had the biggest one I'd ever seen."

Spur walked to the woman. "Do you know

which ranch he worked for?"

Roxanna thought for a moment, then turned back to Spur and shook her head. "I'm sorry. He was just one of the many, not too special except below the waist. He wasn't staying in town, anyway; said he was going back east on the train." She shook her head. "I think he said that." Then her eyes lit up as she looked at him. "Does that help you out?" she asked eagerly.

Spur didn't disappoint her. "Some. At least I know that three men hit the Parkers—as long as this guy was reliable, not just lying or deliberately spreading false information."

"Why would he lie? No. Men don't usually lie right after—unless it's to tell you they love you. They spill their guts on everything. Hell, they tell me things they wouldn't tell their wives or closest friends."

"I see. Thank you for the information, Roxanna. It might help out."

"With what you're doing? What are you doing here, Spur? Why are you in Kearney?"

He shrugged. "Just passing through."

Roxanna crossed her arms on her chest. "If we'd just done it, you'd tell me everything."

Spur laughed. "If we'd just done it you wouldn't be able to talk for five minutes at least."

"I'd sure like to find out," Roxanna said, laughing.

Spur smiled and turned to look out the window. The alley was quiet. A second later he felt a hand on each side of his waist, then they travelled down to his crotch and pressed against his penis.

"I'll promise you anything," she said. "If you'll just get that damned thing out!"

Spur firmly but politely removed the woman's hands as he turned. "Not now, Roxanna."

"Okay, Spur. I give up. You've got to be the stubbornest man around. I know you're no priest—seems like you and Ginny Burriss had a fine time together—but I guess you just don't go for me."

"Where'd you hear that?"

"About you and Ginny? I hear everything." She looked at him pointedly. "And if I hear more about the Parker killings and I think you'd like to hear it, I'll let you know."

"Good." Spur bent and kissed Roxanna's cheek. "Thanks, Roxanna. You're quite a lady."

She smiled and caught her breath. "Sure, Spur. Goodnight, and thanks for coming."

Spur moved out of the room, down the stairs and back into the alley.

Three riders. If the source was reliable—and Roxanna may have a point about men opening up right after sex—that meant he had to find three men. Of course, if he found one, the other two would be easy to uncover.

As he walked down the alley to his hotel, moving through alternating areas of shadow and moonlight, Spur heard a faint sound behind him.

Three steps later, he heard another.

A kicked stone. Leather scraping dirt. The presence of another human being behind him.

Someone was following him.

CHAPTER ELEVEN

JULIUS CRAIG coughed twice to quiet the room, then stood. Twelve men eyed him from various positions in the cramped Craig parlor, and the man sweated. He loathed public speaking, feared and hated it.

"Gentlemen, let us begin."

Craig was a homesteader who had brought his wife and daughter to farm in Kearney County over a year ago. His twelve months of hard farm work had done little to diminish his round face and somewhat rounder body. Thick brown hair sprouted from the man's tanned head and lower face, which had been tamed into muttonchop sideburns and a full moustache which hid his upper lip. His conservative dress —denims, white shirt, string tie—belied the informality of the occasion. His friends had wanted to gather, and Julius Craig happened to have the largest house.

Craig tapped his right hand against his leg as he continued.

"Someone killed Fred Lucas. Someone else killed Al and Gilly Parker and their child. Obviously, we have a real problem here." Craig's fear pulsated in his stomach. He tried to push it away but it lingered.

"Now, I don't know who killed Lucas—I certainly didn't do it—and I don't much care either. I'm sorry to see any man killed, of course, but sometimes . . . ah, things become necessary." Craig's face flushed and blood rushed through his veins and arteries at an accelerated pace. "So tonight I thought we could talk about this and—perhaps, ah, come up with some ideas."

The farmers stared at him, waiting. He had to get the meeting going.

"Ah—ah—"

"Ah hell!" Carl Lanford sprang to his feet. "Craig, I'll take charge here, if you don't mind."

"No. Not at all." Craig gratefully sank back into his chair, his face crimson.

"Good. Now, we all know how bad a year we've had—the locusts coming in and nearly wiping out some crops, the drought, the storm that destroyed the wheat—it's just been one thing after another for farmers in Kearney County."

"Damn straight," an older man said.

"Now we've got another problem; not another drought, or swarm of gasshoppers. No. It's the ranchers. They could be worse than anything else we've had thrown in our faces.

"Fred Lucas is dead. Who killed him isn't important at this time. What is important is that this'll probably stir up more trouble with the ranchers. As sure as hell one of us—or one of our neighbors or friends—is going to get hit by the ranchers. As you well know, they're far past stampeding through crops and tearing down fences. New they're burning down homes and killing women and children." His face was grim as he paused. "It's up to us to stop them before all this gets out of control."

"How in hell you going to do that?" a young man of twenty-two asked.

"I don't know!" Lanford boomed. "That's why we're calling this meeting, so we can come up with some ideas. You have thought about this, haven't you?" Lanford caught each man's gaze singly. "What else has there been to think about?"

"My daughter's getting married next month and I—" one middle-aged man began.

"I don't care about your daughter's wedding!" Lanford screamed. "Not when our lives are at stake! If you get burned down some cold morning you won't have to worry about paying the preacher! Now, any ideas?" Lanford planted his hands on his hips.

Murmurs rippled through the assembled men, but no one voice stood above the others.

"Nothing?" Lanford asked, then shook his head. "Then I guess this doesn't mean anything to you. Great. It's me against them, right?"

"Of course not, Carl," Craig said, rising. "We're all worried—otherwise we wouldn't be here. But worry doesn't always bring solutions. We don't know what to do. Frankly, Carl," he said while biting his lower lip, "we thought you had some plan in mind."

Lanford gazed silently at Craig for a moment, then smiled and cocked his head. "All I can think is to keep watch every night. Hire someone, if you can afford it, or use your young, but have someone alert at all times to stop trouble before it starts."

"What about me?" An older man with a bad eye asked. "I'm all alone. How am I supposed to keep watch?"

"They probably wouldn't touch you, since your farm is so small, Pete."

"We can't afford to hire an extra hand just for that, or let our hands have any less sleep," another man grumbled.

"Goddamn it, men!" Lanford said. "That was only a suggestion."

"What about Sheriff Gardner? Can't he do something about this?"

"Look what he did for the Parkers," someone said.

"There is an alternative." Lanford's voice rose above the others. "We could use their methods."

Craig looked sharply at Lanford. "What in hell are you talking about?"

"Shut up, Craig." He turned back to the men. "It's the only real solution; why didn't I think of it before? We do the same things they're doing to us—to scare them away."

"It won't work," one man said.

"Why not?" Lanford shot back. "What makes you an authority on this? Anything can work if we try hard enough. If we don't do something they'll force us out of the valley. They're scaring you, aren't they?"

"Someone wasn't scared," Pete said. "Someone killed Fred Lucas to avenge the Parkers."

"That's right," Julius Craig said. "Lanford, I don't like what you're saying. Oh, I'm no man of peace but I do know when something's wrong. I'll have no part of your *ideas,* and I won't allow you to spread them in my house!"

"Watch yourself, Craig," Lanford said. "Some day you'll wish you were my friend."

A general ruckus had broken out during the verbal confrontation. Men talked in groups of two or three.

"We'll burn down all the ranches in one week," said one.

"Stampede their cattle so far they'll never find them," another called out. "That way they'll have to leave."

"After that I don't see them giving us more trouble," a gray-haired man said to himself. "Nope, I just don't see it."

Lanford broke from the argument with Craig and stomped his foot four times to silence the men.

"So it's agreed. We'll strike back! We'll show them who rules Kearney County!"

"No!" Julius Craig said. He laid a hand on Lanford's shoulder and shook it. "That's not the way! We've got every right to be here—as much as they do, by God. They simply have to learn that the old ways are gone forever—they've got to stick to their own property, or pay us for passage over ours. This has to be the only solution, the only sensible one. Lanford, you're just asking for trouble."

Lanford brushed the man's hand off his shoulder. "You know we can't teach those ranchers anything. They won't listen to us. Why can't you see that? Stop being so stubborn."

"They're reasonable men. Surely they can see the truth. They have to give in. Let's call a town meeting and get the ranchers and the homesteaders together and work out our problems! We have to stand together, man to man."

Lanford laughed. "Listen to him! Are the ranchers going to listen to us? Hell no. We'll be talking our hearts out while they set our families and farms on fire!" He stared at Craig, then spat in disgust.

Julius watched as the mucus splattered onto his best rug, then looked at Lanford, raging.

"Get the hell out of my house, Lanford! Get off my property! Now!"

Lanford had already turned to leave and didn't acknowledge the man's command. Instead, he clapped another man's shoulder as he walked out.

Julius Craig stood at the end of the room, watching as one man after another rose and walked out with Lanford. Soon only Pete remained in his chair. He rose and moved across the room to sit beside Craig.

"We'll convince them, Julius," Pete said softly.

Craig sighed. "I hope so, Pete. I hope so. Lanford's not really a bad man—just temperamental. I thought—never mind. Let's pray that these men come to their senses."

Spur ducked into a foot-wide alley between two buildings, blending with the shadows as he waited for his pursuer to make the next move.

Spur calmed his breath as he felt for his Colt. Yes, it was still there, ready when necessary.

No noise from the alley. From his position he could see three feet to either side of the alley's walls, and no shadows moved there. The scuffling noise had halted.

Spur tensed, wanting to spring out into the alley, to show himself so that this follower would have to do so as well. But he waited, straining to hear the slightest sound.

Footsteps lightly peppered the ground, moving toward the side alley's mouth. Seconds later a figure moved directly before the opening and passed on, apparently oblivious to Spur's presence. Though it was dark, Spur didn't have to guess that the figure was a man, and that he wasn't the one following him.

McCoy waited five more minutes—nothing. He edged toward the intersection of the two alleys and, after unholstering his Colt, poked his head out from the passageway and waved its barrel back and forth.

No answer.

He moved closer and looked out into the alley.

Nobody in sight.

Spur shrugged and, cautiously, walked into the alley, then turned to his right and moved briskly down it toward the hotel. The man following him must have slipped away.

A second later a large figure burst out from a shadow and blasted lead at Spur. The man's aim was off; the rounds slammed into a brick building, chipping it into dust and ricocheting off crazily.

Spur returned fire, but his rounds did no more than force the man back into the shadows. McCoy ducked behind a water barrel and waited. He detected a flicker of movement and aimed but realized the shadow led into a passageway between two buildings. The man was gone.

He jumped up and ran back a few feet until he found the next passage to the other side of the buildings. Pounding the dirt with his heels Spur made it to the street just in time to see the man rush out across Main Street's eighteen-foot breadth and duck into yet another lane. Spur followed and just as he ran into the blackness he froze—the man was on the ground, face down.

Spur approached him cautiously and kicked the man's legs. Had he tripped and hit his head on a rock, or was he faking?

McCoy turned the man over with his boot toe while aiming two-handed at the downed man's heart. The corpse suddenly leapt into life, raising the pistol he'd hidden with his body.

McCoy's booted foot smashed into the man's hand, sending the gun skidding twenty feet along the dirt. Spur crashed his foot against the man's chest, knocking him flat onto the dirt, then stared down at him.

"Who the hell are you?" Spur asked.

The man shook his head. Spur smelled his boozy breath and felt him shivering beneath his foot. Drunk and scared. Maybe he'd get information from him after all.

"Why are you following me? Who hired you?"

Again the shake of the head. Spur stared down at the man, his face barely visible in the dim light. He was young, Mexican, no more than nineteen.

Spur cocked the Colt and pointed it at the young man's face. Instinctively, he moved back. The man's head hit a wall and he slowly pushed himself up into a sitting position, leaning against the brick wall. Spur's eyes never left him.

"I'll ask this once more, *señor,*" he said calmly. "If you don't answer this will be the last thing you'll ever hear." He nudged the Colt's muzzle against the man's ear.

"He'll kill me," he said. The voice was tight and lightly accented.

"I'll kill you right now if you don't tell me what the hell I want to know! At least I'll let you go after you tell me, and you'll be able to make a run for it, maybe escape. Who hired you?" Spur moved the gun from the Mexican's ear and pressed it against the soft skin in the man's neck.

He seemed almost ready to talk, then fear gripped him. The Mexican shook his head.

Spur savagely dug his boot heel into the man's groin. He groaned and bent double as Spur retracted his foot.

"Talk!" he thundered.

"Okay. Okay!" He moaned once more and rubbed between his legs. "It was Tate," he said, his voice clear and strong.

As Spur's mind raced a gunshot rocked the alley and light flashed a split second before the Mexican's upper body slumped forward, his head bouncing on the dirt between his legs.

CHAPTER TWELVE

SECONDS AFTER pounding two bullets into the end of the alley, Spur heard feet moving rapidly away. He bolted forward, unwilling to let his informant's murderer escape.

He ran out of the side alley into a larger one at the rear of Main. As he moved his mind worked. Tate had someone following him. Which Tate? Surely not Amanda. That left Roscoe.

Hell, Spur thought. Maybe the man was angry at him for poking around the ranch. Perhaps he even thought Spur was sent there as a spy by the homesteaders.

Then again, Roscoe Tate—or one of the Tates—may be responsible for the Parker murders, and didn't want Spur uncovering anything. It was a possibility.

Spur waited for signs that he had been followed. When none came, he was confident it wasn't a trick this time—the man who'd killed his pursuer wasn't coming back.

The agent moved slowly down the alley, then switched to Main Street. He didn't want any more alleyway confrontations that night. Moments later he walked into his hotel room at the Calico, locked the door, tipped his hat to the floor and slept fitfully. He didn't even bother pulling off his boots.

"What the hell are you talking about?" Roscoe Tate thundered. He stood on the front porch of the Tate ranch, barefoot, wearing his underdrawers. It was nearly midnight. "Who told you to follow him in town?"

"No one," the hand answered sheepishly. He was twenty, with a full moustache and beard, close-cropped black hair, lazy eyes and a stupid grin spread over his face that screwed up his eyes. "But we was there, drinking and talking about fucking Roxanna, if we had the money. Well, we needed to piss so we went out in the alley. Who should we see but Spur McCoy? We hid out until Spur had passed us, then Lopez started following the man. I told old Lopez I was tired and was going on back inside, which I did. Then I heard a couple gunshots and so I ran back outside—when I got there Spur had Lopez on the ground in an alley, gun to his head, asking him who'd hired him to follow him. Before I could do anything Lopez said, 'Tate.' I didn't know what to do, so I shot him."

"Who?" Roscoe asked, glancing sharply at the man.

"Who?" the man repeated.

Roscoe punched him in the stomach. "Who'd you shoot?"

"Lopez," he said between coughs and groans.

Roscoe reflected on this news for a moment, ignoring the man's pain. "Is he dead?"

"Yes."' A cough. "I'm sure of it. After I shot him I didn't have much time to check; I just ran. Hid out in Peterson's until closing time, then rode out here."

Tate nodded. "You always were a good shot. That damned Lopez was a fool. No great loss, him. Thanks for your help, Young. Expect a bonus real soon."

The man's face glowed in spite of the throbbing in his gut. "Really? Thanks, Mr. Tate. I figured I had to kill him, even though he only said *Tate* and didn't say which one."

"Nothing else you could have done," Roscoe said. "Besides, Spur McCoy might have thought Lopez was lying to save his ass. If McCoy gives me any trouble I'll be sure to return it doubled. You have any other news to report?"

"No."

"Good. Then let me get back to sleep! I've got to be up early in the morning."

"Fine. Thank you, sir."

The man slipped off the porch and Roscoe closed and locked the door behind him. He walked barefoot back to his room on the second floor, glad that the hand had had the sense to throw a pebble against his window, rather than waking the whole household. He didn't relish the thought of his family knowing his actions—yet.

Tate closed his bedroom door and got back into bed. He stared at the ceiling, wondering what the coming day would bring.

Spur jolted upright in bed, awake instantly as the doorknob's jiggling broke the stillness of his night-drenched room. He fell to his back, motionless, on top of the blankets. Every nerve in his body was alert, ready. He maintained a low, regular breath pattern to disguise his wakefulness.

He waited for two minutes. Spur saw darkness cross his curtained window, then watched as the shadow of the window's center frame slowly crawled upward, rippling against the curtains where they hung in regular folds.

Spur moved his right hand a fraction of an inch closer toward the Colt .45 strapped to his right thigh. The bed creaked.

The shadow halted in perfect synchronization, then continued on to the top. The curtains bent inward for a split second, then fell back to reveal a man climbing through Spur's window.

He half-closed his eyes and continued to watch the proceedings, wondering who it was this time—and if he was from Tate, too.

With his back to the window, the intruder was nothing but a black outline against a lighter background. He was big, though—Spur could see that, well over six feet. Curly hair stuck out around the brim of his Stetson, and McCoy heard the click of spurs as he crossed the floor to the bed.

At the right moment Spur's fist smashed into the man's face, breaking skin and fracturing some thin cheek bones.

The man fell backward as Spur jumped to his feet and drew the invader's six-gun from his holster. Spur came up with both pistols trained on the man's chest.

"Wait!" the man said, whispering. "Don't shoot me, for chrissakes!"

"Why not?" Spur asked. "You were going to shoot me."

"Did I have my pistol out?" the man asked shakily, still in a soft voice.

"No," Spur said. Something was strange here. "What are you doing, then, sneaking into my room in the middle of the night? That's a great way to get yourself killed." Spur hadn't lowered the weapons.

"I was delivering a message," he said. "I wasn't supposed to kill you, just scare you into leaving Kearney County. Honest, that's all."

"Why?"

"So you wouldn't set up law practice here," the man said, with a deadly serious expression.

"What?" Spur asked, then remembered the story he'd told the cowboys at the Lucas ranch. Word sure got around quick. Or was this a bluff? "Who told you to scare me off?"

"I don't know. I really don't!" His eyes were glassy with fear; his voice still quiet. "I just got slipped an envelope by someone in a crowd at the train station this afternoon. I couldn't figure out who'd given it to me. Inside it was a note and a twenty dollar bill." The man swallowed. "Hell, I'd do nearly anything for twenty dollars."

"Why didn't you just take the money and run?"

"The note said they'd kill me if I didn't do what I was told to. They said they'd be watching."

"That's why you're whispering?" Spur asked.

He nodded. "I don't know where they are."

Spur frowned. "Do you still have the note?"

"I brung it with me so I wouldn't forget what to do." He felt in his pockets.

"You can read?" Spur asked.

The man shook his head. "I had a friend of mine read it for me, but I can make out some of the words. And I sure as hell didn't have no trouble finding someone to read it—as long as I was willing to split the money." He continued to dig into his pockets.

"I see. Tell your boss—if he ever contacts you again—that you did just what you were supposed to do."

He smiled and produced a much-folded piece of thick paper. Spur read by moonlight streaming in through the window.

> "Evans, here's $20. If you want it, go to room 201 at the Calico Hotel and rough up the man there. Don't kill him, just scare

him off. We'll be watching. If you run, you're dead."

The note was unsigned.

McCoy handed it back to Evans. "Now get out of here. If I ever see your ugly face again I'll blast you into so many pieces it'll take a week to get you back together again!"

"Yes sir!" Evans said, then walked to the window.

"Forgetting something?" Spur asked.

"Huh?" The man turned around just in time to catch the pistol Spur had thrown to him. He slid it back home. "Thanks."

He was gone.

Spur closed the window, then lay back down in bed, slipping his hands under his head. Things were getting stranger and stranger in Kearney, Nebraska.

An hour before dawn Spur was up. He stripped off his shirt and undershirt, splashed cold water on his face and chest from the basin, then dried and redressed. Fully awake now, Spur tugged on his coat, clammed the hat into position, slung the Spencer repeater over his arm, and left the hotel. He retrieved his horse from Peterson's and mounted. Spur turned east and soon was beyond the last buildings of Kearney. Even the train tracks veered away from the east trail and so he was soon completely isolated as he rode toward Julius Craig's homestead.

Since he had come up with so little on the Parker killings so far, Spur decided to check on the homesteaders nearby to see if one of them had killed Fred Lucas. Spur also needed to know what kind of man Lucas was—perhaps he'd had many enemies and his death wasn't linked to that of the Parkers.

As Spur rode, his horse's nostrils shot out trails of steam into the morning air. He didn't know what to make of last night's skirmish. If Roscoe Tate was guilty of the murders he might have put a man on Spur to follow him around, to make sure he didn't get too close. But then again, Tate might have done it simply because he didn't like Spur, or because he was threatened by all the farmers in the valley.

And the man may have lied, thinking Spur'd let him go if he said any name. But the Mexican in the alley had been afraid, and Spur knew that fear nearly always ensured truthfulness, unless an even greater one awaited.

Evans was another matter. The man's story, plus the corroboration provided by the written note, seemed to indicate that the man wasn't lying. But Spur knew he could have been faking—the note could have been written and the explanation worked out before, in case he was caught.

Then Spur wanted to kick himself for not thinking of something earlier. When he'd asked Evans why he'd been hired to scare him, Evans had replied that it was to keep Spur from setting up law practice.

The note hadn't mentioned that little fact.

Spur hunched over his horse in an effort to warm himself and puzzled it out, trying to get his bearings by the landmarks that the sheriff had given him. There's the red barn. That should be the place. He turned down a lane between fields of new wheat greening the rich earth. As he approached the house he heard a distant shot — apparently coming from Craig's place. Spur pushed the horse to its limit, flying past the fields toward the house. Three men rode before it, firing into the air, then aiming their weapons toward the house itself.

Another attack by the ranchers? Spur grimaced as he raced toward the house, digging his heels deeply into the horse's flanks.

CHAPTER THIRTEEN

SPUR SPED toward the Craig farmhouse, hoping the attackers were too busy to spot him. A quarter mile from the house he leapt from the bay, ground-tied her to a rock, then ran toward the house, his Spencer firmly gripped before his body with both hands.

The men apparently hadn't noticed his approach. He moved in to within two hundred feet of the house, then knelt and aimed at the closest rider. Just as the man lifted his rifle Spur fired, slamming a round into the man's chest. His body jolted backwards off the horse and bounced on the hard-packed earth. The horse galloped away from the house.

Spur ducked behind a pile of straw and waited a second, then darted forward fifty more feet. One of the attackers rounded the house and reared his horse back as he saw his downed companion. He glanced wildly around, pausing long enough for Spur to pound two rounds into the man's chest. Blood spilled out and the attacker's face was awash with confusion as he slumped forward, the rifle falling from his lifeless hands.

Two down, Spur thought, as he ran closer to the house, using a wagon as cover. He moved laterally, settling in behind the well. The third rider stormed up, apparently aware of the situation. He fired wildly, aimlessly in all directions, completely mystified at the source of his companion's executions, then turned and blasted four rounds into a window. Spur heard a scream inside as the glass's shattering subsided. Spur fired once—the shot went wide.

The gunman turned toward Spur and peeled off one round as he rode behind the barn for cover. Spur reloaded the seven shot Spencer and watched from his position behind the well bricks. A minute later he lifted his head above the well to watch the barn. A round hit the water bucket rope, sending the wooden pail crashing down into liquid blackness. Spur fired twice at the barn but had no target. A moment after his fire was returned, he bolted from the well to the other side of the house. No rounds answered his action. Spur walked quietly, avoiding leaves and branches around the house, stopping when he could see behind the barn.

The man hunched there spotted Spur at the same time. The agent bent slightly at the knees as he fired the Spencer, spitting two rounds toward the gunman. The unaimed shot went wide, but Spur's next round ripped through the man's skull, smashing his brain into jelly. With a wailing scream the figure crumpled to the ground and lay still.

Silence returned as the last detonation echoed in the stillness of the morning.

"Hello?" a male voice called from the house.

"Yeah!" Spur yelled. "You all right?"

"We're fine, thanks to you."

Spur made it to the front porch and found a middle-aged man and a young woman of perhaps eighteen standing arm-in-arm, half afraid to step outside the door.

"Julius Craig?" Spur asked.

The man nodded. "I'm afraid you have the advantage."

"Spur McCoy."

"Pleased to meet you, Mr. McCoy," Craig said, and pumped his hand. "Lordy, I don't know what we'd have done if you hadn't showed when you did."

"Do you know why anybody'd want to do somcthing like this to you?" As he asked the question, Spur's eyes darted toward the younger Craig. She gazed at him then, for a moment, her face a mask of passion. Her eyes held his with a hypnotic power that Spur found difficult to resist. With great control Spur forced his eyes and attention back to Craig's words.

" . . . probably ranchers, I'd say. We've been having a lot of trouble last few days." Craig smiled broadly then. "You haven't been introduced to my daughter, have you? Spur McCoy, this is Leah Craig, my pride and joy."

Leah curtsied slightly and smiled. "Pleased to

meet you, Mr. McCoy." Ringlets of rich black hair cascaded down her back, swaying gently as she moved. Her face was tanned, eyes large and clear, her nose strong but not too prominent. Incredibly long lashes dusted her cheeks as she blinked at Spur, then dropped her gaze to his crotch.

What astonished Spur most was her clothing. She was dressed plainly for farm work—denim pants, a man's work shirt, boots. But the way the cloth molded to her body told Spur much of the real woman lurking beneath the masculine exterior.

"Nice to meet you, Miss Craig."

Craig coughed, regaining Spur's attention once again. "This sure is a coincidence," he said. "I was just talking about this kind of thing last night."

"Really?"

"Yeah. Had a big meeting here at the farm, all the homedsteaders who cared to come, talking about the ranchers and the threats they've been making against us."

"Sounds like those threats have become realities," Spur said. "What was the meeting's outcome?"

Craig shrugged. "Nothing. It broke up when old Carl Lanford got up and started yelling all kinds of ridiculous things. Everyone left and that was the end of the meeting." Craig led Spur to the parlor.

"Would you like some coffee, Mr. McCoy?" Leah asked, poised to move to the kitchen.

"That'd be fine, Miss Craig."

She smiled briefly and moved away with a fluid grace despite her trousers.

Craig and Spur sat in rail-backed chairs in the parlor.

"Lord, Mr. McCoy, I don't know that I'd still be breathing if you hadn't come by and saved our skins," he said, shaking his head as if he didn't believe it had happened. "They took us completely by surprise. We'd been up for over an hour, of course, but we were both inside and the hands were out mending fences over on the south side all morning. We were all alone and they could've killed us."

"Glad I could be of help," Spur said. "Now I'd like you to help me, if you can."

"Gladly!" Craig said, a gleam sparking his eyes. "Name it. I owe you my life—so does my daughter," he said as she entered the room with two cups of steaming coffee. She handed one to Spur and the other to her father.

"Tell me about the situation here in the valley. What's going on? Why were you attacked this morning?"

Craig shook his head. "I wish I knew. I guess it's just greedy ranchers."

Spur set his coffee down on a table. "Speaking of ranchers, maybe you wouldn't mind looking at the bodies outside to see if there's anyone you recognize?"

"Not at all," Craig said, rising. He also set his coffee down and then turned to his daughter. "Stay here, Leah. I don't want you seeing those men."

"Aw, daddy, I'm a big girl now. I—"

"Stay here!" he said warningly, and she nodded and sat beside a portrait of her grandfather and sighed, folding her hands in her lap.

Craig and Spur went outside. They approached the first body and Spur tore off the kerchief from the man's lower face.

"No. Never seen him before," Craig said, bending to look closer at the face.

"You sure?" Spur asked, surprised. If the man wasn't a rancher, who was he?

"Positive. Let's check the others."

Moments later, Craig had studied the other two and saw no one he knew or recognized from town. "I don't understand it," he said, puzzled. "Why would anyone but ranchers want to attack me?"

"Does this mean the men who killed the Parkers might not have been ranchers?" Spur asked.

Craig shot him a glance. "Say, you seem to know local history pretty well." He thought a moment. "I don't know. Maybe."

"Unless they hired some guns to do their dirty work for them," Spur suggested.

"Could be. Well, nothing more to be done about it now. I'll just ride into town and tell Sheriff Gardner what happened here this morning."

"Don't trouble yourself," Spur said. "I'll be heading back there soon enough."

"Would you take some late breakfast with us? Leah should be just about ready to put it out."

Spur recalled that he had smelled food in the house. "Sure. I'm grateful for it."

"We can't do too much for you; not after saving us today. You didn't have to risk yourself for us."

Spur shrugged and they walked back to the house.

The meal was fine, and Spur dug into a thick steak, buttered early potatoes, and eggs fresh from the henhouse. Halfway during the meal Spur felt something warm and wiggling press against his crotch. Leah Craig, seated across the table from Spur, watched her father intently as he told his story, and laughed at its conclusion on cue. Spur fidgeted in his chair as the foot continued to caress him, soon producing an erection.

Spur reached down and pushed the foot away, alarmed that the girl's father might notice. Leah gave him a hint of a pout as she retracted her foot, but nothing more.

After the meal, while Leah washed up the dishes with water heated on the wood-burning stove, the two men talked. When Spur decided to leave Leah was nowhere to be found, so Spur shook hands with Craig and went out the door.

As he walked the two hundred feet to where he'd ground-tied his horse he heard a *pssst* to his right. Spur looked and saw Leah Craig standing in a shed, waving to him. Spur started moving directly toward her but she waved him away, then sketched a circle in the air with her hand. She wanted him to circle around and come to the shed from where he couldn't be seen from the house.

Spur nodded and walked on toward his horse,

mounted up and pretended to ride off. It didn't take more than a few minutes to find a field near the shed full of five-foot-high sunflowers. He ground-tied the horse there and made his way to the shed. Not seeing Leah in the doorway, he moved inside and shut the door.

"Hello." Leah lay naked on a homespun blanket spread out on some hay. Sunlight splashed onto her exciting body where it seeped in through warped wallboards. Spur's eyes riveted on the lustrous black patch of hair between her legs. She parted them then and arched her back, thrusting out large nippled breasts.

"Hi," Spur said. He knew what Leah wanted. He hurriedly undressed and then flung himself onto the woman, their naked bodies slapping together. Spur ground his penis against her groin as she gripped his thighs with her legs, lifting her feet to wrap them around his legs.

"Oh Spur, I knew you'd help out a poor farmer's daughter," she said rapturously as he kissed her neck.

His hands sought out her breasts beneath his chest and squeezed them, then his fingernails flickered over her nipples, causing them to harden. He lowered his mouth and sucked one.

"Ah!" Leah said. "Suck it, Spur!"

Spur savored the breast, filled his mouth with it.

"My father always told me this was the best way to spend time, or rather that it would be when I was old enough. And he was right! Every time a man lays on top of me I realize just how right he was!"

Spur lifted his head. "You've done this before?"

"Of course." She smiled, sunlight catching her face, making it glow. "I used to watch the animals around the farm while they were mating, and asked my father. He always told me anything that I wanted to know. I sure am glad."

"So am I," Spur said, then thrust his tongue into her mouth and sought out hers.

She returned the thrashing kiss, gripping his neck with one hand to pull his mouth down harder on hers, and pressed the other between their bodies where she grasped his hardness.

The kiss ended as Spur nibbled her ear.

"Put it in me! Please, Spur, put it in!" She frantically rubbed him as he continued to push it against her belly.

He rose slightly and she removed her hand as he gripped the base of his penis, then pointed it at the perfect angle for entry. Spur watched her eyes as he pressed just the head into her.

"Oh, God, Spur! More!" she cried, as her lashes fluttered and her face broke out in a sheen.

Spur inched into her slowly, then hit home. Leah sighed, and Spur realized she'd been holding her breath. He felt good, strong, horny.

"You like that?" he asked, moving his body slightly to both sides while still fully penetrating the woman's body. "You like me inside you?"

"Yes. Oh, yes!"

Spur withdrew quickly, then rammed his entire length back inside. Leah moaned and her body jerked in response.

"What about that?" Spur asked.

"Yes. Yes!"

Spur knew the woman was enjoying it. He decided a little sexy talk might increase her pleasure. He certainly couldn't complain so far about his own enjoyment.

"What do you want me to do?" he asked, staring into her fathomless eyes as they pressed together at the crotch, motionless.

She returned his gaze, then looked away, turning her head. "I want you to fuck me," she said in a low voice.

"What's that?" Spur asked, holding back from thrusting crazily into her. Each passing second increased his lust.

"I want you to fuck me." The voice was louder, but not by much. Leah wouldn't look into Spur's eyes.

"Look at me, Leah. Tell me what you want me to do."

Unbridled lust flashed over his face then, and snapped her head back to meet Spur's gaze unflinchingly.

"I want you to fuck me. Fuck me like an animal. Please, Spur; you're driving me crazy!" She reached out and pressed down on his buttocks, trying to force a deeper penetration.

"That's what I wanted to hear," Spur said. He

reared back and thrust for all he was worth. Leah sighed and moaned, her breath coming in ragged gasps, their bodies bouncing together and briefly parting, their connection never quite breaking.

"Oh, Spur, fuck me! Like the animals . . ." Leah said in rapture. She groaned and shook as orgasm after orgasm rocked through her body.

Spur pounded on, raising himself on hands planted on both sides of his head. He kissed her passionately as he thrust into her yielding flesh, his tongue mimicking the movement in Leah's warm mouth.

Moments later Spur's control broke and he jetted his load into her in heart-stopping spurts while his body trembled and shook, his hips jerking wildly forward, forcing himself to the maximum depth as the orgasm washed over him.

Spur lifted his sweat-drenched body from hers, shivering in the coolness of the shaded shed. Leah looked up at him dreamily as he stood naked before her, stretching and reaching for his clothing.

"Not yet," she said. "Do you have to go so soon?" She rose to her knees and pouted.

"I have to. I've got to report the killings to Sheriff Gardner. He won't like it if I don't get back there soon."

"Couldn't it wait just a bit longer?" Leah moved toward him on her knees, then bent her head toward his crotch and took his penis in her mouth. She sucked luxuriously.

Spur felt the pleasure spread throughout his

body like electric shocks. "Well, maybe it can wait a few minutes," he said as she cupped his testicles with one warm hand, squeezing them gently as she sucked.

Leah's lips slid along his shaft, coaxing it back to full hardness.

She worked with eyes closed dreamily, occasionally looked up at him.

Spur glanced down, watching himself disappearing into her mouth and felt his knees going weak.

"Leah, Christ, that feels good! Don't stop! Whatever you do, don't stop!"

She pulled her mouth from him. "I won't. And don't you stop. Just go ahead and shoot it off. I don't mind."

Spur took her beautiful head in his hands. As she opened her mouth he guided his erect penis in between her lips, then gently pumped in and out of the velvet-soft, warm and liquidy mouth.

Leah took Spur's thrusts, one hand clamping down on his buttocks to control the depth of his strokes. As Spur began groaning she redoubled her efforts, really working away at him, letting his erection slide down her throat as far as Spur could ram it. She was amazing, Spur thought.

Her hand at his balls squeezed harder, her fingernails gently scraping the sensitive skin. Spur could feel his control break; the woman's mouth was too inviting, hot, needing.

As the Secret Service man banged into her mouth he pulled her head toward him, ramming down it. Leah took it like a pro. Finally Spur let out a yell as his hips became pistons powering back and forth, spitting out his seed into her throat, again and again, finally subsiding, pulling out. He slipped from her mouth and leaned back against the wall, panting. When he opened his eyes he saw Leah Craig still kneeling before him. She licked her lips, stared at his red swollen organ as her hand moved rapidly between her legs.

CHAPTER FOURTEEN

Spur McCoy made the trip back to Kearney in little over a half hour. He rode directly to Sheriff Gardner's office, tied up the horse before it, and stormed in.

He surprised a young man leaning a chair back on two legs, feet crossed and heels placed in the center of Gardner's desk. At Spur's entrance the boy jolted forward, quickly slipping his feet to the floor. A deputy, Spur thought as he looked at the untried, wrinkle-free face.

"Sheriff Gardner in?" he asked.

"No. He's out somewhere."

"When'll he be back?"

"Don't know." The boy's wan face, accompanied by a rich head of blond hair, gave him an insipid appearance. "He said he'd be back when he was back." The boy smiled briefly, showing a broken front tooth.

"Thanks." Spur turned on his heel and strode

out, then moved left and walked along the slightly warped boardwalk, hunting in stores and on the street for the sheriff. He had to report the incident at the Craig farm.

Spur swung his gaze down an alley and saw Gardner standing above a sitting figure who clutched a whiskey bottle in his hand. Gardner was obviously preaching to a town drunk.

Spur paused a moment, planting his hands on his hips, just as Gardner looked up and waved. McCoy motioned back and within seconds the sheriff approached him.

"Ned's not all bad, but he's a slave to the bottle."

"Gardner, there's been trouble at the Craig farm."

He shot up his eyebrows. "Trouble? What kind?"

"Three masked riders attacked the place just as I happened to be riding up there this morning. The men shot in windows, yelled and raced their horses around. I picked them off one by one and neither Mr. Craig nor his daughter were hurt."

The older man blew out the breath he'd been unconsciously retaining. "When you said—I feared that Julius and Leah had been killed like the Parkers."

"No. Though they might have been if I hadn't been there. Craig didn't recognize any of the men; they certainly weren't ranchers from the area, he said."

"Strange. I wouldn't expect that. Who else would be bothering the Craigs?"

Spur shrugged. "Someone could have hired outside guns to do the job."

"Possibly. Looks like I'd better ride out there," he said wearily. "My horse threw a shoe last night. I hope she's put back together by now." He turned to Spur. "Could I ask you to do a favor?"

"Name it," Spur said instantly.

"Stop by my office and tell my son where I'm going?"

"That's your son?" Spur thought of the blank-faced young man.

"Yes. The yellow hair comes from his mother's side—all of it." He clapped Spur's shoulder. "I'd appreciate it."

"No charge."

Gardner smiled broadly and turned toward the livery stable. Spur walked back to the sheriff's office.

Roscoe Tate gripped his whiskey-filled glass shakily, his cheeks burning with rage, as he stared into the square framed mirror in his bedroom at the Circle T.

"Incompetent fools!" he muttered, then downed half the amber contents of the glass.

"It was your idea," Jack Parsons pointed out from the door.

"Goddamn you! You know we couldn't take the risk again. The first time, fine. We caught them by surprise. But this time the farmers have been warned." He lifted the glass again and watched as the last droplets flowed into his mouth.

Parsons closed the door and sat at the desk in the sumptuously appointed bedroom. "Keep your voice down," he warned. "You don't want your family hearing this kind of talk."

The man swung around. "I don't give a goddamn what they think!" he blurted out, but his voice was quieter. "Jesus H. Christ, I can't believe I was so stupid!"

"No," Parsons said in a low voice as he crossed his legs. "We just hired bad men."

"What happened?"

Parsons sighed. "I don't know for sure. Apparently they made it there—but they didn't come back. About an hour ago word got back to me that they'd all been killed."

Roscoe snorted. "Not by that damned peace-loving Craig, certainly. Did he hire any protection?"

"I don't know. But it's not too likely. He doesn't have much extra money now."

"Then how the hell do you explain the way he killed all my men?"

"I don't."

"Goddamn that fuckin' Craig! Why's he making it so hard for me to get him out of my way?"

"I doubt if the attack'll scare him off," Parsons observed.

"Of course not!" Roscoe paced for a few seconds while Parsons sat quietly. He knew how the man worked; after six months' association he'd had time to discover how Roscoe's brain worked. In a few minutes, he was sure,

Roscoe would have another perfect plan. And he wouldn't interrupt the man's thinking if he could possibly avoid it.

In a moment, Roscoe turned and moved toward Parsons, stopping a few feet from the chair.

"There's only one thing we can do to show those damned farmers that we mean what we say, and to get rid of Craig."

"And that is?"

"Hit the Craig farm again."

"What? After what happened this morning?" Parsons asked in surprise. "Where'll you find men stupid enough to do a job like that?"

Roscoe grinned as he looked into Parsons's eyes. "We'll do it. The three of us. Like last time. And we won't just scare them off."

Parsons uncrossed his legs and stood. "What are you saying?" he asked. "That we kill Julius and Leah Craig?"

Tate didn't flinch at the incredulous tone of Parsons's voice. "Of course. What else can we do? If we kill them—and destroy their farm—it'll be the last thing we'll ever have to do here. Hell, I know about your past, Parsons. Don't be so surprised at this. You haven't kept your nose clean, and you certainly don't mind sending men to their maker."

"But women?"

"There's that bank in Cheyenne, wasn't it?" he said, slowly approaching the man. "The banker and that woman, the mayor's wife, who died that afternoon. You killed them."

Their gazes locked then, Roscoe's eyes piercing points of light projecting out with palpable force, Parsons's glazed with fear.

"You're already a woman killer."

Sweat squeezed out along Parsons's forehead and flowed from his armpits. "That was years ago. I was twenty-one. I didn't kill the woman on purpose." He wiped his forehead shakily. "And besides, no one ever proved I did it."

"Yeah?" Roscoe's face turned grimmer. "How about the little rustling business you had?"

Parsons stepped back a few feet. "What the hell are you talking about?"

"Don't play stupid with me, Parsons. I'm not even sure you've quit that. How come you add two thousand head a year?"

"I've accounted for that," he said.

"Not to my satisfaction! Just think what the other ranchers would do if they thought you were the one rustling around here. They'd chop off your balls and feed them to you, then stake you out to dry in the sun, food for the foxes and scorpions."

"No! You wouldn't think of doing a thing like that to me!" he demanded. "I'm your goddamned partner!"

Roscoe smiled. "Of course I won't." He spread his hands out as if in surprise.

"Not if you help me out tomorrow morning," Roscoe said icily. "What the hell's wrong with you, Parsons? We already killed the Parkers."

"That was accidental," Parsons said,

trembling. "We went out there to scare them off—"

Roscoe's laugh halted his words. "You fuckin' idiot! I had no intention of leaving the Parkers alive. Didn't you know that?"

"You never said—"

"Some things are taken for granted." Roscoe paused and paced again. "We'll do it tomorrow morning—the way it should have been done *this* morning! We'll have to go into town, of course—to let our partner know."

"What time?" Parsons had resigned himself to participating. It wasn't that he disliked killing, he told himself. It's just that he knew the Craigs—not well, but he'd talked to them in town. He remembered Leah Craig then—the curve of her hips beneath the work pants she wore, the heavy breasts hanging in her blouse.

"Parsons, you with me?" Roscoe asked. He snapped his fingers before Parsons's enraptured face.

"Huh? Oh, right, Tate." He laughed. "I was thinking about Leah Craig."

Roscoe smiled evilly. "She's a looker, ain't she? It's a shame—shit, we've got to do it."

Parsons laid his hand on Roscoe's shoulder. "Maybe we could kill old man Craig but take her and keep her somewhere, for our own use."

"I knew you wanted to bed her, Parsons. I saw you hungering for her one day in town."

"Why not?" he asked defiantly. "I'll bet she's downright pretty in women's clothes."

"Or out of them."

"Come on, Roscoe! Why not put her up in a sod house or a shack somewhere?"

"It'd be a shame to kill her," Roscoe said in agreement. Then he shook his head. "Too dangerous. She might escape and turn us in."

"We'll see," Parsons said.

Roscoe shot him an angry look. "I'm in charge here. Got that? I make the decisions, the rules."

Parsons blinked in surprise, then nodded. He removed his hand.

"I'll decide about the girl later. We'd better ride into town. We'll show those fuckin' farmers what they get when they kill my men!" He scratched his crotch. "And maybe I'll get Roxanna for a half hour or so."

Roscoe's bedroom door flew open and David Tate walked into the center of the room.

"What the hell are you doing here, little brother? Need help wiping your butt?"

"I'll say this once, and only once. Leave the Circle T within twenty-four hours. You are no longer welcome here."

Roscoe couldn't believe it. Parsons stood in shock looking at Roscoe's younger brother.

"I've decided you're a threat to Father's health and a nuisance to the smooth operation of this ranch. Therefore, you've got twenty-four hours to move out."

"You son of a bitch!" Roscoe threw a fist toward David's stomach, but the man blocked the punch and powered one against Roscoe's jaw. The older brother stepped back, dazed, as Parsons went for David.

"No!" Roscoe yelled, coming back to his senses. "I don't need your help!"

David stood his ground, tensed, waiting for the next blow.

"You have no right!" Roscoe said. "Who's idea was this, anyway? The old man's?" He threw two punches toward David, who easily deflected them.

"I've warned you," David said. "Get off the ranch. By tonight, if you know what's good for you. There's no place for you here." He turned and swiftly left the room, his boots clicking on the hardwood floor.

Roscoe raged and rubbed his chin.

"So, I guess tomorrow morning's off?" Parsons asked.

"Bullshit it is! If I can't stay here I'll go somewhere else." He stepped closer to Parsons. "Could I spend a few days at your place?"

"I don't know," Parsons said.

"Only for a few nights. Christ, we're partners. Maybe you could talk me into snatching Leah like you planned, and I could take her with me when I leave."

"Where are you going?" Parsons had long secretly wondered exactly what the man's plans were. "And what would that have to do with Leah?"

Roscoe shook his head. "Don't change the subject. Will you or won't you?"

Parsons sighed. "Okay. For a few nights. And tomorrow morning's still on?"

"Yes, you goddamn fool! Of course it's still on!"

Parsons paused a moment, his voice lowered. "And we still kill Julius Craig?"

"Of course." Roscoe took a carpetbag from a corner and threw in essentials, all the money he had in the room, and then closed the bag.

"Let's go," he said. "I've seen enough of this place to last me a lifetime."

Parsons followed Tate out of the room, down the hall, and then the stairs. They walked directly past Amanda Tate, who stood near the kitchen entrance.

"Roscoe!" she asked, rubbing pie crust from her hands on the apron tightly wrapped around her waist.

He walked on out the front door.

"Roscoe Tate, come back here!" she said sternly.

As they moved to their horses, Roscoe scowled. "I should kill my brother!"

"If you did, who'd inherit the ranch?"

A gleam slipped into Roscoe's eyes. He stood before his mare and looked at Parsons, then laughed shortly. "I was just thinking about that myself."

"And?" Parsons asked.

"Me."

CHAPTER FIFTEEN

SPUR McCOY noticed two men riding into Kearney—Roscoe Tate and Jack Parsons, he soon realized. Spur ducked into the general store as the men passed by, then followed them, turning his head if either man looked back in his direction.

The men rode out of the business district of Kearney into the broadly spaced streets with clapboard houses standing in neat rows. Two or three of the homes were built of bright red brick that glowed in the hot afternoon sun.

As Spur walked lazily behind them, they stopped before an impressive home, one that Spur quickly recognized as belonging to Rev. Edward Burriss—someone had pointed it out to him. Spur frowned, leaned against a wall, and pulled a cheroot and a stinker match from his shirt pocket. He lit the thin, fragrant stick and inhaled as the men disappeared into the structure. What would Roscoe Tate and Jack Parsons want with Rev. Burriss?

The preacher ushered Tate and Parsons into his home quickly, almost frantically. Fortunately, Ginny was locked in her room. She wouldn't be able to hear them, he thought.

"Christ almighty!" he said after the two men were safely inside, the door shut against prying eyes. Dark drapes hung before the windows, making the interior of the Burriss home dark and cheerless. "What'd I tell you about coming here in the daytime? Anybody could have seen you!"

"Cut the crap, Burriss," Tate said as he walked into the man's parlor and sat. "What if someone saw us? What the hell's wrong with that?"

"I guess it's just that I'm nervous." Burriss's face was pinched with strain.

"Got a drink, Burriss?" Parsons asked.

"Of course," he said absentmindedly, then walked to the cupboard, took down a hidden bottle and poured three whiskeys.

"We've got some more work for you to do," Roscoe said as he accepted the drink.

Burriss looked down at Tate nervously, then sank into a velour backed chair. He shook his head.

"No. Not again. I won't do it, Roscoe. It's too dangerous."

Tate smiled. "Shit, that's just what Parsons said. You're not turning yellow on me, are you, Burriss? You haven't fallen back into the faith, have you, Burriss? That would make things difficult. For all of us."

"No. Of course not." As he spoke panic crossed his face. "What—what kind of work?"

"I wouldn't want you to have to forfeit your share in all this," Roscoe said.

"Speaking of that," Parsons said. "Just how much money do you think you'll finally collect from this scheme of yours?"

Tate shrugged. "I don't know yet. That's my problem, not yours."

"What do you want me to do?" Burriss asked, nervous at Roscoe's lack of response.

"And how do we know you won't run out on us?" Parsons asked. "It'd be easy for you to take the money and leave us here without giving us one thin dime."

"Relax, Parsons." Roscoe smiled and wiped his mouth. "You know you can trust me. Before I head out of town you'll get your fair share for helping."

"Roscoe, I demand—" Burriss began.

"How will David's announcement change your plans?" Parsons asked.

Roscoe shot him a look. "You ask too many fucking questions, Parsons."

Burriss looked from one man to the other, and decided to try a new approach. "What's this? What annoucement?"

"David's thrown Roscoe off the ranch," Parsons said, grinning. Roscoe took a quick swing at Parsons and missed.

"Watch your fat mouth, Parsons!"

"He threw you off the ranch?" Burriss said.

"Won't that make it harder for you to—"

"No. Not at all. Hell, if I have to kill my brother to get it, I will."

"I thought you'd already taken your *inheritance,*" Burriss said.

"I did. But as it stands now, if my brother and father die, even if my mother is alive, the ranch legally comes into my hands."

"What about your mother? Why can't she inherit it? Isn't she in your father's will?"

Roscoe shrugged. "Sure. But she doesn't get the ranch. Father loves her—I guess, if he's capable of any emotion—but he doesn't think she or any woman can run a ranch. 'Ranching's man's work,' he always used to tell us when we were boys. And I guess he believes it."

"Be careful!" Burriss cautioned. "If you're caught, you won't get anything."

"Don't tell me what to do, Burriss. Leave it all to me."

The reverend sighed. "All right, Roscoe. Now what's this about some work?"

Roscoe launched into a vivid description, his eyes snapping.

Spur had just ground the cheroot into the dust with his boot heel when the two men left the house. Within a matter of moments they had ridden back to Main Street where they tied up in front of Peterson's.

McCoy watched the men enter the saloon, then ran down the street, got his mare from the sheriff's office and rode up and tied her near the saloon. If he had to leave quickly he'd be ready.

Spur went into the bar. He scanned the room, searching every face. He couldn't see Roscoe Tate, but Parsons held up the bar with an elbow, his back to the door. The Secret Service agent looked to the stairs. Roxanna? Was Roscoe with her?

He walked to the stairs and ran up them without being seen by Parsons. Spur halted before Roxanna's door, then listened. No voices. Then a soft, sweet humming which occasionally broke into song issued from the room. Roxanna was probably alone, idling away her time. If so, where was Roscoe?

Spur decided he'd better duck into Roxanna's to see how she was, and to question her further concerning that cowboy who'd seen the three riders.

He knocked softly, the humming stopped abruptly, and a moment later the door opened, revealing Roxanna dressed in black silk stockings held up by a lacy, black garter belt. Her torso was tightly encased in a frilly black corset, above which her breasts lay bare, the nipples erect and rose-red. Roxanna smiled as Spur's gaze rose to her face.

"Hello," she said. "Mr. McCoy, I had you wrong. I didn't think you'd ever come back to me. I should have known you couldn't resist me." She laughed and moved back to allow him entrance, then closed the door and turned to him.

"Why don't we start by letting me undress you. Okay?" She smiled and walked to him, reaching out for his belt.

Spur didn't have time to respond or explain; a pounding knock echoed through the room.

"Roxanna!" a voice boomed outside.

"Roscoe?" he asked.

Roxanna nodded and started to speak, but Spur pushed his hand over her mouth. He put a finger to his lips, then looked around the room. The closet. He walked to it and opened the door. It was about eighteen inches wide and three feet long, stuffed with Roxanna's most intimate garments. Spur squeezed in between them. The last thing he saw before he closed the door was Roxanna's smiling face.

"Roxanna, damn it! Are you in there? Are you busy?"

"Yes and no," she said. "Come in!"

At that moment Spur opened the closet door slightly; he couldn't see Roxanna or Tate as he heard the other door swing open, but he had a clear view of the bed. The slips and petticoats, dresses and corsets pushing against him from all sides smelled of the familiar, sweet odor of woman mixed with perfumes and colognes of past times. Spur pushed it out of his mind. Roscoe must have been in a corner of the bar, or out the back, Spur thought. Perhaps in another room upstairs? Either way, he'd get a chance to eavesdrop on him. Maybe it would be useful.

"Ouch!" Roxanna said. "You're hurting me!"

"You know you love it, Roxanna!" Roscoe

growled and Spur heard the sound of ripping cloth. At that point Roxanna's musical laugh filled the room, blending with the man's rougher voice.

"You're paying for that," she said.

"That—and you."

Spur strained to see the pair but they were just out of his line of vision. He heard unstrapping and unbuckling, heavy garments tossed carelessly to the floor, and Roxanna's nearly constant giggles.

"See that big cock?" Roscoe's voice rasped. "It's going right up your cunt."

"I hope so," Roxanna said. "If you can keep it hard long enough."

"Bitch!" A moment later two naked bodies flashed by Spur's vision, then Roscoe pushed Roxanna onto the brass bed and fell heavily onto her.

His hairy body sharply constrasted with Roxanna's milky white, smooth skin. He lewdly ground his groin against hers, then bent to suck one of her ripe nipples. She arched her back and sighed, then threw her legs up until they gripped Roscoe around his deeply tanned back. Her ankles crossed.

"Stick it in me!" she said. "Right now!"

"Goddamn, Roxanna! You're the horniest woman I've ever met. I get a hard-on just hearing your name."

As Roxanna giggled Spur frowned. Say something important, dammit! Roscoe plunged into her, then vigorously pumped.

"I'll show them," Roscoe said between grunts. "Try to make a fool out of me! Nothing's going to stop me now."

"What?" Roxanna said, panting.

"Never mind. You don't need to talk now. Not with your mouth, at least."

Roscoe was silent for a moment after that, then sighed and thrust double-time, sending the bed into squeaks of complaint, bouncing its legs two inches off the floor.

"Oh yes!" Roxanna cried, her face flushed, mouth wide open. Her body slipped across the sheet as Roscoe sweated above her.

"Damn that bastard!" Roscoe said. "We'll show him. Tomorrow morning." The man gave a short, anguished cry as his body trembled, every muscle tensing as he unloaded into Roxanna.

Tomorrow morning? Spur frowned. What was Roscoe talking about? Was the *bastard* a farmer? Were *they* farmers in general?

Spur looked up to see Roscoe's shiny body lying motionless on top of Roxanna. His breath came in harsh gasps, his back pulsing with it.

Roxanna flailed her arms from side to side, trying to push the man away.

"Hey, Roscoe!" she said. "Would you roll off me, please? Jesus, you know how much you weigh! I'm such a fragile thing." She caressed his thighs and back and gently succeeded in slipping out from under the spent man. Roxanna lay back and wiped wisps of hair from her face.

"Whew, Roscoe! You sure know how to ride a woman!"

"Hell, Roxanna," he said, not moving. "You know I got the best cock in the county."

"That I do, Roscoe. Say, what was all that you were talking about? Sounds like you're upset about something—or more rightly, someone."

"What?" he asked groggily.

"You know, about *getting that bastard,* that kind of talk."

Roscoe sat up slowly, looked at the woman, then smiled. "Nothing. Just fucking out my problems, as usual." He reached out and touched her left breast.

"I see. Well, time's just about up. Would you like to pay me now, or later?"

"Shit. Now, I guess." He rose to his feet, stumbled across the floor and retrieved his pants. A moment later he produced a five dollar gold piece from a pocket and handed it to her.

Roxanna gasped. "Roscoe! Surely not all this?" She marveled at the coin.

"Sure. Plenty more where that comes from." He paused a moment, then dropped his pants and sat beside her on the bed. "Roxanna, I may be leaving here soon."

"Why?"

"Troubles. Family problems. You don't want to hear about that. But I wanted to talk to you about something."

Spur broke out in a sweat as the clothing pressed against him; the closet was close and hot.

"So talk," she said, reaching out to stroke his penis.

"Would you ever consider working somewhere else, some other town?"

"Leaving Kearney?" Roxanna's eyelashes fluttered in surprise. "Move to another town? I haven't really. Kearney's my home.'"

"Think about it."

She did, then cocked her head to one side saucily. "I might—if the price was right. I'd also have to be sure I was earning as much as I made here. What you got in mind?"

"Nothing yet. Just plans. But you wouldn't mind working in Denver, or St. Louis, or somewhere else, would you?"

"That depends on who I was working for."

"Keep your mind open, okay? Someday I may have a little surprise for you."

"I'll look forward to it, Roscoe." She gave him one last squeeze and released his organ. "Take good care of that for me, cowboy!"

Roscoe smiled and turned to dress. Roxanna playfully reached out and pinched his butt. "You're a fine figure of a man, Roscoe Tate. Generous too. Now if only you weren't such a damned bastard, you might make some woman very happy one day, I'm sure." But as she spoke she gazed at the gold piece.

Spur felt the sweat intensify, soaking his clothing. Why didn't Roscoe leave?

Roxanna laid the coin on a table before a large, expensive mirror. When she turned back Roscoe was buttoning up his fly.

"Thanks, Roxanna. You're a great woman."

"Come again anytime. And if I don't see you for a while—well, you know you're always welcome here."

"Thanks." He left.

Roxanna fell back onto the bed, sighing as she did so. Spur opened the closet door and stepped from the room, the sudden rush of air chilling his wet body.

"Some show, don't you think?" She laughed. "Some men pay big money to watch what you just got to watch for free. You're not the first man to hide in my closet. And you seemed to enjoy it—you're wetter than I am," she teased.

Spur stared down at her lovely naked body. "I think I've got all that I need. Thanks for letting me listen."

"Did it help you any? I mean, by listening in? I figured that's what you wanted to do."

"Maybe. I'll let you know." Spur left the room and gave his crotch a quick rub to check his growing erection. Tomorrow morning? Roscoe had big plans for the morning. McCoy headed down the hall and into the saloon. He just caught a glimpse of Roscoe and Parsons walking through the swinging doors onto Main Street.

Spur followed.

The men rode about three miles from Kearney, heading due west, Spur figured by the position of the sun. Spur hung back on the trip, hiding for a while behind a slow-moving hay wagon. Finally he saw the men turn onto a trail—above it was a sign with a capital P lying on its side. The lazy P. Parsons's ranch.

Spur turned back toward Kearney at a gentle walk. Something was going to happen tomorrow morning, he thought as he rode. If Roscoe had been partially responsible for the Parker murders, and maybe even organized the attack on the Craig's farm, he might be planning another for the morning. Sure, Spur thought. That fits. But where?

The Craig farm?

Spur decided it was a possibility. One more shot—do the job right this time. Go in, kill or scare out the Craigs. That's what Spur would do. The foiled attempt earlier that morning at the Craig's farm couldn't be allowed to pass into history; that would mean the ranchers had lost control of the homesteaders.

No. They had to complete their mission on the Craig farm. And if Roscoe was one of the men responsible, Spur thought, he'd be riding there early in the morning. Perhaps Parsons would ride with him.

And the third?

Spur shook his head. He knew one thing—he'd be at the Craig place before daybreak. Just in case.

CHAPTER SIXTEEN

"DON'T LET me catch you going out on the street again!" Rev. Burriss said, shaking his ever-present Bible with one hand at his daughter. He stood in the parlor of his comfortable Kearney home. "I'm going out now. I'll be gone about three hours, maybe longer. Just stay here and wait until I come back."

"Wait?" Ginny Burriss said, then laughed. "Wait for what? For you to come on back through that door yelling at me, telling me not to go outside, not to look at handsome men, not to have any damned fun!"

Burriss gave his daughter his sternest pulpit look. "I'll have no cursing in my house," he warned. "The Lord God shall punish thee, O wicked daughter! You are evil. This town's corrupted you, eaten away at your morals. And I won't let it corrupt you further. Stay here until I return!" he thundered.

Looking at her father, Ginny Burriss could

also see the black coat, vest, shirt, boots, and stovepipe hat her father always wore while preaching. As she continued to look at him, she was shocked at the changes she hadn't noticed earlier. Her father looked older; dark circles hung heavily beneath his eyes, and worry lines had furrowed across his face where once the skin had been taut. They'd lived in Kearney for three years and her father had not only turned into a tyrant—he had also grown old.

"Virginia Marilee Burriss, do you hear me?" he asked. "Sometimes I don't know what to do with you, girl. I should hand you over to Satan, for all the good I can do you."

Fatigue rocked through her brain and body. She was tired of his empty threats, tired of the insincere pleas for *getting herself washed in the blood of Jesus.* But she was also simply tired of her father. She knew she couldn't win against him.

"I'm sorry, Father," she said in her sweetest voice, a smile pasted onto unwilling lips. "I'll try harder to be a good child of God." She couldn't remove all traces of a sarcastic tone, but he didn't seem to notice.

Burriss flinched at the unexpected retreat, then frowned. "May He find thee in His favor." With that he stepped out the door.

Moments later Ginny heard the tumblers deep within the lock turn and fasten into place. She spun from the door and surpressed a scream. For months her father had grown increasingly fanatical in his words—but not his actions. Ginny had noticed that he had begun drinking more heavily, going out at all hours of the day and night, even swearing on occasion. Early one night, when her father had stumbled past her on the way to his bed she thought she smelled perfume on him—the expensive French type that some of the fancy women wore.

She sighed and didn't try to understand. She didn't want to understand. All she wanted was to have some man take her away from her father, to help her escape him. Ginny wanted to be her own wild, free self, not the starched, pure-white creature into which her father was trying to change her.

A man. Reverend Burriss had always taught his daughter that men were evil. She should never let them touch her, or return their gazes. And she certainly was never to do the *act of marriage,* as her father called it.

But she had. Several times. The last one was Spur McCoy. Ginny felt herself flush. A tingling spread out from her groin. Without thinking she reached for it, pressing both hands against her *v,* rubbing it gently through layers of petticoats and the stiff dress.

Ginny sat in the middle of the floor on the thick rug, her legs splayed far apart. She hiked up frilly cloth of various shades of pinks and pure whites, then worked her fingers between her legs and finally touched the furry patch. She groaned as she slipped one finger inside, moving it in and out, while another finger snaked up and began rubbing her clitoris.

Shock waves swept through her body as she rubbed herself. Ginny leaned back on one hand while her other one busied herself, her mouth forming an *o* as she shuddered through an orgasm.

She thought of Spur McCoy—his tanned, muscular body, his huge erection. Her fingers moved faster as she remembered his rough touch on her soft skin, how she knelt before him and he rammed his penis down her throat.

A series of cries and gasps issued from her throat as her hand became a blur between her legs, its caresses plunging her into paroxysms of delight and ecstasy.

There were others, too; other men, other times. Good times, she remembered, searching for a new fantasy, a new way to break the monotony, to quench her insatiable desire for sex. There was the cowboy who she'd bumped into one night when she was out looking for her father—the young man who'd opened his pants and showed her his hard penis in the moonlight, then put it in her.

Then there was Mr. Marshall, the general store owner, who'd closed early one afternoon and, after pulling down the window blinds, spread her out on the counter and took her in utter animal lust.

Ginny's body rocked with orgasms, her mind racing from scene to scene of her brief sexual life. Suddenly she stopped, almost gasping as the explosive action of her fingers ceased.

This was wrong, she told herself. Masturbation was evil, a tool of Satan to tempt the wicked. Her cheeks burned as she thought of the burning pools of Hell, of the Devil with his pitchfork, infernal fire, wailing sinners. Eternal damnation.

She should stop, she told herself. Stop, wipe your hands and pray to God that she never touched herself again. She should ask Jesus to cleanse her of wicked and evil thoughts.

Ginny Burriss sat for a moment, her hand frozen above her genitals, then shook her head. Her father was wrong. The Bible was wrong. It's wrong *not* to experience these delights, she told herself. That is what life's all about. Otherwise, God wouldn't have given us sex organs, she thought.

With this Ginny's hand pressed against herself again, hard. Her other rose to her breasts, squeezing the nipples, pinching them, cupping and rubbing the sensitive skin there.

She thought of every man who'd lain between her legs; the disgusting ones, the thrilling ones—and the feelings they'd aroused in her. Her hand was no match for a good, hard man, she thought briefly before all rationality was swept away on the crest of a wave of passion.

Her body shook as she fell back onto the rug, one hand jabbing violently at her crotch, the other squeezing her breasts alternately, while the sexual flush spread out across her face, neck and chest.

Ginny Burriss, wrapped in passion, didn't hear the tumblers within the lock rotate, nor the front door swing open. Two seconds later, however, she heard a loud intake of breath—shattering her passion, and forcing her head to look up at her father's incredulous face.

"Christ—shit—Ginny!" He didn't look into her eyes. "Slut! Whore! How dare you pleasure yourself on my best parlor rug! I'll kill you. I'll kill you now and let the Lord take charge of your soul. That's all I can do now!" he said threateningly. Burriss swung the door closed without taking his gaze off her body.

Ginny was too stunned to move for several seconds. Then she removed her hands, straightened her skirts, and started to rise. Only then did she notice that, although she'd covered up her body, her father's eyes continued to rest on her crotch. He hadn't stopped looking there since he'd walked into the room, surprising her.

"I won't say I'm sorry, Father," she said. "This isn't the first time. I do this every day, sometimes several times a day. When you go out, when you lock me in my room, or when you're asleep at night."

"Abomination!" He looked up at her face, finally.

"And it feels good."

"Heathen slut!"

"What did you expect me to do? Sit quietly in the corner, hands folded, waiting for your return? You never let me go to the dances with the local men. When one comes to call on me, you tell them I'm not home. Since I couldn't have many men, I pretended I had one."

"Ginny!" her father said.

"Why don't you try it, Daddy?" Ginny said viciously. "Or do you already do it? Do you feel yourself at night, Daddy?"

Rage prevented Burriss from speaking. He took two halting steps toward his daughter.

"I'll bet you do," Ginny said, sneering. She faced her father fearlessly. All her hesitation, her weariness of her father vanished. Maybe she didn't need a man to break off from her father. Maybe she could do it on her own. She was nearly nineteen—plenty old enough to be free, to do what she pleased. "I'll bet you pull your thing every day, Daddy! And then pray to God afterwards to forgive you for being such a lowly sinner. Or do you, Father? Do you really pray—have you ever really prayed—or are you acting all the time?"

"Filthy slut!" Burriss slammed his hand down hard against Ginny's face, knocking her to the floor. She crumpled and screamed. "I'll teach you to speak to a man of the cloth that way!"

"You're no preacher, Father. And you're sure no Christian!" Ginny rubbed her cheek, trying to stamp out the pain. "You drink and swear and lay with Roxanna Stafford—don't think I don't know what you do when you go out!"

He stared at her in astonishment for a moment, then smiled evilly. Ginny looked at him in horror as she rose. Then she saw the distortion at his crotch—the way the material bulged out at the front of his pants. Her father was aroused. Her father—

"So you want a man inside you, do you?" her father asked, throwing all pretensions of Christianity away. Ginny had never seen her father this way. "Isn't that why you do such things?"

"Stay away from me," she said, pushing her hands out before her, but fear clutched her throat. She felt behind her—the wall. If she could make it to her room she could wait until he cooled off.

"You want a man? Huh? Well, daughter, you're damned well going to get one. Little lady, I'll make you see God. Or the devil, in this case."

"No!" she cried. "Father! It's a sin! That's what you taught me, remember?"

"What the hell do you care about sin? Or me, for that matter? Come on, Ginny. You know you want it. Any cock'll do, isn't that it?"

"No!" She bolted to the right, but her father easily caught her.

"Stay right there, little lady." He grasped one of her hands in his, and after pressing his knees against hers to hold her body in place, he lowered her hand to his crotch, then pushed it hard against him. "Feel that?"

Ginny held back the urge to vomit, then cried out in rage and disgust. She kicked her father's shins but he didn't seem to notice the blows. His evil face, inches from her, shot out hot breath that struck her like poisonous fumes. Gathering every ounce of energy she jabbed her fingers savagely against the man's erection, then repeated the motion and pulled her hand free as Burriss moved his hand to cup and protect the area.

"Shit! Jesus Christ!" Burriss yelled, bent over at the waist, one hand rubbing his damaged genitals. "You've nearly unmanned me, wicked girl!"

"Feel that, Father?" she said. Ginny turned and ran into her father's room, then slammed the door shut and locked it. Feeling calm, as if she wasn't participating in the action but merely observing another moving about on a stage, Ginny Burriss shoved a chair up beneath the doorknob and then walked to the window. She was glad she'd run into her father's room—her bedroom had been specially designed without windows.

Ginny pulled the curtains back, slid the window open, hiked up her skirt and petticoats, and stuck one booted foot out the window. With a bit of straining and stretching she was soon outside.

Her pulse pounded in her ears and before her eyes as she walked, then broke into a run. She turned down Main Street and headed toward Sheriff Gardner's office. He should know what to do. Surely he wouldn't side with her father. Then she stopped. No. The questions, the trial, the looks of her neighbors. She couldn't do it, couldn't go through the shame. Desperation clouded her thoughts; she turned to the right, then the left, stumbling over her feet, her hands hanging limply at her sides, not knowing where to turn, and the scream she'd earlier choked down tore from her throat as she fell to the dusty road.

CHAPTER SEVENTEEN

Should I tell Gardner? Spur wondered as he stopped the horse in its tracks, one hundred feet from the sheriff's combination office and jail. Spur paused for a moment; he didn't have proof that Roscoe Tate was responsible for the Parker murders, nor that he and Jack Parsons were planning on striking the Craig farm in the morning. But it made sense, fit the facts, and it was the most that Spur had to go on.

Spur began moving the horse toward the sheriff's office again. As he passed an alley he heard the sound of approaching feet—then watched as a young woman collapsed onto the street, screaming.

"Hey!" he called, springing off the horse and running to her. He recognized Ginny Burriss. "Ginny! What's wrong?" He reached down and helped her to her feet, but it was a few seconds before she opened her eyes and allowed Spur to touch her again.

"Are you all right?" he asked as she rubbed her eyes and looked around her. She blushed slightly.

"I must look a mess."

"You look fine, Ginny."

"I'm sorry." She lowered her head for a moment, then stared up at him earnestly. "I was afraid, and I was just running anywhere—and then everything seemed to close in on me—and that's all I remember."

"Why were you running?"

"To get away from my father."

"What's he done now?" Spur asked, remembering the scene her father had made in his hotel room.

"He—he—he's chasing me. I hurt him." Ginny shook her head. "No. I can't tell you any more. It's too awful." With those words she collapsed into his arms and shook as she cried.

"Ginny, I'm sure you have nothing to worry about," he said softly as he stroked her hair. "If your father's after you, we'd better get off the streets."

"Please!" she said between sobs. "I don't want him to find me. I never want to see him again!"

"Then you don't have to."

She stopped crying, sniffling a few times, and wiped away the moisture from her cheeks. "Okay."

Spur could see the woman was deeply troubled by something, but it was obvious he wasn't going to learn what that was—not now, at least.

He took the horse's reins in one hand, put an arm around her shoulder and started off toward the Calico Hotel, but Ginny violently tore away from the contact.

"No! Don't touch me. If he sees me—or if anyone sees you touching me—he'll explode!" Her eyes were wild.

Spur raised his hands in defeat, then dropped them to his sides. A strange girl, he thought. Her father had turned the young, vibrant, sensual woman of a few days ago into a blubbering, timid mouse. What could have happened to her that had done that?

"You're not going back home?"

She didn't look at him as she shook her head violently. "Never. Not when he's there. I'll wait until he's gone—maybe Sunday morning when he's preaching—and then go in and get all my things. I'll put all my money together and go somewhere where he'll never find me."

"How will you live? Your money won't last very long. What about after that?"

"There are ways—for a woman to make money," she said slowly.

"Ginny," Spur began.

She shot him a look and stopped walking. "Why the hell not? My father already thinks I'm a whore. Why shouldn't I go ahead and become one? If only for a while, until I save up enough to live on?" She laughed bitterly. "I'd hate to disappoint him."

"We'll talk about this later," Spur said, glancing at several men and a pair of women who'd looked toward them, attracted by

Ginny's loud voice.

They walked to the hotel in silence, the horse accompanying them.

Once inside Spur's room, Ginny splashed water on her face, bending over the basin. Spur admired her fine backside then, remembering how exciting and bold she'd been in bed. She'd had none of the maidenly reserve that too many women maintained, even while rocking through orgasm after orgasm. Spur had enjoyed her immensely.

"What happened at your father's house?" Spur asked when the woman had finished patting her face dry. Where a few moments ago there had been redness or puffiness, her face was now freshly pink, glowing, radiating beauty.

"It's too awful," she said. "I don't want to talk about it. I can't think how I'd tell you. It's—beastly."

"Try me," Spur said. "After what we've done, we're at least good friends by now."

She smiled once—and her face lit up. She sniffled again and sat in the straight back chair that was pushed up near Spur's bed, then lay her hands in her lap and folded them.

"Well, he'd just gone out," she said with perfect calm and dignity. "I was in the middle of the parlor, and suddenly I thought of when I'd snuck in here and surprised you, and then had fun together." She looked down at her hands. "That was one of the best times I've ever had, Spur, in my whole life! And sometimes when I think of things like that, I just have to touch myself there, feel myself, reliving the moment. You know what I mean?"

"Go on," Spur said.

"Well, I was in the middle of the parlor doing that—and my father walked in! I thought he would kill me, at first—he was so furious at me doing such a wicked thing. That's what he said, at least. But after a while it seemed like he was more than angry—and—and I saw he was getting excited. He wanted to lay with me, like men and women do! Spur, I didn't know what to think, what to say. Ever since we came to Kearney he's been a wicked man. He used to be gentle, a true Christian in every sense of the word. Now he's become a different person. He goes out at all hours of the night, sometimes early in the morning, before the sun's up."

Spur's brain latched onto that piece of information, but he didn't interrupt Ginny's narration.

"So I told him it was a sin, but he didn't care, and thought I didn't either. And he—he made me touch his hard—well, you know. His man thing." She squirmed. "I wanted to retch; I felt myself getting sick. So I jabbed him hard in the crotch, twice, and ran for the closest room. I locked the door, pushed a chair under the knob, and climbed out the window. I was just running from the house when I collapsed in the street."

"I see," Spur said. "You jabbed him in the groin?"

"Yes. I didn't know what else to do—and I was afraid imagining what he might make me do if I didn't stop him."

"You're a very resourceful girl," he said.

She stiffened her back and composed her face. "I'm a young lady," she thought for a moment. "Well, a young woman. Maybe not a lady anymore."

"My apologies," Spur said. "Any fool could see you're a young lady!"

"So I'm leaving Kearney and never want to see my father again," she said suddenly, as if to test the plan's reality.

"Are you going to the sheriff's office? You could have your father arrested."

"I—I don't know. I'm not sure I want to go through all that—and if I told Gardner I know I'd have to see my father again, go to trial—" She sighed. "I just want to collect a few things and leave." She stood then, and kissed him lushly on the lips. "Thanks."

"For what?"

"If I hadn't remembered the time we did it, my father wouldn't have caught me playing with myself, and I wouldn't be breaking free from him right now."

"I see," Spur said. "Do you have any immediate plans?"

"What do you mean?"

"If you want, you can stay here for a while—a few days, if you wish. Until you can get the things you want."

"That would be wonderful!" she cried, clasping his shoulders, her hands traveling down to his biceps, where she couldn't possibly touch her thumb to her fingertips while they were wrapped around his powerful muscles. "And maybe we could do it again—sometime soon? Not now, but maybe later?"

"Of course."

"But if I'd be in the way—I wouldn't want to put you out. If you have a different girl in here every night, I can find somewhere else to stay."

McCoy smiled. "No need."

She relaxed then. "Wonderful. Do you have anything to do right now?"

"Yes. I was on my way to Sheriff Gardner's office."

"Why?"

Spur smiled shortly. "Business."

"I see. I'm sure I can find something to do."

"Keep the door locked, if you want. And if you go out—"

"I'll be careful," Ginny said, shivering. "I don't want to give my father the chance."

"Fine."

She raised herself up on her toes, lifting her face at the same time.

It was the most obvious kiss proposal Spur had ever seen. He leaned down and their lips touched. Spur's tongue probed, broke through the sensuous lips, and slipped into her hot mouth. He pulled her to him then, pushing his crotch against her body, feeling her erecting nipples jabbing his chest. His penis had throbbed to full erection by the time the kiss ended, and it was with an effort that Spur pulled himself back from the woman.

"Goodbye, Ginny."

"Bye."

Spur left the room.

* * *

Sheriff Gardner snorted. "Where's your evidence?" he demanded of the man standing on the other side of his desk. "You don't have one single shred of evidence, Spur."

"I'll admit that, Gardner, but it's the—"

"And there's a big hole in your little scheme. According to your sources three men attacked the Parker place, right?"

"Yes," Spur said, standing across the desk.

"Roscoe and Parsons are only two. Who's the third?"

"I don't know."

Gardner nodded and gave a short chuckle. "I'm sorry I got so riled up there, but that's just the kind of thing that I was thinking about two weeks ago."

"Why didn't you move, then?" Spur asked.

"No evidence. Couldn't do a thing. I had ideas—but that's all."

"You suspected Roscoe Tate and Jack Parsons?" Spur asked.

Gardner paused, nodded, then shook his head. "Yes. Well, no. Maybe not those two particular men. I suspected all of them, but I never had the chance to prove my suspicions."

Spur slid into the chair before the desk and faced Gardner. "That's what we can do now—tomorrow morning. I'll ride out there and if no one shows, I'll know I was wrong. If some men do show with thoughts of trouble, I'll know I was at least partly right. And if Roscoe Tate and Jack Parsons arrive there around dawn—with a third man—and attack the Craig farm . . ."

"Okay, okay," Gardner said. "Go ahead. Do it."

Spur smiled. "I wasn't asking for your permission. I have jurisdiction over you here. I simply wanted your opinion."

"Sounds good to me," he said slowly, "although a long shot."

"I'll let you know what happens." Spur began to rise from the chair.

"Hold on, Spur! It could be too dangerous for one man. I know you think you can do it alone—and you did once, I'll give you that. But you won't get lucky again. It just makes more sense to have more than one man there—in case your fears prove real."

Spur nodded. "Maybe. But I like to work alone."

"So how about me and some men going out there to back you up?"

Spur looked hard at the man. "If you can keep them back, well out of sight."

Gardner nodded. "I'll round up the men quietly, only the ones I trust the most. Then we'll ride out of town at different times, heading different directions, but meet at the Craig place—some time late tonight, early in the morning. And you?"

Spur shrugged. "Probably the same." The thought of all those extra men made him uneasy. The raiding party could discover them and change plans—and Spur might never find out who killed the Parkers. But the backups might come in handy, Spur conceded, if they were secreted correctly.

"You know, if you're sure it's Roscoe Tate and Jack Parsons—"

"Which I'm not," Spur butted in.

"—you could follow them tonight, or even watch their ranches."

"Could," Spur said, musing over the idea.

"Don't worry about my men," Gardner said. "They won't get in the way unless they have to." He shook his head. "I hope you're right—and I hope this puts an end to the problems here in the Platte River Valley."

"My sentiments exactly," Spur said.

"But I've got doubts. Still—" he shook his head. "Any other news to bother me with? How's the investigation into the Fred Lucas killing coming along?"

"I was going to ask you the same thing," Spur said. "I've been concentrating on the Parkers."

"I haven't had any luck on it, either," Gardner said. "I've tried."

"I've also got a little story to tell you."

Gardner looked at him in surprise. "Story?"

Spur launched into a description of the trouble between Burriss and his daughter Ginny. He didn't leave much to the imagination. When he was finished Gardner was grim.

"I knew Burriss had gone bad, running around and causing some trouble, but I had no idea he was capable of trying to commit incest. The man's changed. How's Ginny taking it?"

"As well as can be expected."

"Why didn't she come to me?"

"She didn't want to cause any trouble, and she wants to leave Kearney as quickly and quietly as she can. Could you arrest her father—and get a conviction—without her help?"

"Don't know," Gardner said, scratching his head. "But I know Burriss won't be welcome in Kearney for much longer. If I can't use the law to force him out—I'm sure the citizens around here will do the trick." He smiled ruefully. "He's not the first *preacher* to be run out of town."

"I'm beginning to wonder about Rev. Burriss. He doesn't sound much like a Bible man. Ginny described what he's been doing lately—and I don't like the picture she painted."

"Burriss has gone bad; no one will deny that. Still, he's the only preacher we've got and people keep on going to church every Sunday to hear him preach." He laughed. "Every Sunday we hear him ask God to forgive our sins, and his as well. Maybe he thinks that makes him pure."

"Wouldn't know."

"I'll set out rounding up the men. If not before, I'll see you at daybreak at Craig's?"

"Probably," Spur said. "I just might follow one of the men after all, as you suggested. Let's wait until two hours after sunrise to call it quits. If they haven't shown by then, I was wrong."

"Sure," Gardner said, then laughed. "You're the boss."

CHAPTER EIGHTEEN

SPUR STRETCHED out a leg to loosen the stiff muscles, then tucked it back under him. He'd been crouched over in a shadow in front of the Lazy P ranch for nearly three hours. No sleep for him tonight, he thought ruefully. He was sure it would be worth it. And he'd had worse experiences.

After leaving Gardner's office, Spur had ridden back to Jack Parsons's ranch. He moved carefully toward the house—both horses stood there where they'd been left hours earlier. Both Parsons and Tate, then, were still inside.

Spur spent the time thinking, going over and over the facts, to see if his conclusions were correct. No matter how many times he did this, Spur McCoy always had the same result: Roscoe and Parsons and another man had killed the Parkers, or were involved in the killings, if they hired other men—and that they were going to attempt the same thing with the Craigs on the coming morning.

He was sure Gardner and his men were in position by then, or soon would be. Spur hoped that they damn well wouldn't get in his way. He disliked the idea of their presence—hell, he was sorry he'd told Sheriff Gardner his thoughts in the first place. But the backup men could come in handy, if things didn't happen according to plan.

He looked around him with a start when the faint sound of a horse and rider tattooed itself into his brain. It approached from directly before him, where the trail to Kearney stood out clearly in the moonlight. Spur, realizing he might be seen by someone approaching from that direction, moved further into the shadows, and then ducked around behind a bush.

A few minutes later Spur could see who was riding up to the Lazy P. A big man—a light-colored hat—but Spur couldn't see the man's face, not even when he passed within twenty feet of him. He frowned. Who'd be riding out to Jack Parsons's ranch at this hour of the early morning?

The third man? The one who'd helped them kill the Parkers?

Spur grunted, then ran forward to follow the man. The unknown rider dismounted and tied the horse up before the farmhouse, then walked directly in without knocking or pausing, as if expected.

Spur moved back to his shadowy corner near

the gate and frowned. It was a long wait to daybreak. Should he ride out to Craig's place now, or wait to see if the men leave? Spur decided to stay put; he just had a *feeling* about Roscoe Tate.

He pulled the coat tighter around him and leaned back, relaxing into the position.

Spur was startled out of a light sleep by the slap of moisture on his face. His Stetson had fallen back against the tree trunk he'd been leaning against, squatting on his toes. The droplet bolted him into a standing position. He pushed the hat forward onto his head.

Night. He must have dozed off for a couple minutes, no more. Raindrops fell heavily around him, sending up splashes of dust as the liquid hit the dry-as-bones Nebraska soil. Spur raised his face into it for a few stinging seconds to wake him fully, then turned to examine the surrounding area. The sun hadn't yet streaked the eastern sky with its first colors.

A door banged shut somewhere far away, causing a dog to bark. "Shit," Spur muttered. The rain stopped. He saw the three men move to their horses in the distance. They swiftly mounted and rode directly toward Spur and the gate. He ducked back away from the trail and moved quickly toward his horse.

He didn't want to miss any of the action he knew would be coming at the Craig farm.

Spur didn't bother waiting for the men to catch up with him; nor did he decide to follow them at a distance, to make sure they were headed for the Craig farm. He didn't think they were.

He *knew* so.

Spur cut across the completely flat land for several miles. His mount's eyes were clear and good, for she avoided all obstructions even in the moonlight. He saved time by not following established trails and roads that had been etched into the plains by centuries of use—long before any ranchers or farmers had settled the area.

His horse tired and began to falter on the last mile, so Spur slowed her to a walk.

"'Good girl," he said, rubbing her neck. "Not too much farther." If he was reading the stars right he was moving in the correct direction.

As he approached the Craig farm deep purple tinted the east, showing gathering storm clouds. Dawn was approaching.

He moved his horse into a thicket of hickory trees, tied her up, rubbed her down for ten minutes, keeping his eyes alert. He stood about a hundred feet from the gate which led into the Craig farm itself. Spur crossed the ground quickly, looking for a place to hide until the men showed—which could be at any second. Sure enough, as he ran toward the henhouse full of clucking chickens and a vociferous rooster, Spur heard the men's horses moving quickly toward him. He had just made it inside the henhouse when the three men discreetly slowed their horses to a walk, then finally dismounted, walking beside them.

"Damned sure of themselves, aren't they?" Spur said to himself. As they grew closer Spur could see the kerchiefs wrapped around the men's lower faces. No way to identify them—although one of the hats looked exactly like one he'd seen perched on Roscoe's head recently. He was sure the men were Roscoe, Parsons and one other.

The men had apparently decided on a different approach than the one they'd used here last at Craig's—or rather, their hired men had used. As a rooster pecked at his boot Spur scanned the area visible between the door and jamb as the men broke up—one larger man moving to the rear of the farmhouse, the other two evenly dividing up the property between them. The two in front—the only ones Spur could see—stood about sixty feet from the house.

Now, Spur's nerves screamed. Raise your Spencer and blow the two men to hell, before they can hurt Julius Craig or his daughter Leah. Spur had to fight the urge to open fire on the men. He had to do this in accordance with the law—by the book. Especially when the sheriff was watching. Spur wondered where his men had hidden—he didn't see any sign of them. Gardner must have done a good job.

The two men stood motionless for a few moments, then one raised his rifle toward the kitchen window. Before the man could shoot the sharp, crackling explosion of a discharging rifle ripped through the early morning quiet, from behind the raiders, to their right, from a clump of trees.

The chickens broke into a new chorus of cackles as Spur watched out the door. The two men immediately ducked and ran for cover; Spur glanced at the area from which the shot had originated, silently cursing the man who'd fired early. Spur aimed two shots toward an overturned table behind which one of the men had ducked. Both men had apparently been spared from the trigger-happy idiot. Now Spur almost wished he'd been the one to shoot the early round—at least one of the men would be nothing but dead meat by now.

Hot .44 slugs flew through the air towards him as the two men bombarded the entire area. They occasionally shot toward the henhouse but concentrated most of their fire toward the clump of trees. Spur saw a flicker of movement in the corner of his eye; then turned and aimed. A man near the house ducked out of sight before Spur could fire. He was the third man, coming to the front to help out the other two, or was he pushed there by gunfire?

Spur couldn't tell how many men were shooting all around him, but he was convinced he'd never seen so many lousy shots in one place, from one group of men, in his life. After a few seconds Spur heard the farmhouse windows shattering, then someone shooting from within the house. Good, Spur thought. The Craigs were fighting back.

McCoy finally saw his victim. It was the second when a target and weapon line up and the moment seems frozen in time, and he held his breath until the connection between life and death had been made.

One of the men rose from his hiding place and ran across the yard, apparently in an attempt to remove himself from the fight. Spur blasted two rounds at him, leading him perfectly. The head and shoulders shook, the arms were thrown up and the figure wobbled grotesquely, spasming as it fell to the earth backwards. It lay motionless.

One down.

As Spur calmly surveyed the area, fresh from his first blood of the fight, he saw too late the figure of a man rapidly leaving the area on horseback. The man turned back for a second in fear—and Spur clearly saw the face. It was the fallen minister, Burriss!

McCoy cursed the man as he fired at what was apparently the only other man there. He wondered if it was Roscoe or Parsons.

Dawn threw riotous colors over the area where the clouds had broken up, charging it and the earth with an incredibly vivid crimson light. It cast a surreal feel to the otherwise earthy scene of carnage.

Spur kept firing at the hidden figure, but the man didn't make a mistake—didn't show himself too long, or even on the same side of the obstruction twice in succession. Spur wondered how long the man could hold out.

When he realized that the man hadn't returned fire for a minute or so, he stood tensely for a few seconds, then abruptly whistled. The shooting, which had been sporadic at best, stopped around him. He ducked back down and waited a moment. The man didn't fire. Was he dead, unconscious, out of ammunition—or crafty?

"Come out of there," Spur called out. "Show yourself. You can't possibly save yourself now. Your friends are dead, and you'll join them in two seconds if you don't get your butt out where I can see you."

"Fuck you!" the voice said, shaky but strong and deep. Spur recognized the voice instantly.

"Come on, Roscoe!" he yelled. "Let's talk this thing over. Cooperate with me, and I'll let you off easily."

"Not a chance, asshole! Goddamn it, I should've had you killed when I had the chance! I was right about you! You're nothing but trouble. Why don't you go back where you came from and leave me alone!"

"Too late for that. Let's talk."

"Fuck you," the man repeated.

Spur waited a moment, then lightly moved out over the rough ground as the rain started again. The sky spat out a drenching downpour toward the parched earth, which effectively muffled the sounds of Spur's movements as he approached the upturned table. When he was ten feet from it, he bent at the waist and scrambled up to it, then sprang up to his full height before it, aiming down behind the table.

Empty.

The man was gone.

Spur swore as he looked around—and just

caught a pair of feet disappearing around the back of the house.

He ran after Roscoe as the rain continued to pound down. The man couldn't have gone too far—Spur rounded the house and again caught the sight of the departing Roscoe darting around the other side, splashing in the instant puddles.

This is absurd, he thought, and abruptly turned, then ran the opposite direction, stopped, and aimed chest-level at nothing.

As quickly as it had started the rain stopped. Roscoe appeared before him, his head turned back to glance behind.

"Looking for me?" Spur asked.

Roscoe jerked his head and glanced wildly up at him. The mask was half-torn from his face, revealing enough for Spur to firmly identify him. Roscoe's hands were empty.

"Shit!" Roscoe said, then started to move.

"No," Spur said sharply. "Don't run. If you so much as spit I'll scramble your brains with hot lead."

Roscoe stood motionless.

It was only then that Spur saw the small stains on the man's clothing—one on his right thigh, another in his left shoulder. The rain had smeared them into long streaks.

"Tell me about the Parkers," Spur said.

"Fuck you. Why the hell should I tell you anything? You're not the sheriff."

Spur lowered his aim slightly. "If you say one more word without answering my question I'll blow your balls off."

The man's throat tightened visibly as he stared at the Spencer aimed at his crotch. He nodded.

"Yeah. Fuck yes I rode out to the Parkers the other week! Me and Burriss and Parsons. But look at you!" he said, sneering. "You and those men out there watching us. You killed Burriss and Parsons. How's that different from what happened to the Parkers? That was an accident."

Spur laughed. "Accident?"

"I swear it's the truth!"

"Bullshit. You killed those three people. Why?"

"Because—hell, because I hated old man Parker and I wanted all the homesteaders out of Kearney. We set fire to their house, yes, to warn the other farmers."

"And you shot and killed Al Parker?" Spur asked, guessing.

"That's right." Roscoe rubbed his shoulder. "I'm shot," he said.

Spur ignored him. "Why did you want the homesteaders out of Kearney County? You're no rancher; your family told me that. And you don't seem to be the type to stick around this cowtown. What's your scheme? Waiting around for your father to die for your inheritance?"

"I wanted to clear out the homesteaders so they wouldn't interfere with the Circle T. It was on its way to becoming the biggest outfit in the area. I figured as soon as it was going as well as it ever would, I'd take as much money as I could and leave here forever."

"And do what?" Spur asked.

"Maybe open a saloon; I don't know." The man grimaced as he touched his shoulder.

"You hired those three men to come here yesterday morning to kill the Craigs?"

"No! Not to kill them," he said. "Just to warn them to leave here." He looked up at Spur in disgust. "I suppose it was you who killed them," he said accusingly.

"Damn right! That's my job. They were threatening the Craigs. Anything else you want to confess before I turn you over to Sheriff Gardner?"

"No," Roscoe said, then bent at the waist as it pained. He fell to the wet ground.

Spur stood still. "Roscoe?"

The man lay motionless.

"Roscoe?"

His face was half-pressed into the muddy ground. Spur saw the man's hand flash into action, then the glint of steel. He aimed and fired before Roscoe could raise the hidden derringer from his boot. The round ripped through Roscoe's chest, slamming him back to the ground. His head rolled at a strange angle, the eyes glazed and lifeless, unblinking as massive droplets of water hit them and slid off.

Spur sighed. He walked warily to the corpse and, after pushing it several times and looking at the man's eyes, decided that Roscoe Tate was officially dead.

CHAPTER NINETEEN

TWO BODIES. Spur looked at the downed men as he walked to the farmhouse. Sheriff Gardner limped out from the front door of the house and greeted Spur halfway. The rain had stopped, and the wind had split the clouds and pushed them away. A deep blue sky shone overhead.

"Come on out, you men," Gardner called.

From various strategic locales around the farm ten men appeared.

"You were right," Gardner said. "Obviously. It was Roscoe Tate all the time."

"You all right, Sheriff?" Spur asked as the two men stopped three feet from each other, the posse gathering around them.

"Sure. Just fell and hurt my leg in there, dammit! I'm fine." He looked at his men. "But I'm not so sure about these guys. Which one of you men fired early?"

He stared hard at the group; no one said a word.

Spur looked at the men curiously. They were farmers, to a man, which may have accounted for their lack of expertise at handling firearms. Men from Ohio and Pennsylvania aren't necessarily the best shots.

"Come on," Gardner said. "Tell me. No use trying to hide it. I'll find out soon enough."

"I've got to go," Spur said.

"What's that?"

"Burriss left—he was the one who rode out. I've got to follow him and bring him in."

"Right," Gardner said. "Go ahead. I'll finish up here."

"Spur!" a musical voice called out.

He glanced toward the farmhouse where Leah Craig stood in the doorway. She ran to him, wrapped her arms around him and pressed her face against Spur's chest.

"I worried about you out here!" she said, then pulled away from him. "I mean, I'm so glad you're safe. Thank you for saving my life again."

"My pleasure, Leah."

"Not now," Julius Craig said from the house as he appeared in the doorway behind his daughter. "He's got to get on and grab the good reverend before he slips out of town." The man grimaced as he touched a freshly-bandaged thigh. Leah had apparently ripped away the trouser leg and dressed the wound herself.

"You hurt bad, Craig?" Spur asked.

"I'll live."

"Get out of here, Spur," Gardner said, then smiled. "Thanks for your help."

"Sure," Spur said, then broke into a trot through the mud toward his horse. As the goo slapped against his boots Spur tried to forget how good Leah Craig had smelled, pressed up against him.

Rev. Edward Burriss hurriedly unlocked his front door, pushed it open, and slammed the key back into the lock as he closed it. He ran to his bedroom where he extracted a thick leather wallet from behind a picture. He glanced inside it—the neat stacks of hundred dollar bills were in place. He was glad he'd changed the church funds into these convenient bills last week. Those *donations* from Roscoe Tate sure had beefed up the coffers.

Burriss threw the money into a saddle bag, then added a shaving mug, brush, soap and comb. He looked at the large Bible lying on a table near the fireplace. He turned from it, then sighed.

"Shit."

He went to it and picked it up, then stuffed it into the bag. It might come in handy soon. He might have to pose as a preacher. Again.

Burriss couldn't believe his incredible luck in escaping the Craig farm that morning. And he hadn't been followed on his way back. He hoped both Roscoe and Parsons had been killed, thereby silencing them forever about his involvement with Roscoe's crimes.

Of course, he couldn't count on this, so he decided to leave Kearney. No sense in hanging around waiting for trouble.

He didn't flinch at the thought of his two partners lying dead on the muddy ground back there. They had been necessary evils. Now that he'd given up all pretenses to following that stifling, dull, stupid religion he could put up with some small problems—especially when he saw the possible money to be made.

Burriss shut the saddle bag, pulled the straps tight and hefted it. He pulled his pocket watch out—five till ten. The next train came through at 10:30. With luck he'd be far gone from Kearney by noon.

Where should he go? Burriss snorted as he gripped the bag and walked toward the door. He didn't care where. As long as he could hide out and—

Burriss looked at Ginny's bedroom door.

Ginny. He'd forgotten Ginny. Was she there? A quick check of her room ruled that out. Ginny, his pride and joy—no, his disappointment, he remembered bitterly. The girl was a slut, and she certainly wasn't his daughter any more. He pushed his feelings for her aside and hardened his face. Edward Burriss had no reason to stay in Kearney. Not any more.

He moved to the door, turned to survey the house, knowing this was the last time he'd do so, then reached for the knob.

Spur saw no signs of Burriss, but the man had headed west—probably toward Kearney. Trusting his instincts, Spur nudged the horse in that direction.

She was rested, frisky in the cool morning air.

Spur pushed her as much as he could, trying to figure out what Burriss was doing. Probably leaving town.

Too bad Gardner hadn't already arrested Burriss—then he would have been out of the way. But the sheriff had said there were some problems with that—Ginny not wanting to testify. Too late now.

Spur pulled up in back of Burriss's home. An exhausted horse stood there, sniffing the greenish water in the trough. Burriss must have just arrived.

He tied up the horse, walked to the front of the house, moved onto the porch and reached for the knob. It began to turn before he gripped it, so Spur laid himself flat on the wall next to the door's hinges. It swung open, halted a moment, then moved back.

Spur was ready as Burriss appeared from behind the door. McCoy knocked the man backward with a hard fist to the jaw, then pounded twice into his gut. He sprang back, light on his feet, feeling the glow of satisfaction from beating Burriss. A bag skidded across the porch where the reverened threw it.

"Going somewhere?" Spur asked.

"You're—the man with Ginny! What the hell concern is it of yours whether I'm going somewhere or not?" Burriss' face contorted with pain.

"Kearney doesn't let murderers leave town," Spur said. "Or men who try to sleep with their daughters."

Burriss backed away, stumbling when he

stepped off the porch backwards onto the walkway leading to the street. "Leave me alone. I don't know what you're talking about. I'm a man of God."

Spur laughed. "Gardner and I both heard Roscoe Tate say you were the third man in the Parker killings," Spur said with satisfaction. "He told us just before he died."

"He's crazy," Burriss said, sweating. "He named me at random. I haven't done anything wrong. Roscoe's just mad at me because I won't let him marry Ginny."

"I saw you this morning at Craig's. Let's go."

"Where to?" Burriss asked, rubbing his stomach.

"Jail. We usually hang men who kill women and children."

Burriss moved to the right, but Spur stuck out his foot and caught it under the man's legs, sending him sprawling to the ground. As Burriss looked up he saw Spur's Colt .45 out and ready.

"Don't try that again," Spur said.

"None of it's true! It's all lies!" Burriss said, real fear tinging his words.

"The Parkers. Two weeks ago. You were one of the three men. You helped kill the Parkers. Admit it!" Spur said.

"No." Burriss shook his head, his eyes wide open. "I—" He finally looked down. "I didn't want to. I found out what he was planning to do, and faced Roscoe. He gave a very generous donation to the church and said there was more if I joined him. He also threatened me—said if I didn't agree to do whatever he said he'd kill me. What else could I do?"

"Told Gardner, had Roscoe locked up. If you had the Parkers would be alive today. Come on, Burriss. You're a cold-blooded killer out to get as much money as you can, no matter what stands in the way."

At the mention of money Burriss glanced over to the fallen saddlebag on the porch. Spur followed the man's gaze, then carefully walked to the porch, keeping his eyes toward Burriss. He reached behind him with his left hand and pulled the bag off the porch.

"What's this?" Spur asked.

Burriss looked defeated. Spur felt inside the bag and soon found what he was hunting for.

"Where'd you get all this money, preacher?" Spur asked as he brought out the bills. "There must be four, five thousand here. Religion's a good business, wouldn't you say? I'm sure the church could use this. Maybe they'll hire a real preacher next time."

Spur slung the bag over his shoulder and pulled the man to his feet, then walked him to Main Street, then down it to the sheriff's office, his Colt pressed against the man's spine.

Several men and women looked at them as they walked down Main Street, but none said a word. Few faces seemed surprised at the spectacle of their preacher being taken to jail.

Once there, Spur again saw the blank-faced

boy sitting behind the desk. This time he looked different—his face was red, hair ruffled beyond repair, sweat pouring off his body and soaking his clothing. Then, in a moment, Spur knew.

He walked Burriss into one of the open cells, pushed him into it, and swung the door shut.

"Put this in the safe," Spur barked, slamming the saddlebag onto the desk.

The boy jumped and followed the man's orders. While he did so Spur walked to the gun rack behind the desk. One of the rifles had been fired recently—he could smell the gunpowder in the barrel.

"You're Gardner's son, right?" Spur asked as the boy dialed the last digit on the safe lock.

"That's right," he said, then pulled the handle to the right. The door opened and he stuffed the bag inside.

"And you were there this morning," Spur said. It was not a question. "You went without your father's permission, then either got scared or trigger-happy and fired the early shot."

The boy stood and stared at Spur in astonishment.

"How did you know?"

"Never mind. Your father doesn't know," Spur said. "Not from what I could tell. Am I right, that you went there without his permission?"

The boy nodded. "He told me I had to stay here. I'm bored sitting here behind this desk all alone, playing solitaire, whittling. So I snuck away this morning and went out there."

"You could have ruined my chance to bring in the killers," Spur said sternly.

"I'm sorry." The boy looked at him blankly, but his cheeks were apple-red.

Spur coughed. "Tell your father when he gets back that I'll be in to see him later."

"Okay," the boy said, still smiling.

"And now you won't be so lonely. You can talk to old Burriss back there." Spur smiled and left the jail. He went to the Calico Hotel, cleaned up, and made it to the kitchen, where he sweet-talked the cook into making him some flapjacks and frying a couple eggs. Spur helped himself to a cup of fresh coffee and sat alone in the dining room, sipping it, trying to drive the chill out of his bones.

He wolfed down the meal as if he hadn't eaten in days, then went outside. Lucas. The Parker case was finished. That left the killing of Fred Lucas.

He could question each farmer in turn, and finally force the guilty party to reveal himself, but that would take a week or more. Farms were scattered all over the county.

Spur sighed and winked at Roxanna as she strolled by, a middle-aged man at her side.

"Spur!" he heard a man call behind him.

Spur turned and saw Gardner limping toward him.

"What's up, Sheriff?"

"Something so important I had to ride all the way back here to tell you about it, and to check. I was right."

"About what?"

"About Fred Lucas. Seems he was wanted for murder in Wyoming two years ago."

CHAPTER TWENTY

"LUCAS WAS wanted for murder?" Spur asked.

Gardner nodded. "I'd gotten a wanted poster on him some time before he moved here, but forgot all about it. I found it in my office in the bottom of a drawer." Gardner produced the poster. It didn't have a picture, but Fred Lucas's name dominated the page.

"Seems he killed a woman in Cheyenne two years ago, trying to rape her. Her husband tracked down the man's name but he'd left town by then. They never caught him."

"And he's been living right here under your nose all these years?" Spur asked.

"I can't believe it myself."

"Why's this so important you had to ride back here from the Craig farm to tell me?"

Gardner smiled. "The name of the woman Fred Lucas killed was Kathryn Lanford."

Lanford. Carl Lanford.

"Lanford killed Lucas," Spur suggested.

"It seems likely. One thing puzzles me. Why didn't Lanford kill him a long time ago? He's been here a year."

"I don't know. I'll ask him."

"You know how to get to the Lanford place?"

"No."

"Ride east for two miles, go north through the corn fields for about a mile, then pick up the trail heading back east again. It's the small farm with a house that has twisted chimneys—two of them."

"Thanks for your help."

"Better late than never," Gardner said, solemnly.

Spur rode through endless rows of short, vibrantly green corn fields. Just when he'd figured he'd ridden a mile the fields abruptly changed; now young wheat struggled up toward the sun. He found the trail and headed toward the east, then rode down it between corn and wheat.

Spur found the house with no difficulty; the chimneys were indeed built of bricks and twisted to make spirals. Smoke rose from one of them. The farm wasn't large, but then again Lanford wasn't a family man, Spur thought grimly as he rode up to it.

Spur tied his horse up before the house and walked toward it.

"What the hell do you want?"

An overweight man dressed in muddy clothing approached him, a shotgun in his hands. Spur smelled boots and stale sweat as the man neared him.

"I'm looking for Lanford."

"Not here." He eyed Spur suspiciously.

McCoy paused. "Where is he?"

"North fields."

"Thanks."

He left the man and rode north. Spur found Lanford on his knees, bent over, a horse standing quietly beside him in the middle of a wheat field.

"Lanford?" Spur asked, then dismounted.

The man looked up in surprise. "Yes?"

"Spur McCoy. Remember me?"

"Who?" Lanford said, then shook his head in confusion.

Spur drew his Colt.

"Wait a minute," Lanford said, rising and dusting off his hands on his pant legs. "What's going on here?"

"Did you kill Fred Lucas?"

Lanford didn't seem surprised by the question. "What makes you say that?"

"As I understand it," Spur said, uneasy at the man's attitude, "Lucas killed your wife."

"That's right. How do you know?"

"Gardner found Lucas on an old wanted poster, saw your wife's name, and figured it out."

"I'll be damned," Lanford said. "I didn't think he had it in him."

"You want to tell me what happened?" Spur asked.

Lanford nodded. "I first met Fred Lucas in Cheyenne about two years ago, a year before I moved to Kearney County. I was there with my wife, Katie. We were visiting relatives—my brother's family, staying in a hotel downtown the night before the trip back east. That night Katie said she had to go out for a walk. She couldn't sleep. The window was stuck and it was a hot night. I said I'd go with her; she said that this was the west and everyone knew that women were safe here. I pulled on my boots but she made it out of the room before me, ran down the stairs and went outside. By the time I got out there she was gone—nowhere in sight." He stopped for a moment. When he continued his voice was tighter. "A few seconds later I heard a scream." Lanford swallowed loudly. "I could always recognize her voice, even when she was screaming. I followed it and found her and Fred Lucas struggling in an alley. He had half-ripped her blouse off, and had one hand between her legs." His face screwed up with emotion as he continued. "I saw a flash of metal between them as I ran toward them. Katie pulled out the derringer she always kept tucked inside her dress in case of trouble while we were travelling. Somehow, he got hold of it and fired, sending a bullet into my sweet Katie. She died before I could reach her." He bent his head back, staring at the sky. "Lucas slugged me and ran. I found out his name but that was it. After a year I stopped looking for him and finally settled here, decided to try my hand at farming."

"When did you realize Lucas lived in the area?" Spur asked.

"Only a few days ago. That day we talked—in the saloon, remember?—I saw Lucas for the first time. He was the one in that stand-off with the farm boy. I finally recognized him."

"So you decided to kill him?"

"That's right. Pay the goddamned bastard back! I knew killing him wouldn't bring back my Katie, but I had to do it."

Spur eased up on his arm.

"Don't move," a greasy voice said from behind him.

McCoy started to turn but a round slammed past him at close range.

"I said it, and I meant it," the man growled. "You all right, Mr. Lanford?"

"I'm fine, Otis."

"What's going on here?" he asked.

"None of your goddamned business!" Spur said.

"You shut your mouth!" Otis said. "Drop that weapon. I want to see it hit the ground. Now!"

"If you kill me I'll kill Lanford," Spur said, his arm directed at the man's chest.

"Shit," Otis said. "What should I do, Mr. Lanford?"

"Do what he says," Lanford's voice sounded tired, lifeless.

"But—" he started.

"You want to get me killed?" Lanford asked.

"He doesn't," Spur said. He spun around and saw the fat man with the dirty clothes standing there. "Throw your rifle down."

"Damn. Damn!" he said. "I don't know what to do, Mr. Lanford."

"Otis," Lanford said, as Spur glanced back at him. "Drop the rifle. Now!" he barked.

The man nodded and laid the rifle reverently on the drying mud.

"Now back away," Spur said.

Once Otis had done so, Spur turned to Lanford. "Get up."

Lanford did so. "Otis!" he began. "You stupid son of a bitch!"

"Now stand behind our loyal hand," Spur said.

"Why?"

"You're going to tie him up." Spur tossed Lanford a length of rope from his saddlebag and watched as he did the job. He checked the knots; they were good and sound.

"Otis?" Spur said. "I want you to start walking."

"Walking? Where?"

"That way." Spur pointed toward the north. "Just keep walking until you get out of breath, then turn around and come back. If you try to follow us or bother me again I'll fill you with so many holes you'll breathe through your belly."

"Mr. Lanford!"

"Move!" Spur ordered.

Otis started walking, looking back at them every few steps. The man was slow, Spur thought. He laughed and tied Lanford's hands behind his back, then helped the man into his saddle.

"Where are we going?" Lanford asked.

"Gardner's hotel."

As they rode, Spur behind Lanford's horse, rifle in hands, the agent continued to ask questions.

"Why kill Lucas now?"

"I thought, after the Parkers were killed, if Lucas was murdered everyone would think it was a kind of blacklash for the Parkers. Thought it would throw off suspicion. And one day I just told myself that he had to die—I couldn't take it any more."

"Why didn't yo give the facts to Gardner and let him handle it?"

Lanford laughed. "Where's the satisfaction? That man murdered my wife. If I didn't kill him I'd never be able to rest at night. Seeing him hang wouldn't have done it."

"You know you'll probably hang?"

"Sure," Lanford said.

"You shouldn't have taken the law into your own hands. That's what you pay Gardner for."

"Don't you see?" Lanford said as they bounced along. "I couldn't live until Lucas was dead. Now that he is, I don't care what happens to me. Since Katie's been gone—" he shook his head.

"Maybe the judge will be lenient," Spur said. "I'll give you a good report. You didn't give me any trouble. But that Otis—"

Lanford laughed. "Otis! Hah! He's not too bright, but a damn good watchdog. I hired him on a few weeks ago when the ranchers got busy."

Spur nodded. "Lanford, you neary started an

epidemic. If you hadn't killed Lucas the Craigs probably never would have had the trouble they've seen."

"I know," he said. "I felt responsible for that, in part. But like I told you—now that he's dead, nothing else matters."

They rode the rest of the way in silence, while Spur tried to figure out how to halt the tensions in the area between farmer and rancher.

CHAPTER TWENTY-ONE

AFTER SPUR had deposited Lanford at the jail he headed for the Calico Hotel.

"Ginny?" he said as he walked in. She must have gone out. Spur stripped to the waist, poured fresh water in the basin, washed his face and chest, then shaved. After a night spent crouching in the shadows Spur felt dirty.

Spur splashed the last remnants of shaving soap from his face and toweled dry. As he turned back toward the bed the door opened—and Ginny Burriss walked into the room.

"Oh!" she said in surprise.

"Hello."

She ran to him then, her breasts bouncing gently as she hurried across the floor. They kissed; tongues clashing through lips. He raised his head.

"Ginny," he said.

"Hmmmm?"

"About your father—"

"I know," she said. "I heard all about it."

"I'm sorry."

"Why? The very fact that he's capable of doing such a thing proves he's not the father I used to have. I wanted to break free of him; I guess this is about as free as I can get." She looked at him. "What'll they do to him?" Ginny asked, hesitantly, as if not wishing to hear the answer.

"Don't think about it," Spur said, smiling. "You've got other things to worry about."

"Like what?" she asked. "Do you mean business? Selling the house?"

"No." He pulled her closer and stuck his tongue in her ear. "Like this," he said, between licks.

Ginny shivered. "Sounds wonderful."

"Glad you approve." He kicked the door closed, locked it, then lay her down on the bed.

Ginny squealed as his hands flew over her, unbuttoning, unfastening, pulling off, down and up, gradually denuding her to reveal her magnificent young body—large breasts, slender waist, curving hips.

"Jesus, Ginny!" Spur said. "You've got a beautiful body. And what great tits!" He took one in his mouth.

"Why do I get the idea you like tits?" she asked playfully, running her fingers through the hair matted on his chest.

"Because I'm a tit man. I've always loved them. Can't help myself."

Her hands fumbled at his crotch as she moaned, feeling the hardness straining against the cloth, yanking the cloth away from the buttons. Ginny pushed his pants down below his hips and then slipped his short drawers down.

She gasped as his penis sprang up.

"Spur, you've got the biggest cock I've ever seen!" She gripped his shaft, squeezed it gently, and sent ecstasy through Spur's body.

He jumped up from the bed, pulling out of her hand, and tugged his clothing off, then stood next to the bed, holding himself.

"Put it in me," she said. "Fuck me as hard as you want. Ram it inside me and fill me up." She touched his penis again, making it jerk in response. "I want to be covered by your hairy body. Come here, Spur McCoy." She spread her legs wide and parted her lips.

Spur pounced on her, then knelt between her legs and held them high. He scooted her forward a few inches, laid her feet under his arms, and guided his penis to her slot.

Gradually, painfully slow, Spur pushed into her. Ginny practically screamed out in need, finally pushing herself back against him, driving it into her until her buttocks touched his hairy thighs.

"Oh, yes!" she said, eyes staring dreamily at him. "That's it! You're way up inside me! Oh God, I'm going to come any minute. And I'm going to make you come!"

Spur kissed her, then withdrew and plunged back in. Ginny gasped as he drove down into her, moving her head slightly from side to side.

Ginny just seemed to suck him in, Spur

thought as he continued to pump. Their bodies worked together precisely, hips moving in counterpoise to enhance their lust. Spur savagely thrust into Ginny, attacking her nipples with his mouth; licking, gently biting and sucking.

"Wait, Spur," Ginny said in mid-sigh. "Let's do it standing up."

Spur stopped in mid-stroke. "Really?"

"Yes. Come on; I know it'll be fun. I've—thought about doing it this way." She squirmed beneath him.

Spur rolled to one side and watched as Ginny got to her feet and bent over, her hands on the wall for support, exposing her beautiful hard-as-apples bottom and lips.

He grunted at the sight, feeling his penis spasm. Spur stood and moved close behind her, then pushed easily into her soft wetness. They both sighed at the incredible feeling. Spur gripped the woman's waist as he pumped into her.

She had damn good ideas, Spur thought as he listened to the woman moan and pant. She slammed her buttocks back against him, meeting his strokes, juicy sounds coming from their crotches.

Just as Spur was completely caught up in passion, when his brain kicked off and he was nothing more than an uncontrolled lust-blinded animal, Ginny pulled away from him and stood. Spur nearly yelled when he felt cold air around his shaft.

"One more," she said, pointing to the chair in the corner.

Spur looked at it and shook his head. "Jesus, Ginny! I don't know—how would you do it?"

"Sit down and you'll see!" she smiled at him and stuck a finger up into herself.

He swallowed and slapped down in the chair. Ginny raised herself until she sat on Spur's lap, facing him, her legs straddling the chair's arms. Spur positioned his hands under her bottom and she slowly sank down onto him.

McCoy didn't know how much more of this treatment he could take. She raised off him a second, then plunged down so hard it made her choke. She repeated the motion, and reached behind her to cup his testicles in her hand, pulling gently at them, giving them a yank once in a while, sending shock waves through his nervous system.

Spur kissed her breasts as they bounced before him, then leaned his head back against the wall, his lips parted, sucking in breath as Ginny continued to ride him. The feeling was unbelievable.

"Oh, Spur, I've dreamed of this!" Ginny cried as she impaled herself. "And it's much better than the dreams. I wonder if that's true about all my dreams."

"Dreams?'"

"That's right," she said. "I daydream a lot." She tensed up around him with hidden muscles, nearly sending Spur over the brink.

"That's all," he said. "No more playing

around." He firmly locked Ginny's ankles around his waist, then told her to grab his neck. Spur gently leaned forward and stood, still planted deep inside her. He slowly walked to the bed, bouncing hard into her each step. Spur gently laid her on the mattress then, holding her legs widely spread, pulled out and rammed into her at lightning speed, feeling the sexual tension increase, the pressure grow more intense at his crotch.

Finally he gasped as his pent-up sperm gushed up into her. His body shook, jerked erratically, his hips jamming forward, riding up on her so that she could share his pleasure. Ginny's body moved with his as she sighed through her own pleasure, wrapping her legs more tightly around Spur's torso.

McCoy shot his last and slumped forward, then moved over to lay face up on the bed beside Ginny. Her legs slipped back to the mattress, and she laid a hand on Spur's thigh, then touched the tip of his penis. She trailed out a long, glistening string of his essence.

"Spur," she said.

"What?" His voice was hoarse; he coughed and tried to control his breathing.

"I've—I've decided what to do."

"Just now?"

"Yes. My father's in jail, and he'll hang before long. I know that. There's nothing to keep me here in Kearney. I'll sell as much as I can, have the rest shipped back home to my grandmother—my mother died giving birth to a dead baby—and make some money."

"Money?" Spur asked.

Ginny lifted her eyebrows twice, then fluttered her lashes suggestively.

Spur couldn't conceal a look of surprise. "You're going to do it?"

"These last few minutes," she said. "Weren't they wonderful?"

"Of course."

"Then wouldn't it make sense to do it all the time?"

"Of course; if you can handle it."

"I think I can. That's why I've definitely decided to become a fancy lady." She looked triumphantly into Spur's eyes. "It's the only thing I can do."

"And I helped you make this decision?"

"Yes. If we'd just had a terrible time, I'd probably become a nun, or get married right away—if I could find a man who'd want me. No; this is what I want to be." She smiled. "And if they're all like you—'"

"They won't be," Spur said. "You'll have smelly cowboys, ancient old timers, men who'll want to stick it up your—well, all kinds of men. All shapes, sizes and colors. You ever sleep with a Mexican man?"

"No," she said. "Not yet. But I've dreamed about it. And I don't think badly about a person, just because he may happen to be Mexican, or Indian, or anything! As long as a man has one and knows how to use it, fine! Let's do it!"

"That's good," Spur said. "I hope you're happy with your new career." He kissed her. "Where are you going to go?"

"I don't know. Anywhere off the plains. Maybe San Francisco. I heard they had trees up there; I love trees." She sat up and rubbed her eyes. "So much to do. I really should be going." She bent and kissed his chest. "Thanks for everything you've done for me."

She dressed, Spur helping her by holding up garments until she could slip into them. Completely dressed, she walked to the door and turned back to him.

"For you, Spur, no charge." She winked and was gone.

Spur lay back on the bed; naked, exhausted. He woke when he felt something wet and warm against his penis. A head moved there, long black hair hiding the face. Who was it?

The unseen mouth swallowed his shaft and sucked in earnest, licking, tongueing the sensitive underside.

Spur lifted the head—it rose and the hair fell back from its face revealing Leah Craig smiling at him—with her mouth full.

"Leah," he said.

She pulled off him. "Hi, Spur. I just couldn't let you go without personally thanking you for your help this morning." She lowered her head to the task at hand.

Spur laid back in shock and amazement. He thought he was too tired but Leah's magic soon had him fully stiff again. Spur found his old energy and strength back in force and grabbed Leah's head, holding it still while he pumped into her mouth. After a few seconds of this he relaxed and let her do the work.

Spur's leg dangled off the side of the bed, but he was too awash in pleasure to notice when he began slipping over the side of the bed. Before they realized what had happened they were both on the floor, the sheets between them.

They stood, laughing, and Leah undressed.

"I knew you wouldn't mind if I came right in," she said, "since the door was open. And when I saw you laying there naked, I couldn't help myself."

"Sounds reasonable to me."

Leah stripped off the man's work shirt, the heavy pants, and boots to reveal her perfect body. She lay on the bed next to him and pulled Spur to her. Lying on their sides they plastered their bodies together. Spur cupped her breasts in one hand as they kissed, his eager erection throbbing between them.

She slipped down, lowered her head to his crotch, and greedily enmouthed him again. Spur shivered. He moved with her until he sat on the edge of the bed while Leah knelt before him.

Spur's balls slapped against her chin as she swallowed him, snapping the fuse inside his groin. He pushed down into her throat as he spurted, gripping her head, ramming deep six more times before gently releasing her.

Spur laid her back on the bed, exhausted, gazing at the ceiling as Leah sucked the last from him, blessing the day he'd first come to Kearney County.

CHAPTER TWENTY-TWO

As Spur walked into Gardner's office he saw a woman standing, her back to him, talking to the sheriff.

"I certainly don't blame you," she said.

Spur recognized the voice before she turned around—Amanda Tate.

"Mrs. Tate," Spur said, tipping his hat and setting down his bag.

"Mr. McCoy." She smiled slightly and approached him. "I'm glad I have this chance to see you before you leave."

"We were just talking about Roscoe," Gardner said, standing on the opposite side of his desk.

"I'm sorry, Mrs. Tate."

"No need." She stiffened her back. "He was a bad apple, that's for sure, and it wasn't your fault that he murdered the Parkers, or attacked the Craig farm. You did what you had to do. That's in the past now."

"How's Mr. Craig feeling?"

"My husband?" She smiled. "It's the strangest thing; he woke up this morning feeling much better. He even took a walk around his room. I can't say why, but it looks like he's on the road to recovery."

"Glad to hear that," Spur said.

"Well," she said, pushing her hands back into the gloves she held, "I should be getting back home. I hear Wesley outside yelling to me." She put out her hand for Spur to take. "Thank you again for all your help."

"My pleasure." He kissed the gloved hand and released it.

"Goodbye, Spur." With a smile to the sheriff she left.

"A fine woman, Amanda is," Gardner said after a few seconds. "Too bad she had such a piss-poor son as Roscoe."

"That's not her fault," Spur said. "Everything finished up here?"

Gardner nodded. He motioned toward Burriss's cell. The man sat in the corner, eyes downcast.

"He's been quiet—not a work from him all day."

"He's got a lot to think about."

"I'll say. You leaving us?"

"Yes. I wired back to my office that this job was completed. Within two hours I received a reply. My next assignment."

"Fine," Gardner said.

"There's no problem here, is there?" Spur

asked. "If you think I should stay around for a few days, I could probably do it."

"No need, McCoy. I can handle things from here on in."

"Think there'll be any more trouble?"

"No. I won't tolerate it. I've been too easy. Hell, you never would have had to come here in the first place if I'd gotten off my butt and worked with my suspicions! You've shown me that can be the solution. I'll also admit I was afraid of the situation."

"Afraid?"

"I worried it would end up worse if I messed with it. But from now on in—I'm in charge."

"Glad to hear it," Spur said. "If you ever need me—you know where to reach me."

"St. Louis?" Gardner asked.

"Right. I'm never in my office, but they relay any important messages to me wherever I am."

"Thanks again. I don't know what I would have done without you."

Spur smiled and walked to the door.

"Take care of yourself!" Gardner said.

Spur left thc office and walked toward the train station.

"Yoo-hoo!" a high voice said.

Spur looked to his right and saw Roxanna Stafford walking to him, dressed in a spectacular pure white satin creation with cascades of ruffles.

"Hello, Roxanna," Spur said.

"Going somewhere?"

"Headed to the train station. I'm late."

"The station?" Roxanna was shocked. "You're not leaving Kearney, are you?"

"Yes."

"But—but—hell, Spur McCoy!" she said, exasperated. "You led me on all this time, saying you owed me, and now I catch you trying to sneak out of Kearney without even saying goodbye! Don't I deserve something for all the help I gave you?"

"I was going to stop by and see you, but I'm behind schedule." He meant it.

"You're seeing me now," Roxanna swung her hips back and forth lewdly. Two cowboys riding by whooped, and Roxanna turned to blow them kisses.

"I have to catch the five-ten," Spur said. "Otherwise, I'd have to wait another day. I can't afford to do that."

"Come on, Spur—one for the road. It won't take long. Hell, I'll even do it here." She put her hand to her dress and pulled down its front, revealing more of her splendid breasts. "Look good, don't they?"

Spur debated a moment—if they hurried—

No. He didn't have the time. Besides, Leah and Ginny had already wrung him dry. He doubted he could do it again so soon.

"Sorry, Roxanna. Not this time."

She sighed. "I don't like a man who turns me down," she said, "but I'll live. Next time you're passing through look me up, or lick me up!" Roxanna laughed.

"I'll do that."

"Hey, I heard you caught Roscoe, Jack and Rev. Burriss all with their hands dirty," she said, snickering. "That's what you were doing all this time in Kearney, right? That's why you asked me all those questions, listened in on Roscoe and me in the closet. Right?"

"Yes."

"Heard you were some government man, working for the Secret Service. You heading on to your next job?"

"That's right."

"Well—hell," she said, then lunged at him. She threw her arms around him and pressed her mouth to his.

Spur recovered from his surprise and returned her kiss, their tongues lashing each other. Spur heard an old woman shriek at the sight of such unbridled passion on the street in broad daylight.

"Whew!" Roxanna said. "That was sweet. Takc care of it," she said, still pushed up against him. "I wouldn't want anything to happen to it before I got a change to play."

"I'll try."

She smiled and walked away.

Spur set down his carpetbag on the floor of the Kearney train station, thinking of the people he'd met in the past few days. Suddenly a hand tapped his shoulder.

Spur spun around. Ginny Burriss stood before him, dressed for travel, holding two bags.

"Going my way?" she asked.

Spur smiled and kissed her, then took her bags and lifted his own as the train puffed up.

"You finished your business here?" Spur asked as the sound died down.

Ginny nodded. "One man's wanted the house for years, and he bought it on the spot. Paid cash. With that money and what I'll get from my father I'm pretty well set. So I've decided to go on an expedition to see what I can find in the real world out there. I wouldn't mind sharing part of it with you," she said invitingly.

Spur smiled. They climbed the steps and entered the train.

Perhaps it wouldn't be so boring a ride after all.

SPUR

MOUNTAIN MADAM

Chapter One

Brother Benjamin leveled the sawed-off shotgun at the man beside him riding the fancy palomino horse. It was dark, yet the horse was easy to identify and so was Deputy Sheriff Conners who covered the Wallowa Mountain side of Union County in the state of Oregon.

"Deputy Conners, you best ride along with us, we need to do some chewing on the rag."

"Yeah, you're men from the Center, I see. Hey, go easy with that scattergun. That thing can hurt a man. Just put it up, and we can talk a lot better."

"Don't sass me, Deputy Conners. I got the shotgun on you. We're heading back toward the Center where nobody will bother us. We think there's something down the road a piece you should see."

The speaker was a middle-sized man, riding a lean, rawboned bay with skitterish ways. He had a full beard and a hat pulled low over his forehead.

"You must be one of the Brothers from the Center. Be glad to ride up with you and have a long talk. That's part of my job in this end of the county." Deputy Conners looked at the shotgun, then at the three men who rode behind them. All three had shotguns and wore homespun pants as well as shirts that marked people from the Center.

"You're the head man up there, ain't you? Brother Benjamin as I recall." The deputy had been warned that the Center, as they called it, was a mite on the suspicious side, and he had never ridden up there but once to introduce himself when he took over this far eastern part of Union County that extended up along the sides of the Wallowa Mountains.

The three men remained behind the two front horses as they moved out on a trail that wound to the southeast along Catherine Creek for a ways, then headed due east. They came to a grove of trees along the stream, and Brother Benjamin stopped.

"Far as we need to go," Brother Benjamin said. He lifted the sawed-off ten gauge shotgun and fired one barrel from less than six feet. Deputy Sheriff Conners caught all of the buckshot in the side and chest as he turned to look at the rider beside him.

The rounds blew him off the horse and dumped his lifeless form on the ground eight feet away. The horse panicked and raced off to the east, then circled and headed back to its barn near the small settlement of Union, some six miles from the murder scene and 11 miles east of La Grande, the county seat.

Brother Benjamin watched the horse go, then slid out of his saddle as did the other four men. Two of them brought shovels from their horses and looked around a moment, then found a spot that should be clear of tree roots and began to dig.

Twenty minutes later the four foot deep narrow grave was dug and the body rolled in; they unceremoniously shoveled the dirt back in, covering up their foul deed. Then the top was spread with leaves and branches and dry grass so it looked the same as the rest of the surrounding landscape.

The men had not said a word as they worked. When they were through Brother Benjamin nodded.

"Let's go," he said. They mounted and rode at a canter another eight miles east into the mountains. They came to a lookout point on a little used trail and stopped. One of the men gave the cry of the night hawk. Far off another man made a night hawk call. The four riders continued through a narrow pass and down a slope into a valley about two miles long and half a mile wide that was circled by the Wallowa Mountains.

In the distance they could see the lights of the Center and rode there quietly. After they stabled the horses the four men went at once to the log cabin that served as the mess hall. It was the largest building in the Center and was used not only for meals but for holding meetings, for services on Sunday and for fellowship on cold winter nights. It was heated on three sides by fireplaces and was usually the warmest building in the Center.

Two women saw the men come in and quickly went to the warming ovens of the efficient wood stoves and served up dishes of family style food, rushing back and forth with coffee, fresh sliced bread and whatever the men asked for. The women wore simple dresses, both exactly alike. The fabric was homespun, one of them made from wool, the other from linen. The fabric was roughly textured, similar to the men's shirts and pants.

When the men finished eating, they went to their respective cabins. The men lived eight to a cabin as did the women. In the end of each unit was a narrow separate room with an outside door. These were bundling rooms and were reserved by either the man or the woman for sexual encounters.

When Brother Benjamin went to his cabin he proceeded directly to the bundling room, knocked and then entered and barred the door. Only then did he look at the bed. A woman sat up on the narrow straw-filled mattress. A coal oil lamp burned in the room shedding faint light. It was turned low because coal oil was expensive and was one of the few items they had to buy from the outside.

"I am here as you instructed, Brother Benjamin, but I am not at all pleased," the woman said. She was sitting tall, her long neck suggesting a lean, fit body. Her hair was brown, her features refined and pretty without being beautiful. Now her green eyes glinted as she stared at the man.

She was fully clothed and on top of the quilts even though it was chilly in the unheated room. Her arms were crossed defiantly over her breasts as if protecting herself.

"I know your rules and your laws, but I am not a member of your society. I have no wish to have sex with you, but to avoid any talk that might harm you, I will spend the night here, if you do not touch me."

Brother Benjamin laughed dryly. "Now I understand why you have not become pregnant. You have been with us for almost a year. None of our other women go so long without conceiving. We must produce our own new members of the Center. Our women must become pregnant as often as possible. But now I see you have not been bred. That will be taken care of nightly by me until you conceive."

Although it was mid-August, the nights grew chilly on the 4,000 foot high valley on the sides of the Wallowa Mountains. Brother Benjamin pulled off his homespun shirt and sat on the bed beside her.

"Angelina, you were well named by your late father. You have the body and face of an angel, but the heart and mouth of a viper. We have pulled your fangs, and now we will recreate you in our own image."

He reached for the buttons down the front of the homespun blouse.

Angelina slapped him.

Brother Benjamin slapped her in return, jolting her to the side and slamming her to the bed.

"Never hit me again or I'll break your arm. We want your arms here, since you are our finest weaver. We need your skills and your babies. Why can't you be happy and fulfilled as the other Sisters in our group?"

"Because I am not a cow to be bred for my offspring. You touch me again and I'll kill you in your sleep."

"You'll never have a chance," Brother Benjamin said. His hands pulled her up so she was sitting, then he grabbed the sides of her blouse and ripped them apart, tearing the fabric, ripping out buttons and revealing the soft white cotton chemise that covered her large breasts.

"Take if off," he commanded.

"No."

Brother Benjamin sighed, then he ripped the cotton with his strong hands and yanked it off her neck. Her breasts shook and jiggled from the motion, and he smiled.

"Yes, a fine figure. I had only guessed before. You will make a good mother."

"You mean a fine brood bitch. I'll never submit."

Brother Benjamin nodded. "I know." He pushed her backwards to the mattress and grabbed the woolen rope already secured to the bedpost and tied it around her wrists.

"You see, sweet Sister Angelina, it doesn't matter what you want or how you talk. You will be bred once every twenty-four hours for the next thirty days. It is a system that seldom fails with our healthy women. Sorry to say I won't be here every day, but I'll be around often enough to let you know I'm still in charge. You will be in this or another bundling room every night for a month.

"Each time you are bred you will be instructed in the ways and the truth of the Movement Of Natural Man. And you will be converted to our ways. If at the end of the thirty days you have not seen the light, then you will be sacrificed to the Great Spirit as Mother Earth has instructed us. Your blood will be drawn to fertilize our fields, and your body will be divided and used to enrich and to bless our gardens."

He stared at her as he pulled down her skirt and soft cotton bloomers.

"Sister Angelina, do you understand what I am telling you? Simply put, you either convert to our way of life—or you die."

Angelina lay there perfectly still. He did not have to tie her ankles to the bottom of the bed. She submitted, let him fondle her breasts and arouse himself, then enter her and systematically plant his seed as deeply as he could.

She was no virgin, but she had been entered only once before since she had been captured by these people as they ran from their former homes in upper New York state. It had been a long trip. She had let herself be seduced the first time because the young man said he loved her and together they would escape when they reached the next large town.

He had been lying to her, and since then she had shamed each man into inactivity when brought to the bundling rooms or wagons set aside for lovemaking. She had discovered quickly that there was no love or marriage in the Movement. Free love was encouraged, and all children were cared for by the extended family of adults. No child had one mother. His birth mother was quickly forgotten, and he or she became one of "the small ones" who were cared for by all of the women. The natural father of the child was almost never known.

There were 35 women and 24 men in the Movement. Four men had been jailed in New York, and only one had found his way back to the group in this Oregon hideaway. At one time they had recruited new members. Now they produced them much as a dairy herd produced new milk cows by breeding.

She shivered. It was her bleeding time and she was sure she could not conceive then. Somehow she had to get away, but how? There were horses and saddles, but women were not permitted to ride.

She could dress up like a man possibly. She would start stealing men's clothes. Yes, it was a chance. Angelina kept working on the plan.

She did not sleep. Twice more that night Brother Benjamin planted his seed and twice more she lay comatose and let him. With her hands tied, she had no chance to kill him. She had heard that a hard upward blow with the bones on the side of the wrist against the bottom of the nose could kill a man. It would drive small slivers of cartilage and bone up through the nose cavity and into the brain. Maybe she should try it if she ever got the chance.

Brother Benjamin rolled away from her and gathered his strength. What a beautiful body she had—fine, wide hips and big breasts. He reached over and fondled them again, then lay back close to her on the small bed and knew he must get some sleep. There was much work to do tomorrow. It was August already, and the harsh winter would be on them soon. There was firewood to stockpile and much meat to dry in the hot sun. They had to organize hunting parties to bring down the elk and deer, then butcher them out and dry the meat into jerky the way the Indians did for hundreds of years. There were berries to pick and dry and the fall harvest from their gardens to gather and process.

They had been there only two years now, so the fruit trees were not producing yet, but the garden and the wheat and flax were in good supply. Corn was a bit short this year, but they would save the best ears for seed for next year. Their herd of cattle had grown, but still they could use only the one and two year-old steers for fresh meat and for drying.

The sheep had done the best, so there would be plenty of wool for the women to spin and weave this winter. Winter was cloth-making time for the women and breeding time for the men; it was the time for telling stories, educating the youth and sharpening their skills with dominoes and checkers.

Brother Benjamin thought about the dead deputy sheriff for a moment. He had been a meddler. With his disappearance there would be others searching for him, but when they could not find any trace of him, they would give up. There was nothing to tie the Center or the Movement to this missing sheriff deputy, and there never would be.

A new deputy might be assigned, but he would know about the Center and be warned to steer clear of it.

Benjamin reached over and caught one of Angelina's big breasts as he turned on his side to go to sleep. The Movement was the best thing ever to happen for him. He could have a different woman every night if he had the strength, or he could concentrate on one for a week. Yes, the good life. If a meddling outsider had to be eliminated now and then, it was a small enough price to pay.

He squeezed her breast, but Angelina didn't respond. She would. Within three days she would be responding, and after a week she would be the one assaulting him in their nightly sexual encounters. Just wait. She would give in. They always did.

Chapter Two

Spur McCoy leaned back in the chair in the sheriff's office in the Union County courthouse and explained it again.

"My name is Spur McCoy, and I'm a member of a small group of federal peace officers known as the Secret Service. We work directly out of Washington D.C. Our boss is William Wood, director of the Secret Service. He's appointed by the President."

"Yeah, I heard you. Just why the hell are you here in La Grande. We doing something wrong?" The question came from Bryce Johnson, the elected sheriff of Union County now in his third four year term. Johnson was four-foot ten-inches tall, a writhing bundle of energy who dressed in cowboy gear and had a twin set of pistols on his gunbelt. He swaggered more than walked, was

46 years-old and bald on top; as futile compensation he wore a fuzzy, haphazard moustache. He had trouble reading without spectacles but seldom wore them when anyone was watching. He almost never sat in the swivel chair behind his desk, preferring to sit on the desk with his feet on the chair. That way he was a little higher than anyone sitting in the guest chair.

"You have on report a missing man named Duncan Currier," McCoy explained. "He was estimating the timber supply up in the Wallowa Mountains and hasn't been heard from for two months."

"Yes, I remember the case. We didn't find anything on it, nothing at all. The man simply vanished."

"Then three weeks ago a man came to town and checked in at the Trail's End Hotel and never checked out. His name was Victor Denning, and he was a mining engineer. He was found a week later beside the road, dead of a severe case of buckshot. Both men were employees of the Federal Government. My job is to find out what's going on in this county and why government men are being killed and missing. I'm here to help your department, not criticize you."

"Oh, yeah, good." Sheriff Johnson wiped a growing line of sweat off his forehead and smiled. "Well, now, we sure as hell want to take any help that you can give us. You know anything else about the two men?"

"Not a thing. I'd like to see your reports on both cases and anything that was found on or around Denning's body."

"Sure enough. We've got both in our unsolved files which are not too big yet, and we'd sure like to keep them that way. They're right out here."

A half hour later, McCoy realized he knew little that he hadn't already been told in his telegram of instructions from General Halleck in Washington.

Currier, the timber estimator, had been cruising the Wallowa Mountains to establish a preliminary report on the value of the timber in the mountains for some projected sale. He simply vanished and had not been heard of for two months.

Denning, the mining engineer, was supposed to be checking out a gold mining claim on federal land near Mt. Fanny, a 7,100 foot mountain in the northern part of the Wallowas and almost due east of La Grande. But his bullet-riddled body was found more than 20 miles south of that near some hot springs. There was no blood on the ground where the man was found, indicating he had been shot somewhere else and brought there and dumped.

It was almost noon so McCoy left the courthouse and found the Grande café. He had vegetable soup, two cups of coffee and an order of toast and jam. He asked the waitress where he could find a good map of the area.

She grinned and waved down the street. "The Union County Library, right down there half a block. Meg over in the library has a good map you can copy with tracing paper, that real flimsy stuff."

He thanked her and walked down to the library which obviously had once been a store of some kind. Inside he found racks of books along the walls, two tables and chairs, and no readers. From below a high counter emerged a swinging red swish of hair tied near the head and let fall so it looked for all the world like a pony's tail.

Then the girl's whole head popped into view,

and a pert freckled face and large brown eyes went with it. A most pleasing combination, McCoy decided. She grinned, and her eyes sparkled.

"Hey, a patron, a man who can read! Look who walked into my library! You're the first person here all day." She was a tall girl, five-six at least and slender with a tiny waist.

McCoy chuckled. "You're the librarian, Meg?"

"Indeed I am. Though I'm mostly a volunteer, the county pays me enough to live on. How can the Union County Free Lending Library be of service to you, sir?"

"I want a copy of Walt Whitman's *Leaves of Grass*."

Meg looked up, her brows raised. "Oh." She frowned. "I'm afraid that was not one of the books the Library Council agreed that we should have on our shelves. It's considered a little too naughty for most of us."

"Just checking," McCoy said with a grin. "What I really need is an accurate map of the county that I can make a copy of for my personal use. Would that be possible?"

Her frown evaporated. "Sir, you are a tease. Yes, of course we have a good map. I'll even furnish you with the tracing paper and a soft pencil to do the job. Right this way."

She led him to a desk, produced a fine printed map of the county and spread it out for him. Then she produced a sheet of tracing paper and the pencil.

"Trace to your heart's content," she said. She paused a moment, watching him. A grin curled around her pretty face. "Maybe what I should do is get a larger supply of maps instead of books." Just then the small bell over the door tinkled, and she looked up.

"Mrs. Culbertson, how nice to see you." Meg moved to the front of the small library, and McCoy enjoyed watching her walk away. The skirt she wore was just a bit tight and provided an enticing hint at the real Meg Tackett that was underneath.

It took him 20 minutes to trace the map and put in all of the detail that he wanted. By the time he finished the first lady had left, but two more came in and were at one of the tables looking through books.

McCoy took the map back to the desk and handed it to her.

"Meg, it's been an adventure. I like the way you've done your hair. Makes you look a little like a Buckskin."

She laughed. "I don't know whether to hit you or thank you. Glad you could use the map. Sure you don't want to check out a book?"

"I'm not a county resident. Maybe later."

He folded his traced map, put it in his pocket and walked outside. Spur McCoy was hard to miss. He stood six-two and weighed an even 200 pounds. His green eyes stared at a world that was not as gentle as he would prefer and that he was trying to straighten out.

His reddish brown hair was a little longer than most men wore it. He wore a low crowned black Stetson, and showing under it was a tanned face that had seen a lot of days and nights outdoors.

He moved with a fluid grace reminiscent of a cougar stalking his prey. The big Colt .45 that hung at his side was honed to a hair trigger, and he could shoot the wings off a fly at 40 feet. A friend described him as good on a horse and with a rifle, at home in the woods or the desert, and good enough as a cowboy to make a cattle drive and pull his load.

McCoy looked back at the library, sure that he would see that pretty girl again. Next he wanted to talk to the District Attorney and see if he had any kind of an investigation going into the two cases. After waiting five minutes for the man to finish talking with someone, McCoy went in.

The D.A.'s name was Lawrence Sloma. McCoy introduced himself, presenting his credentials. The D.A. was tall and slender, maybe 35, pale, sandy hair, clean shaven, and wearing a proper black suit, vest and white linen detachable collar. His dark blue tie vanished inside his vest. He read the letter of introduction and handed it back to McCoy.

Just as McCoy started to ask about the two cases, a man hurried into the room and gave the D.A. a message.

"Terrible, just terrible!" he exploded. He looked up at McCoy. "Pardon the outburst but we just found out that one of the Deputy Sheriffs assigned to the southwest part of the county is missing; his horse galloped into the barn last night with blood all over the saddle and down his flank. They dug a .32 caliber shotgun slug out of the horse's side."

"The deputy could be the third killing in this area in the past month," McCoy barked. "Three men dead or missing with no logical explanations. I'm sorry about the deputy. Have you had any investigations going in the other two cases, Currier and Denning?"

"No. I have a small staff—me—and I'm kept busy on routine matters around the office and with the court and the County Commissioners. I work closely with them."

McCoy took out his map. "Mr. Sloma, could you locate these three problem areas for me? Where was this most recent one?"

The District Attorney showed McCoy where the little settlement of Union was and that the horse showed up coming from the east. He pinpointed where the only body was found and Mt. Fanny where the mining engineer was supposed to be working.

"The body was at least twenty miles south of his location near some hot springs," the D.A. said. "As for the timber man, he told friends he would start on this side of the ridges and gradually work over to the far side. That could cover forty or fifty miles across part of Wallowa county as well as ours. Hard telling where he could be."

"Of the three men, Currier is the least likely to be in trouble. He is an experienced mountain man and knows the whole state of Oregon, I'd guess."

"Still damn suspicious." McCoy put an X on the map near the Wallowa Mountains.

"I hate to say it, but chances are the deputy is dead. One shot could go low and hit the horse. The rest of them probably blasted the man right out of his saddle."

"That's what I'm afraid of. I'm riding out there in the morning to check it. You want to go?"

"Why not right now, Sloma? I'll rent a horse and meet you at the livery stable in ten minutes."

District Attorney Sloma stared at McCoy for a minute.

"Damn, you believe in getting things done, don't you? Fine. I'll be there."

The two riders covered the 11 miles to the village of Union in about three hours. They went at once to the sheriff's substation and found a new deputy in charge. He had just ridden in from La Grande. He showed them where the horse and the saddle were and said he'd also show them to the sheriff who would come out the next morning.

They examined the saddle, and Spur found another of the .32 caliber slugs imbedded in the leather.

"That still leaves eleven or so slugs," McCoy said. "Plenty to do murder. Look at this." He pointed to several small burn spots on the saddle.

"What is it?" the D.A. asked.

"Powder burns. The shooter had to be well within ten feet to get those kind of powder burns on leather. At that range the spread of buckshot is less than eighteen inches, depending how long the barrel is."

The deputy showed them the barn where the horse had returned. McCoy spent 15 minutes walking around the barn, then made a half circle around the far side of the barn where the horse had come running in.

The D.A. followed McCoy.

"What are you looking for, McCoy?"

"Found it. Look here." He pointed to a set of horseshoe prints in the soft soil. "These prints are made by a horse running toward the barn. See how the front of the hoof has thrown some of the dirt and grass behind it. I'm going to get my horse and see how far I can follow these tracks. In this country it should be easy."

"I'm coming with you."

The two riders worked ahead steadily, usually finding the hoofprints every few yards as the animal made nearly a straight line for its barn.

The first hour they covered a little over five miles. They had skirted Catherine Creek when they saw the prints turned to the east.

"What's up in there?" McCoy asked the D.A.

"Nothing that I know of. Not any ranches or farms or timber cutters. Just wilderness."

They followed the tracks again with McCoy now walking.

"The horse was galloping along here," McCoy reported. "An animal like that won't gallop more than a quarter of a mile even if it's in a panic. This mare must have been scared out of her eyeballs."

After another 200 yards McCoy stopped and studied the ground.

"Well now, Sloma, come take a look."

The two men stared at the ground. It was easy to see the dried blood on the grass and rocks and leaves.

"Somebody did considerable bleeding right there," the D.A. said.

"That red stuff does tend to run out of a body long as the heart is pumping. Don't walk around. I'm looking for boot prints. Somebody picked him up and dug a grave nearby. Shouldn't be too hard to find. They must have done it at night considering when the horse got back to the barn. Hard to cover up everything at night. We have another three hours of sun. Lots of time. I just wish I'd brought a shovel with me."

McCoy went on his hands and knees and studied the ground. There were no boot tracks. Instead he found a wide heel print and then another. Sturdy farmer-type shoes. He pointed it out to the D.A. who only shrugged.

"Haven't seen any shoes like that for sale in town. Don't know where they could have come from."

Ten minutes later the shoe prints led them to the grave. There were dozens of prints around the grave. McCoy brushed off some of the leaves and grass and twigs. Some of the dirt was still damp.

"Haven't had a rain here in three weeks," the D.A. said. "That moist ground came from down a ways. Damn well looks like a grave to me."

McCoy carefully spread the leaves and branches back over the grave. "We'll leave it the way it was in case somebody checks it," McCoy said. "Now let's ride back to Union and get a couple of shovels and another horse and a lantern or two. Don't think it would be a good idea to get this close to a body and let it be snatched away from us."

It took them 45 minutes to ride hard to a farm near Union, borrow two spades and a horse and a rope, and ride back to the grave site. No one had been there.

McCoy tied his horse and went to work at one end of the grave. The D.A. took off his jacket, hung it on a tree and began digging at the other end.

Suddenly McCoy dug up a foot. They used more care then, and just before it got dark, they pulled the body from the grave.

Sloma stared at the man's face and nodded. "Damn sure that's Deputy Winston Menagat. Let's get him tied to the horse and out of here."

"You want to fill in the hole?"

"Hell no! Somebody might be watching us right now with a rifle and be sighting in."

They tied the man over the back of the horse, lashing the man's hands and feet together under the horse's belly. Then they rode off.

Three hundred yards up the creek, a 16 year-old boy wrote on a pad of paper. He had written down a complete description of both men including their approximate ages. He wore homespun shirt and pants, and when he stood up and started trotting back up the hill toward the Wallowa mountains, his shoes had wide heels and wide soles—the kind of shoes that weren't for sale in eastern Oregon.

Chapter Three

The village of Union didn't have an undertaker. Since Deputy Menegat was from La Grande, the D.A. and the Secret Service Agent stopped at the Union sheriff's office and reported the death, then rode on to La Grande.

It was nearing midnight when they arrived. After they left the body with Charlie the Digger, McCoy headed for his hotel. It had been a long day. He'd taken a room at the La Grande Inn as soon as he had gotten off the stage, and now he went up to room 214. He walked to the door quietly and tested the knob. It was locked. He looked up and down the hallway but saw no one.

A moment later he turned the key in the door and stepped inside. McCoy struck a match, saw the room was empty, locked the door and pushed the straight chair's back under the door handle. Anyone coming in would make one hell of a noise.

He stripped, dropped on the bed and fell asleep at once.

The next morning, McCoy shaved in cold water, had a quick breakfast and was waiting for the sheriff when the lawman came to work about eight.

The small man glowered at McCoy. "Sloma told me about it last night. Thinks you're damn near to God. Still it was good work.

Lots of times when a lawman gets gunned down you can track it right back to something the man's done, something wrong or out of line. Couldn't be with Menegat. A model citizen and lawman. Married, didn't cheat on his wife. He hadn't even been at the Union office long enough to make any enemies."

The small sheriff sat down on the top of his desk and put his cowboy boots on the swivel chair.

"McCoy, what I'm saying is that young man was cut down on purpose but not for anything he done. Something foul is afoot here."

"Agreed," McCoy said. "All we have to do is figure out what it is and who's doing it."

"That's my job," the sheriff said with a touch of rancor.

"Agreed, but it's also my job. No reason we can't work together. Right now you know everything I know."

"Same here," the sheriff said.

"I'll stay in touch," McCoy said as he headed out the door.

He went to the Grande Café for a cup of coffee. The same little waitress who had served him breakfast and dinner the day before came up with a full cup.

"Anything else?" she asked.

He held out his hand. "Yeah, I'm Spur McCoy. What's your name?"

"Polly Smith." She was maybe 19, fresh and eager and a little on the chunky side. Her dark hair was pulled into a soft braid at the back of her head, and her dark eyes glowed as she shook his hand.

"Hi, Polly Smith. Thanks for the coffee."

She grinned. "You're new in town, and you ain't no cowboy."

"How do you know?"

"Hands—no rope burns or scars on them. Hands take a beating working cattle with a rope. My daddy used to be a cowboy." She watched him a minute and nodded. "Well, I got to get to working or I'll get whupped."

McCoy watched her a minute, then sipped the coffee and took out the map. He erased the X near Union and put it out about six miles east. That didn't change matters much. Still there were two X's for dead bodies in the southern part of the county near or south of Union, and one question mark in the Wallowas north of Union.

Something had to be going on, but what? The sheriff said that these two killings were the first with no reason for over five years. He downed the rest of the coffee, waved at Polly and walked down the street to the newspaper office.

The La Grande Evening Observer sounded like a daily but couldn't be in a town this size. The owner must hope to keep publishing long enough for the town to grow to a size that could support a daily.

As soon as McCoy opened the door, he was hit by the unique smell of a newspaper office. The combination of the smell of stacks and stacks of paper that mingles with the acid tang of printer's ink gave off a distinctive aroma that could never be forgotten. A small counter cut off the front of the building. A dozen feet away was a wall behind which the printing work was evidently done.

A young man hunched over a desk. He wore garters on his long sleeves to keep them out of his way and a green visor shading his eyes. He looked up and rubbed his eyes.

"Yep?" he asked.

"Wondered if I could look over your past issues?"

"Help yourself. Last six months are there on the sticks." He went back to work, editing something on the paper in front of him.

McCoy found a pair of dowels about three feet long with clips on both ends. One of the dowels remained behind the paper; the other one was laid across the center of the opened pages and then clipped together at the bottom to the back dowel. Now the paper could be hung on a rack and leafed through, but kept intact.

He turned to the first issue six months ago and read at least part of every story on the front page. That should cover all the important news in a town this size.

Church meetings, city council election, dead horse on Main Street, twins born, a barn raising where a barn burned down—the usual small-town happenings.

There was nothing of major importance, at least to an outsider. He watched for something big like a new rancher, a big mine strike, a big timer operator buying up timber rights.

Page after page he examined and checked. Some of the stories he read, but nowhere did he come up with any major project that would call for murder of public officials.

He frowned. Public officials. All three of the dead or missing had been government officials or employees. He hadn't thought about that before. Was that significant?

Could be. At this point anything might be significant. He left the papers and walked over where he could watch the man behind the counter.

"Sir, could we talk a minute?"

"Sure." The young man pushed back and came to the counter. He was maybe 30, had a printer's ink smudge on his cheek and a no-nonsense expression.

"Morning, I'm Hans Running, editor and publisher of the *Observer*. And you're Spur McCoy in town working with the sheriff."

"Right. You hear about Deputy Menegat?"

"Working on the story now. You found him. Nice bit of tracking. Are you a state lawman?"

"No. I'm an interested party. I have a question for you. What is happening in the county that could cause the deaths of three public officials."

"Three? Who else?"

"Victor Denning, the federal mining engineer, and Duncan Currier, the timber cruiser."

"Currier isn't dead yet."

"He's dead, just not found yet. A man like Currier doesn't get lost in a forty mile section of mountains. He could crawl out in this much time with two broken legs."

"True. I have no idea what's happening. Tried to figure it out. No big land deals cooking, no big ranches being sold. The railroad sure as hell isn't this far yet. I have no idea of any big economic or social or business changes about to happen."

"There must be something."

"You're a federal lawman," Running said.

"Yes, but don't tell anybody and don't print it. It will make my work easier to get to the bottom of this."

"Wish I could help."

"Just don't say anything in the paper about any conspiracy or tie the three together, all right?"

"Wasn't going to because I can't tie them together. Wish I could. The sheriff is stumped, but then he never has been tremendously curious or good at his job. I better get back to it."

McCoy said good-bye and walked out of the newspaper office.

What the hell now? He should try to find out where the two dead men stayed when they were here in town. That might be productive, but he doubted it.

How about a couple of beers? He'd take his mind off the problem and maybe his subconscious would solve it for him. McCoy headed for the best looking saloon along the two-block long street. He could see at least eight saloon/gambling houses. Most of them probably also had cribs upstairs for those so inclined. He walked into the Gaiety Saloon and saw that it was well named.

A piano player plinked away even though it was only eleven o'clock. The mahogany bar was 20 feet long with mirrors behind it and a variety of bottles there he figured were mostly for decoration.

A sweeping staircase took customers to the second floor. Every ten steps up there was another two foot high painting of a fetching girl, most dressed scantily and all in provocative, smiling poses. Evidently some starving artist had taken his portrait fees out in trade.

McCoy stepped to the bar and tossed down a dime, and the bar keep drew a beer for him.

Instead of giving it to McCoy, he slid it down the bar to the far end where a woman sitting on a high stool caught it.

"Your beer is down here, McCoy," she said.

She didn't look like a whore. She wore a conservative dress that showed none of her bosom. It was not overly tight and covered her ankles. She wore a little makeup but was not one of those painted whores the proper women of the town complained about.

McCoy walked down the length of the bar and put one foot on the brass rail.

"Sorry, I don't know your name," he said.

"Sue, Sweet Sue, Silly Sue. Most anything you want to call me. Don't get the wrong idea. I run this place. I know everything that goes on in town, and I don't tattle on nobody."

"Then why the little game?"

"Wanted to meet you. See if you're as goodlooking as all of my girls tell me."

"So?"

"Those girls of mine know good stock when they see it. They truly do appreciate a fine specimen of a man."

"Thanks. Now why the inspection?"

"You always all business?"

"No, but I never pay for pleasures that are available free."

"Wise man, but enough of your kind and I'd have to rent rooms by the night instead of the hour. I been figuring you. You got to be lawman. You could be state or federal, but the federal folks don't know Oregon is out here yet. You're interested in murder. So am I. Deputy Menegat had been fair and honest with me when he worked here in town. I want his killer."

"So do I. Did he have any enemies?"

"Not that I've been able to think of. Hear you're a tracker. What about the horse prints of the killer around the murder site? Find any of them?"

"Lots of prints. It's a highly traveled section out there. No way to make any sense out of the prints. By now they have been run over, mashed down and obliterated."

"Last night?"

"By the time we found the body it was too late to see much of the prints, but they were jumbled, nothing for sure, not even able to say for sure the prints came before or after the killing. No help. Sorry."

"You're the tracker."

"What about the cruiser? He spent quite a bit of time in this area, didn't he?"

"Now and then. I've seen him in my place time and again. Don't know much about him. I'll talk to the girls."

"The mining man was out of Portland. I haven't heard anything from a telegram I sent the police there."

"Probably won't. Portland cops don't like nobody."

"So, any suggestions?"

Sue lit a long, black thin cigar and blew smoke at him. "Yeah, a couple—but you ain't in the mood, I can tell. You know anything about the Movement of Natural Man, known hereabouts as the Movement?"

"Nope. Never heard of them."

"Bunch of weirdos who live out beyond Union. A damned commune. They say they're self-sufficient except for sugar and salt and a few things like axes and hoes. Got a place going in a valley out there. Must be about two dozen men and more women than that. Free love. No families, no marriage, just free fucking—and the kids that come belong to all the men and all the women. From what I hear a woman can't ever tell for sure who the father of her kid is."

"A religious group?"

"Not so you can notice. They just go their own way, plant their crops, birth their babies, make what they need. Once every three months two of the men come to town to buy necessities. Well, not buy, really. They got an arrangement with the stores in town to barter what they have to sell for what they want to buy. Sometimes they sell grain or potatoes. They are big on potatoes and chickens out there."

"Why would they want to kill a deputy sheriff?"

"Not saying they did, just trying to get you up to speed here with the community. While you're getting educated on La Grande, remember the Gaiety Saloon has the best pieces of ass you'll find in this town. Satisfaction guaranteed or double your money back—or one free poking."

McCoy laughed. "I'll take your word for it. I've got a mind to go over and talk with the general store man. What's his name?"

"Maynard Geiger, old friend of mine. I used to see him every Thursday night. His wife died about six years ago. We got on good until I retired to the business end of things."

"Instead of the other end?"

"Oh, that end still works fine. It's just damn particular who it entertains. So when you feel the need, come see me—a gift from one friend to another."

"Much obliged, Pretty Sue. Now I better run."

McCoy went outside and was just about to step off the boardwalk in front of the Gaiety Saloon to cross the dusty La Grande street when he saw a footprint in the half-inch of dust that stopped him. The print was identical to those he had seen around the grave site of Deputy Menegat. It had to be a brand new mark in the dust. He looked up eagerly trying to see where the prints went. The second one pointed across the street with the wide toe and the nearly square heel. The print was so flat he didn't think the shoe had any arch in it at all.

McCoy looked up anxiously and began to follow the plain set of shoe prints across the street.

Chapter Four

Spur McCoy followed the tracks nearly to the middle of the street before he lost them in a jumble of wagon wheel marks as well as hoof and boot prints. He checked the far side of the thoroughfare but it was jammed with wagons parked nose to tail. There were no more of the strange looking shoe tracks.

They had been adult size, and the stride was good, nearly as long as his own, so the man was probably near six feet tall. That was about all he had to go on.

McCoy continued down the boardwalk to the general store. Inside he found the owner, Maynard Geiger, and talked with him.

"You probably know more about the people from the Movement than anybody in town, I'm told. What can you tell me about them?"

Geiger was slender, trim and of average

height, about five-nine. He had a moustache and long sideburns and a healthy head of brown hair.

"Nice folks, I'd say. Always kind and polite when they come in. Usually the same two gents come and always on a Tuesday. They figure that's my slowest day, which it is."

He poured some six penny box nails from a keg into a wooden bin. "Yep, I'd say they are smart, too. Seem to get by without a lot of things most folks around here think are essential. Like them new foot warmers we got in last winter. People bought every one I had the first day soon as word got around. Never seen nothing like it.

"I apologized when the Movement men came in because I was out of them, and they said they wouldn't think of owning one. I do straight barter with them. They bring in sacks of flour, potatoes, dried beans and squash and punkins in season. They're good farmers out there. Got a new little mill they use to make flour from their own wheat. My wife won't use nothing but Movement flour now."

"Sound like fine, hard-working people," McCoy said. "I'm trying to get to know the country. Might want to settle down here someday."

He bought a nickel sack of horehound candy and walked out sucking on one of them. Nice gentle people up there at the Movement. So where did he start looking next? Had he missed something in that long telegram from General Halleck? He went back toward the hotel, scuttered out of the way of the stage that came in about this time every day and got to the porch of the La Grande Inn before the dust from the four big wheels and the team of six could blow his way.

Upstairs in his room, McCoy checked the telegram again. There was no hint of any cause, no suggestion for a line of investigation, just a go and do it order. He slumped on the bed and sat there staring at the telegram.

His door jolted open, and he saw nothing but the bottom of a woman who backed into the room dragging a mop and bucket. Her skirt was hiked up to show both of her bare legs to the knee, and he was pleased to see that they were slender and shapely.

The woman grunted, tugged the heavy bucket in farther and then closed the door. She stood, wiped her brow, then pushed one hand back and lifted her skirt and scratched her bottom, revealing her good legs right up to her bloomers.

"Well, now," McCoy said.

The girl whirled around, eyes wide, then she covered her face with both hands.

"Oh, my! Nobody was in here. I just checked a couple of minutes ago and the place was empty. Time to scrub the floor. Where did you come from?" She peeked out through her fingers.

"Sorry, I can leave right now and come back."

When she let her hands down from her face, he saw a line of cleavage through the open neck of her blouse where she had unfastened two buttons.

"No need to leave. You have beautiful legs."

She blushed. "That was . . . I mean." She shrugged. "Warn't supposed to be anyone here."

She let down her arms now, and her breasts pushed hard against the thin blouse.

"You look worn out. Why not sit a bit and rest? What's your name?"

"Becky."

"I like that. Becky, come and sit down and forget about the mopping for a minute. Been working here long?"

"Most two years now. Good job." She frowned. "It be all right for me to sit a spell?"

"I'm sure it will. I won't tell the owner if you don't."

She smiled. "That's right nice of you. What's your name?"

"Spur McCoy."

She looked up quickly. "Oh, yes, the new gent in town. I've heard about you. Doing all sorts of things, you are." She sat on the bed and the mattress sagged and they swayed together until their thighs touched. She didn't seem to notice.

"How long you be in our town?"

"Long as it takes to do my business."

Becky turned to him and leaned forward. "Mr. McCoy, would you like to relax a bit and have some fun? I'm in no hurry this afternoon." She reached up and unbuttoned another fastener on her blouse and then the next, and the creamy white sides of her big breasts showed plainly.

"Becky, I'm in no hurry myself. You'd not mind doing this, just to be friendly to a stranger in town?"

"Be my pleasure." The last button was loose and she pushed both sides of the blouse back, pulling them from her skirt until her breasts swung into glorious view. "The twins say hello to you, Mr. McCoy."

He brushed them with his hands, then reached down and kissed her waiting lips. Her mouth was open, and she made a strange little noise in her throat. When the kiss ended she pushed forward and a moment later had eased McCoy back on the bed with her laying on top of him. She caught his hands and brought them up to her breasts.

Spur caressed them, tweaked the enlarging nipples, and then decided some caution was needed.

He kissed both her breasts, rolled her over, eased off the bed and took three quick steps to the door. He pushed in the key from the dresser, locked the door and turned the metal shaft halfway around so it couldn't be pushed out.

Then he slipped the back of the straight chair under the door handle so the chair rested only on its back legs.

"Just to insure our privacy," he said.

She sat up watching him, and when she saw him lock the door she eased out of the blouse. She wore nothing under it.

"Well, now, Becky, what a pretty picture," McCoy said.

"Look all you want to, Mr. McCoy, but they do like to be kissed and petted."

She went down on her hands and knees on the bed, and McCoy slid under her and stared up at the hanging peaks. Gently she moved one toward his mouth. He opened it and accepted the gift, licking her tenderly, then sucking half the big orb into his mouth and chewing on the morsel. He finished by nibbling her enlarged nipple until she yelped in pleasure.

She pulled away and gave him the other one to lick and kiss and chew on. When that was over she sat up and unbuttoned the fly on his pants.

"You sure you want to explore in such a dangerous place?" he asked her.

Becky grinned. "Oh, yes, the good part. I love all parts of a man from his broad shoulders to his slender hips, but the best place of all is right here."

She spread back his underwear then found the opening and slid his erection out.

"Oh, glory!" she breathed. "Wonderful, just—oh, my God, he's beautiful!" She bent and kissed his rod, then rolled on the bed with her knees up and her hands at her own crotch as she jolted and shivered and stormed into a series of orgasms that left her sweating and moaning on the bed. Reaching for him at last, she pulled him down so she could lay on top of him. She started a slow grinding motion with her hips against his erection.

Her eyes fluttered open, and she smiled. "Christ, what you do to me! You set me off like a firecracker. I'll never get enough of you. May I undress you? I want this glorious, wonderful hot feeling to last forever!"

She kissed him then, a long, hot, demanding kiss as she ground against his manhood. When they separated he laughed softly.

"Undress me all you want to, Becky. I'm ready anytime that you're ready."

She peeled his clothes off slowly, one at a time, taking her leisure at it, exploring the sandy-brown hair on his chest, kissing his nipples, then kissing the hairy trail down his belly and stopping where the fur vanished under his short cotton underwear.

"You're a marvel, so big and so strong and so . . . so damn sexy!" She looked up and moved her face close to his. "I got to tell you. I can't lie no more. It was all a lie about me not knowing you was here and backing into the room so I couldn't see you and all. And I—"

He kissed her mouth to quiet her.

"I know, I understand. I'm glad you came. I needed you."

"Really?"

She brightened. "Oh Lordy, but I am glad. Sometimes I see a beautiful man like you and I touch myself and then my hand gets down to my crotch and before I know it I'm crazy and hot to fuck."

She ducked her head and grinned at him.

"I said the bad word. Usually I can't even say it unless—you know—unless I'm really doing it. Then it's easier."

She inched his underwear down until his penis sprang free, and she squealed in delight.

"Such a big, strong boy. I hope he works. Found a man once who just couldn't do it. He kept trying and trying. Does big cock here work?"

"You'll have to wait and see, won't you?"

"Enough of the waiting." She stripped off his shorts, then went to her knees on the bed and unfastened her skirt and bloomers and pushed them down both at once until she was naked as a newborn puppy.

She stood on her knees over him, held out her arms, then cupped her breasts and held them up. "Well, what do you think of Becky's naked body?"

"Fucking good!" McCoy said and pulled her down beside him and began working one hand up and down her soft inner thighs. He would come almost to her crotch, then detour and work back down again. At last she grabbed his hand and pushed it against her wet crotch.

"Rub me, damn you, rub me hard."

He did and found her clit and she climaxed again, tearing into a longer series of spasms than she had the first time. She began to cry halfway through and couldn't stop until the last shattering orgasm drilled through her and dropped her spent and sobbing on his bare chest.

"I'm sorry," she blubbered. "When it's so good I always cry because I know this can't last forever and that makes me sad. Does that make you sad?"

She wiped her eyes. "Damn, you've got nothing to cry about. You haven't even cracked your nuts yet. Come on, fuck me, big man!"

She rolled over on the bed, spread her knees and held out her arms.

McCoy was ready. He went between her white thighs and thrust and hit her hole and lanced in so fast he thought he might have missed. She crooned and laughed and pumped upward against him until their pelvic bones grated together and she winced.

"Damn, I think you found my tiny little cunt hole. Now you fuck me good or I'm gonna tell everybody in town you're no good in bed."

He made sure she couldn't say that.

Ten minutes later he couldn't hold off any longer. He put her legs on his shoulders, lifted her until she was almost standing on her shoulders on the bed and pounded into her with so much force that she yelped in pain and delight as he roared into his own shattering orgasm.

After his final thrust he let her lie back down, and she panted a dozen times before she could speak. He had triggered her again inside, and there was a glow of wonder on her face. She wrapped her arms around him as he collapsed on top of her and held him that way tightly inside her for ten minutes.

"Oh, yes!" Becky said softly. She let go with her arms, and he rolled to the side and lay on his back still recovering. She leaned up on one arm and stared down at him.

"Son-of-a-bitch, that was the best cock fucking I've ever had. Not even my cherry picking was that good. Shit, but that was good pussy punching. I'm gonna be here tonight when you get back. No matter when you come back I'll be here panting and waiting for you, all naked and worked up and ready. So you rest up good."

She jumped up and pulled on her clothes, kissed his wilted manhood and pushed her bucket and mop out the door. As she went she hummed a little tune without any real melody to it. Just a happy sound as she moved down to the next empty room to mop.

McCoy followed her to the door and closed it and locked it, then lay back down on the bed naked, lacing his fingers behind his head. Now that was a nice way to ruin an afternoon. It was entertainment at its best, but it didn't do a damn thing to get the case solved. Who was killing off the government workers?

He dressed slowly, trying to think it through again. He first thought the railroad was coming in. That would account for the timber cruiser finding too much timber to be given away to the railroad. The mining engineer could have found mineral rights on some of the land and that could mess up the route the road wanted to take.

But he had checked in Portland. There wasn't any applications on file for any of the railroads to extend their service into the wilds of eastern Oregon.

What did that leave? Land speculators? He had thought through that idea too during his four hour layover in Portland. The U.S. Land Office there said they had a branch office in Pendleton, some 50-odd miles from La Grande. The office there had reported no inquiries about any large scale land purchases. Nor was there any large group that would go in and homestead long stretches of rivers by gerrymandering their claims 20 yards wide and five miles long so they could tie up water rights to rivers for 50 or 60 miles. None of that.

McCoy got up and dressed slowly. Something had to turn up. He had to make something happen, get somebody nervous, make somebody take a try at killing him—but how? He snapped his fingers and finished dressing and hurried down to the newspaper office. Inside he found Hans Running still at the desk.

"Mr. Running, I'd like you to help me solve these murders. Are you game?"

Running looked up, his blonde hair tousled around the eye shade. He grinned past the wire-rimmed spectacles he now wore.

"Game? I've got an idea how we might do it. You tell me your idea first."

McCoy did. The ideas were almost the same. The two put their heads together and composed the story that would be on the newspaper's front page on every porch and store in La Grande bright and early in the morning.

Chapter Five

A man stood at a second story window on Main Street staring down at the jumble of wagons, horses, buggies and pedestrians below that usually clogged La Grande's two block business district.

Down there somewhere was a man he had to kill. He wasn't even sure who it was, but someone was starting to dig into the disappearances and killings, and it was absolutely mandatory that such activities be stopped. The sheriff was bad enough. This outside agitator was too good at his work to stay alive for long.

The man turned and touched the purple birthmark marring his left cheek. He had learned to live with it, not in spite of it. Now it was a kind of badge for him, proving that he could be a success without being handsome and perfect.

Frank Virgadamo smacked one double-up fist into his palm and growled. It had to be done soon, damn soon. He had been surprised about the death of the deputy sheriff. At least that wasn't anything connected with his operation.

Frank walked to his desk and sat in the swivel chair. There were only two pieces of paper on the large desk. If he didn't need something now it was properly filed in a drawer where he knew how to find it.

He stared at the paper. One of his people said the man's name was Spur McCoy and that he was staying at the La Grande Inn. Perhaps the time wasn't quite right today. He'd see what tomorrow brought.

His plans took time. He had money to raise; he had people to keep in line. Most important he had the big group to placate, to make sure they were happy.

Frank rubbed his face with his left hand. He had created the habit as a way to hide his birthmark. Now it was so ingrained that he didn't even realize he did it.

His face was thin, closely shaven. Not even a beard would cover up the birthmark, not unless he let it grow three inches long. He hated beards. The rest of his body was trim and hard. He'd come up the tough way and now wanted to enjoy some of the benefits.

He wondered if Billie Jo was busy. He looked at the man who sat in a chair at the far side of the room. Why not take some of the benefits?

Frank took an envelope from his desk and a $20 greenback from his wallet. He wrote on a piece of paper, then folded it around the bill and put them in the envelope and sealed it. On the outside he wrote the name, Billie Jo.

Frank motioned to the man at the far side of the room and he came to the desk at once.

"Yeah?"

Frank handed him the envelope. "Give this to her if she's downstairs. Otherwise hand it to Sue over at the Gaiety Saloon. Understand?"

"Yeah. Can I have a beer while I'm there?"

"Make it two. I'm going to take a nap." The big man went out the door, and Frank walked over to a day bed, fluffed a pillow, then stretched out on his back. What else should he be doing to speed up the whole process? Why in hell did it take so long to get anything done? He felt the anxiety building up and tried to relax. He wasn't supposed to get excited, not that way. Now with Billie Jo he could get excited all he wanted to. His doctor had told him so.

Angelina threw the shuttle through the warp and pressed the lever with her foot to tighten the weave. Yes, she was good at her work, but others in the colony were as good. Benjamin had a special appetite for her; she knew that now. Since the first time he had raped her two nights ago, he had had his way with her twice more. To protest publicly would make her the butt of the women's jokes, and she knew how cruel women could be. She would endure it, but not forever.

Already she had a man's hat and a pair of trousers. She had stolen them from one of the smallest men so they would fit her. Now she had to find a shirt of the homespun variety, and only two men were small enough for their shirts to fit her. One was a lad of only 16. She wondered if he had made love yet? Such activity was encouraged among the young people, but there was no young girl near his age. It gave her an idea. The night before she made her try she would seduce the boy and he'd give her his shirt.

She threw the shuttle again. Day after day she did little else but weave the drab, dull, blue homespun yarn into cloth. There had to be more to life than this.

She found no pleasure in how well the colony provided for itself. They were almost independent. Only coal oil for their lamps and a few other items had to be bought in town.

What else would she need for her ride? A horse and saddle. That would be hardest and had to be obtained the night she rode away. At night she could get through the lookout post with no trouble. She had learned to ride on the farm, so that was no problem.

Food? She could take along some jerky. It wouldn't take her that long to ride to the town of Union she had heard about. If there was no sheriff there, she would ride on to La Grande where they had stopped briefly two years ago. It certainly was big enough to have a law officer. There she would ask for protection. Then she would need to find work to earn money for a stage ticket away from there, back to New York eventually.

She worked harder at her weaving since she had a quota. If she got more done than that a day she could have a few minutes to herself to walk among the trees or play with the dogs or their puppies.

Angelina looked at the two other women weaving in the special cabin set aside for such production. Yes, soon she would be out of here! She smiled at the thought.

When she looked up again, Brother Benjamin watched her.

"It's good to see you smile," he said.

She spoke low so only he could hear. "You can bet that I wasn't thinking of you when I smiled. Now you see that my smile is gone when I see you. I was thinking of my home and farm in New York."

"Forget New York. Your home is here."

"My home will never be here."

"You are still a difficult woman, but you are my new challenge. I will tame you. I will make you yearn for me."

Angelina laughed. "Never in a thousand years, Benny."

He hated it when she called him that.

"We'll see about that. I'll be at your cabin tonight. Make sure you reserve the bundling room."

"It's already reserved."

"I'll be there anyway, and we'll use the great outdoors. Bring a blanket."

"Bastard!" she said softly yet with great feeling.

Brother Benjamin only smiled and went out the door.

One of the other women looked up. "Well, Angelina, it seems you've caught the eye of Brother Benjamin. It can't hurt. Try to get something special from him. Some of the men will do little favors if you're exceptionally nice for them."

"With Ben I've heard he likes a little bit of a fight from his woman," the second weaver said. "I didn't have the nerve to try it when he bedded me. Wish I had."

They stopped talking when another man came in to check on their work. He was the foreman of the clothing operation which included the raising of the flax and the sheep and everything else through to the finished goods.

He paused beside Angelina's loom.

"Angelina, are you busy tonight?"

"Of course not," she said with a bright smile. "I'll be at your cabin's bundling room at seven."

The man smiled. "Good. I've been waiting my turn." He nodded and walked away.

The closest woman laughed softly when he left. "Now that will be interesting. Benjamin is going to be truly angry with you."

Angelina smiled. "Good, I hope he'll be furious."

The rest of that afternoon and evening, Spur McCoy worked with Hans Running at the newspaper. He collated the two big sheets of paper and folded them in half twice and stacked them in piles.

They printed 150 copies. By the time they were folded and placed in each store front and door in town, it was nearly one A.M. McCoy waved tiredly at the still bouncing Hans Running and walked with slow steps to the La Grande Inn. When he got to his room he unlocked the door and eased it open. A shaft of moonlight coming in the window showed Becky, the hotel maid, sleeping on his bed.

McCoy closed the door gently, locked it and put the chair under the handle. Then he looked closer at the girl. She lay nude on top of the sheet, one hand thrown over her head, the other cupped around her crotch.

He slid out of his clothes except for his underwear and edged onto the bed beside her. For a moment she didn't stir, then her hand reached out and found him. She pressed against his back with her breasts, spooning against him until they matched perfectly. Then she continued to sleep soundly.

McCoy grinned and relaxed. Just before he went to sleep he felt her arm come over him and reach for his crotch, but she couldn't get it that far. She mumbled something in her sleep, then settled down.

Neither of them awoke until nearly seven o'clock the next morning.

Becky woke up with a squeal.

"Why didn't you grab me when you came in? Damn, now I don't have time. I've got to be at work soon, and I need to go home first. Oh, damn!"

McCoy grinned. "Hey, I thought you liked me for my mind. Why all this talk about sex all the time?"

She giggled. "Yeah, you don't like fucking at all." She jumped out of bed and pulled on her clothes. "Next time, Buster, you wake me up or I'll tell everyone you're a lousy lover." She kissed him and hurried to the door. She looked back, shaking her head. "Damn, what I missed last night. Next time I'll wake up as soon as you get in the room. See you tonight."

When she was gone, McCoy got up and dressed, then shaved in the cold water and combed his hair. He had a leisurely breakfast at the Grande Café. Polly left three people sitting so she could come over and talk with him.

"Hoped you'd come in. Is it true what I read in the paper this morning?"

"All true, Polly. You know what's going on?"

The newspaper story was a banner headline that screamed *Three Murders By Secret Syndicate*. The story was less explicit, but it got across the point that the three killings in the county in recent weeks were all part of a huge plot to defraud the people of Union County. It stated that certain police agencies were hard at work tracking down the last of the clues as to the identity of the culprits, and arrests were expected at any minute.

It was vague but threatening, and Hans Running and McCoy hoped it would smoke out the real syndicate behind this big plot—whatever the hell it was.

"Golly, I don't know a thing about this. You mean all this happened right here in La Grande and Union? Nothing like that ever happens here."

"We've got two dead bodies, murdered, and one missing man who probably is also murdered. Makes you stop and think, doesn't it?"

Three people came over to talk to McCoy while he ate his shredded potatoes and sausages and three eggs. It was an interesting meal.

One man said he had seen a lot of suspicious activity going on at a barn near the edge of town, but he figured it was just Old Charlie still getting in operation. Never could tell, though.

The next man said he had seen the deputy sheriff get killed. He was up that way two nights ago when he saw three men jump the deputy with sticks and club him, then use hunting knives and carve him up. This man obviously hadn't seen the killing, but McCoy didn't tell him that. He thanked him, pretended to write down his name and said he was sure the sheriff would be contacting him.

A woman came up just as McCoy was about to leave. She was hesitant, and he smiled at her. "Good morning, I'm Spur McCoy. Do you have something to tell me?"

She looked away and then nodded. "Mr. Currier stayed at my boarding house when he was in town. He . . . he told me there was something strange going on up in the Wallowas. He said he wasn't sure just what it was, but that on this cruising run he hoped to get to the bottom of it."

"Sit down, please," McCoy said. "What's your name?"

"Mrs. Burton, Mrs. Hazel Burton."

"Thank you. About Mr. Currier—did he give you any indication at all what might be strange up in the Wallowa Mountains?"

"Not a thing. He did say there could be some danger. He told me the less I knew the less danger I would be in. Whatever do you suppose happened to poor Mr. Currier?"

"That's what we're going to find out, Mrs. Burton, and it probably will be best if I don't talk to you any more in public. Tell me where you live in case I need to contact you again."

He memorized her address and quickly left the café. He hoped nobody who was involved in this matter had seen her talking to him.

Outside he realized that he was a target. He walked past two store fronts, turned to see who was behind him, then walked casually into a men's clothier. He stood near the door watching outside, but no one came past who seemed interested in where he had gonc. No one stood at the window and looked in.

He asked the owner if there was a way to the alley, thanked him and hurried out. McCoy grinned at himself. How was he going to get any leads unless he did make himself a target? That made sense. At the next vacant lot, he cut through to Main Street and walked half a block, found himself still alive and began to wonder if this had been such a good idea. It would alert whoever was doing the killing and might not give him any kind of a lead.

Then someone came up behind him quickly. He whirled around only to see a star on the man's leather vest.

"Sheriff Johnson really wants to see you, Mr. McCoy," the deputy said. "He's madder than a wet turnip right now. I guess he read the newspaper, too, this morning."

"Think it'll work?" McCoy asked as he walked the half block to the court house.

"Think what will work?" the deputy asked.

"Nothing," McCoy said. If the deputy didn't figure out the ploy, maybe the killers wouldn't as well and go ahead and try to kill him. McCoy just wished they would hurry up and try.

A second later he heard the sharp report of a rifle, and the deputy sheriff to his right stumbled and went down.

Chapter Six

Spur McCoy dove to the left, away from the sound of the shot, rolled once and scrambled into the door of the closest store before the rifleman could get another round fired. From the floor, he stared around the doorjamb at the boardwalk. The deputy sheriff lay on the planks holding his left shoulder. Blood dripped though his fingers.

"Get to the doctor!" McCoy bellowed. "He isn't after you. I'm his target. See where it came from?"

"No. Across the street somewhere." The deputy sheriff stood and walked down the boardwalk toward the doctor's office a block away. He left a trail of bright red blood from his shoulder.

Another bullet slammed through the open door

of the store, and this time McCoy saw the blush of blue smoke from the powder. The sniper lay on top of the hardware store. It was a two story building, so the man could drop down to the one story roof on either side.

McCoy looked at the shop he was in for the first time. It was a seamstress's store with two frightened women cowering at the back near a partition.

"Get in the other room, ladies," McCoy ordered. Then he sent four shots from his six-gun into the false front around the top of the hardware store building. He figured the gunman was gone.

McCoy came out of the shop running, his gun trained on the top of the hardware. No shots came. He tore across the street, barely missed getting run down by a team of four towing a big wagon, and jolted up the steps and into the hardware. He waved his weapon and raced through to a back door and out into the alley.

No one came down the ladder that went up to the second story roof of the hardware. He watched the roofs on either side. There were a dozens places the bushwhacker could be hiding. McCoy faded into some shadows across the alley from the hardware building and waited and watched. After five minutes no one had come down from the roof of any of the adjacent buildings. Some of the roofs probably had access to the inside.

He decided to give it another five minutes. Well before that time was up, he saw a head peek over the false front of the store next to the hardware. The man seemed to be checking the scene. A moment later he started down the ladder to the ground. He had a rifle strapped across his back, leaving his hands free for the descent.

McCoy waited for him to get halfway to the

ground, then he came out of the shadows on a run and blasted one round into the ladder just above the man. The man looked over his shoulder at McCoy just as the second round from his .45 smashed into the climber's leg, making him fall ten feet to the ground.

"Don't touch that six-gun or you're a dead man," McCoy bellowed.

The man's hand started for it, then slowed and stopped. He groaned and rolled on his side, his hand away from the weapon.

"You must have broke my damn leg," the bushwhacker screamed.

"Not sorry about that at all. You shot at me. Who hired you to kill me?"

"Don't know what you're talking about. I was inspecting the roof for leaks."

"With a rifle? Sure you were."

McCoy cocked the six-gun and aimed it at the man's legs.

"Which knee joint you want me to shatter, your right or your left? Either way you'll never walk good again."

"By damn, no!"

"Who hired you?"

"Some guy in a saloon. Never saw him before. Big guy, missing a front tooth. Bigger than you are."

"What saloon?"

"Damned if I remember."

McCoy fired, deliberately missing the joint but searing some flesh off his upper leg with a creasing shot.

"Damn! Okay, it was the Rusty Hinge Saloon."

"What was the man's name?"

"He didn't tell me his, and I didn't tell him mine."

"What's your name?" McCoy asked as he cocked the weapon again.

The man stared at the gun, down at his left leg that was bleeding and at his right with the crease.

"Shit! Ned Odekirk."

"On your feet, Ned. You get to walk down the alley to the courthouse and the jail."

"Can't walk, got a shot-up leg."

"Tough! Drag it then. I'm not going to help you. I'll take your iron and that long gun."

McCoy lifted the weapons from the man and prodded him. He stood and hobbled along in front of the McCoy.

"Guess you know you wounded that deputy walking with me. Should be good for five years in the state lockup over at Salem."

"Five years?"

"Yep, at least. Especially if you don't remember any more about the man who hired you."

"He had a gap in his teeth where one upper was gone. He was six-three, I'd say. Brown hair combed straight back. Wore town clothes, dressed good, suit and a tie. Didn't talk as good as he dressed. Never seen him in town before."

"You're doing good, Ned. You might get out of this alive yet. I figure this big guy won't be too happy you missing me that way."

After locking up Ned the sheriff came and stared at him in the last jail cell.

"This the bastard who shot my deputy?" Sheriff Johnson asked, his small eyes furious.

"He's the one. Better send somebody for the doctor. He can use some patching."

The sheriff motioned to a deputy who left in a rush.

"I questioned him with some persuasion,"

McCoy said. "I think I know everything he knows about the man who hired him."

They walked back to the sheriff's office where McCoy told him what Ned Odekirk had said.

"I think he was telling the truth. He had lots of reasons not to lie to me."

"Good enough. We'll hold him for attempted murder on a police officer. That's good for ten years. I'll want you to write all of this down and sign it, McCoy."

"The glorious paperwork. Sometimes I'm sorry I learned how to write."

"My deputy is going to be all right. He got a slug in his shoulder that the doctor is digging out. He's using that newfangled ether, so Rob shouldn't hurt too much." The small man wiped his hand over his face and stared hard at McCoy.

"He was aiming at you, of course. Was this what that newspaper story was all about?"

"Stirred up somebody. We have a small lead. I'll talk to the bartender at the saloon. Might learn something more."

"Might not. The Rusty Hinge is the worst saloon in town. They can't even get the whores to work there."

"Sounds like fun. What's the bartender's name?"

"Depends who is alive this week. They change a lot. Place is owned by an ex-bank robber who brags a lot, but I got no paper on him."

"Is it open now?"

"Only saloon in town that stays open twenty-four hours a day. Tried to get them to close down after two A.M., but the owner threw me out. No law against it, he told me—and he's right. I've got the city council working on a saloon closing law. Two A.M. sharp."

"I'll head that way."

McCoy left the jail, and on his way to the Rusty Hinge Saloon, he passed the store front that had been turned into the Union County Library. McCoy opened the door and walked in. The pretty redhead stood behind her tall counter checking out a book for a woman with two children in tow.

She looked up, saw him and smiled.

"I'll be right with you, sir," she said.

He went to a shelf of books along the wall. They were alphabetical by authors. She was right. There was no Walt Whitman on the shelf.

A minute or two later, she walked toward him smiling. "Now, can I help you find a book? A reference book of some kind, I would think. Surely nothing in fiction."

"Actually I was looking for a novel by Alexandre Dumas, the famous French novelist and playwright. Do you have anything by him?"

"I'm afraid not. No French authors—just yet." She grinned like a little girl. "You're teasing me. You're not really here to find a book, are you?"

"Actually no. I was on my way past and wanted to stop by and see if you were actually as pretty as I remembered."

She closed her eyes for a moment. "Sir, that is pure flattery, and we both know it isn't sincere." She turned with a stern look on her face, but the edges of the smile were still there. "I do have a lot of work to be doing."

"Fine, I'll browse. That is permitted, isn't it?"

Her stern expression cracked and then broke, and Meg Tackett giggled.

"Entirely permitted and encouraged." She stared at him openly, looking up and down.

"You are staring, you know," he said.

"Yes, I just wanted to see if you were as handsome as I remembered."

They both laughed.

"Could I take you to dinner tonight, Miss Tackett?"

"Oh, my." She frowned a minute, then smiled. "Yes, I don't see why not. I'd like that."

"Good. Shall I pick you up here? When does the library close?"

"At five."

"I'll see you here at five and we'll have an early dinner. None of the best restaurants in town will be crowded at that time."

Meg couldn't stifle a giggle. "Mr. McCoy, I like you. You make me laugh."

He nodded and went out the front door. Right now he had a date with a rough and tough barkeep, and he knew just how to handle him.

The Rusty Hinge actually had rusty hinges on the door that squeaked gratingly as the door opened and closed. Inside there was a wooden floor but it looked new. The bar was set up on two 50 gallon wooden barrels and made of unpainted pine planks. Two side by side constituted the entire bar. Behind the bar a man stood with a three day's growth of beard and a scowl. He held a baseball bat in one hand and pointed it at two men about to fight.

"Outside both of you or I'll cold cock you. Got that?" the barkeep thundered.

The two quieted down, then walked outside. The barkeep put down the baseball bat, picked up a cloth and looked at McCoy.

"You want a beer?" he asked.

"Yeah, a beer and some talk." McCoy moved to the end of the bar, and when the barkeep came with the beer, McCoy punched him hard in the belly with his left fist. His right hand drew the .45 and pushed it into the soft flesh under the man's chin. His head came down to lessen the pain of the belly blow, but the pressure of the muzzle in the soft flesh eased his head upward to avoid that greater pain.

"In back," McCoy said, grabbing the man's arm and walking him backward through a door and into a supply room.

"What the hell?"

"I'll ask the questions, stupid," McCoy spat. "I'm looking for a big guy, six-three, with an upper tooth missing in front. Fancy dresser, a town kind of man. He was here this morning. What's his name?"

"Hell, I don't know no names. Don't know yours, but I'm gonna find out."

McCoy pushed the revolver barrel harder upward. "Just how the hell you think you'll find out when your brains are splattered all over the room here? You know where the first slug from this iron is going when it slams through your mouth and then the roof of your mouth and into your useless brain? Hell, it's going out the top of your head and taking the last bits of your life with it. You're a dead man if you don't tell me his name."

"Christ, easy. He's Landower. Only name I ever heard. Travels sometimes with a slick guy about forty. Neat, clean, but he's got a birthmark on his left cheek. Big damn purple thing, big as a silver dollar."

McCoy let the six-gun down and rubbed the man's chin. "Now that wasn't so tough, was it? I'm McCoy, if you want to know. Who are you?"

"Ace. Everybody calls me Ace."

"Fair enough, Ace. Don't tell anybody I was in

here or that I asked about Landower. Can you remember that? If you have trouble remembering it, think about that .45 slug blasting through the roof of your mouth and out the top of your head."

McCoy turned and went out the front door, listening to the shrieking of metal on metal as the Rusty Hinge door closed.

Chapter Seven

The sky was dark with no moon at all showing among the bright array of stars. The one-horse buggy rolled forward at an even pace of four miles an hour. It had just left Union, heading toward the hills on a little used track. Another mile or two now at the most, the man holding the reins thought.

He hunched his shoulders against the strain of the long drive. He was not used to handling a buggy or a horse for that matter, but there was no chance anyone else could come along and drive for him—not even Landower, who knew too much already.

Frank Virgadamo sighed and looked out at the trace of a stream he was following as it wound toward the foothills of the Wallowas. The message said he would meet the man a mile or two outside of the little village. That had to be pretty soon. Should he keep moving, or stop and let the man find him? Keep moving. If both stopped and waited they could be all night finding each other.

Frank Virgadamo rubbed his face with his left hand, covering the birthmark on his left cheek. Old habit, he thought as he realized he was doing it. He slowed the horse, then stopped her and listened. He could hear nothing but the buzz of some night insect and a cricket or two calling for a mate.

He moved the horse ahead again.

Without warning a man on a horse charged toward him out of the deep, dank blackness.

Virgadamo stopped his animal and reached for the derringer in his jacket pocket.

"Benjamin here, don't shoot," a voice said from the back of the horse. Then the horse was close enough that Virgadamo could see the dull blue of the homespun. He held the reins as Brother Benjamin rode up to the side of the rig.

"You bring the necessary equipment?" Benjamin asked.

Virgadamo held up a bottle of whiskey and two glasses. "Never without the necessities of travel," he said. "Come and sit up here. There's plenty of room for two, and we can be partly out of the night wind."

A few minutes later they had cracked the bottle's seal and poured the amber liquid.

"Nothing like a good shot of whiskey to get a business deal moving along at the right level," Virgadamo said. "But go easy. I understand you have no strong drink in your community."

"None that's known to be there," Brother Benjamin said with a sly smile. He sipped the whiskey, nodded, then looked up at Virgadamo.

"Now, we've kept our part of the bargain. We've turned away anyone coming close to the valley. It's still a secret. Have you raised the cash and credit you need yet?"

"I'm going back to Portland in a week or so, and by then it all should be set up. Raising a hundred thousand dollars for a venture such as this is not easy."

"But with the profits that can be made . . ."

"Many are doubtful, some are smart, and it's not a sure thing. We know where we think it is, but until we get there and go to work, no one can be sure."

"Another two months is all my men need," Brother Benjamin said. "By then it'll be too cold to work anyway. We'll be ready by the middle of October. After that you're on your own."

Virgadamo scowled for a moment, then shrugged. "We've had plenty of time. If I don't have the money by then, I'll move in anyway and get proof. Then the backers will come screaming, wanting a part of the project."

"So you better get back to Portland and raise money." Brother Benjamin emptied his glass and poured it half full again. He kept the glass and stepped down from the buggy.

"Next time you want to talk, think it over carefully. The fewer times we meet the better. I hear some newcomer is giving you problems in town."

"He is, but not for long."

"I heard that your man missed him twice."

"Haven't you heard that the third time is a charm?"

"Let's hope so. I've got too much work invested in this project to have to stop now."

"Is it getting better?"

"In some places; in other places—nothing. My problem." Brother Benjamin mounted his horse, gave the trim man a mock salute and rode into the darkness toward the Wallowas.

The meeting had not been one that Brother Benjamin needed, he decided. It had been to reassure Frank Virgadamo that everything was in order and progressing according to plan. The man was weak. He might never do what he wanted to do, but that would not be Brother Benjamin's fault.

It was still early. He wondered where the girl was. He always thought of her as the girl, the girl with the big tits and the pounding, tight little ass. Best woman he'd ever had in the Movement. He'd try her cabin on the chance she was there. She was and came to the door reluctantly.

"Get a shawl. We need to have a talk."

"I'd rather stay here. I'm tired."

"We're all tired. We're supposed to be after a hard day of work. Still we need to talk."

Angelica shrugged, stepped out the door, closed it and leaned against it. "Talk."

"Not here. Somewhere that's more private. Up behind your cabin a ways."

"Oh sure, out in the trees where there's some nice soft grass? That's all you ever think about, isn't it?"

"Not at all, if only you knew. And you *could* know if you were a little more loyal to me."

"Loyal? You use me like a whore then say I should be loyal to you?"

"This won't last forever. I told you that. It could be all over for some of us sooner than you think." They had been walking into the edge of the pines in back of the cabins.

"So you're going to run off with all the spare money around and you want a woman along you can turn into a free whore for you."

"Not what I had in mind."

"Then why do you insist on making me feel like a whore? Don't you think a woman has any feelings? Don't you think a woman might want to pick out the man she beds?"

Brother Benjamin stopped a minute and pondered it. "Yes, I guess that's true, but it's not terribly practical. It's the men who have the sexual need, the drive, the feelings."

"Women have needs, too. Why can't you be a little nicer? Raping a woman is one thing. Even seducing her would be a lot better."

He stopped her, put his arms around her and stared at her in the soft darkness. "Angelina, would you mind if I kissed you?"

"No, I wouldn't mind, but I don't want you to."

"Oh. Then would you let me kiss you? Please?"

"Hey, this is better. Sure, go ahead, but go slow. Remember, I'm not a two dollar whore you just bought in La Grande."

"Damn right you're not. No two dollar whore I ever saw had beautiful, wonderful, big tits like you do."

"Breasts! Call them breasts or I'll kick you in the balls."

"Breasts, big beautiful breasts. They just make me feel like I want to kiss you."

She made him go a slow step at a time, and it took him nearly an hour before he got her skirt hiked up around her waist and her bloomers off.

After it was over they lay side by side.

"You were saying something about going away. Just a few of us?"

"Might only be two, if you want to go."

"Wow! I'd give a lot to get away from this place. Some of the men kidnapped me in New York, you know that?"

"I've heard. That was when Brother Joshua was the leader. I didn't know about it until you told me a few days ago."

"It's true." She sat up and put his hands on her breasts. "So when are we leaving?"

He shushed her. "Not another word about it, you hear? The whole thing could blow up in my face. You just be patient. I'll put you on restriction like you're pregnant so the other men won't bother you."

"How long is it going to be?"

"Two months at the most, but it could be a lot less than that. Be patient a few more weeks and I'll know for sure."

She liked the feel of his hands on her bare breasts. She trembled, but she had to find out. "Are . . . are we going to have any money when we leave? I've been poor all my life, and it's no fun. Will there be any cash?"

"Yes, sweet Angelina, there will be plenty of money. I'll buy you gowns and diamonds and a fur coat."

"I hope so." She pulled his face close to hers so she could see him in the darkness. "Then we've got a bargain? I'll be your woman if you get me out of here when you go."

"We've got a deal, a contract. If things work out, I might even marry you."

She pulled him over on top of her. "Great, good. Now one more quick fuck to seal the bargain, then I need to get back to the cabin and go to sleep."

When Angelina got back to the cabin, she waited until the other women were sleeping, then she checked her hidden cache of clothing. She had one pair of pants and a shirt she had taken from a clothesline yesterday. It was a little large, but she could push most of it in to the pants. She had a man's hat, and her shoes were the same as the men's.

So she was ready. Now she had to figure out who would be guarding the horses. She knew one man slept in the barn, so he could watch for Indians or rustlers. They had never had any problems, but they tried to think ahead.

She would have to club him with a stick and then tie him up and gag him. That wouldn't be too hard. She was desperate and would do anything to get away.

That made Angelina think about Brother Benjamin's plan to sneak away from the group. She didn't know how there could be any money around. If they sold more in town than they bought, there would be a credit. Maybe some of the stores gave them cash for the surplus. But how could that be very much? She slid under the quilts and tried to sleep.

She would have to leave soon while the moon was dark. A full moon would make getting away that much harder. That meant it had to be in the next day or two. She would be ready. Tomorrow she'd check on the stables, spot a horse and see where the saddles were. She could ride, but she'd need a saddle.

Run away with Benjamin? Not a chance! Use him here to help herself—yes. Whatever he had in mind would be worse than it was here. She had to play for time, anything for the next day or two so she had her chance to get to La Grande. Yes, she had to get to La Grande and talk to the sheriff.

* * *

In La Grande, Meg Tackett stared at her pillow in the small house that she rented from the hardware store owner. It was two bedrooms, and she had hoped to find another single woman to share the expenses but had no luck so far.

She tried to sleep, but again the vision of Spur McCoy came floating in to distract, confuse and excite her. He was by far the most handsome man she had ever seen. And he was nice! That's what surprised her. When she came here from Portland to take over the library, she had been warned by her mother to expect all sorts of men who would try to seduce her. She hadn't had that trouble at all.

Oh, some of them asked her to dances and to the opera house whenever a traveling stage troupe came through, but there had been no stampede to try to win her hand.

Spur McCoy could do it with almost no problems at all. He was such a gentleman—and educated, too. He knew about the book by Walt Whitman. She bet not another soul in La Grande had even heard of Walt Whitman.

That made her smile. The book had some rather risqué parts in it. One of the poems was about a man's private parts. She had read it and now blushed just thinking about the words.

Spur McCoy was one of the nicest men she had ever met. There was a sense of danger about him, though, as if he lived for the moment and would as quickly seduce her behind the rows of books as shake her hand.

That was one of the reasons she was so taken with him, but he was here on business. She wasn't sure what kind of business, but he seemed to be in and out of the sheriff's office a lot. Law business?

She guessed it was. He had certainly helped find the murdered deputy sheriff at the edge of the Wallowas.

So he would be here one day and gone the next, and she'd never see him again. Maybe, just maybe, she should ask him to kiss her. She had never done a thing so forward in her life. It would be cheap and terrible.

But the more she thought of it, the more she decided she wouldn't have to ask to be kissed. Maybe sometime they would just be close together and she wouldn't exactly run away from him. Yes, she figured she could work out something like that. Drop her handkerchief or show him a passage in a book or something.

Meg thought about it again and smiled. Yes, she would think of some way to do that. She wiggled her sleek, trim body in the beg, cuddled the pillow under one arm and thought about how delicious it would be when she kissed Spur McCoy.

Chapter Eight

That same afternoon, Spur McCoy picked up a note from his box at the hotel. It said simply:

"Might be able to give you some help. See me when you can. Sue at the Gaiety."

McCoy turned around and walked out of the hotel and down the street to the best drinking/gambling/whorc housc in town. Suc saw him come in and drew a beer, motioned to follow her and walked to a back table.

Sue had on another town dress, modest but a little tight, covering her to her throat and wrists with the skirt sweeping the floor.

"Thought I might have some news for you, if you're still looking."

"Always like to hear news," Spur said.

"One of my girls has a new sometimes regular who likes to have his entertainment all night in his office. Strange sort of bird from what I hear.

He sends an envelope to me with a twenty dollar bill in it, and the lady in question takes a stroll to his place and goes in through the back door.

"Now there's nothing strange or unusual about this, but somewhere I heard you were interested in a gent who had a front top tooth missing and who wore a dark suit and tie when his real occupation is that of bouncer and strong arm man."

"This is sounding more interesting all the time. Is the guy about six feet tall and broad-shouldered?"

Sue nodded. "Sure is. Big guy. Doesn't talk much."

"You have any idea who he works for?"

"Billie Jo told me. There's no name on the door and no company name she could see, but she got a look at a letter addressed to him. She likes to know who she's with, especially on an all-nighter."

"So?" McCoy probed.

"Gent I've never heard of before—Frank Virgadamo. Slick guy, Billie Jo says, suit and tie and vest, all very proper. Slender and sharp, except for the round purple birthmark on his left cheek. The thing looks almost like a brand, Billie Jo said. He kept it turned away from her most of the time."

"Where is that office?"

"Second floor, above the Saddle Shop. There's a front stairs and a back stairs."

"Convenient."

"Only the one door up there. Looks like a whole group of rooms, but she just saw only the one."

"Got it. Thanks. Thank Billie Jo for me." He tipped the beer, finishing it. "Sweet Sue, I owe you."

"You have time to pay me back right now?"

"You mean . . ."

"I got me a big hankering, big man, and you're the only one who can fill the bill. Right now?"

"This early in the afternoon?"

"Don't make no never mind to me. When I want some, I want some. Come on."

"Love to, Sue, but I can't right now. I'm working, remember? If I don't get this situation figured out I'll be laid out on the undertaker's slab. Give me a few days. I pay my debts."

"Oh, damn. It's tough to get turned down."

"Not turned down, just postponed. Promise. I'm going to pay a social call on the man over the Saddle Shop. Billie Jo isn't there now, is she?"

"No, that was last night."

"Good. Thanks for the beer. I'll be back."

As McCoy came into the street a thin rain began falling. It hadn't rained in La Grande in a month, which wasn't unusual. What was strange was it raining at all during the month of August. He headed down the street and stepped into the doorway of a store out of the shower.

Lawrence Sloma came out of the next store and made a dash across the street and down toward the courthouse. Something must be damn important to get the tall man running through the rain. The tails of his black suit flapped as he ran. For a moment he stopped in a store doorway, then ran to the overhang that extended from the front of the General Store over the boardwalk. He wiped rain off his face, then charged for the court house.

McCoy wondered what was so important in the county building.

District Attorney Lawrence Sloma scurried into the main door of the courthouse just before the real thunderstorm struck. He wiped his face with his hands, then used his white handkerchief to finish the job and tried to dry his hands.

By the time he got to the County Commissioner's meeting room, the three men were all there and about ready to start.

Alonzo Harwick looked up and nodded.

"About time, Sloma. You call a special meeting you better have something important to talk to us about."

The D.A. went to his seat at the side of the long table and faced the three men. "I have. I've been working on it for over two months, but I've kept it quiet. Now I think it's time to act. Recently I had a break in the case when a young man defected from the Movement of Natural Man colony and came and talked with me."

"Sloma, I don't see how we have a leg to stand on dealing with those folks."

"Oh, but we do, from both a legal and moral standpoint. Let me set out the particulars. I'll go to the grand jury if you think I need to, but we have enough legitimate violations of laws and statutes that I don't see why that's required.

"First, the entire colony is on federal land. They are squatting on land not owned by them and as a consequence are using county facilities and services without paying any county property taxes. That's a misdemeanor.

"Second, they are a society that practices free love, with none of the men and women in the group married. I can charge them with child endangerment, with fornication, with living in an unmarried state. On this charge alone we have more than enough legal power to put every man there in county jail and send the women back to their home states with the children.

"The whole situation is one of massive moral turpitude that is a tremendously bad example for our young people and the residents of this county."

"So what do you intend, Sloma?" the chairman asked.

"These people are an abomination to the good name of Union County. I propose to issue warrants for the arrest of each of the twenty-five men on the property on charges of cohabitation and sexual intercourse with women other than their legal wives."

Elton Jessup, the oldest man on the commission, rubbed his chin. "Can you win on such a charge? Seems to me to be hard to show evidence."

"We can win. There are thirty-six children in the Center, and they were born by these women. Someone had to impregnate them. I also have a former resident who will testify to the outrages that happen there. No woman who is with child can tell you for sure who the father is. Typically it could have been one of six, eight or ten different men.

"Now, say we can't win the cases. We will keep up a barrage of legal charges against them until it becomes so uncomfortable for them that they will leave the county.

"I also have sent letters to the U.S. Lands Commission, detailing these outrages and hoping that federal officers will arrive any day to evict these squatters."

"Sloma, you seem worked up on this point," Harwick said. "Why?"

"My job, Commissioner, is to uphold the laws of the state and county and to prosecute any law violators. I intend to prosecute these people to the full extent of the law as long as they stay in Union County."

He looked at the three commissioners as they all thought about it. Two conferred quietly, then the chairman looked at the man on each side of him.

"Are we ready for a vote?" They nodded. "All in favor of endorsing this action against the Movement of Natural Man say aye."

All three voted in favor. District Attorney Lawrence Sloma pushed his papers together, put them in his leather briefcase and smiled.

Spur McCoy stayed under the protection of the store doorway to keep dry. He looked at the store again and realized it was the former store that was now the library. He wiped some of the wetness off his face and opened the door.

Meg stood at the window looking out, watching the rain.

"Hi!" she said with a big smile. "Isn't this rain wonderful? I love to see it rain."

"Nice for the ducks and the winter wheat crop, as we used to say," McCoy answered.

She looked up, surprised.

"I never knew that you were once a farmer."

"Wasn't. Just heard the farmers saying that somewhere. Kansas I think it was."

"Did that map do you any good?"

"Yes, helped me figure out the county at least a little. You probably still don't have *Leaves of Grass*."

Meg laughed. "No, and don't expect it any time soon, not with the Library Commission that we have in the county. Terribly conservative."

"I don't like poetry that much anyway."

"Are you looking for any particular book today?"

"Nope, just getting out of the rain. This is the driest spot in town."

Now they both stood near the front window, watching the rain. Suddenly the downpour was over. The eaves still dripped, but now people began coming out of stores and shops. A wagon moved down the muddy street. A woman tried to cross the sea of mud and slipped and fell seat first in the goop. Two men helped her up, and then one of them fell down.

"Looks like La Grande is coming back to life," Meg said. She watched him with curious eyes. Her hair was down today, combed out and forming a golden red river halfway down her back.

"Well," McCoy said, "thanks for the use of your dry place. I better get on with my journey."

"Careful crossing the street," Meg said and waved.

McCoy walked up the boardwalk a half block, then took his life in his hands and stepped down into the muddy street to cross over to where the Saddle Shop sat on the other side. His first few steps were careful, then he got more confident.

Halfway across he heard a rig coming behind him. He glanced back and saw a team of blacks coming at him. They were running and pulling a light wagon. He stared for a moment, and when he saw the driver wasn't turning, he began a frantic scramble to get out of the way.

For a moment he didn't think he would make it. Then he took one last leap and the lead black missed him by the width of a harness strap. The animal came so close that McCoy could feel the horse's hot breath out of its flaring nostrils.

Mud spurted on him from the wide steel wheels as the rig hurtled past. He started to draw his revolver, but the driver had hunched down behind the front seat.

McCoy took a step toward the rig to follow it, but his footing gave way and he fell forward. Just as he fell the booming roar of a shotgun exploded and buckshot spewed out of a hole at the back of the wagon that was only eight feet ahead of him. The buckshot screamed over his head where he lay in the mud.

McCoy drew his six-gun and put two rounds into the back of the wagon as it raced away. He then stood and ran after the rig, slipping and sliding. He reached the boardwalk where he had good footing.

He raced down to the corner, sloshed across the muddy street and then down the next street which had no walkways. He saw the blacks and their buggy turn at the next corner to the right.

By the time McCoy had reached the corner, he saw the rig standing halfway down the block. The horses were breathing hard, the reins were tied to the seat, and no one was on board.

"Be damned!" McCoy thundered. He looked around. There was no one in sight. He looked in the bed of the wagon but found only the wet boards and a discharged shotgun shell.

There were two shops on the street and several houses. He went to the first building and saw that it was the blacksmith shop. He walked inside, found the forge and backed up to the friendly heat.

"Need anything, or just warming your backside?" a heavy voice said from nearby. At the same time a hard hammer slammed down on red hot iron on an anvil.

McCoy saw the smithy, working some iron.

"Thanks, just waiting around. Did you see who drove up with that pair of blacks over there a couple of minutes ago?"

"Nope, been working."

"Mind if I wait and see if they come back? Got a small bone to pick with them."

The smithy grinned. He was maybe five-ten and had arms like oak tree trunks. The hammer hit the iron again.

"More'n welcome to stay, just so you don't talk too much. Hate big talkers. Oh, you best turn around slow like or you'll burn your ass off on one side."

"Yeah, thanks."

For an hour McCoy watched the wagon and the pair of blacks. Nobody came anywhere near them. He waited another hour and still no one showed up.

McCoy gave up on it. He said good-bye to the smithy, walked out the front of the shop and turned back toward town.

A rifle shot blazed in the clean, cool air, and the round sliced through a quarter inch of McCoy's upper left arm before he dove to the right behind a watering trough.

Chapter Nine

McCoy cursed his own stupidity for coming out the front of the smithy shop. He should have figured someone would be waiting for a good shot. He grabbed his upper left arm–not too bad a wound. Then he checked his position. The watering trough was two feet high and six feet long. Across the street somewhere a sniper lay waiting for him to move again. He looked out from the far end but could spot no blue smoke from the shot.

The bushwhacker was behind a house or shop or in some dense brush over there. He was close because there was no time between the sound and the slug. He checked again, but there was no escape path using the watering trough as protection. He lifted up and dropped down at once but drew no fire.

A moment later a rifle snarled again, this time

three quick shots from a repeater. The shots came from the blacksmith shop's big door behind him.

The smithy's big voice came a minute later. "Get back in here, stranger. I'll cover for you." The rifle cracked again, and Spur came to his feet, sprinting for the cover of the smithy shop 20 yards away. The big blacksmith fired twice more as McCoy made his dash for shelter.

The blacksmith put down the Spencer that looked like a toy in his big hands.

"Two of the bastards are over there by that yellow house, one on each side of it, laying down with rifles. Somebody around here don't like you."

"Damn true. Thanks for the rescue. I'm in your debt."

"A hundred dollars in gold would make me feel better," the blacksmith said. McCoy looked at him, and the big man burst into a hearty laugh. "That always gets a man's attention. Hell, I hate bushwhackers. If a man wants to fight, he should come out in the open and fight."

"I'm on your side," McCoy said. "Mind if I use the back way out of here?"

Ten minutes later he moved toward the Saddle Shop again. This time he came down the alley behind it and went up an outside staircase to the second floor. There was only one door which he opened cautiously. It led into a hallway that had four doors off it. One of them had to belong to Frank Virgadamo, but which one?

He tried two and found them locked, then he heard someone coming up the front stairs. He hurried down the hall to the back door and eased outside but left it cracked so he could see along the hall. He saw a large man in a suit and a smaller one also in a dapper suit and vest. As the smaller man turned, McCoy saw a purple birthmark on his cheek. Virgadamo himself!

Confront the man right now? No, he didn't have enough evidence. He had only some hearsay and little else. He would go after Virgadamo when he was sure he could put him behind bars for good.

McCoy eased down the outside stairs and went up the alley. It was almost dark. Another day gone, but he was making some progress. He checked his watch—nearly eight o'clock.

"Oh, damn!" McCoy said aloud. He had forgotten his supper date with Meg Tackett. Quickly, McCoy walked down the dark street to the library, but there was no lamp burning in the window. He had missed her and didn't know where she lived. Oh, damn! He kicked the boardwalk and continued on to the café. He might as well have something to eat. He'd have to apologize tomorrow.

Polly grinned when he came in. She put him at a table near the back and told him she'd been saving supper for him. He didn't have to bother ordering. She was gone for a while, and when she came back she had the biggest steak he'd seen in years. It was an inch thick and filled the platter. Surrounding it were side dishes of two vegetables, mashed potatoes and brown gravy.

Polly kissed his cheek, then sat there grinning as he ate.

Down the street two blocks, a man leaned against the mouth of the alley across from the courthouse. He was of medium height and wore the faded blue homespun of the Center, but he had a leather jacket on over the homespun shirt. Evidently the man was watching for someone.

Brother Benjamin rested as he waited. It had

been a hard, long ride and he was tired, but no matter how tired, there was a matter that had to be attended to.

He watched various people come from the courthouse after a long session, and at last he saw the man he wanted.

The man was tall and slender with sandy hair. He wore a black suit, vest and starched collar. District Attorney Lawrence Sloma was late, and he hurried past Main Street and up two blocks toward his home where he lived with his wife and one child.

Sloma never got home.

A block from his house Brother Benjamin caught up with him and called softly.

"Sir, are you the district attorney?"

Sloma turned slowly, his hand on a derringer he had started carrying. "Yes, I am. Who are you?"

"Oh, you wouldn't know my name. I'm from the Center—you know, the Movement of Natural Man. I'm getting out of there, and I figured if you ever wanted somebody to testify against that pack of hyenas, I'd be more than pleased to do it."

Sloma relaxed and grinned. "Matter of fact, I'm looking for someone to testify."

"Good, but I can't talk here. Somebody might see me. Over there in the alley, behind that house?"

"Fine with me," Sloma said. "I'll need to know your name and where I can find you. Are you staying in town now?"

"Sure, I'll be glad to tell you, but over there."

They walked into the deep shadows of the alley. A moment later total darkness closed in, and Sloma stopped.

"No one can see us here. Now what's your name, and exactly what can you tell me that will help me in my suit against the Center?"

The only answer Sloma got was a slashing blow of a six-gun butt as it smashed down on the side of his head. The steel jolted cruelly into his flesh, staggering the D.A. Then a second blow on top of his head smashed him to the ground and into unconsciousness.

It took Brother Benjamin ten minutes to run and bring his horse. He draped the unconscious form over his saddle and took him through connecting alleys out to the edge of town. There he dumped the D.A. in some high weeds and rode back to the man's house. He found the door to the small barn in back open, went in, saddled the D.A.'s favorite horse and led her out.

A half hour later, he was ready. Now both horses were a mile out of town on the northeast road to Pendleton.

Brother Benjamin used a rock and smashed it twice against the side and top of Lawrence Sloma's head. He touched his throat feeling for a pulse. There was none.

Now he hoisted Sloma up and pushed the D.A.'s left foot into the stirrup of the D.A.'s own horse. He let Sloma fall and twist, holding his foot and boot so it locked into the stirrup and wouldn't come out. He led the horse for a while.

Sloma's shoulders and head bounced and dragged on the hard road. After a quarter mile, Brother Benjamin mounted his own horse and came up behind Sloma's. He jabbed the mare in the hind quarters with his knife, short sharp jabs to infuriate and frighten the animal. It screeched in pain and took off at a gallop, dragging the D.A. behind.

Brother Benjamin spurred after the frightened mare, jabbing her a dozen more times so she continued to run back toward La Grande. He pushed the animal almost into town, then turned and rode away, making a large circle around La Grande and heading back to Union and the Center. He would stay in Union with a woman he knew there before he went back to the Center.

Brother Benjamin took a long breath. It was done. It had to be taken care of quickly. He had been surprised when Bellyache rode all the way to the lookout at the Center. The lookout brought Brother Benjamin to talk to Bellyache, and then the two of them had left at once.

Bellyache had made a quick ride from La Grande once he heard the news. The D.A. was going to file charges against all the men in the Center. Brother Benjamin had given a five dollar gold piece to Bellyache who screeched in delight and said he'd spend a week in Union and not go near La Grande.

Then Brother Benjamin had ridden. It was a four hour ride that he made in three hours, and then he got there only when the night session of the County Commissioners broke up. He knew a lot about the D.A., knew about his love for horses and riding and that he kept a horse in back of his house.

After that it was just a matter of doing what he had to do. He thought through it as he rode slowly toward Union. There was not a chance anyone could tie him or the Center to the tragic, accidental death of the District Attorney.

But Bellyache was a small problem. Tonight he would be in Union getting dead drunk. By sometime tomorrow Bellyache would have accomplished his heart's desire, drinking himself to death. Of course Brother Benjamin knew that he would have to help matters along a little, but Bellyache would be passed out and thrown out of his favorite saloon well before midnight. All Brother Benjamin had to do was find him and help him to his own private heaven or hell.

Yes, it would be a good night's work. Two more months and he would be ready to leave this country. Two more months and another ten thousand dollars! He smiled as he thought about it and kept riding for Union.

After McCoy finished the steak dinner, he thanked Polly, slipped out and headed for the doctor's office. It was connected to his home so the doctor was always available. He was the only doctor in town.

The medic was in his sixties, had been in town since it began and knew everyone. He looked at the wound and snorted.

"Hell, it's just a scratch."

"Sure, Doc, but I've seen men die from scratches like that. Take care of it for me. You have any of those new medicines that kill all the bad things?"

"They got it in Portland, but I can't get any out here yet. Maybe next year."

The doctor washed off the wound. It was about a quarter of an inch deep. Another inch in and the rifle slug would have broken his arm, shattering a lot of bone.

The doctor treated it, put on some salve and said there was no use in trying to stitch it back together. He wrapped the wound tightly so it would grow together.

"See me in a week if it breaks loose. Now can I go back to my book?"

McCoy said he could and was out the front door before he thought to ask the doctor where the librarian lived.

As he walked back to Main Street, he reviewed

his case. He had one suspect who might know something about the vanishing and dead men. At least Virgadamo had hired men to try to kill McCoy, but beyond that it was a blank, a total mystery. He should be making some progress by now.

The death of the deputy sheriff must be tied into the Center, the Movement of Natural Man, but not even the D.A. had any proof of this, only the shoe prints that evidently came from the Center.

McCoy gave up for the time, went into a saloon and played quarter limit poker. He spent three hours there, and it was nearly ten o'clock when he heard a shout outside. He was a loser by five dollars. He crowded outside with the others to see a deputy sheriff riding down the street fast. He pulled in at the sheriff's office and jumped off.

McCoy ran that way with some others and soon the word was out. The district attorney had just been found dead on the north road.

"Looks like he fell off his horse and his foot caught in the stirrup and he got dragged to death," the deputy said.

"Hell, not possible," a voice said from the crowd. "Sloma is an expert rider. He'd know how to get his boot loose. Not a chance he got killed accidentally that way."

McCoy saw the sheriff coming, stuffing his shirt into his pants as he marched down the street toward his office. McCoy hurried into the sheriff's office. This had to be tied into the other killings, but how?

Chapter Ten

The sheriff listened with a scowl as the deputy explained it to the sheriff.

"Let's get out there," the small man said. "McCoy, you get a horse and come with us. You seem to be the tracking expert around these parts."

The deputy had left the body where he found it, the boot still firmly twisted in the stirrup. McCoy asked them all to stop and leave their horses 50 yards from the body.

"Sheriff, I'd like to ask you to put a guard on the road down there about a quarter of a mile or so—no make it a half mile beyond the body and another guard here—and detour all traffic around this section of the road until tomorrow noon. Then we'll have a good chance to look at the tracks in the daylight."

"Yeah, good idea," Sheriff Johnson said. "He

sent one deputy each way, making sure they went off the road and telling them to detour everyone, especially wagons and the stagecoach.

The deputy who had brought the lantern lit it, and the four men left walked up to the horse. McCoy and the sheriff and the other two looked at how the boot was twisted in the stirrup. When all had studied it, McCoy twisted it the other way and pulled the boot out of the stirrup.

The horse was still winded. McCoy bent and touched the jaw of the attorney. He was not yet cold.

"Hasn't been dead more than an hour or two. Strange how slow a body cools down."

They moved the lantern down so they could look at Sloma's head. One side of it was ground half away by the long dragging.

"That's not right," McCoy said. "A horse like this might panic and tear off, but after a hundred yards she'd get tired and quiet down and stop. Unless somebody was forcing her to run. Anybody report hearing any shots out this way tonight?" McCoy asked. The deputies shook their heads.

McCoy looked over the body quickly, unbuttoning the vest and shirt. There were no wounds or marks on the chest or near the heart.

"If he wasn't such a good horseman, I never would have thought about foul play," the sheriff said. "Sloma here was raised on a ranch. Could ride by the time he was three. He was one of the best bareback riders at our annual rodeo that's coming up in a few days now."

McCoy turned the body over and checked his back.

"I don't see any other marks on him other than the dragging—unless he was shot in the head. Of course he could have been beaten on the head and then dragged."

McCoy stood up, took the lantern, patted the mare and walked around her. She was a gentle animal. Why would she suddenly bolt and charge away even though she knew she was dragging something? He ran his hand down her back and patted her hind quarters.

His hand came away sticky. He lifted the light, and they all could see the spots of blood on the mare's right hind quarters. The body had been dragged by the left stirrup.

The sheriff nodded. "Damn, if somebody was jabbing me in the rump, I'd damn well run away from it as hard as I could."

"Let's get Sloma in for the doctor to take a look at him," McCoy suggested. "He might be able to tell if there were any blows to the head before death."

They brought up a horse, draped the still flexible body over the saddle and walked the remains of Lawrence Sloma to the doctor's office.

McCoy used his heel and made a big X on the ground where the horse had stopped. "Might as well get the horse down to the livery stable and have the man there put something on those cuts," McCoy said. "I want to see what the doctor finds on Sloma."

They left the murder scene, with the guards stationed at both ends of the half mile stretch to detour traffic until at least daylight.

Doctor Kenny was slow getting out of bed. He growled at them when they showed him the problem.

"Damn, nice young man. I liked him."

"Then show us how he died," McCoy said.

"Didn't just have a scratch on his arm, tell you

that," the medic shot back. Then he grinned.

He stretched the dead man out on a table, lit four kerosene lamps that had mirror reflectors and angled the light on the battered head. Now they could see the extent of the damage. One half of the top of the head had been scraped off by the long run. The doctor pointed to a half-inch indentation at the edge of the skull.

"Anybody got a six-gun?" he asked.

The sheriff handed him one of his .44 Colts, and the doctor placed the end of the butt in the depression. It fit almost exactly.

"That mark wasn't made by a rock along the road," Dr. Kenny said. "Somebody hit Sloma damn hard with the butt of a pistol well before he was dragged on the road. That could have killed him. He was beaten before he was dragged by that horse. I'd say he was dead first. The scrapes on his neck and face and head haven't bled much. A wound bleeds only so long as the heart is pumping blood through the veins and arteries. Like when you stop pumping at a well, the water stops flowing."

McCoy checked his watch. It was 12:30. "Gentlemen, I'm going to get some sleep. I'll be up at dawn to take a look at those tracks and try to follow any leads that I can turn up."

No one was in McCoy's bed when he opened his door. He locked it and used the chair, then went to sleep almost at once.

By daylight he had saddled his rented horse from the livery and was out to where the first guard stood wearily at his post. McCoy left his horse there and began walking the route. It was clear where the body had been dragged.

Less than 200 yards down the road he came

to a second set of horse prints on the road that were just to the right of those made by the mare dragging Sloma. They continued back down the road and stayed with the death drag even when it went from one side of the road to the other.

They had been right. Somebody had driven that mare forward. He went back to where the double set of tracks stopped. They turned sharply off the road into the open land a half mile outside of town. At first the tracking was easy. He told one deputy to bring his horse, then told both of them as far as he was concerned they were released from their guard detail.

McCoy led his horse as he tracked. There were no distinctive prints, no broken shoe, no small one, nothing to set these prints apart from any others. As long as they were the only prints around, he was safe.

The rider was making no attempt to conceal his trail. Why? Was he so confident it would never be found? Or did he know that soon he would come to a highly traveled roadway and the tracks would be impossible to read among all the others?

The trail soon turned and circled around La Grande, then angled for the road to Union. A mile later it hit the Union track, and the single mount's prints were lost in a host of others, some new, some old. He tried to track them, but by then it was after eight o'clock and a half dozen farm wagons had been up and down the road. McCoy gave up and rode back to the sheriff's office.

The sheriff was having breakfast. McCoy reported his findings, confirming what they had decided last night.

"But the trail led to the Union road and then I couldn't follow it any more. Too much traffic."

"So it could have been someone from the Movement of Natural Man," Sheriff Johnson said. He told McCoy how the County Commissioners had approved plans by the district attorney to use legal means to roust the free love commune from Union County.

"They must have heard about it and sent a killer here to stop Sloma," Sheriff Johnson said.

"Could have. But wouldn't that be fast? The County Commissioners only approved it yesterday afternoon, and then Sloma gets killed less than six or seven hours later?"

McCoy stopped and lifted his brows. "Yes, I guess there's time enough, but, damnit, we have no proof."

It was ten o'clock. McCoy was starved so he went for breakfast at the Grande Café. It was the first time that he noticed the banners going up on main street.

"Grande Ronde Rodeo". The signs were all over. It was four days away. All at once everyone was talking about the rodeo. Even Polly, the waitress, was all enthused bout it.

"It's our annual celebration, our big holiday. Everyone is in a party mood, and all sorts of wild things happen," she said. Polly grinned. "In fact I had my first real kiss behind thc grandstand at the rodeo one year."

"You feed me well enough you might get kissed again this year," McCoy teased.

She fed him good. When the flapjacks and brown potatoes and eggs and toast were gone, he had a second cup of coffee. It was the midmorning lull.

"Hey, could I hire you to move some heavy things back in the storeroom?" she asked.

"Sure, why not? I don't seem to be able to figure out what I'm working on."

"The district attorney's death?"

"Yeah. Where is this moving job?"

She took him to the storeroom that was just in back of the kitchen. It had a separate door and one high window. She showed him a heavy box of apples that he lifted and put on a table.

When he set the box down she stepped close to him and kissed him. His arms came around her so she wouldn't fall down. It was a demanding kiss, and when their lips parted she sighed.

"Hey, do that again," she said. Her mouth was open, and he drove into her, fighting with her suddenly active tongue.

When that kiss ended she caught his hand. She led him to the door to the storeroom, slid a bolt in place, then pulled him to the back where three blankets were spread on the floor.

"I have naps back here when things get slow. Right now I'd like to have a nap with you." She unbuttoned the fasteners on her blouse.

"Hey, now, Polly."

She shushed him. "Spur, I'm a big girl. If I want to mess around a little, it's all right. I'm not exactly a virgin, so don't worry about that."

She opened her blouse and her breasts came out, larger than he guessed. Thumb-sized nipples surged hot and filled with blood. He could almost see her nipples pulsate. She caught his hands, pulled them to her breasts and smiled.

"Oh, yes, Spur McCoy, that does feel delightful. So good." She put her hands on his crotch and quickly found where he was getting hard. She rubbed, then undid the buttons and pushed her hand inside until she could grasp his manhood.

"Oh, my, Spur McCoy, you feel good, too!"

She kneeled down and pulled him with her.

"McCoy," she said watching him closely, "I really want you to fuck me right here and right now. How about it?"

"You won't be missed?"

"I have a deal with my boss. Now come on." When she kissed him again, McCoy was through playing coy. He pushed her down on her back and kissed her breasts. Then he sucked one into his mouth, and she began to wiggle out of her skirt. When he came up for air her skirt and bloomers were off, and she had worked his erection out of his pants.

"Hey, you don't even have to undress. Just slam that big stick into my pussy right now. It's been too damn long since the last time."

She spread her legs and pushed him between them.

"You don't want any more . . . ?"

"Now, damnit, fuck me now!"

McCoy knew an order when he heard one. He lowered and angled and then tried to slide into her. She was as tight as a virgin.

"Told you it had been a long time." She put some saliva on her hand and coated his purple tip, then urged him to try again. He found the spot, went past a small hinderance and then slid into her as smooth as honey on a hot biscuit.

"Yes, yes, yes!" she said as she humped upward to meet him. "That is heaven. There is nothing so good as a great man buried in my pussy and him squishing me into the floor. Course it's a little better on a featherbed."

She hadn't even hinted at an orgasm on her own yet. He pumped hard a dozen times, then gave himself some room and pushed his hand between them. His finger found her small hard node.

"What are you doing?"

"Helping out."

"Don't count if you have to cheat."

"Not cheating. Some people just don't match up right, and I can't touch your little clit with my cock. Isn't cheating at all." He twanged her clit six times, then six more, and she started breathing heavy, then moaned and a minute later sailed into a wild climax that shook her like a maple leaf in a fall wind. She vibrated and panted and squealed and then went through one more series of spasms that left her winded with tears seeping out of her eyes.

"Oh, God, but that was terrific!" she whispered when she could breathe again. "So wonderful! Nobody ever did that for me before—I mean right when we were fucking."

She glowed for a minute more; then her eyes went wide. "Hey, I beat you. You ain't had your turn yet." She began rotating her hips under him, squeezing him with those inside muscles.

He stroked and waited, pounded and paused, and then when she was twisting and turning and slamming upward at him, he at last spilled over the top into a grunting, pounding, yelping climax that left him weak and exhausted.

"Now that was a fuck!" Polly said. She hugged him and pushed him away. "I got to get back to work. You stay here and recuperate long as you want to. Anytime you want to get a really good one, you come around. Hell, I ain't had one like that in two, maybe three years."

She kissed his cheek, pulled on her bloomers, her skirt and her blouse, and she was up and gone a minute later.

McCoy lay there still panting. He wasn't 16 any more; he knew that. Hell, at 16 he could climax six times in an hour and be ready for more. Not now. Damn, but that was a fine one!

He rolled over and sat up on the floor. The floor? Like they were a pair of kids behind the outhouse. McCoy grinned, stood up and adjusted his clothes, then buttoned his fly. How long had it been since he'd taken on a woman that good with his clothes and even his shoes on?

McCoy chuckled as he went out the door of the storeroom. Now maybe he could figure out what the hell was going on here in Union County. At least four men killed, and nobody seemed to be able to figure out why.

He had to figure it out and fast, or he might be the next one to meet his maker.

Chapter Eleven

Angelina watched the other seven women in her cabin. They had only candles in their shelter, and they had to be blown out by nine P.M. For an hour after that, Angelina lay silently in her bunk listening to the other women. Two talked quietly for a while.

One was expecting her first baby anytime, and she felt alone and frightened. In their communal living, alone was one feeling that Angelina never had. At last the two women said good night and went to sleep.

It must have been another hour before she felt it was safe to get up. She pulled the men's pants and shirt from under her straw mattress and put them on. Then the floppy hat. Outside she picked up a walking stick that many of the men carried and moved with longer steps than usual in what she hoped was a manly stride toward the stables.

They had mostly work horses, trained to the plow, but there were six riding horses as well for the men to use working the cattle. She had chosen a small bay mare and hoped that she was gentle.

The man who usually slept in the stables was not there. She figured he was bundling with someone for the rest of the night. Quickly she took a halter, entered the small corral and found the mare. She stood near two others.

The bay didn't seem to mind that she was being haltered and taken out at this time of night. Angelina slipped the halter in place, led the animal to the gate, opened it and took the mare out, then closed the gate silently.

It took her longer than she expected to get the saddle on. At last she took the mare into the barn and stood on a wooden box so she could boost the heavy saddle on the back of the bay. The mare turned and stared at her once, not used to being saddled in this manner.

At last the cinch was tight with the saddle firmly anchored, and Angelina stepped into the stirrup from the box and lifted her leg over and into the saddle.

Now as she turned the mare to leave the barn she saw a man standing in the doorway.

"Well, now, what do we have here?" the man said. She didn't recognize him from his voice. "You ain't planning on running away, are you, boy, on one of the Center's horses?"

Angelina still carried the thick walking stick she had brought from the cabin. She kicked the bay in the ribs, and it charged forward. This sudden move caught the man at the door by surprise, and he stumbled to the side as the mare drove forward.

Angelina swung the walking stick hard with her right hand and felt the stick sting her hand when it hit the man on the side of the head. He had started to shout something, but the words never got out of his mouth as he sighed and slumped to the floor.

"Now you've done it!" Angelina whispered to herself. She slowed the mare to a walk and turned so she could ride behind the stables and into the edge of the woods away from the other buildings. Yes, she had to walk the horse. If she galloped out surely someone would hear her.

She walked the animal for a quarter of a mile, then lifted her to a canter and worked across a trail through the wheat field and back to the main road down the valley toward the lookout point.

That was when she heard the pistol shot. It came plainly echoing down the valley from the Center buildings. The one shot was a distress signal. It would bring out half the men, eager to find out what the trouble was.

The signal was seldom given, and always it was something important. She dug her heels into the flanks of the bay and galloped for a half mile down the valley. Nearing the lookout point she had no idea if they kept a man there on guard at night or not. She took no chances, slowed her mount and edged into the woods on the far side of the narrow end of the valley.

For a moment she stopped and listened. She could hear activity back up the valley. Then she could hear horses pounding hard down the trail. She hadn't counted on them coming after her so quickly.

She pushed deeper into the woods and began to move downstream along the far side of the valley where no one could see or hear her. When she came opposite where the lookout should be, she heard a man talking. Two men!

How had they got there so quickly? She couldn't understand their words, but it was enough to know there were two of them and they were watching for something. Soon the men from the Center would be there, and they would know who was missing. She was sure they had made a bed check of everyone as soon as the shot was fired.

Angelina kept moving. She rode down the side of the valley to where it widened. Still she kept to the far side. She was going out of her way, but perhaps they wouldn't think to look over here. No one could track her until daylight at least.

There were no ranchers or farmers out this far. She had heard there were no other settlers until a mile from the little town of Union. How far that was she had no idea. Her only plan was to watch the stars and ride northwest. That should put her onto a trail that would take her to Union. There she would find the deputy sheriff. She had heard there was one there and that he had been curious about the Center. He would protect her. He had to—he was a lawman.

Now she heard nothing behind her. The valley spread out into the broad and long flat floor that extended for miles and miles. She stopped and stared up at the stars. She found the big dipper and followed the pointer stars of the cup down to the North Star. Yes, there it was! She headed directly toward that for about an hour.

When she had done that and crossed over two small streams, she turned to the left, which would be west. Union had to be out there somewhere. She came to a small rise and looked to the northwest but could see no lights. She checked to the west and thought she saw a blinking light, but then it was gone.

Far behind her she heard a rifle shot, echoing plainly in the cool night air. They were searching. At least they had no idea which direction she would go. She was sure that someone would guess that she had headed for Union, and they would ride in that direction.

She had heard it was only seven or eight miles to Union which should be a two hour ride. Then she remembered the river, Catherine Creek. It flowed near Union and began up near the Center somewhere. No, it didn't start up there but flowed past in the valley below. If she could find the river she could follow it downstream to Union.

Now she made sure she was traveling to the west, keeping the North Star on her right. After a half hour she found a small creek and turned and followed it downstream. It should empty into Catherine Creek.

Fifteen minutes later it did, and the stream swung more to the north. She followed it and then slowly became aware of sounds behind her. She stopped to listen.

Horses! Three or four of them, and men talking. She turned away from the stream, found a patch of brush near a small feeder stream and worked her bay well into the brush.

Less than five minutes later, the horsemen came past. She could make out the shadows in the partial light. There were four of them, and she could hear them talking.

"Hell, she can't be this far. We missed her."

"Brother Benjamin said go all the way to Union if we had to, so we go all the way. I figure we won't find her until it gets light anyway. We get to town and wait."

"Maybe a saloon will still be open," another voice said.

"Sure, and what you going to use for money?"

That stopped the talk, and they continued on.

Angelina sat on her horse and shivered. What could she do now? If she went on down the river into Union they would find her. If she stayed here they would surely find her on their way back.

She scowled for a minute. There had to be an answer. Then she nodded, rode forward toward the river and worked downstream again, not moving as fast as the men ahead of her did.

Angelina decided she would give them time to get into the small town where they soon would get tired waiting. Then they would lay down somewhere and sleep until morning. While they were sleeping she would ride on past and head for La Grande. Yes! They didn't think she could go that far!

She had heard the men say it was 11 miles from Union to La Grande. There would be no danger getting lost then. They had talked about a wide wagon road all the way. All she had to do was be careful while she was going around Union.

She rode for another half hour, not sure how quickly her little horse was walking. She came around a small bend in the stream and saw lights to the right. Catherine Creek turned to the left there, but the trail headed for the lights.

So did Angelina. She came on the first house sooner than she figured she would. It was a simple frame structure with no lights on and a small shed out back. Ahead she could make out the outline of more buildings.

One of them was a saloon with yellow light coming from the windows, showing a store across the street. She rode forward, then saw another street. She turned that way and worked through the two block long town and found the trail coming away from it and heading for La Grande. She stopped in the dark shadow of a two story building and watched the trail.

The glow of a cigarette showed across the street and ahead. She heard voices that were soft and low. At last some phrases came through plainly.

"Hell, I don't care what Brother James said. I ain't sitting out here while he's there in that saloon trying to get a free drink."

Two horses pulled away from shadows across the street and rode back toward the center of town.

Angelina waited until she was sure they were well down the street. Then she walked her bay the opposite way along the street which had turned northeast. It was a good wagon road. Stages probably even used it.

She walked the bay for a mile, then lifted her to a lope and made better time. Now all she wanted was to get to La Grande where some lawman would be on duty even at night and she could tell him her story. Surely someone would believe her.

As she rode, she worked out a plan. Yes, she would charge Brother Benjamin with rape and kidnapping! That would make the sheriff sit up and take notice. Even if he was afraid of the Center and the 24 men there, he would have to do something. Maybe there was a newspaper in the town. If so, she would go see the editor and tell him her story, and then the sheriff would have to protect her. Yes, it was a good plan.

It took Angelina three hours to ride the 11 miles from Union to La Grande. She had no way of knowing what time it was. When she saw the first small farm at the edge of town, she watched for ten minutes to be sure no one was waiting for her. At last she rode past and soon came to other houses, all dark, and then at last the main street.

Here a few lamps burned in stores, but she couldn't find the sheriff. Then she saw the courthouse, and on the second trip down Main Street she turned in and followed the sign to the sheriff's office. She had to pound on the door three times before anyone came. Then a sleepy deputy unlocked the door and stared down at her.

"What in the world?"

"Good evening. My name is Angelina Potter, and I'm from the Center, up from Union. I want your protection. Six men are chasing me, and I don't want to go back there. Please let me talk to the sheriff. I want to file a complaint against the men, charging them with rape and kidnapping."

Deputy Wilson shook his head in surprise. "You want to file a complaint?"

"Yes, sir. I just rode in from the Center, and I'm tired and wonder if I could stay here tonight so the men who are chasing me can't capture me. I'll be glad to stay in one of the cells. You do have jail cells, don't you?"

"Yes, ma'am."

"Then kindly show me to one so I can get some sleep. I want to be awake when I talk with the sheriff in the morning. Oh, what time is it, please?"

"Time?" Deputy Wilson pulled a watch out of his pocket and turned it to the kerosene light.

"Ma'am, the time is nearly five o'clock. It'll be light in another hour."

"Fine, where can I sleep for a while?"

"I don't know if I should . . . I mean I've never . . ."

"Young man, just show me to a cell and lock me in. I promise that I won't shoot you or anything."

At last Deputy Wilson nodded, took her to the jail cells that were empty and found two blankets and a pillow for her to use on the narrow bunk.

It was all a dream. He knew in the morning when he met the sheriff they would both have a good laugh about it.

Spur McCoy had a visitor that morning at his room in the hotel as he was shaving. He answered the knock with his Colt on full cock and relaxed when he saw that it was Sheriff Johnson himself.

"You're up early this morning, Sheriff. Mind if I finish shaving?"

"Hoped you would. I have a small problem over at the office I think you can help me with. You were with our late D.A. when you found the deputy's body up the other side of Union, and you later decided it must have been the work of men from the Movement of Natural Man up there, right?"

"True, Sheriff."

"Come on over to the office soon as you're ready. We may have found ourselves a good witness."

"Against the Center?"

"I'm hoping so."

"I'm ready. Don't surprise me."

"We've got a woman who claims she rode away on horseback last night. The men chased her, but she got away in the dark and rode in here about five this morning. She's sleeping in a cell. Claims she wants to file rape and kidnap charges against the number one man up there, a Brother Benjamin."

McCoy laughed. "Sounds like manna from heaven. Sometimes, Sheriff, it's better to be lucky than to work hard. This could be your lever to rout out that bunch. Did the district attorney give you any arrest warrants or papers to serve on the men up there before he died?"

"Didn't have time."

"Then let's get them for murder as well—two, three, maybe four killings."

An hour later the three of them sat around a corner table in the Grande Café talking over breakfast. The woman had asked for a comb and had combed her hair and scrubbed her face before they left the jail. She kept on the homespun blue men's shirt and pants and collected a few stares from the people they met.

She ate breakfast as she told the sheriff and McCoy how she escaped and then let them ask questions.

"Did you hear anything about men from the group killing a deputy sheriff up there," the sheriff asked.

"Heard something about it. Rumors. Not sure if it was true or who might have done it. Nothing I could give as evidence in court."

"Why were the men up at the Center afraid of the deputy?" Spur asked.

"I'm not sure. But during the last four or five months something secret and strange has been going on. Everyone at the Center must produce something, cloth or food or wood or babies or something. I was a weaver.

"But ten of the men would go to work in the woods every day, but they never brought back anything, not wood or grain or berries or anything. Brother Benjamin, the leader, went with them. Nobody complained about it, but several of the woman talked about it. Soon they were told to be quiet and forget all about the ten men or they'd be in trouble. The men supposedly were doing something important.

"Women up there are like brood mares on a ranch. All they have to do is have babies and keep quiet. They have to work and produce food and goods as well, but the men treat us like animals."

The sheriff nodded. "I've heard enough. You come by later today and we'll fill out the forms and file your complaints of rape and kidnapping. What will you do here in town? Where will you stay?"

"I don't know. I don't have any money or any clothes. Nothing but the horse. I could sell her for maybe twenty dollars."

"I've got an idea," McCoy said. "There's a lady I want you to meet who is looking for a roommate. If you like each other it just might work out."

Ten minutes later when the library opened, McCoy led Angelina Potter into the storefront. Meg looked up, saw McCoy and smiled, then looked at Angelina and lifted her brows.

"Meg, this is a friend of mine I want you to meet. Meg Tackett, this is Angelina Potter. She's just escaped from the Center of the Movement of Natural Man. I know you're hunting a roommate. We need a place for her to stay. Could she stay with you for a week or two?"

"Well, nice to meet you, Angelina. This is quite a surprise."

McCoy took Meg to the side and explained the situation.

"She needs a friend, a safe place to stay and a job if we can find her one. Oh, I'll give you twenty dollars for her board and room for the first month and another twenty so she can get some regular clothes. It's a project for you."

"McCoy, it isn't the money . . ."

"She's charging one of the men up there with rape and kidnapping."

"Oh, dear! Oh, my, how terrible for her. Of course she can stay with me. First we'll get her some clothes."

When they went back to find Angelina, she had a book from the shelf and was reading it.

"A real library! I'm impressed."

Meg grinned. "Me, too. I'm your new roommate. The first thing we do is close the library and go buy you some town clothes."

McCoy left with the two women making plans. He went across the street and was about to step up to the boardwalk when he saw a shoe print in the slightly damp dirt of the street. There had been a dew last night.

He bent and checked the shoe print again. It was a mark exactly like the ones he had seen around the deputy sheriff's shallow grave and like the one he had seen in town once before. He saw that the line of prints crossed the street from the direction he had come. Since there hadn't been much traffic yet this morning, this was a good set of prints that he could follow.

Chapter Twelve

Spur McCoy walked across Main Street carefully watching the ground. Twice he stopped to sort out the flat-soled shoe prints where a wagon had crossed them. He found them again as they continued to the other side. Toward the boardwalk they became irregular, and at one point he figured the man had fallen to his knees.

Hand prints in the dirt showed where he had pushed himself erect and walked on. The prints angled along the boardwalk past two stores to where the wooden walk ended at an alley, and the prints turned into the space between stores.

Twenty feet into the alley, McCoy found the owner of the shoes. He sat in the dirt, leaning against the wall in a spot of sunshine and cuddling a bottle of whiskey. McCoy checked his shoes and found they matched the prints he had been following. The man was in his forties and passed out.

McCoy shook him without success. He roughly pulled the bottle out of the man's hands, and that brought him back to the land of the living.

"No! My bottle. Give me back my bottle!"

He glared at McCoy through whiskey-fogged eyes. The man blinked and scowled. "Who the hell you think you are, stealing a man's property?"

"I'm a friend of yours. I'm trying to help you. Where did you get enough money to buy a whole bottle of whiskey?"

"Earned it. Yeah, working man. I earned it."

"Good for you." McCoy gave him back the bottle and squatted down beside the drunk. "Still got the job?"

"Hell, no. Just a once in a while job."

"Nice shoes. Never seen any like them before. You be careful I don't steal them from you next time you pass out."

"Can't do that. I got these shoes from a friend." The man giggled. "He don't know I stole them off him. He don't care. He died last month."

"What's your name?"

"Bellyache."

"That's it? Just Bellyache?"

"Yep." He tilted the bottle, took a shot of whiskey, coughed, screwed up his face and let out a long satisfied sigh. "Yep, just Bellyache."

"Fine. How about a pull on that whiskey?"

"Hell, no. Go get a bottle of your own."

"Not a friendly cuss, are you?"

"Hell, no. Get out of here and let me alone. It's time for my morning nap."

McCoy stood up and scowled at the drunk for a moment. Then, deciding he was telling the truth about stealing the shoes, McCoy went back to the street.

More preparations were at hand for the rodeo. He saw a dozen horses led down the street toward the rodeo grounds at the far edge of town. The people had built temporary corrals there for the bucking broncs. There was one permanent corral to hold the bulls that some foolish men would try to ride. Loading chute pens had been made to hold the animal about to be used, with gates that swung open quickly.

He walked two blocks down and watched the men working around the area. They put in a lot of time to make the show a good one for the town and surrounding area. Evidently it was the biggest celebration and holiday of the year.

Dozens of men were in town with their toughest bulls and unbroken horses. By using a horse for a dozen rides in the bucking bronco contest, it would give them a head start on breaking the animals back at the ranch for range work.

McCoy saw three cowboys herding about 20 three-month-old calves into a pen at the side of the corral. They would be used for calf roping. All of the skills used in the rodeo were ones that any good cowboy should have to work the range. The land around La Grande was ideal for cattle raising, and there were more than a dozen big ranches. The men from the ranches sometimes worked as teams to see who could gather the most winning points in the various contests.

McCoy went to the post office in the General Store. The clerk went over to the small partitioned-off section and checked the general delivery box. She handed Spur a letter from Portland. He nodded at the return address and tore it open. It was from the U.S. Land Office in Portland and was right to the point.

"Mr. McCoy,

Our records here show no trace of the name Frank Virgadamo, either as a buyer or homesteader of federal lands. No one by that name has on file any application to buy federal lands in the Oregon, Idaho or Washington area.

We wish you well in your work."

Three days ago he had sent a letter to Portland on the stage asking about Virgadamo, but evidently he wasn't known to the office. He could be working under a different name now. This had to be a land grab deal somehow, but he still had no idea why the federal men were killed.

He thanked the postmistress and went outside to check with the sheriff. The County Commissioners had appointed the other lawyer in town to be the temporary District Attorney until one was elected next year.

"Has he moved ahead on any of those warrants that were going to be issued?" McCoy asked.

"Don't think so, but he has written up complaints for that young woman. I'll be going out there soon to serve them on this Brother Benjamin."

"Sounds good. I'd suggest you take two well-armed deputies with you. Shotguns would be advisable."

Sheriff Johnson looked up quickly.

"Think I might run into trouble out there?"

"I'd almost count on it, Sheriff." He told the lawman that he had found a place for Angelina Potter to stay. "She should be safe enough during the day. I'll suggest that she stay inside during the nighttime. I'd hope that your deputies would keep a sharp eye out for any of the men from the Center who come to town in their homespun shirts."

"We'll do that, McCoy. How is your investigation coming along? Don't seem like it's doing much."

"I know. I've found the guy who evidently is trying to get me buried, but I can't prove it yet. When I do, you'll be the second one to know."

McCoy left the sheriff's office and noticed that the library was closed, so the ladies presumably were out buying clothes. It had been a good idea pairing them. He wandered on down the street toward the rodeo. He had been to a few of them. They were usually hard riding, hard drinking affairs, with the cowboys from all over the region in town to ride for the glory of their spread. Some of the ranches had their own distinctive neckerchief colors.

A dozen tents had gone up in back of the rodeo grounds. More tents would sprout as more outfits came in with bulls and calves and broncs to be ridden. It was shaping up as a real celebration.

He walked down to the arena, and before he knew it he had been drafted to help set up bleachers. They were on risers around the fence where the bucking broncs would be ridden. He worked for two hours, then went back to Main Street for some dinner.

He ate at the Grande Café, but Polly was too busy to more than stop by and brush against him.

"Hope to see you later," she said softly and was gone.

After his meal, McCoy made the rounds. He met the new D.A. and told him who he was and what he was trying to do there in La Grande.

"Anything I can do to help you with this Center problem might also help my case. Who knows?"

The D.A. turned out to be an intense young man who had thrown himself into his new job with a surprising intensity. His name was Adolph Nanning, and he promised complete cooperation with McCoy.

He checked with the sheriff. Nothing new. Then he went to see Sweet Sue at the Gaiety Saloon and whorehouse. Sue sat at a back table with one of her girls. When she saw McCoy come in she sent the girl upstairs and motioned to him to come and sit down.

The barkeep brought them two cold beers, and Sue grinned.

"Hey, haven't seen much of you lately."

"Right. I'm not supposed to have this much fun, so I have to stay away from your place and work."

They both chuckled.

"We know anything more about Virgadamo? Sometimes men talk in the heat of passion. Did Virgadamo?"

"Not that Billie Jo told me. He's not all that passionate, I understand. More a wham-bang kind of a guy."

"That's not good news. How is the rest of life going for you, Sue?"

She laughed. "You making talk or you really want to know?"

"You're a new friend. I'm interested."

"So I'm alive. I'm making a little money. My barkeep is stealing me blind, but he's the only one in town who will put up with me. I'm a bitch to work for. The girls love me like a mother. That means I have to mother them, and now I've got another fucking pregnant whore."

"A problem of the business. Haven't you figured out how to prevent that?"

"Sure, total abstinence, never get exposed. But that really shoots the hell out of my business." Sue laughed, but it was without humor. "Damn, maybe I should just sell out and go back to Portland to live the life of a grand lady. I could go to the opera and the concerts, give money to charities and get written up in the newspapers."

"Sounds damn boring to me," McCoy said.

"Yeah, I agree. When you going to come around to my room for some sexy relaxation on the house? We'll call it an early birthday present from me to you."

"Love to, but right now I'm going to go rattle Virgadamo's cage. I'm going to pay him a social call and see what he says. Should be interesting."

"Don't get yourself shot."

"Try my damnedest. Already got shot once in the arm. That's enough for this case." McCoy finished the beer, reached over, kissed her rouged cheek to her delight and walked out of the saloon without looking back.

He went directly across the street to the Saddle Shop and up the stairway beside it. At the top of the stairs he turned right, saw the door that they had used before and, seeing no sign on it, knocked. Someone said something inside, and McCoy opened the door.

He walked in and saw the small man behind the desk with Landower right beside him.

"My name is Spur McCoy, and I understand you want to see me."

Before either man could say a word, McCoy drew the six-gun and trained it on both of them.

"It's time we have a nice long talk. I'm getting annoyed the way you keep sending men to try to kill me. Why in hell are you doing that, Virgadamo?"

"What?"

"You heard me, Landower, put your hands on top of your head and lace your fingers. Virgadamo, keep your hands on the desk or die in two seconds!"

"You're a madman, McCoy. You come charging in here and threatening me. I should call the sheriff."

"I don't think you want to do that, Virgadamo, do you? He might ask too many questions. You don't like people asking questions. Right now the sheriff thinks you killed the District Attorney."

"Not true. I've never met the man."

"Just want to warn you, Virgadamo, that you better pray that I stay healthy. If another person tries to shoot me, or if I trip over a chair and break a leg, I'm coming up here shooting. You'll be dead before I open the door, you understand that? You send your bully boy here after me and he's dead before he turns around. Just want to make sure that you understand I'm through with your bushwhacking."

"I don't know what you're talking about. Mr. Landower and I are legitimate businessmen searching for a place to open a new operation. This looks like the town. Your threats will be put in a letter and sent to the sheriff."

"Won't do any good. Nobody over there can read. We deal in basics out here, Virgadamo, life and death. Like the way Victor Denning was killed, that federal mining inspector, and the way that Duncan Currier, the timber cruiser up there in the Wallowas, met his maker."

When McCoy said the names Landower sucked in a quick breath, but Virgadamo was better controlled. His eyes widened just a little and his nostrils flared, but then he was back to normal. It told McCoy enough.

He backed slowly toward the door. "Don't move, either of you, for five minutes. I'd hate to have to shoot you before you had a chance to draw."

McCoy went out the door and closed it, then flattened himself next to the wall and waited. Less than 20 seconds after he left the room, the door came open slowly and Landower looked out.

McCoy's six-gun slammed down across the side of his face, smashing him to the floor where his own revolver dropped from his hand.

McCoy picked up the weapon then went down the stairs to the street. He left the building and worked down to the overhang section. When he looked back at the two story building over the Saddle Shop, he could see the shadow of a man standing behind the curtains at the window.

McCoy waited there at the side of a store and watched the stairway near the shop. No one came down it. He leaned there another five minutes, then pushed out from the wall and headed for the library.

A man eased away from a wall ahead of McCoy and stopped, his feet wide, his hands at his side in the classic gunfighting pose.

It was Landower.

McCoy dropped his hand beside his tied-down Colt and walked forward.

"Whenever you're ready, McCoy," Landower shouted. "Now's the time for action instead of you always using that big mouth of yours."

McCoy walked to within 20 feet of the other man. A woman screamed. People on the boardwalk between and behind both men scampered out of the possible line of fire.

McCoy eased into position and waited.

"Anytime you want to die, Landower, I'm ready."

Chapter Thirteen

McCoy saw Landower's face work just a minute, as if this showdown wasn't such a good idea. McCoy remembered what an old gunfighter told him. It was to get any advantage on a man you could in a shootout; it was your life you were putting on the line. One of the best ways was to be first to draw. That way the man drawing first had a fraction of a second advantage. The other man had to see the draw, recognize it and then react and start his own draw.

The small fraction of a second could mean the difference between life and death if both men were equally fast.

McCoy saw the hesitation again, then he moved. His right hand leaped upward, palming the gunbutt and jerking it up. As it rose his fingers closed around the grip and his trigger finger eased into the trigger guard opening.

He lifted the weapon just high enough so the muzzle would clear the leather. At the same time it was coming up, his thumb found the hammer tong and he drew it back until it clicked on full cock.

Then as the weapon barrel cleared the leather, he started it moving forward, at the same time aiming it at the target. It was much like pointing your finger at an object.

All of this happened in a fraction of a second, and then the roar as the big .45 caliber six-gun went off. Firing was not a conscious movement. It was automatic. When the muzzle was on target and the angle right, his finger squeezed the trigger.

Then his thumb cocked the weapon again for a second shot.

There was only one six-gun report. McCoy's fast draw completely outclassed Landower. His weapon wasn't out of leather when the .45 slug tore through his shirt, splattered a rib and drove half of it into Landower's heart along with two big chunks of the broken .45 slug. Landower died before he slammed backwards onto the rough planks of a new section of the boardwalk.

A deputy sheriff ran out of a store where he had taken cover. Sheriff Johnson hurried up. McCoy slowly slid the weapon back in his holster and walked up to the body.

"It was a fair fight, Sheriff," the deputy said. "I saw the whole thing. The dead man there challenged Mr. McCoy. Stood on the boardwalk and challenged him to draw. It was fair. Mr. McCoy just drew a hell of a lot faster than the other man."

"His name is Landower," McCoy said. "He works for Frank Virgadamo. He's the man who's been hiring men to try to kill me. This time he tried it himself."

McCoy filled out a paper at the sheriff's office stating that the death of Landower was the result of a fair fight in a shootout. The deputy signed it.

Sheriff Johnson nodded. "No damn big loss, if what you say about him is true. What about Virgadamo? You have any evidence against him yet? Anything that will hold up in court?"

McCoy told him about the talk he had with Virgadamo that afternoon. "I don't know what he'll try next. Evidently his little scheme isn't quite ready to be finished yet. He isn't working on a land swindle scheme. I checked with the land office in Portland."

"So what's left?" the sheriff asked.

"Timber, a lot of valuable pine up in the Wallowas. Then there could be water rights. Control the water up here and you control the grazing. Doesn't seem to be much in the way of mining, but that's always a chance."

"He better stick to beef," the sheriff said.

McCoy headed out the door, this time determined to talk to the woman from the Center. They were both at the library, with Angelina in a bright yellow dress and her hair done up in a yellow ribbon.

"Who's your pretty girl helper?" McCoy asked Meg.

Angelina grinned. "I'm so thankful for the way you two have helped me. I just never expected anything like this."

Meg had a small frown on her face. At last she went to McCoy and touched his arm.

"That man on the boardwalk. He really tried to kill you? I heard some people say he challenged you. And that you drew and shot and he . . . died."

"That's right."

"I don't understand. Life is so precious. How could . . . I mean, I don't think I could ever kill someone."

Angelina came and put her arm around Meg. "Miss Tackett, you are an idealist and a wonderful person, but you don't know a lot about the harder side of life. This man came at Spur and said you try to kill me and I'll try to kill you. If Spur hadn't drawn, right now he'd be the one in the street being hauled off to the undertaker. Out there it's kill or be killed in a situation like that."

McCoy nodded. "Meg, that's what happened. It was either die myself or try to kill or wound him so badly that he couldn't fire. I'm not good enough to shoot the gun out of his hand. I don't know anyone who is. Those are fairy tales. This is reality."

Meg shivered, then lifted her brows. "I'm learning. At least you weren't hurt."

McCoy touched her hand. "You don't have to change. Stay just the way you are." He paused. "Now, I need to talk to you, Angelina, about the Center. You said ten men were working on some kind of a secret project up there. Let me tell you what I'm doing here."

He briefed her about the three dead men and the dead D.A. and what his job in town really was. She nodded.

"So I'm trying to find out if that secret project has anything to do with why those two government men were killed."

"Spur, I wish I knew. They were so tight-lipped they never even talked about it when they were . . ." She looked at Meg. "They didn't joke about it or whisper or anything. It was like they had a secret pact. Everything else up there was open and common knowledge."

"Angelina, I see only one way to find out. I've got to go up there and follow the men to wherever they go and see what they're doing."

"Oh, no, they'll kill you! They have a good security system and lookouts and everything."

"You got out, Angelina."

"Yes, but I knew the system and the territory. Also I was plain lucky."

"I have to get in there. It could answer a lot of questions I have."

"Well, then, there's only one way. I'll have to go along and be your guide." She held up her hands. "Now, shush. I got out so I can get us both back in, and I know the general direction the men go. We might not have to follow them, maybe just go in that direction at night when they aren't there."

"Angelina, you can't go back in there," Meg said. "I'm afraid you won't be able to get out."

Angelina laughed. "Yes, we will. I have an idea, a plan. They'll never even know we're there if we don't want them to." Angelina grinned. "We better plan on going in after dark, which means we can leave anytime now. I'll get changed back into my work clothes. Those pants make riding a horse a whole lot easier." She grinned. "Luckily we haven't taken my Center clothes to Meg's place yet."

She ran to Meg and hugged her. "You're like the sister I never had. Now don't you worry your pretty little red head about us. I'll bring him back all safe and sound."

She hurried into the back room to change clothes.

* * *

An hour later they had eaten a big meal at the cafe, got their horses saddled and rode out on the road toward Union. McCoy had a Spencer repeating rifle in the saddle boot and two extra tubes of seven rounds each taped around the barrel. It wasn't the best way to carry the extra rounds, but if they got into a fight with the men from the Center, the tubes would provide him with a quick load for 21 rounds.

They were just away from town when McCoy glanced over at Angelina. "You've ridden a horse before," he said.

"I was a farm girl back in New York. I love to ride. We'll have eleven miles to Union, then about seven or eight on up to the Center. Of course we won't be going directly there. Everytime I saw the men leave, they went out to the north. That must mean they went over the ridge of the valley we were in and into the next valley north of us."

"So why don't we head for that valley, ride up it and see what we can find?" McCoy said.

"You are quick and smart. I see why Meg thinks so highly of you."

"She does?"

"She hardly talked of anything else most of the time I've been with her."

"Well, that's good to hear. I admire that lady as well."

They rode on then without talking. It took them a little under three hours to get to Union and by then it was an hour from dark.

"We better not ride into the village," Angelina said. "There could be one of the buyers there from the Center, and he'd recognize me right away. I don't even have on my Center hat to hide behind."

"We're a little early to be heading up that way

so close to the Center, don't you think?" McCoy asked. "We can ride out along one of the streams and take a rest. The horses would love that."

They turned to the left a half mile before they came to Union and rode into the country, then to the north. They passed some cattle grazing, then came to a stream and followed it a ways before they found a good spot. It had more brush and trees than most of the area along the small creeks. They rode in and were safely concealed from any prying eyes.

They both let their horses drink at the water, then ground tied them so they could chew on some of the sparse grass.

McCoy threw stones in the water for a minute, then sat down in a splotch of sun where it came through the trees.

A moment later Angelina came and sat beside him. She watched him a moment, then she laughed softly.

"Oh, yes, I can see exactly why Meg is so smitten with you, Spur McCoy. You are what every woman wants—big and handsome and gentle and thoughtful. What else could a woman wish for? But Meg is shy and still a virgin, I'll bet. She isn't exactly sure just what she wants yet.

"I *am* sure, and I'm no virgin. Besides, I want to repay you somehow for helping me out today. You've been kind and charming, and now I want to do something thoughtful for you." She had been working at her homespun shirt, and now she pushed it open and let it fall off her shoulders. There was nothing under it.

Her breasts were large, pointed and tipped up, and she held out her arms.

"Spur McCoy, right now while there's time, I want to make love with you, quickly and wild or soft and slow, whatever you like best."

McCoy smiled. "Angelina, this isn't something you need to do. You're charming and beautiful, but there's no need."

She moved close to him, reached to his crotch, opened his fly and worked her hand inside.

"But I have a need. For a year I made love when someone else wanted me to. Now for a change I want to do it when I want to. Can't you understand that?"

She pushed him down gently in the grass and lay over him. She lowered one breast into his mouth and kept fondling his genitals, working up his erection. She pulled her breast from his mouth and moved off him, quickly stripping down her pants and underwear. Then, naked, she stood on her knees and moved to him. She lifted over him and moved higher, spreading her thighs so he could look up at her vagina.

"Angelina, you have a powerful argument."

He pulled her down and chewed on her breasts again, then helped her take off his pants. With them off and his shirt unbuttoned, she had him sit up and spread his legs. She came to him sitting almost on his crotch, her feet on both sides of his torso. Then she slowly eased his erection into her wet and ready vagina.

When he was fully inserted they sat facing each other, her arms around his neck. He humped at her gently, then she shook her head, put her hands down on his hips and lifted herself almost off his rod, then dropped down on it.

McCoy grunted in surprise. She did it again and again, then she screeched and her whole body shuddered and spasmed again and again until the orgasm worked its way through her slender body.

"Oh, God, what a good one!" she shouted. Then she grinned. "I've always wanted to do that. Out here no one can hear us." Then she held him tightly and rolled over, lying flat on the grass with him over her.

"Your turn, wonderful Spur McCoy. Please fuck me so hard I'll be sore inside for a week!"

He tried.

But she had so aroused him that long before he was ready he felt the juices rush forward as he drove into her eight times and then fell exhausted on her slender body. She kissed him and kissed him as he recovered.

They made love again, softly and so gently that Angelina cried she was so moved. Then they lay in each other's arms, watching the last of the sunlight fade from the sky.

"Don't tell Meg about this," Angelina said as they were dressing. "I don't want her to know. She idolizes you. She wouldn't understand. I'm sure she wants you to be her first lover."

They rode then, keeping a half mile from the trail up to the Center. They didn't see or hear anyone on the trail, and when they came near the spot where the lookout would be, they rode due north until they found the next valley and turned up it in the dark. Now there was a partial moon which helped.

"The valley here should be two to three miles long," Angelina said. "If this is where they come, they might be working in any part of it. Some of the women think they're building a new headquarters with new, bigger cabins and a huge common hall. I'm not so sure."

They rode through the darkness, letting their horses pick the way. The stayed in the middle of the meadow so they could see both sides. Nowhere did they spot any fires, any lights or any buildings.

A half hour later they came to the end of the valley. The small stream that flowed through the center of it wandered to the left and into a small ravine. There it dashed and chattered as it fell down small falls and jumbles of rocks.

They dismounted from the horses, tied them and explored in the darkness. There was clearly no one around. McCoy found a pitch stump, kicked it apart and took out a long piece of pitch wood, nearly totally made up of dried turpentine. It blazed up into a perfect torch as McCoy lit it with a match.

Now they explored the rapid water farther into the narrow canyon. Fifty feet up the waterway, McCoy stopped.

"Look, a sluice box," McCoy said.

"For mining gold?" Angelina asked.

"Absolutely. And look at the shovels and gold mining pans. See where they have dug into the ground around the edges of the stream where it could have overflowed and left a deposit of gold dust. That's what the big secret is. Those ten men have been mining gold and not telling anyone."

"And Brother Benjamin talked to me about going away with him, leaving the Brotherhood. He said we would have all the money we needed."

"Which makes you think he's about ready to run away and steal all of the group's gold dust. Let's see if we can find where they hide the gold."

It took them two hours and two more pitch torches, but at last they found it. The miners had made a small lean-to 20 feet up the side of the canyon. Under the thick roof of pine boughs there was a wooden box three feet long and a foot wide and six inches deep.

Inside they found leather pouches, each containing gold dust and small nuggets.

"Now I believe you," Angelina said. "How much gold is here?"

He lifted one of the pouches. "Gold dust is heavy," he said. I'd guess there are five pounds in each of the pouches."

"How much is that worth?"

"Gold is worth twenty dollars and sixty-seven cents an ounce—or about three hundred and thirty dollars a pound. Ten pounds is over three thousand dollars."

"Forty pounds is over twelve thousand dollars, and Benjamin is going to steal it all. I hate him! Think of all those men who have been working all this time, only to be cheated. Let's take it all with us so we can give it back to them."

"We can't. Then Benjamin would know he's been found out, and he'd ride away and never have to pay. Since I've seen this, I think he's probably the one who killed the deputy and the district attorney. He could also be working with Frank Virgadamo in La Grande. He might have killed the timber cruiser and the mining engineer as well. Now the best thing we can do is get out of here with our lives; then later we'll plan how to trap Brother Benjamin."

"Just a small memento," she pleaded. "I earned it."

They found an empty leather pouch and poured into it a little bit of the gold dust from six or seven of the full pouches. McCoy kept hefting it. When it got to be about ten ounces he stopped. They put everything back the way it had been and hurried to their horses.

It was well after midnight when they reached the other side of Union, found a secluded spot of woods and went to sleep snuggled next to one another. Both were too tired to think of making love.

Chapter Fourteen

Spur McCoy and Angelina were up with the sun. She kissed him good morning, then they saddled their horses and rode out, anxious to get back to La Grande. They arrived before eight and had breakfast at the Grande Café. Polly at first wouldn't serve them, then at last she did so with a couple of unfriendly jabs at McCoy.

They surprised Meg at the library, and she was so pleased to see them that she hugged them both.

"Yes, Meg, we found out what we needed to know, but we can't tell anyone yet," McCoy said. "It's extremely important that we keep it a secret. Any news here in town?"

"A little," Meg said and smiled. "I've been elected Rodeo Queen."

"How wonderful!" Angelina said. "You'll get to do all sorts of things. You ride, of course."

"Yes. They told me last night just before I closed the library. A committee does it, and I was surprised."

"Hey, I'm happy for you, Meg," McCoy said. "Now every young cowboy in the area will be watching you. I'd say you'll get about four proposals before the rodeo is over. Be choosy."

They all laughed.

McCoy left them there and went to see the sheriff. Nothing new had happened. He hadn't heard anything from Virgadamo.

"I think I know what this conspiracy is all about," McCoy said. "Now I just have to prove that Virgadamo and Brother Benjamin from the Center are working together. I'm not sure how yet, but there is a connection."

"What did you find out up there?"

"Can't say yet, Sheriff, not until I know I have both of them dead or arrested. Then everyone will want to know. What we need to do right now is arrest Virgadamo on murder charges. He hired Landower to kill me, and Landower got killed. That makes Virgadamo guilty of murder. That's the law most places. What I want to do is get him in jail and make him sweat a little. He might admit to some lesser crime to get out of the murder charge."

"I don't know, McCoy. The juries we get around here are just common folks."

"The murder charge will never get to a jury, not until we have some real evidence. Let's see what we can wring out of Virgadamo. He doesn't look all that tough."

The sheriff agreed at last, and they set off to get Virgadamo. On the way they passed a quickly built two-by-four stud wall make-believe jail in front of the General Store. A man with a big cardboard badge reading "Sheriff" came up with three others and arrested McCoy and put him in jail. The lock on the door was cardboard, too.

"You're found guilty of not wearing a cowboy kerchief on rodeo day," the "judge" told him. "Your sentence is a fine, a donation to the county library fund."

McCoy donated a ten dollar gold piece, was given a receipt and let out of the make-believe jail.

"Bunch of damned foolishness," Sheriff Johnson sputtered.

"Sure, but the library should make some money. Meg needs a lot more books over there."

"I know. They arrested me last night, but I got off for a dollar."

A moment later they climbed the steps beside the Saddle Shop and knocked on Virgadamo's door. They heard nothing but McCoy pushed the door open anyway.

Virgadamo was busy packing his things in a box.

"Going for a little trip, Mr. Virgadamo?" McCoy asked.

He reached for a drawer, but the sheriff had out one of his six-guns, trained on Virgadamo.

"Not a move, sir, or I'll be forced to fire."

He stopped. "I was just trying to find a clean handkerchief," the well-dressed man said.

"Don't matter. You're under arrest for murder. You instigated the shootout between your hired man, Landower, and Spur McCoy. Such an act is a felony. Since a death happened during the commission of that felony, you are thereby charged with that death, and so arrested."

"That's insane. I've never heard of that before."

"You're hearing it now," McCoy growled. "You

want to bring your shaving gear or start growing a beard in your jail cell?"

They went out the back door and down the alley to avoid the growing number of people on the streets. This afternoon the rodeo would begin with the bronc busting.

At the jail, they searched Virgadamo and pushed him into a cell. Then McCoy began questioning him.

"Virgadamo, the time has come to tell all. I know everything about your little secret with Brother Benjamin. What I can't figure out is why you're giving him so much time. Why didn't you move in right away and have it all? Why wait this long?"

"I don't know what you're talking about."

"Of course you do. Your secret is safe with me. Hell, I can't profit from any of my cases anyway. I could have grabbed all of those leather pouches, I guess, instead of just one for evidence. Now just why are you waiting so long?"

Virgadamo shrugged and lay down on the cell's cot.

"My guess is that when it's time for Ben to move, you've guaranteed him transportation, a new set of identity papers and probably a place to stay in Portland until he figures out what he wants to do. Yeah, that would interest Ben."

"You're guessing, McCoy. You don't know nothing."

"You don't think so." McCoy took from his pocket the leather pouch they had brought from the mining creek. He opened it so the prisoner could see the gold dust inside. "So where do you think I found this?"

Virgadamo looked at the pouch, then inside it. He wilted. "You bastard! No, you could have got that anywhere. At the bank."

"Sure the bank buys this sort of item all the time around here. You can pick it up out of the gutters."

The prisoner slumped on his bunk, shaking his head.

"So you tried and you lost. Tell me what you know about Brother Benjamin and I'll see about getting this murder charge dropped."

Virgadamo sat up straight. "You could do that?"

"I could try. How did you and Ben get together?"

"I knew him back east. He said he had a sure thing. Wrote me a letter. He needed some help on the outside. He said he had the slave labor, and we could clean up. He'd take the surface stuff, and I could find the mother lode and put down my claims. All he wanted was six months."

"But hard rock work costs money, lots of money," McCoy said. "Where did that come from?"

"I had a little, enough to set up a company and then work some friends in Portland for the rest. I got half of what I needed and ran out of friends. Nobody else wanted to buy into an idea. I had to wait until Ben got gone, then I could go up there and do some showing to prospective investors."

"But then a timber cruiser stumbled on the digging and had to be taken care of, right, Virgadamo? Did your man Landower do the job or did Ben?"

"Don't know nothing about that, not a thing. You'll have to ask Ben."

"We will, believe me. What about the mining engineer? You must have known he was in the area. You took care of him just in case he got down toward the southern Wallowas, right?"

"Not me. I didn't even know he was around until I saw that story in the newspaper. A surprise to me all the way."

"Yeah, I'll bet. You had most of your cash invested in this project. You weren't going to let some federal mining inspector spread the word about a new gold strike. Then there would be a thousand men swarming over that valley and no chance for you to tie down the mother lode."

"You're guessing, McCoy. What a court wants to see is evidence. You don't have any."

"Fine. I'll tell the sheriff you aren't cooperating, so we'll go ahead with the murder charge."

"Hey, I told you a lot."

"Not enough. We'll let you sit here and think about that trap door on the gallows and how it suddenly drops and the hemp tightens around your throat and that big hangman's knot slams against your head, snapping it to one side and breaking your neck. Then there's nothing but blackness for all time. You'll be hanged and dead and that'll be the end of you. Think about it, Virgadamo. I'm going to go see the rodeo."

McCoy walked away and left him. Now they'd let him stew for a few hours. So far it was falling into place nicely. That's why Ben wanted two more months, so he could take off the cream of the mining gold and be gone.

He told the sheriff they were making progress, but he still didn't tell him about the gold strike. "Going to let him stew for a while," McCoy said. He went out the door of the courthouse and could hear the cheering of the crowd. The broncs were first for riding.

He walked that way and watched the next man up get thrown after three seconds. Then somebody called to him.

"McCoy, where you been? We been hunting you. You're next on bareback riding. Get on up here."

"I didn't sign up to ride."

"Hell, you didn't. Got you on my list."

"I don't even have any spurs."

"Hell, borrow mine." The cowboy bent down, pulled off his spurs, fastened them on McCoy's boots and led him to the chute. Two minutes later he stood on the chute above a wild-looking roan that was foaming at the mouth.

"Sit on her and grab the one rein and all you got to do is stay on her for seven seconds. Spur up high. The judges always like that."

A minute later he heard a man with a big megaphone announcing him as the next rider.

"You ready?" the same cowboy asked.

"Hell no!" McCoy said.

"Great. Drop down—now!" He pushed McCoy onto the horse's back. He found the rope that was the only rein. Then the side of the chute opened and the bronc went out and fishtailed, then bounced straight up in the air three feet and came down on all four planted feet.

"Spur that bronc!" somebody shouted, and Spur leaned back and lifted his legs high on the neck of the horse, spurring down as he was flung from side to side and up and down. At last he heard a whistle and two cowboys rode alongside of him. He grabbed one in desperation and slid off the still bucking bronc, letting it race away.

There were cheers and whistles as the man with the megaphone blared out the news.

"And we have a new leader in the bareback bronc riding—Spur McCoy with a clean ride—and the judges are awarding him ninety-two out of a possible one hundred points. Let's hear it for Spur McCoy!"

"Yeah, that's the way, McCoy!" A high voice pierced through the cheers. He looked over and saw Meg in her new cowboy hat and fancy cowboy shirt on the rail. Beside her stood Angelina in a bright red dress, screaming her head off.

Somebody ran up to McCoy with his gunbelt and his six-gun, and McCoy carried them as he headed for the girls. Then suddenly, Angelina stopped cheering and turned. McCoy saw two men in dull blue homespun grab Angelina and carry her off.

"No!" McCoy shouted and ran for the fence. He scrambled over the top of the rails and found Meg crying.

"Somebody grabbed Angelina!" Meg screamed. "They ran off with her that way."

Spur looked but all he could see were hundreds of rodeo fans cheering for the next rider. He ran, buckling on his six-gun belt as he went. It took him several minutes to get to the street, but the kidnappers had the same trouble. Just as he got there he saw two riders moving quickly away from the rodeo grounds. One of them was riding double, and he could see Angelina's red skirt billowing out around the rider.

A man had just stepped down from a big black as he got ready to watch the bronc riding.

"Sir!" McCoy shouted and ran up to him. "Somebody just kidnapped a girl. Can I borrow your mount? I'll get him back to you. I'm a federal lawman."

The man looked surprised, then nodded. "Sure, of course. He's a good one. Lots of speed."

McCoy stepped into the stirrup and into the saddle, then pulled the big black stallion's head around and worked out of the crush of people to the street. Then he galloped down Main after the pair of kidnappers.

He couldn't see them now, but he was sure they

wouldn't hide in town. He wished he had his Spencer rifle. No time for that now. He dodged around a freight wagon, passed two more farm wagons and at last saw the riders about 200 yards ahead of him. There should be no problem. This strong big black stallion should be able to outrun either of those horses, especially the one carrying double weight.

At the edge of town he had gained 50 yards on them. He saw one man turn off at the last house in sight and jump off his mount. McCoy ignored him for the moment. The other man was stretching out ahead and angling toward the river.

The first rifle shot slammed within inches of McCoy, and then he knew quite well what the man off his mount was doing. His job was to pin down McCoy while the other man escaped.

McCoy bent low on the far side of the big black and headed directly for the house the sniper hid behind. Two more shots came, one grazing the black in the hindquarters. It bellowed in pain but stayed under control.

Another 20 feet and McCoy slid off the black, hit the dirt and rolled behind the wellhouse. Two more slugs slammed into the small building but missed him.

McCoy took stock. He was on foot with only a six-gun against a rifle. The other man was doing a delaying tactic. How did he beat those odds? The man lay at the far corner of the house, firing around the corner.

McCoy first had to keep the sniper's head down. McCoy pushed a sixth round into his .45 and crouched. He waited until the sniper fired again, then he burst from behind the well and fired five times at the corner of the house as he sprinted the 20 yards from the well to the near side of the house. The slugs slapping into the corner of the house kept the Center man from leaning out to fire.

Now McCoy was in good range for his six-gun. The rifle wasn't a big factor anymore. What would the other man do? He would run. McCoy worked around the far side of the house, checked at the corner, saw no one and ran along to the other side where the sniper must be. He reloaded as he moved and came up to the far corner with six rounds ready. Just as he looked around, the sniper stepped into his saddle.

McCoy bellied down, held the Colt with both hands and snapped off six rounds. The fourth one snarled into the sniper's left shoulder. His left arm flew up, and the weapon spilled from his hand. The fifth shot was high, but the sixth hit the rider in the side as he turned. He screamed and slumped in the saddle, but the horse moved only a dozen yards and stopped. Slowly the sniper fell out of the saddle, hit the ground hard and didn't move.

McCoy ran to find his black. He was grazing on sparse grass near the wellhouse. He leaped onto the black and took off in the direction he had seen the double mounted horse heading toward.

He couldn't see a thing. All he could do now was ride in that direction and hope that he could find some distinctive tracks to follow.

Chapter Fifteen

Spur McCoy found the tracks a quarter of a mile from town. The prints were deeper than usual since the horse carried a double load. They angled straight for the trees along the river, and McCoy knew the folly of following them right into the brush. It was a prime spot for an ambush. He figured the pair would be heading upstream.

Both men had worn the faded blue homespun so they must be from the Center.

It was the Grande Ronde River that came through La Grande. It flowed almost due east out of town after rising high in the Blue Mountains to the west of town. About four miles out from La Grande, Catherine Creek emptied into the Grande Ronde which then turned due north and then northeast to dump into the Snake River.

So if the Center man had counted on using the brushline to escape, he would be going four or five miles out of his way. He should be cutting down southeast to hit Catherine Creek.

McCoy figured this out in a few seconds. He turned downstream on the Grande Ronde, charged for the brush and slid into the greenery without incident. He stopped dead still and listened. He heard three kinds of birds but heard nothing of a horse or riders. Slowly he worked upstream, keeping to the edge of the brush so he could check the open country in case the kidnapper decided to head southeast the way he should be going.

McCoy went 50 yards, then dismounted, tied his horse and moved ahead slowly, not moving a branch, not breaking a dry twig. It was another ten minutes before he heard the first indication that someone was ahead.

He stopped and listened again.

A woman crying. She had to be Angelina.

Then a voice came booming through the brush.

"McCoy, I know you're out there. I'll make a bargain with you. You go out in the open, put down your gun belt and a rifle if you have one. Lay them on the ground. Then I promise not to kill this woman. That's the only way it will be. She's wanted back at the Center, and she's one of our people. She belongs to us. So far all I've done is punish her for running away. I'm authorized to do this. That's why she's crying.

"You have two minutes to go into the open and drop your guns. If you're not there in two minutes, I'll cut a four inch slash in Angelina's cheek. If you're not there in another two minutes, I slash her other cheek. If this pretty woman is disfigured, McCoy, it's your fault."

McCoy immediately knew he had lost this round. He walked directly into the open, took off his gun belt and dropped it in the dirt. Then he moved away eight feet and sat down on the ground.

"Yeah, good, McCoy. You follow us and the same thing's gonna happen again, you understand me?"

"Yes, I understand."

There was a flurry of sounds and a small scream of pain. A moment later a horse came out of the brush and headed southeast toward Catherine Creek. He caught only a quick glance of Angelina where she sat in front of the big man who rode in the saddle behind her.

Then they were gone.

Now it was a contest between the two horses. McCoy jumped up and ran for the woods. He strapped on his six-gun and raced back to where he had left the big black. His task now was to ride farther and do it faster than the bay could do with a double load. It sounded reasonable. He kept to the brush along the river for a half mile until he was well out of sight of the other rider. Then he angled to the southeast as well. He had to get to Catherine Creek, then ride wide of it and circle around the kidnapper and do it before they got to Union.

With any planning at all, Brother Ben would have sent two men to get the girl and two to four more to Union to wait for her arrival and bring her back to the Center.

He rode the black hard for a quarter of a mile, then paced him at a canter for a half mile. The bay and the kidnapper had to be walking. Four miles an hour. Three hours to Union. McCoy knew he could do eight miles to the hour on the black at a gallop, but the big horse could stand that only a quarter out of every mile. If he cantered at six miles an hour the other three quarters of a mile, the black should be able to make nearly seven miles in an hour.

The kidnapper couldn't do much over four to five. In an hour he should be two miles ahead of the kidnapper and could angle to Catherine Creek and lay his trap.

He rode hard, monitored the health of his horse every quarter mile and saw that the black stallion was holding up just fine. Once he did two quarters at a gallop. He checked his watch, and when he was sure he had been pushing hard for 50 minutes, he swung over to where he could see Catherine Creek, then rode straight for it.

He found what he was looking for quickly. The wagon road passed close to the creek at this point. The road actually slanted through a stand of trees and brush along the creek. Trees had been chopped down and the stumps pulled out to make a smooth passage through the stand of timber.

For a moment, McCoy wished he had a piece of strong thin wire to stretch across the roadway, but since that would hit Angelina first, it was just as well he couldn't implement that plan. He looked over other possibilities. A road block would do no good, since the horse would simply be ridden around it.

At last he decided on the only sure way of doing the job without hurting Angelina. He found his hiding spot and then took the big black stallion back in the brush and out of sight. He checked the roadway and found no recent hoofprints of a double loaded animal. He had to be ahead of them.

McCoy waited behind a pair of towering pine trees a yard from the side of the road. He had a good look far down the roadway and would have lots of notice that they were coming. Then at the proper moment he would sight in and fire. It had to work.

He waited for 20 minutes and then heard a noise downstream. He could just see a horse coming around a small bend a quarter of a mile away. He couldn't tell for sure if it was the same bay or not, or if it had a double rider.

Damnit, he had to wait!

Five minutes later he could see the flapping red dress and knew it had to be Angelina. The closer they came, the better he could see them. Angelina had slumped down, her dress bunched around her waist. Her legs must be rubbed raw by this time. The kidnapper was a big man and rode tall in the saddle.

For a moment, McCoy thought of changing his plan, but he considered the odds and knew he had to go with the original logic.

They rode closer.

When they were only 50 feet away, McCoy kept behind the pine. He held the Colt with both hands and rested his left arm against the pine tree. He'd have just one shot.

Now he could hear the horse breathing. There was a creak of the saddle and then the steady clopping of the hooves against the hard road. He saw the nose of the horse come around the tree. McCoy tracked it a moment and fired.

The big slug hit the bay in the head just under the eye, and it screamed and stumbled, then went down. The two people on its back slid with the animal, but Angelina clawed her way over the falling horse, scrambled to her feet and ran toward the sound of the gun.

McCoy didn't watch her. He was sighting in on the twisting, turning form of the kidnapper.

McCoy fired once, then again, and the man on the far side of the horse screamed in agony. He tried to sit up, then fell forward on his face in the dirt, his nose digging a small furrow in the deep dust until he stopped moving.

Angelina ran into McCoy's arms. She was crying, but this time it was from relief and joy and a little terror as well.

Neither of them said a word. McCoy still hadn't looked at her. His gaze was still on the body beside the dying horse. But the kidnapper never moved. McCoy relaxed, lowered the weapon and looked at Angelina.

She had a bruise on one cheek, and one of her eyes had turned black. She whimpered as he held her.

"I never thought I'd see you again," she said, still crying. "He was so mean!"

"He won't hurt you any more. None of them will. We're getting a bodyguard to stay with you every place you go from now on."

She motioned toward the creek; they went down there, and she washed her face.

Angelina looked up,her eyes bright again, a smile working through her anger and the edges of her shock.

"Hey, I think it's time we ride back to La Grande. I know that Meg is just going to worry herself sick until she sees us."

Angelina borrowed his knife and cut a slit in her dress front and back, then she tied each half around one leg to prevent any further chafing. Then they mounted and rode away.

It was dark when they at last came into La Grande. A simple little kidnapping and shootout couldn't stop the rodeo. Tonight was the first of three street dances. Half of Main Street had been blocked off, and men with rakes and shovels had removed all of the horse and cow droppings and shoveled away part of the dust to make a fairly hard dancing surface.

Two orchestras played, one on each end, scratching out Virginia reels and fancy two-steps.

Angelina and Spur watched the dancing a minute from the back of the big black, then they rode on to the nearest orchestra. Spur stepped down from the saddle and asked the leader to make an announcement at the next break asking Queen Meg Tackett to go to her house, that she was needed.

They rode to Meg's house and found her already there waiting. She burst into tears when she saw Angelina. They vanished into the house, and McCoy went to give his report to the sheriff on the two new dead bodies.

When he was finished writing the report on the two deaths, McCoy realized he was hungry enough to eat an entire bear. He gave the sheriff the paper and nodded. "Food next," he said. He frowned. "Looks like it's about time we take a ride up there and collar that damned Brother Benjamin before he gets anybody else killed. I'll be back tonight and we can talk about it. How is our star jailbird?"

Sheriff Johnson sat on his desk and snorted. "Some fancy lawyer was in and tried to get Virgadamo released on bail. I told him we don't have bail until the circuit court judge comes to town, which isn't scheduled yet for a month. He screamed something terrible, so I locked him in the cell next to Virgadamo and they had a nice three hour talk. The man says he's going to defend Virgadamo."

"Fine by me. Food next."

He ate four entire steaks, and Polly was flabbergasted.

The rodeo dance was still in full swing when McCoy went back to talk to the sheriff.

"How long they dance?" McCoy asked.

"Until nobody is left on the floor," the sheriff said. "Last year it was twenty-two minutes after four A.M. But this time there's half a dozen couples out there who swear they won't stop at least until the sun comes up. Both bands are taking turns, now that it's down to just fifty or so people."

When they settled down in the office, McCoy uncorked a fresh bottle of whiskey, set two glasses on the sheriff's desk and poured each half full.

"Time for a small celebration, Sheriff," McCoy said. "We're closing in on the bastards."

"Then tell me what the big secret is."

Spur still had the small sack with the ten ounces of gold dust in it. He took it from his pocket, and handed it to the sheriff.

The small man opened the bag, looked inside and snorted.

"In this county? The prospectors gave up fifty years ago."

"Not all of them. I'd say it's a fairly rich deposit. Hard telling where the mother lode is, but somebody will find it. You can see why we can't make any announcement until after we get our hands on Brother Benjamin."

"Sure. Half the men in the county would be up there trying to find out how to file a claim."

"You better be ready to send about three deputies up there as well to keep the peace. But first we have to get Brother Benjamin. What would you say to gathering up about twenty men with rifles and heading up there tomorrow morning?"

"Easy for me to say so. Don't know if we can find that many men who want to get shot at."

"Shouldn't be too much shooting. Try to get men who have had war experience. They'll know what's going to happen if it does come to shooting."

"Sounds reasonable. You want to start out about eight?"

"Let's make it nine. I've got to get some sleep sometime."

When McCoy got to his room at the hotel he found Polly pacing the hallway outside his door. She rushed inside with him, and when he told her he was too tired even to kiss her, she stormed out and screamed at him all the way down the hall.

Then McCoy got some sleep.

Chapter Sixteen

Spur McCoy woke up at six A.M. as usual. He was still tired, so he turned over and went back to sleep. It was after eight when he got up, still tired.

There had been too many assignments in a row—too much killing, too much shooting, too much running and chasing and far too many problems.

Damn but he was tired!

This was not a good way to start out with a posse going after a killer. He groaned and got up and dressed.

At the Grande Café, Polly wouldn't look at him. When she came with his eggs and bacon he caught her hand.

"Pretty girl, we didn't get married, right? We didn't sign any pacts of undying love, correct? You're a grown woman. You know how these things happen."

"Who was the slut with you last night?"

"That's the girl who ran away from the Center and is helping us solve some crimes around the county."

"I'll bet she's a big help in your bed, too."

"That would be her business, just like your little games in the storeroom, right?"

Polly took a deep breath. "Yeah, I guess. Still I'm mad as hell."

"A little anger gives some spice to life. Now get me some more coffee." He patted her soft bottom, and she grinned and hurried away.

When the posse formed up they had 15 men, including the sheriff and McCoy.

"We go with what we've got," McCoy said. It was a bright, crisp morning, a reminder that winter would come quickly to the high country.

They passed through Union, took a small break and then pushed on for the valley that Angelina had told Spur about. It was about six miles out of Union and well past the place where Spur and the D.A. had dug up the dead deputy sheriff.

McCoy skylined the Wallowas to the left and came to a spot he figured should hold the entryway into the valley they hunted. For the past two miles they had been following a fairly well-traveled trail.

Now it passed through a narrow place between two ridges, and it was here he figured the lookout would be posted. Somewhere on the slopes over them they heard two rifle shots in quick order. Some of the men ducked, but the rest grinned.

"That shooting isn't at us. It's a signal from their lookout," McCoy told the men. They settled down. Now the Center knew someone was coming. They would be on their best behavior. Would they fight?

McCoy figured they wouldn't, not with the law against them and 15 rifles. Angelina said they had 24 men, but that was before he had put down at least two of them.

As they rode into the valley, they saw how well it was tended, how neatly the fields were laid out and how the cattle were fenced into the less productive farming area. The small stream had been diked and dammed in three places so the overflow would angle into irrigation ditches.

They could see buildings ahead, and about a half mile from the structures a line of horsemen appeared from the brush along the creek and stretched across the road. Each man had a rifle. There were 12 of them.

One man rode out ahead of the others. All wore the men's homespun shirts and the floppy hats McCoy figured they must have bought from some mail order catalog.

McCoy and the sheriff rode out in front of their men. The posse had been split into two rows which now fanned out across the road facing the other force.

The front riders came within ten yards of each other and both stopped, then the riders behind them stopped.

Sheriff Johnson sat as tall as he could in the saddle and stared at the man he faced.

"I'm Sheriff Johnson of Union County. Tell your men to put down their guns; we're not at war here. We've come searching for one man by the name of Brother Benjamin."

"There's no one living here by that name," the lead man said. He was about 30, over six feet tall and had a full but carefully clipped beard. "We came out here to protect our land and our homes."

"This isn't your land. You're squatting on land owned by the United States Government," McCoy said. "Your homes are made of logs owned by the government. You have no claim to either the land or the buildings. We know that Benjamin lives here. He's your leader. Is he off working on his special secret project?"

"How do you know . . . ?" The young man frowned and turned, then another man rode forward. He was older, in his forties, and he came closer.

"My name is Brother Andrew. Yes, Brother Benjamin does live here and is our nominal leader. We are a commune, and each man, woman and child lives here in harmony with the others, all working for the good of the group. How do you know about the secret project?"

"I've been there, to the valley over the ridge. I know all about it. I also know that Brother Benjamin plans on leaving your group and taking with him everything of value that you have."

"But we have no worldly goods," Brother Andrew said.

"Oh, but you do. The secret project in the next valley is a gold mine, and we figure that Brother Benjamin and his ten workers have taken out about sixty pounds of gold dust from the stream so far. That's almost twenty thousand dollars in hard cash."

"But that's impossible," Brother Andrew said. Surprise and shock flooded his face. "I'm second in charge here. He would have told me."

"But he didn't," McCoy said. "I was at the place yesterday. I saw the gold washing pans and the sluice boxes. It's there. I also found more than a dozen leather pouches filled with gold dust."

"He never told us."

"He's trying to steal it all from you."

"The gold panning stream is on government property as well?"

"Yes, and as of right now it's open for staking claims. You folks better get over there quickly before word spreads to Union and La Grande. Then five hundred men are going to be charging up here with stakes."

Just then ten more men from the Center rushed up the road from the buildings. Some were on horses, some came at a trot, each with a rifle.

"What's the quickest way over the ridge to the next valley?" McCoy asked.

Brother Andrew talked to one of the newcomers.

"These are the men who had worked with Brother Benjamin at the gold mine. He sent them on ahead to defend the valley."

"Why didn't he come?"

"He said he would stay behind and bury their gold to protect it for all of us."

McCoy rode up to Brother Andrew. "Quickly, take us to the mine. He's not saving it. He's stealing it and running away. Ride man, and show us the way!"

Brother Andrew shouted something at the other men, then all charged along behind Brother Andrew and McCoy. They streaked down a lane that crossed the fields and up the slope on the far side. It wasn't too steep for a horse, but they were slowed to a walk as they worked up some switchbacks in the trail. At the top McCoy looked down on the valley.

He couldn't remember much of it, since he had been there at night, but he knew where to go on the stream.

"Go to the top of the valley," he called. They came down the slope to the valley and then raced forward. By the time they got to the diggings,

Benjamin had left. McCoy ran up to the small lean-to and found it knocked flat and the wooden box thrown open and all of the gold gone. He went back and told the men.

The ten who had worked the diggings screamed in protest.

"That was to be our treasury," one of the men bellowed in rage. "He promised us that all the gold would be owned by the whole commune, as everything else is."

The men who had not known of the mine could only look on in wonder.

"You men stay here and stake claims if you want to," McCoy said.

"How big is a claim?" somebody asked.

"A hundred feet along the stream and from rim to rim on the ravine," McCoy shouted. Then he went back to the flattened lean-to and began to search for tracks. The man would have his horse close by as he loaded on the gold. Yes! He found the tracks after five minutes of searching.

The tracks did not go back to the diggings, where they would have been totally obliterated. He saw the men below coming to a quick agreement. The men who had been panning and digging the area had first claim, the others in the commune could stake next, and what was left over was for the members of the posse. They went to work cutting stakes and making their marks on them with stubs of pencils some of the men carried. Even the sheriff and two of his deputies staked claims. The ones above the original diggings would be the richest, McCoy knew, but he didn't stop to tell them that.

He was on a one man job, and even the sheriff seemed to recognize that. Anyway he'd have a hell of a time pulling the posse away from the gold field.

McCoy walked, leading his horse. The hoofprints he tracked showed deeper than usual in the soft mulch of the pine woodland. He doubted if Benjamin had 60 pounds of gold in the saddlebags, but it was a fair estimate. This guy was a real bastard, and McCoy looked forward to meeting him face to face.

After ten minutes of tracking, McCoy left the miners far behind and kept moving ahead. He was riding now. He had a Spencer repeater carbine in his boot and an extra box of shells. Benjamin must have panicked when he heard the two rifle shots and sent the men to help defend the valley. He also must have figured his time had run out, partly because his men in La Grande hadn't captured Angelina and brought her back.

After a half hour, it was plain that Benjamin wasn't headed to the commune or Union or La Grande. He had angled past the top of the commune's valley, taken the next ridge downward, came out of the fringe of the mountains and turned due south.

McCoy tried to remember the map. What else was below Union? At last he had it—a small settlement called Baker. It had been on one of the old wagon train routes into the Oregon Country.

Once McCoy had the general direction he could make time. He spot checked the trail, riding at a gallop for a quarter of a mile, then dismounting and checking the land critically until he found the trail again. This way he could travel faster than Benjamin was moving.

McCoy hadn't brought any food. He hadn't figured on a long chase and now wondered how long it would be. He came to a small rise. Generally the trail had led downgrade toward a long valley that he figured must be the upper reaches of Catherine Creek or some other stream.

He stopped on top of the rise and stared ahead, first a general overall scanning. He saw nothing moving. Then he cut the area into a dozen squares and concentrated on each one. About halfway through he saw a dark blob moving. It was a horse and rider maybe three miles ahead of him.

The line seemed to be due south and angling to the west. He studied the terrain. If he tracked the man he would have two hills to climb. But since he knew where the man was, he could angle to the west, keep to the valleys and cut off at least a mile.

He put the horse into a trot, figuring he could do seven miles an hour and not exhaust the animal. He came to the point where he had seen the other rider and examined the tracks. Yes, the same ones. He followed them to the next rise and checked ahead.

Now the speck was much larger, maybe a mile away. Again he figured out a better path than Benjamin had taken. Evidently Benjamin was working a compass direction and didn't want to take any chance of getting lost. Benjamin would have no food, except maybe some emergency dry rations kept in a getaway cache. He needed to find some settlement before dark.

An hour later, McCoy edged up to some brush near a stream. The water flowed southeast here, not northwest the way Catherine Creek went. He had tracked Benjamin for the past 20 minutes from less than 100 yards.

McCoy had kept to the brushy areas and the ravines in this mostly unforested series of shallow valleys. Now it was time to settle things.

He had moved to a spot slightly ahead of the thief and now levered a round into the Spencer.

He hadn't fired it before so he wasn't sure just how it would zero in. Most rifles had a tendency to fire slightly high or slightly low and to one side or the other. For critical work, a marksman needed to know that. He didn't have that advantage now.

McCoy was 100 yards away and leaned against a cottonwood tree to steady his aim. He centered the sights on Benjamin's chest and then led him a little and squeezed off the round. The horse stopped. McCoy had planned on a little bit of forward motion so the bullet slammed into the fleshy top of the animal's neck. The sorrel bucked, screamed in pain and threw the unprepared Benjamin to the ground. The horse took off at a run.

For a moment Benjamin sat on the ground in shock, then scurried for some cover. There was none. McCoy had planned it that way. McCoy sighted in again and this time caught one of Benjamin's legs as he scrambled behind some low growing sage. Even from that distance, McCoy could hear the screech of pain.

McCoy rode out from the brush and came to within 50 yards of the thief and lifted the rifle.

"Benjamin, you want to die here or go back and face trial for the murders of the timber cruiser, the mine inspector and the deputy sheriff? We've got all sorts of witnesses glad to testify against you after you double-crossed them. What do you say?"

Benjamin fired at him, but the shot fell far short.

"No handgun can carry this far, Benjamin. I can sit out here and shoot your worthless body to pieces. You'll never live to enjoy any of that gold."

There was no response. Benjamin was hidden behind the sage. McCoy walked his horse to the side, moving to a better angle. When he could see behind the sage, he realized the man was not there!

He rode 20 yards forward and saw a small ravine that had been formed from drenching downpours and runoff that had taken the top soil with it. The small ravine worked to the left toward the stream.

McCoy rode hard toward it, moving down the gully as it got wider and deeper. Soon it was deep enough so a man could stand up and run. He rode faster searching for the desperate fugitive.

The shot came as a surprise. It hit Spur McCoy in the shoulder, and before he knew it, he was falling off his horse toward the ground.

Chapter Seventeen

Spur McCoy twisted in the air as he fell. The bullet in his shoulder hurt more than any wound he could remember. He fell on his right side and rolled, trying to avoid his wound, but half his weight went on the arm as he turned and it brought a guttural roar of agony.

His right hand grabbed at his six-gun. It was still in place. He drew it and watched the lip of the small gully. Brother Benjamin was down there somewhere within pistol range—or he was trying for McCoy's horse.

He looked around, frantic for a moment, then he saw the animal nibbling on some grass 50 feet from the ravine. Nothing moved along the barren soil on top of the ravine. He inched forward, pulled his six-gun and cocked it, then got to his knees for a better look. His left arm hung at his side, hurting but not useless.

McCoy stood for a minute, and his gaze swept the ravine immediately in front of him. Then he dropped down. He drew no fire. Where was the bastard? He listened and heard a faraway call of a blue jay. Closer he heard rocks rolling down the side of the draw.

He turned and again checked the sides of the ravine that he could see. For the second time he stood, and this time he saw Brother Benjamin. He was less than 20 feet away and held the weapon in his left hand. His right pants leg was dark with fresh blood.

At once McCoy threw himself to the ground just before the six-gun aimed at his heart went off and missed.

Benjamin had no cover down there!

McCoy crawled the best he could, using one hand and watching ahead. He had another three feet before the lip of the draw would drop away and he could see in the groove.

He crawled six feet parallel with the gully, then went toward the lip. He had the six-gun up now and watched where the man had been. His eyes swept both sides of the area as he inched forward, revealing more and more of the ravine.

Benjamin was gone from where he had been. A dark, wet spot showed on the sandy soil. Another spot of blood wet the soil to the left. Benjamin had moved that way.

Then a figure jolted up from a rock in the gully and fired.

McCoy saw him as soon as he lifted and swung his weapon that way and fired once, then again, then a third time.

Two rounds left. Any gunman worth his powder knew how many times he had fired each weapon and how many shots were left.

McCoy dropped out of sight and waited a moment. McCoy rolled away from the haze of blue smoke and then moved toward the rim again. Brother Benjamin sprawled half behind the big rock. His head and shoulders showed plainly.

A long, low wail of anger, pain and turmoil bellowed into the air from the man.

"Who the hell are you, McCoy? Virgadamo promised that you would be in your grave before he did anything else."

Lightning rumbled in the hills behind them. Angry clouds moved out of the Wallowas and blew toward the pair.

"That leg broken?" McCoy asked.

"Damn near it. Hurts like thunder."

"Where else you hit?"

"Side. You hurt me bad. I'm not walking much any more."

"I'll come down and patch you up."

"You try it and you die sliding down the gully! I got forty more rounds. I counted them. I might not be going anywhere for a while, but not a chance you gonna capture me. Hell, no!"

"What do you have against living, Benjamin?"

"Lots if it all finishes for me on the end of a hemp rope."

"That is a good argument."

"Those brothers back at the center gonna be damn mad that I took off with the gold. That horse I was riding is the richest horse in this part of Oregon right now."

"You get your sixty pounds of dust?"

"Closer to seventy-five pounds. I knew somebody had been at my supply. I always folded the tops of the pouches a certain way."

"You should have left that night and vanished."

"Hindsight is always so damn easy," Benjamin

said. "You got some lead in your hide, too, if I heard right."

"Shoulder." They were quiet for a time. The winds blew stronger then; a gale was whipping sand and dust at them.

"Gonna rain," Benjamin said. "I live here. I know."

"So come on out and we'll keep dry somewhere. I got a poncho soon as I catch my horse."

"Not a chance. I'm not leaving. I'm not a good enough shot to kill you, McCoy, but I might wing you once even if you stay up there. You try to come down here and you're a dead man right along with me."

"Can't let you do that, Benjamin. That's cheating the county out of a hanging."

"Hell, I'm bawling like a baby you make me so sad."

"Since we're having an even-handed conversation here, what happened to the timber cruiser? He stumble on your diggings and start to spread the word?"

"About the size of it. He came in one day about noon, just pleased as a pussy cat. I told him it was private land. He laughed at me. Said it was all U.S. government land. He should know, he said. He worked for the government estimating how much timber was on the slopes.

"Then he got on his horse and said he was leaving. He even told us to get proper claim stakes put up every hundred feet along the stream.

"When he started to ride off, I had to shoot him. Not a chance we could let him ride out with what he knew."

"The deputy?"

"He was a fool. He met one of our women in town on her only trip and went crazy over her.

He was coming out to see her, so I shot him."

"The mine inspector?" McCoy asked.

"Hell, he was sniffing around, got too close and figured what we was doing. So he had to be done away with, too. None of this gonna do you any good. I'll deny it all when I get out of here."

McCoy looked at the mountains but couldn't even see them. It was raining bucketsful just half a mile to the west.

That's when Brother Benjamin fired. He shot four times with his six-gun, and one of the rounds came so close it nudged McCoy's hat off before he flattened out and masked himself with the lip of the gully.

"Had to try," Benjamin said when the sound drifted away. "Didn't expect to do no good."

Spatters of rain hit them. McCoy buttoned up his light jacket but knew it wouldn't do much good.

A minute later the rain smashed into them full force. It had rained for five minutes, and both of them were soaked through to the skin just waiting it out.

McCoy heard lightning and thunder to the west as another surge of the storm washed toward them. When the thunder died he thought he heard something else, but it faded. Then he was sure he heard a rumbling and roaring, a sound almost like a freight train.

"My God, Benjamin, get out of that damn gully!"

McCoy stood and ran to the very edge of the ten foot ravine. There wasn't time. Fifty feet up the arroyo he saw the water coming. The cloudburst upstream had triggered a flash flood that drained millions of gallons of water into this runoff route.

Benjamin lifted up to look at the water and laughed. "Told you, McCoy, that you wouldn't take me alive, you lawman bastard!" Benjamin shouted. Just then an eight foot high wall of water, mud and branches smashed down on Benjamin. He screamed until his head went under the roiling, surging flood and swept him downstream.

McCoy moved back from the edge so he wouldn't fall in. He watched, but Benjamin's head never came to the surface.

As quickly as it had started, the rain blew past him and the sky cleared as the thunderstorm moved on to the west. Soon even the flash flood tapered off to a slow foot wide trickle.

McCoy got up and looked for his horse. She stood splay-legged, head down almost between her legs, waiting out the rain. He walked up and wiped off the saddle, then lifted onto it. The Spencer was still in place. He checked his shoulder. It was bad, but he'd had worse. He took his kerchief and with one hand and his mouth tried to tie up the shoulder to stop the bleeding. He couldn't get a knot tied.

The bullet hadn't come out, but he could still move his arm. The slug went in up high, but he didn't think it had hurt the shoulder joint.

It took him 20 minutes to find Benjamin's horse. The mare hadn't run far and had huddled down when the rain came. She watched McCoy as he walked his mount toward her. She shied off to one side, then walked off 30 yards and stopped. This time she waited until McCoy took her reins. He checked and found both saddlebags were lumpy with leather pouches of gold. He turned and headed back to the Center.

Two days later most of it was sorted out. The gold, all 32 pounds of it, was returned to the Center. Brother Andrew said he had talked with the people, and they were going to moderate their life style; all those who wanted to could get married. They would start to look for a tract of land to homestead and rebuild their commune. The gold would be their treasury as they had planned.

In town, the doctor dug the rifle slug out of McCoy's left shoulder, treated it with some salve and bandaged it. He told McCoy to give the arm complete rest for two weeks. The sheriff removed the three murders laid to Brother Benjamin from the unsolved file, and the little town settled down to getting ready for winter.

McCoy decided to withdraw charges against Frank Virgadamo with the stipulation that he leave the county and preferably the state as soon as possible. He was charged four dollars a day for his upkeep in the jail according to the county statute.

In the library, Angelina hefted her own leather pouch of gold.

"I don't understand. Is this still mine, or do I have to give it back to the Center?"

"Looks like it's yours," McCoy said. "They don't know you've got it, and I'm not about to tattle on you."

She put away a book she had been reading. "Brother Benjamin. I knew he was a rat. I mean most of the men up there were on the gentle side—kind and thoughtful. It wasn't such a bad life, not really. It was interesting, trying to make everything that we needed, even down to the shoes. Oh, yes, you found out about the flat soled shoes, didn't you? One of the men decided shoes were easier on our feet and legs when they didn't have higher heels."

Meg came up with a stack of books and put them on the desk. "We're getting a lot more people coming in now, and the make-believe jail at the rodeo brought in a hundred and forty dollars. I'll be able to buy maybe two hundred books with that much money."

"Angelina, what are you going to do now?" McCoy asked.

"Not sure. Mr. Geiger, down at the General Store, said I could come to work for him. He wants to get in dishes and lots of clothes and appeal more to the women buyers. I might just do that."

"You can live at my house—our house," Meg added quickly.

"If I do, I'll share the expenses." She twirled the ten ounces of gold. "Or I could cash in my gold dust and take a ride on the stage to the nearest train and go east until my money ran out."

Sheriff Johnson opened the door, looked in, spotted Spur and entered.

"Figured I might find you here. Things have quieted down considerable. Course I still have three deputies up at the gold strike. Never seen a creek swarmed with so many men so fast. By the time the town folks got up there the creek was claim-staked right up to where the water wasn't more than a foot wide. Now the latecomers are looking for the mother lode. Guess that means I'll have to find out how big a hard rock claim is supposed to be."

"I hear you staked a good claim up there yourself, Sheriff," Angelina said.

"Well, yeah. One of the deputies promised to work it for me on his time off. Don't reckon that I'll get rich." He turned to McCoy.

"Had another problem. It's about our late district attorney. You said Benjamin confessed to those three killings. He say anything about doing in Lawrence Sloma, our former D.A.?"

McCoy thought about it a minute. What would it hurt? Benjamin had the motive. If the rain hadn't come so fast they would have made it to Sloma.

"Matter of fact I forgot to mention that. He said that Sloma would ruin them and foil his whole gold panning scheme if he served those warrants. So Benjamin had to kill him. He was trying to buy two months more time to pan out the gold."

The sheriff nodded. "Good. Gets the last unsolved case off the books. Now I can run for reelection with a clean slate." He waved to the women and left.

That afternoon, Meg had arranged for her and McCoy to go on a picnic down by the Grande Ronde river. It was pleasant. The sun was still warm enough, and the ground had dried off. They spread a blanket, and she brought out fried chicken and a gooseberry pie.

"First something else," she said. Meg leaned over and kissed Spur. His arms came around her, and she sighed contentedly.

"I could get used to this," Meg said.

McCoy kissed her again and felt her tremble. It was a long kiss, and when it ended she started to move away. Spur held her and reached for her lips again. It was a secluded place, and he was more than interested in her.

Meg pushed him away gently. "Mr. McCoy, I have a rule about kissing. Twice in a row is my limit. The man who kisses me the third time will do it only after he slips a wedding band on my finger."

She watched McCoy and laughed. "My, such a look of fright passed over your face. I do believe I scared you something terrible."

McCoy laughed softly. "That you did, sweet girl, that you did. Let's try the chicken, then I have to get ready to ride in the morning. I have to get to a telegraph where I can report in to Washington D.C."

Meg nodded a bit wistfully. "I know. I didn't really figure on you for that third kiss."

McCoy nodded. Bested, he thought, bested by a beautiful redhead. But what the hell—it had been interesting.